Mother Love

by

Ann McCauley

PublishAmerica
Baltimore

First printing

ISBN: 1-4137-2950-9
PUBLISHED BY PUBLISHAMERICA, LLLP
www.publishamerica.com
Baltimore

Printed in the United States of America

Acknowledgments

I could never have written this book without my wonderful parents, Cynthia and Roy Himes, who believed in me and taught me to believe in myself. When I was a young girl Dad told me, "You're a writer…." So I *always* knew it was true.

My writing friends Susan Anderson and Edie Hanes…thanks for your patience and years of encouragement in showing me the ropes.

Special thanks to my dear friend Ingrid Fokstuen for your comments and encouragement as first reader, my daughter Shiela Cleveland for your plot assistance and my *soon to be famous* actress friend Lizbeth Allen for answering my questions about character development. To nurses Corky Johnson and Mary Pearre for answering my Honduras questions and the Peace Corps' Honduras desk staff for your patience and courtesy in answering my numerous inquiries. Finally my cousin and friend Maureen Johnson for your excellent editorial advice and my friend Lynn Graham for your invaluable proofreading expertise.

Many thanks to all of you *and* my heartfelt gratitude….

Ann McCauley

Enjoy!
Ann McCauley

I dedicate this book to my best friend and husband, Widad. It took us a long time to find each other, but you were definitely worth the wait! I'd have been lost without your ongoing encouragement throughout the frustrations and doubts of bringing my first book to completion. And to our five children, their mates, and ten grandchildren, you never stopped amazing and inspiring me!

Chapter One

BARBARA
August 1998

Barbara forced herself to turn the tape recorder on and began to speak. "You may not want to hear all that I have to say. But you're all adults now and perhaps you will learn something from the mistakes of your parents....

"It's been two weeks since your father died and I think it's time you hear the real story about your parents. My deepest hope is for you to understand your father and me, our family and yourselves better as you finally learn how we came to be the way we are. I believe understanding brings acceptance and with acceptance comes peace. And peace, my loves, is what I bequeath you.

"Since Bobby left this morning; I've been wandering around the house, almost in a daze. The reality of widowhood has settled in, I'm really alone for the first time...or am I?

"I know I'll be okay. I'm 52, yet I know better than anyone that I've lived the life of a widow for the past fifteen years. I've wanted you children to someday know the truth about us...I'd made some decisions even before your father's untimely death. Well, anyway I hope this will help you understand that we both tried in our own ways. Each of you can decide if you think we made the right choices.

"It was only two weeks ago Charlie frantically pounded on the window by the piano. It was a miracle the glass didn't break. I turned off the vacuum when I saw the panic in his eyes. 'Barbie, Bill's bad, it's his heart. He's in Lewiston ER.'

"Charlie made the thirty-minute drive to Lewiston General Hospital a wild ten-minute ride. Yet it somehow felt like a tedious two-hour commute. He was choking back sobs as he tried to explain the situation.

"'We were on the tenth hole; it happened so fast…oh God.' He and Bill had been best friends since grade school.

"Charlie was probably the only person in the world Bill had ever been loyal to besides his parents and you children. He screeched to a stop at the ER and I ran in. A friend from nursing school spotted me and rushed me to Bill's cubicle.

"The crash cart was by his bed, IVs were dripping, monitor wires and beeping machines seemed to be everywhere. I found my way to him in spite of the room full of nurses, techs and doctors. I was shocked by his pasty gray color and I covered his hand with mine. I was shocked at the cold clammy feel of his skin. I gently squeezed his hand to reassure him.

"'I'm here, Billy.'

"He looked at me through frightened teary eyes and in a soft raspy voice said, 'Barbie, you're the only woman I've ever loved…thanks for stickin' by me.'

"For a few brief seconds it was like thirty-three years had simply slipped away and it was just Billy and me before everything got so crazy.

"But his hand had felt so cold. I remember crying silently, 'Billy…Billy….'

"And then he was gone. I felt numb.

"The house feels emptier than ever. I don't know if I can stand to live here with all these ghosts…or are they just memories? I'm sitting shivering in front of an unlit fireplace reminiscing about my life as Mrs. Bill Malone. I just don't have it in me to light a fire this evening; guess that's why we have these heavy old afghans.

"Bill's never going to walk through that door again. He'll never sit across the dinner table from me again. Never again will he make me feel like an unwanted relic from our 1965 courtship. His deathbed vow of affection was far too little too late.

"But today I can't seem to take my eyes away from our wedding portrait displayed among the photographs of you children on the piano across the room. I was so in love and so trusting of Bill on our wedding day.

"My father had wanted me to finish college and take my time courting and I'd really wanted to please my parents. Mother insisted if Bill loved me, he'd find it an honor to court me until I finished college. They didn't know Bill though…or maybe they did.

"Bill's persuasive tactics broke my resolve…as you know, your father was a charmer and he was used to getting what he wanted. And just what had he wanted? I've long suspected that perhaps what Bill had wanted most was to avoid the draft and Vietnam. Marriage and instant fatherhood had been a quick and easy deferment. For me it was a solemn vow of commitment. Ours was a short but exhilarating courtship; when Bill Malone decided he wanted to make Barbara Olson his own, he did. My family had always been reserved. Bill's charm had literally swept me off my feet. The wedding photograph masked the humiliation I felt as a pregnant bride. I'll never forget the pained expressions on my parents' faces when I told them…our wedding was a small subdued affair much to the dismay of the Malone clan.

"However the reception plans were intercepted and paid for by the Malones. Six hundred of their closest friends to a sit-down dinner with the best food and catering service this town had ever seen. The band played for hours and then a limousine had suddenly deposited us at the airport. Our honeymoon was at the Grand Marquis Hotel on Nassau Beach, Bahamas.

"I had never traveled further than school trips had taken me. I was awed by the profound beauty of the Bahamas beaches and the blue crystal clear coral reefs. But the purging of morning sickness was even more overwhelming.

"One afternoon I finally felt well enough to adventure out to look for Billy who couldn't stand to be cooped up in the hotel all day…only to find him lying between two gorgeous women on a beach blanket. He was in the process of applying suntan lotion with great care to the one in the skimpy yellow bikini.

"Bill looked up, surprised to see me. 'Barbie, let me introduce you to Julie and Margot. They been keeping me company while you've been sick. They're real nice girls, they fly the friendly skies of United, how you feelin', doll? God, what a way to spend a honeymoon!'

"Julie rolled over on her back and greeted Barbara with a coy smile. 'So nice to meet you, Mrs. Malone. Oh, Billy, you missed a spot right here,' and she pointed a long red manicured nail at her ample breasts.

"Bill turned his attentions back to his new friend, 'Okay, sugar, why, you're just a little tease.'

"Margot, in an equally revealing bikini, was leaning over Bill as Barbara turned to walk away. Margot purred, 'Now it's my turn, Billy.'

"I walked away from that beach scene, alone on my honeymoon. I was stunned and angry. It was obvious they'd all been drinking. But that didn't take the sting away. I walked and walked. I forgot about dinner and didn't get back to the suite until long after sunset.

"When I opened the door, Bill was sitting on the edge of the bed. He hurried over to me, real concerned like, 'Barbie, for God's sake, where have you been? I been worried sick!'

"I looked at him through teary eyes for several long seconds and then slapped his face as hard as I could.

"Bill stepped back in shock. 'What the hell is wrong with you? I bring you to paradise and this is my thanks!?'

"His audacity amazed me. 'You call this paradise, I'm sick half of every day while you're out playing with your bimbos! Paradise!'

"'So this is the kind of wife you're gonna be. Those girls were just havin' a little fun. They mean nothing. Whiney bitch you are...I'm outta here!' And with that he was gone for the next four days of our honeymoon. That was the first time I ever saw his mean side...and it proved to be an omen for our future.

"When we first returned from the honeymoon, my parents thought my sullen mood was because of my pregnancy. In the sobering months to follow, I became fully aware of what a very spoiled selfish immature man I had married. Yet, I was determined to somehow make our marriage work.

"Bill's excitement about Billy's birth was unrivaled in my family's more conservative show of joy. Billy, Jr. filled a gap in my life. Bill was an excellent provider, thanks to his family's business holdings. Jessica came two years later. Followed by Janie in 1970 and Bobby in 1974. Your father's excitement and pride in each of your births was genuine. He loved you above all else.

"You children were wonderful distractions for me. I think you nurtured me as much as I did you. I was your first teacher and friend. I remember having a real struggle with Bill's mother. But I was not about to have a stranger come into my home and take care of my children! Besides I wasn't interested in the Country Club scene...not when I had my babies at home. And thank God I had my babies.

"Bill was home for holidays, most birthdays and rarely missed any of your baseball, basketball, football games, music or dance recitals. He always sat beside me; your father was the perpetual president of your fan clubs! His enthusiasm for you children was sincere. To unknowing eyes we probably looked like an ideal family. But we always traveled in separate cars because Bill would have to stop at the Club for a drink, go back to the office or leave on a business trip. Many nights he didn't bother to come home at all. His absences were something we didn't talk about; I always explained, 'Dad has business.' You never mentioned his absences but surely you must have wondered.

"I went along with whatever excuse he offered. My emotions were numbed for at least ten years after that honeymoon. I left a naive bride and returned ten days later a stoic wife. And stoic I stayed all those years. I had vowed during those long days of my honeymoon to avoid more confrontations with your father.

"I have to admit I felt pretty damn relieved that he had the heart attack on the golf course rather than with one of his paramours. Also, that he hadn't named any of them as beneficiaries in his will. God knows he had been generous enough as they came and went…I know of at least four new cars he had bought for his 'associates,' as he liked to call them. Expensive clothes, trips, jewelry and Lord knows what else.

"You're asking yourself, how did I know? Well, I paid the bills and your father was a pioneer with plastic spending! I think he really wanted me to know.

"I remember the day your Grandmother Malone and I became friends. It was an autumn afternoon in 1975. She came to call on the pretense of visiting 'the grandchildren.' After about thirty minutes of polite chatter and formal hugs for each of you, she calmly stated, 'Barbara, I think you and I need to have a talk. We have more in common than you realize.'

"I had just put Bobby down for his nap and helped you older three with your jackets to go outside to play. 'Of course we do…we have Bill and the children….'

"Truth of the matter was, I had detested your grandmother's lifestyle: country club gatherings, servants, golf, bridge and only associating with the wealthy. I think she sensed my feelings. As you know I never could get into that lifestyle. I had to become involved in volunteer work because it was long established that 'Malone women did not work.'

"I will never forget her clear soft voice as she said, 'Barbara, dear, you don't have to pretend with me. I know what you live with; Billy is his father's son.'

"I walked over to the window to watch you children play in the piles of leaves you had made in the backyard. Your grandmother stood beside me and gently put her arm around my shoulder. 'They are truly beautiful bright children, Barbara. You have taught them well. One day soon you may have to make a decision that may have a lifelong effect on those four young lives.'

"When I looked into your grandmother's murky gray eyes, I saw a warmth I had never before sensed from her. Then she went on to say…

"'There are some things in marriage we must overlook for the sake of the children. These days I hear of young women leaving husbands who stray…I've read there is a generation of children growing up without fathers, broken families, remarriage, and tangled family lines.'

"I looked at her straight on and told her, 'Mother Malone, please don't worry about us. I will never leave Bill and he will never leave me.'

"'Barbara, I know how hard it can sometimes be. If you ever need a friend, I'm here for you.'

"We sat down to finish our tea, holding each other's hands and through misty eyes, we knew we had each found a friend.

"And that was the end of the discussion. You see I made a decision to stay married to your dad years ago and ignore his philandering the best I could. And I refused to discuss it with anyone.

"One day a few months later my friend Alice tried to talk to me about marital infidelity. I simply told her in my very best icy voice, 'Alice, dear, different people have different expectations from marriage. Now, what was that special spice you put in your stew? It was so tasty.'

"Alice wasn't my best friend without reason. She never again pressured or pried into the state of my marriage.

"Yet even with you children, a lovely home and no financial worries, I knew quite well something was missing. I grew up in a family where my parents were each other's best friend. I am glad you've all had close relationships with your Mormor and Morfar Olson. They have shared so much with you in their quiet steady way. Even though they are in their golden years, they still sparkle! Especially for each other and their grandchildren. You have learned Swedish family history and recipes, how to fish, play cards and common decency, thanks to the hours you spent with them during your childhood.

"Even though I made a sincere commitment to stay married to your father, there were times when his indiscretions hurt so deeply that I was unable to maintain the stoic front. During those times I quietly went home to my parents and cried on their shoulders. They never once said, 'I told you so.' And I always gained the strength to return to my life as your mother.

"There was the time Bill brought home an 'associate.' They were both pretty well smashed. You children were all under six. I was always afraid Billy may have remembered that awful night. I lost my temper and shouted at your father, 'Take your slut out of our home! Don't you dare ever bring any of them here again. If you do, I'll take the children away…I will *not* accept this, Bill.'

"He had fire in his eyes but seemed to realize he had crossed the line of demarcation. That was the last time he was ever quite so brazen. I never mentioned that night to Bill nor did he mention it to me. And so the pattern of our marriage was established, such as it was.

"We continued to share the same bedroom whenever Bill felt the urge to sleep with me…until 1985. Mostly he lived out of his office. He called home at least once every day to keep up with your schedules.

"When I first found the ulcer, I thought it would go away; it didn't. Then I remembered the rash a few weeks earlier and reluctantly called Dr. McNeal. After he examined me, I was most unhappy to answer his probing questions.

"'Barbara, these are routine confidential questions but I have to ask you, how many sexual partners have you had in the last month?'

"'For heaven's sake, Doctor! I'm a married woman. Only with my husband.' My face felt like it was on fire.

"I had to undergo penicillin therapy to treat the syphilis. And worse than that tell your father, so he and whoever else would undergo the treatment also.

"That was the day I truly became a widow, that fateful day in October 1983. Bill came home that night about 10:30 with the familiar odor of whiskey on his breath as he pecked my cheek in a cool kissing motion.

"I looked at him and said, 'We have to talk.'

"He made it a joke. 'Ooh, this sounds serious. What's up, Barbie?'

"I told him I had been to the doctor that day.

"He became animated. 'Are we gonna have another baby? That'd be great; the world can't have too many Malones!'

"I told him I was not pregnant and then checked to make sure you children were all asleep. Then I returned to the family room. (Strange that I am sitting here in the same room this very day, talking into a tape recorder….)

"I looked straight into his incredible eyes. 'Bill, I have syphilis. Dr. McNeal started my antibiotic treatment today. Since you are the only man I've ever been with…he says you must get treatment also….' I could not hold back the flood of bitter tears.

"Bill stared at me blankly, then he walked over and hugged me. 'Aw, Barbie, I'm so sorry. God, I don't know how this could've happened….'

"I pulled away from him. 'There is only one way it could've happened, you bastard! And you will never give me another disease.' I was unforgiving and told him I was through pretending.

"I told him I had ordered twin beds for our bedroom and they would be delivered the next day; that we would share the same bedroom for the children's sake. But he was never to try to touch me again.

"Bill had never seen me so angry and determined about anything; maybe it was all those years of holding everything in…. Considering the facts of the situation, he stared out the window for a few minutes and then slowly turned with sagging shoulders to go to bed alone.

"That was a night for soul searching and little sleep. By morning I had made several life-changing decisions. I decided to finish my degree. And someday when you were all grown and gone, to do something unique with what was left of my life. No offense, but something that had nothing to do with being a 'Malone.'

"Bill was subdued the next day. I fixed breakfast for the family just as I did every morning and I marveled at you children's enthusiasm and energy for life. I felt such deep maternal pride and love. Billy, you were a senior in high school and excited about your dreams for a future without limits. Jessica, sweet sixteen, both of you willing to chauffeur Janie and Bobby to their practices and games. That gave me a newfound sense of freedom. I dared think about my own future for the first time since our marriage.

"Bill had insisted on giving you both new cars for your sixteenth birthdays. I had not wanted you to have cars so young but was relieved to see how unaffected you seemed to be by the Malone trappings. There was no way to stop Bill from indulging you children.

"A few days later I asked your father if he had seen a doctor yet, and he replied with a terse, 'Yes, it's been taken care of.'

"I then informed your dad that I had decided to go back to college to complete a degree in nursing.

"He whirled around and looked at me square. 'Why?! We don't need the money. Malone wives do not work!'

"I felt the hair on the back of my neck bristle. He sounded like his old controlling self again. I held my ground and told him in no uncertain terms that I wanted my degree for myself, my parents, and our children. And that there was always a need for qualified volunteers.

"He stared at me as though seeing me for the first time, but said nothing more about it. We both recovered from the syphilis physically but the scars it rendered to our marriage never healed. And I've lived more or less as a widow ever since...."

The abrupt ringing of the telephone startled Barbara. She turned off the tape recorder to answer the phone. It was Charlie. Again. She wasn't quite sure what to think of his persistent concern. "Hi Barbie, Beth and I were wonderin' if you'd like to come over to dinner tonight."

"Thanks, but I'll take a rain check...it's real nice of you to ask me again. Hey don't worry about me, I'm doing okay...."

"Yes, they've all gone back to their lives. But really, the empty house is fine. It's home, you know." She laid the receiver down and hoped Charlie would back off.

Bitter memories flooded Barbara; enough was enough! He of all people should know that Bill was seldom home and being alone was nothing new for her....

Barbara walked over to the desk and sorted through the stacks of mail that had accumulated during the last two weeks...mostly sympathy cards. Then a large white envelope fell to the floor; she reached to pick it up and couldn't help smiling. "My word! I've been so preoccupied with the funeral...." Barbara had been interviewed several months ago and almost forgotten about the Peace Corps. She slowly opened the envelope and found the letter of acceptance, officially known as "the invitation." She eagerly read every word.

"I'm in! I can hardly believe it!"

Back to the recorder. "As you all know I found ways to use my nursing degree in spite of Bill's ban on working. I organized Lewiston's first Well Baby Clinic through the local Red Cross, providing free early childhood immunizations for the working poor. And I taught Red Cross CPR and First Aid.

"About eight months ago, I sent for information about the Peace Corps, thinking this might be the time for me to really go 'to work.' Bobby was almost finished with law school, you were all busy with your careers, finding yourselves and making your marks in the world...it's only natural that you spread your wings.

"I completed the entire application the day it arrived. Two months later I made an overnight trip to Washington, D.C. No one even missed me. I passed the physical and the personal interviews. My credentials were in order. I didn't know until today's mail that I'd been accepted. I feel a sense of purpose for the first time in many years. Yes, the Peace Corps sounds like an even better idea now than it did before. I will be serving two years in Honduras, and my training starts in November.

"Billy, I do wish you and Liz a lifetime of true friendship and joy in your future marriage. What are you waiting for anyway? Liz is a peach and I am so happy for you both. You share a common interest in your teaching careers and I believe all the students whose lives you touch will be richer for having known you. I am so very proud of both of you. I appreciate your phone calls; your voices are like fresh air in my sometimes stuffy life. Follow your dreams and know you are blessed. Some people *never* find their true soul mate.

"Jessie, you are such a beautiful young woman and already showing signs of career success as a supervisor/trainer in the Physical Therapy Department at the University Clinic. I realize we are not as close as when you were a preteen, but I hope someday we again will share the secrets of life as we did back then. I miss you so very much. And I am truly proud of your dedication and achievements. Indeed, I appreciate your phone calls even though we seldom go deeper than superficial pleasantries.

"Janie, my volatile beauty! You were always so full of life, so creative and such a mimic…even as a small child. Sometimes I've wondered where in this world did we ever find a child such as you! But wherever it was, I've never stopped being thankful for the privilege and challenge of being your mother. When I see you in those TV commercials, I have to smile and check my pride so as not to be too boastful. True success will come if you remain diligent; you are extremely talented. I miss you but it is important for you to follow your dreams.

"Bobby, you have grown and gone now, too. A lawyer. Your dad was so proud of you! As am I. Guess he had enough need for lawyers in his life that having a son enter the profession made him feel like he owned a piece of the 'brotherhood.' I know adjusting to the demands of the legal system probably seems a bit overwhelming at times, but you made it. Passing your boards the first try. Hang in there and serve your apprenticeship and you will find your way. My baby, my son, the lawyer…I miss you, yet I am so proud of you. Let your conscience lead you and you won't go wrong.

"My sincerest wish is that you all make time in your hectic lives for each other. It will not just happen, you all live miles and miles apart in different cities. If you make the effort to be friends, not just siblings…it will be a choice you will not regret. The relationship one has with a sister or brother is often the longest relationship of a lifetime. You know each other so well and, of course, there will be times you will irritate one another but heaven help anyone outside the sibling fold who tries to criticize your sisters or brothers. You had this when you were young. I think it's still there if you allow it to surface!

"When I look at the sky on a starry night, I always think of my dear Katlin. I know my life would've been much harder if it hadn't been for my sister. I believe having sisters and brothers is like a constellation of stars, you always have someone to connect to…. She's been gone for five years and I still find myself thinking, 'I've got to tell Kate about this.' I'm so glad I still have Eric. We talk at least twice a month and when we do, it's really from the heart. I've always wished he hadn't moved so far away. But that's just a selfish streak in my thinking. He's found success and I know he is happy living in California.

"I hope you each receive this tape in the spirit it is being sent. I loved your father back then and he returned his love to me, to the best of his ability. He and I didn't have a healthy marriage, but we did have a marriage and we were both dedicated to our children. Sharing our story with you is not an apology. It is not a position proposal (my side, his side). It's simply an explanation to help you understand us all better. Nothing more and nothing less."

Chapter Two

"I started this tape almost three weeks ago and I hardly know what to do next, I've been soo busy. First of all we're not poor people. You're all healthy, well-educated young adults. You've entered adulthood with certain advantages. Each of you has an excellent education, debt free, I might add. You have chosen your own career paths. Your ambitions match your talents. Bill was so very proud of each of you. And so am I.

"When the will was read, I couldn't tell how any of you really felt about your father's decision to leave everything to me. I was really quite surprised. We had never talked about it and I'm not going to make any major decisions about it at this time. Since none of you have ever indicated any interest in the family business, I certainly don't expect you to now.

"I often felt that if your father would have had to struggle more to obtain success that he might have been a better person. Everything that most people strive for was handed to him. Therefore he expected immediate gratification in whatever he attempted. I know his parents thought they were doing right by their only child, but I don't think Bill was ever truly happy with himself. Maybe that's why he felt so much pride and unabashed love for his children…he had a little more input with you than with his 'puppet positions' in the family business.

"The trusts will provide each of you with some security but not too much. You each will continue to receive $15,500 per year from the trusts your father established several years ago. I want you to experience the satisfaction of achieving personal success and earning your own way. Maybe that's part of the reason I feel the need to give something back at this time in my life. I know many people think being a rich man's wife would be just the thing. But it wasn't for me. I married so young that I never had a chance to have a career or make a worthy contribution to society...other than you four children. You have been my one solid link to sanity, my pride and my joy.

"I first started thinking seriously about joining the Peace Corps when Bobby was doing his research paper on poverty in Central America three years ago. Mormor and Morfar were shocked when I initially mentioned it but they have slowly realized that this is the right choice for me, especially now.

"I'll be closing the house with all valuables placed in a vault at the bank and in the two grandparents' homes. Morfar will keep an eye on the house; you children will be welcome to spend holidays and visits home with either Grandmother Malone or my parents. They're all in extremely good health for their ages. Even Grandmother Malone has come around and reluctantly supported my decision to join the Corps.

"Since we have all been blessed far beyond our needs, I think you should know that I plan to give most of my inheritance to charity (I have yet to decide which ones). I want all my children to feel the joy of personal achievement. And I know you will. Please don't plan on further inheritances unless your grandparents decide to bequeath you. I will decide while I am away if I will keep the house. It's awfully big for just me.

"I will start intensive cultural and language training on October 28th, two days of intense orientation in Washington, D.C., and then onto Honduras for three months in country training. My nursing background and Spanish language skills are highly regarded. When I passed the physical, the final interviewer couldn't hide her enthusiasm and bumped me up to train as soon as possible. (For applicants my age, the physical is sometimes the big elimination factor!)

"I hope you are not too shocked with my decisions. If you would like to, after a few months you could even travel to visit me. I should be on my first assignment by the end of January. I have to admit that sometimes I feel a bit dizzy, things are suddenly happening very fast. I've had so many changes in the last three months. Well, that's enough news from home for today. I want to get these tapes in the mail to each of you. I have to admit that I am truly excited, yet ambivalent about all the unknown factors. When we talk next time, you will at least know about my mid-life plan of adventure! And I hope share some of my joy."

"I love each of you more than you could ever know."

Chapter Three

BILLY

"I can't believe she's doing this, yet I've always known Mom was a bit different than the other kids' mothers. Honduras! My God, they're not even civilized there, not where they send Peace Corps workers anyway."

Liz smiled and touched his face softly. "Bill, I think it is a great thing for her to do, especially now. I know you're concerned for her safety but I'm sure they try very hard to send the volunteers into 'safe zones.' I'd be so proud of *my* mother if she'd ever consider doing something altruistic. Your mom has had a rough life despite all the trappings. Give her your blessings, how about it, Billy?"

"I don't know...I'll have to call Jess, Janie, and Bob. I can just imagine the girls are flipping out over this. Why didn't she just call? Why this stupid tape?"

Liz smiled and paused before sounding more like his conscience than his fiancé. "How far would you have allowed her to go before interrupting her, asking her questions or trying to influence her to change her plans?"

Liz walked over to the window and gazed out at the park. It was a sunny August afternoon. "Besides she only had to say it once this way. Don't you think this must have been an emotionally draining experience for your mother? I wonder how many of the young mothers out there are living double lives for the sake of their children? God, Bill, she was so young when you were born and she hung on all those years. She must have been so lonely. I can't imagine. Yet, she maintained a wistful devotion to your father...." Liz shook her head with a cynical thought. "My parents were never into pretending for the sake of their child."

Bill remained very quiet as he rewound the tape. "I have to listen to this again. I just can't understand why she told us all these rotten things about Dad. Why after all these years? He's not even around to defend himself. I know he was away a lot when we were growing up, you know...I can vaguely remember the night they had the major row and there was some woman in a red dress with Dad, but really Mom made our lives seem so normal...that this tape makes me feel like I'm in some sort of a twilight zone. It's my mother's voice, and she is telling me things that I don't want to hear. Liz, do you think if we set a wedding date that maybe she'd cancel the whole Peace Corps thing to help with the wedding?"

"Jeez, Billy, I can't believe you just said that! We have already agreed to a quiet wedding with just us and two attendants *if* you ever decide to set a date. We don't need your mother to change her plans for us; do you know how selfish you sound when you talk like that? Please just promise me that you will never be your 'father's son' in the husband department."

Before he could answer, the telephone's shrill ring interrupted them.

"Hello...Bobby, my God it is good to hear from you! Yes, I've listened to the tape."

BOBBY

"Bill, I'm in shock here. I just can't believe our mother would go off and live with some tropical primitive tribes. Why didn't we have any idea what was going on with her? My God!"

"Bob, I know this is a real shock, but once you stop and consider what her life has been like...."

"Wait a minute, okay, Billy, so you're on her side. I think it was just too callous to send us a message like this on tape."

"I felt the same way at first, but then I realized, with a little bit of help from Liz, that we would have questioned her every step of the way."

"You're damn right I'd question her! Dad's gone so now Mom is running off to the jungles! I can't figure why she told us all that garbage about Dad.... And how does she get the nerve to blame *my* research paper on this cockamamie idea?"

There was a long silence between the two brothers who hadn't taken the time to even call each other since their father's funeral...no bad feelings, just self-absorbed in their own lives.

"Bill, when was the last time you were home? I guess I haven't been home since the funeral. I mean, I do call Mom every week just to check in and see how she's doing. I tell her about my work; she's always been a good listener. She makes me feel like I'm the most important person in the world when I talk to her."

"Maybe that's why I call her, she is so damn proud of 'Bobby the lawyer' but if only she knew how unimportant I am here at this firm! Hell, my office is barely a tad larger than my bedroom closet at home. And most of the law partners in the firm don't even know my name."

Again silence. Only this time it was interrupted by sounds of sniffling.

"Hey, Bobby, are you okay?"

The sniffling sounds continued but Bobby managed to answer, "Yeah, Billy, it just hit me pretty hard when I listened to Mom on that tape; I listened to it while eating Chinese and reading today's paper. I was so angry I immediately tried to call her. She's disconnected the answering machine and was either out or refusing to answer. Then before I called you I listened to it again. She sounds very firm about the whole deal."

Another long hesitation, then Bill hesitantly asked, "Bobby, are you free this weekend? Do you want to go home and spend some time with Mom? That is if she has time for us to come home! Sounds like the ground rules are shifting in the visitation department."

"I think I can arrange it; do you think we'll be able to persuade her to forget the Peace Corps? And what about our rightful inheritance? That is not my area of expertise but I don't think she can just cut us off like this! I know Dad would never have done this. I'll bet Grandfather Malone wouldn't have let her give our inheritance away."

"I doubt we'll be able to persuade her to change her mind about anything. She is a class act in stubborn resolve. Guess she had to be to survive her life with Dad. Mom will probably be busy if she suspects an ulterior motive for our visit. Actually she's probably about swamped. Maybe we can volunteer to help her with whatever needs to be done. Oops, there's a beep on my call waiting, I'll call you back tomorrow. Chill, Bobby, we'll talk to Mom and everything will be as normal as can be…for our family."

JESSICA

Jessica paced around her small apartment waiting impatiently for her brother to answer his phone, "Come on, Billy, pick up! I have to talk to you now!" Of course, no one could hear her but she felt some relief from the great frustration she felt from simply waiting. Patience was not one of Jessica's virtues.

Yet, she managed to get along well at work as a physical therapist. Her ability to empathize with the disabled was a winning combination with her unrelenting determination. Most of her clients worked harder for Jess than they would for any other therapist, and consequently progressed faster.

It had been a long day *and* then to come home and receive this tape from her mother. "Come on, Bill...." Then he answered.

"Billy, this is Jess. Did you get a tape from Mom today?"

"Hi, Jess, good to hear your voice again! How are you? I'm fine, thanks for asking! Yes, I got the tape and I've listened to it three times, pretty amazing actually. I thought I knew my mother and yet I feel like I'm listening to a stranger. I realize she is an exceptional person that...."

"Cut the crap, Bill!" Jess had no tolerance with her older brother (or anyone else for that matter), who tried to explain their feelings in a philosophical manner. "I think she's gone off the deep end. I don't appreciate all the shit she said about my dad, now that he's gone and can't defend himself. It's not fair. As far as I'm concerned she enabled him to live like he did just as much as the Malone money!"

"You sound like your old spitfire self, Jess. But do you think you might be just a bit hard on Mom? All she wants to do is go practice nursing in the jungles of Honduras for a couple years. Remember, this is a woman who sacrificed her career years to provide a home for us."

"You seem to be overlooking the lost inheritance part! How dare she? Daddy would never have allowed this! God I miss him. He knew who he was and he liked being a Malone. He relished strutting around the club...Mom has always been so, so, well, boring! It's no surprise he wandered!"

Bill swallowed hard in a feeble attempt to remain calm. He knew they could always count on Jess for radical opinions. He wondered if she might actually enjoy spreading dissension.

In an effort to appease his sister, he said, "You know, Jess, she did say she wouldn't make any rash decisions. She's closing the house up, but not liquidating. All she did was join the Peace Corps! Give her a break. She is your mother."

Another sibling was silent on the other end of the line. What a night he was having. Finally Jess replied in a somewhat softer voice, "Okay, maybe you're right, Bill. Guess that's why I called. Janie left me a semi-hysterical message just minutes before I came home. She'd received her tape today too. It's a really weird way for families to communicate, kind of unnatural. But I'm not calling Janie back; I just can't deal with her tonight. She can be so annoying."

"It took me a while to calm down and a little common sense chastising from Liz. But after listening to the tape three times, I understood. This had to have been very hard for her. This way she only had to say it once. And you know if we had been there…we would have argued with her. She'll call us when she's ready. Bobby said she's disconnected the answering machine and was not home or else just not answering tonight. All her cards are on the table. I don't think it really matters what we say or do. Our mother is a resolute lady and it sounds like she's made up her mind."

"So, I'm not the first to call you either. How's Bobby feel about the whole thing?"

Billy attempted to minimize his brother's response. "He felt a bit shocked and confused at first just as we did."

"God, I don't think I've talked to him since the funeral, I get so caught up in my work and life. I do try to call Mom every two weeks and honestly she never mentioned anything about the Peace Corps to me." Jess spoke in a dejected monotone.

Billy hesitated. "I think I know the answer to this but have you been home since the funeral?"

Jess sighed. "No I haven't but I do call. She could have told me. Besides, I live four hours away; and that's when traffic isn't too heavy. Anyway, it's only been three months."

"I know you work hard, Jess, but maybe we should all try to visit her before she leaves for training. What do you think? Could you get a long weekend?"

"I don't know, I'm not making any promises now. I think I'll listen to the damn tape again and see if I can gain some of your calmness, big brother. Hey, how is your sweetie, Liz? And I do mean sweetie. You're a lucky couple."

"Liz is great, she sends her regards and wanted me to tell you she'd be very proud if her mother would join the Peace Corps!"

"Oh God! Does she want me to retract my good feelings about her? Have you two set a date yet or are you going to live in sin till death do you part?" Jessica couldn't help but grin as she spouted off to her brother.

"Jess, you'll be the first to know when we set the date. Also contrary to your preconceived assumptions, Liz and I have separate apartments and addresses! Also want you to know that we plan to have only two witnesses and a Justice of the Peace when and if we do take the big step. So, no hard feelings, okay?"

"Jeez, Billy, I think I struck a nerve...sure, whatever. I hope you realize how fortunate you both are. It's a jungle out there and it's full of jerks. Dating is a big pain these days."

"Sorry to hear you talk like that, sounds like you've almost given up on finding a mate, Jess."

"Whatever. But you better not forget to tell me when you and Liz take the big step. I'm going to listen to that tape one more time. Good chatting with you and please stay in touch."

"Okay, Jess. Good talking with you too. Try to stay cool."

JANIE

"I suppose I better call big brother Bill, but first I'll finish this joint." Janie was much calmer as she inhaled her favorite stress reliever.

She held the tape in her hand. "My mother thinks I'm a surprise package. My God, she's an original trip to Mars and back!"

Janie slowly placed the tape in the player to listen to it again. This time her mellowed mind remained calm and tears slowly trickled down her cheeks. "Follow my dreams! My life has become a nightmare...I've lost count of how many men I've slept with to get the few breaks I've had. Everyone just uses everyone. It's nothing but a wretched jungle. When I tune in the current TV shows, especially the sitcoms, I feel so pissed off. I can act circles around those half-starved idiots. I guess I just haven't slept with all the right people yet. Oh, Mother, if you only knew...."

The phone rang just as the tape was ending for the second time. "Hello...Billy. It's great to hear your voice, it's been awhile. When are you coming to New York again? There's always something cooking in the Big Apple." Janie's voice droned the words in an unnatural cosmic rhythm.

Billy hesitated. "Are you okay, Janie? You don't sound quite like yourself."

(Yet he instinctively knew what she did sound like, he'd escorted enough stoned kids to the Rehab Detention Center in the H.S. He knew.)

"Oh shit, yes, I'm okay, it's not every day I receive notice from my mother informing me she's joined the Peace fuckin' Corps and leaving the country, closing up the family home and giving away my rightful inheritance. Other than that everything else is just perfect." Another silence between Malone siblings.

"You know I'm still not used to the idea that Daddy's gone. I always had the idea that if I wanted to, home would always be there...sometimes I get so lonesome here in the city that I feel almost dead myself." A muted sniffling sound was all that broke the silence.

"I understand how you feel, Janie. But she's only going away for a couple years and we can go to the grandparents' whenever we want...."

"Billy, cut the shit, that's not the same and you know it! They'd have me arrested; they watch my coming and goings like private investigators. I gotta have some space."

"Okay, Janie. Okay. You know, I love your orange juice commercial, any luck with auditions lately?"

"Oh yeah, Billy, I'm gonna be the next Meryl Streep! Can't you just tell?"

"Listen, Janie, I don't know what's going on with you. I can tell you are having a rough night; maybe it would be best if we talk tomorrow after you get some rest. I'm exhausted and I have to get up bright and early for the salt mines. What do you think? Can we talk tomorrow?"

After another long silence, he heard the familiar sniffling sounds and then his sister spoke. "Hey Bill, sure, thanks for calling the black sheep, Baa-Baa; that means good night in sheep talk."

Janie put the phone down. Staring at the window, she fell asleep in the chair with her jeans and t-shirt on. Another night without dinner; she had simply forgotten to eat again.

BILLY

Billy put the phone down with a feeling of great sadness. He looked at Liz, and knew he was a lucky man to have her in his life.

"You know how we were thinking of going home to Lewiston this weekend? How would you feel about going to New York City instead?"

Liz closed the book she was reading and gave him a puzzled look. "Must be pretty worried about Janie if you're thinking of postponing the visit to your mother; what's up?"

"Janie has always been a free spirit. She managed to charm her way around Mom and Dad, she was always so energetic, petite and somehow so vulnerable…we were all guilty of excusing her excesses. I'm really worried about her now. She sounds like a very angry lost soul. She also sounds stoned and like a lonely young woman in a city too big to notice her."

Liz put her hand on Billy's and without hesitation said, "New York sounds great. We could leave Friday right after school, we should be there by 11 p.m. Do you want to bunk at Janie's or in a hotel?"

"Maybe we should stay with her so we get a clear picture of how she's really doing. Thanks for being so understanding, Liz. I have to call Bobby and let him know of the change in plans."

Bobby answered on the third ring. "Hey, Billy, twice in the same night. Not bad for the Malone boys! What's up?"

"Well, I just talked to Janie and she is not well. Liz and I are driving over to New York this weekend. I'm worried about her. Sorry. I know I told you I'd go with you to see Mom. But maybe you'll have a better chance to really talk to her if you go alone."

"No problem, Billy. What's wrong with Janie other than she is Janie?"

"I'm not sure, she's taking the whole thing, Dad's death and Mom's joining the Corps, very hard. She sounded out of it and quite stoned."

"What is happening to our family? Jeez! Are you sure she wasn't just a little tipsy?"

"I'm sure, Bob. Remember what I do for a living, we have to herd the potheads out of class several times every week. Maybe it'd be best if you didn't mention our concerns about Janie till we know how bad it is this time."

"Sure, but don't you think Mom should know? It seems to me before she goes off nursing strangers in another country that she should make sure her own family is well."

Billy paused and then rephrased his request for his brother. "Please, no discussion of Janie's problem until I talk to you Monday night, what do you say?"

"Okay, Bill. You win. But I really think Mom should know."

"Maybe she does know. And maybe she is at her wit's end with Janie. Janie is so full of herself that she drives people away. When she was younger, it was considered cute and she's always been such a beautiful girl." Bill was embarrassed to have expressed his secret thoughts about his youngest sister.

"You know, you may be right. Don't worry; I have so many things to talk to Mom about that I won't have time to talk about Janie."

"Thanks, Bobby, and good luck."

"Hey, I'm not the one who's going to need the luck, Bill! You're the one who's going to see our fruity sister. Good luck to you, sir."

Three days later Billy and Liz were on their way to New York City and feeling more than a little apprehensive; Janie had not been enthusiastic when he called her back and suggested this weekend. Nor had she discouraged their visit.

They arrived by ten o'clock and felt very lucky to have found a parking spot on her block. "At least she lives in a decent neighborhood," Billy muttered as they gathered their things from the back seat of his beat-up Honda.

Before they had a chance to ring the security bell, the ornate door swung open and Janie flung her arms around her lanky brother. "Oh God, I can't believe you're really here! I've missed everyone so much. And Liz, it's so great to see you again too." With that she let go of Billy and latched onto Liz.

"Come on up, I want you to meet Arnie, he's cool. You'll like him. You must be starved, I've got food. I'm so happy you're here!" She sounded like a four-year-old on Christmas morning.

"It's great to see you too, Janie. How have you been? You look kind of pale and like you've lost even more weight." Billy tried to sound cheerful.

"No way, it's just these sweats, they're so baggy that they give an illusion of thinness. Well, here we are…*mi casa es su casa, bienvenido*!"

"Oh Janie, your apartment is lovely. You really have a flair for decorating and it smells good too." Liz set her bag by the door and walked into the living room admiring the decor.

A tall young man swaggered out of the kitchen. He was wearing an apron. "Arnie, this is my big brother Billy and his fiancé Liz. Billy, Liz, I would like you to meet my friend, Arnie. We met at one of my auditions. We didn't get the parts but we found each other. He's a struggling actor, too." Janie smiled at him sweetly.

Arnie extended his hand to Billy and Liz, and they exchanged pleasantries. Janie announced the buffet was ready. The travelers had already eaten but hadn't the heart to tell their hostess.

The awkward silence was broken by Liz. "This is delicious, Janie, I didn't know you were also gifted in the kitchen."

"I'm not, Arnie did it all for me. It took all my energy just to clean the apartment. Well, you know after waiting tables all day...sometimes I'm just pooped." Janie gave Arnie another radiant smile.

Billy toasted his hosts. "My compliments to the chef and to my little sister, the ever gorgeous Janie Malone. And to a grand weekend in the city for all of us!"

They all raised their wineglasses and joined in the toast. "To a grand weekend in the city!" The wine loosened their tongues; they small talked about movies and books.

About an hour later Arnie suddenly announced, "I forgot to tell you, babe, but I have an early audition and I gotta have my beauty sleep...I'll call you."

Janie jumped up with a perplexed expression on her face. "Well, good luck. And thanks for all your help. I couldn't have done it without you."

"Nice to have met you, folks, hope I see you again sometime this weekend." He gave her a slight peck on the forehead; she seemed to have slipped something into his hand. And then he was gone.

"Arnie seems like a nice young man. Is he someone special? He sure is a good cook," Billy commented as his sister returned to the room.

"Yeah, he's a good cook and he's special and all that but Arnie and I are just pals, that's all," Janie answered in a tired, monotone voice with a distant look in her eyes.

Liz gently asked, "Well, is Arnie a good actor?"

"Being good has nothing to do with making it in this business...yes, he's phenomenal. But he kinda runs hot and cold. Everyone I meet in New York seems to." Janie was no longer the enthusiastic young girl who planned on taking New York by storm.

"You don't seem to be so keen on New York anymore, has something happened to change your mind?" Bill tried to sound casual and relaxed. He felt neither emotion as he spoke.

Janie looked like a scared schoolgirl as she slowly looked around the funky apartment; hesitantly, she softly began. "Yeah, I'm not so sure anymore...about anything really. Back in Lewiston, I was somebody. I was Homecoming Queen for two years; I always had the leads in the school plays, even the Community Playhouse productions. Here I'm nobody but the perky little cutie who does a few stupid commercials. By New York City standards I'm not even considered really pretty...just cute. Hell, those ads barely cover the rent. I have to work as a waitress, and can you imagine, I make more money as a waitress than as an actress. If it wasn't for the trust from Daddy I wouldn't be able to survive here, and to tell you the truth I don't know how much longer I want to live like this."

Liz looked at Janie, seeing a new side of the complicated unhappy girl. "Have you considered any alternative choices you could make in your life?"

Janie looked at her guests, then tossed her head as if to shrug off the question. "You two look really tired. Why don't we turn in and resume our talk in the morning. I did manage to trade with a girl at the restaurant and have the whole weekend off. You can sleep in my bedroom, it's all made up with fresh sheets. Towels are on the dresser. I'll sleep on the sofa."

Billy smiled at his little sister. "Sounds like a great idea. Good night, Janie."

Two days later Bill and Liz drove down the highway in silence lost in their thoughts, their hands barely touching as his right and her left arm rested on the console. The weekend in New York City had left them both emotionally drained and tomorrow was the first day of another demanding week of teaching.

Chapter Four

BOBBY

Bobby headed back to the city for another week of legal drudgery. "I feel good, I didn't think that I would now...." He sang along with an old James Brown song on the radio, freely changing the words to suit his euphoria.

The weekend home had not been what he expected. His thoughts were in a tailspin. How was it possible to be twenty-four and feel like he'd met his mother for the first time? And on top of that discover that she's...well, she's all right.

Even though he hated his job, spending a few days with his mother helped him see that dues must be paid. And life goes on.

The middle-aged secretary from hell greeted him tersely as she glanced at the clock. "Good morning, Mr. Malone. Running a little late again, are we?"

Bobby bowed as if greeting royalty to the secretary he viewed as little more than a spy for the big boys upstairs. "Top o' the morning to you, dear lady, please be sure to add my tardiness to your list for Mr. McDowell."

He immediately tackled the mounds of paperwork stacked on his desk. But his mind was on his mother's plans...even though he didn't like what she was about to do. He smiled and shook his head. It was a feeble effort to clear his mind. "I've got to concentrate. I have to concentrate. I must concentrate."

On cue, Miss Lears popped into the cramped office to see if he needed anything. "Did you call me, Mr. Malone? I thought I heard you talking and your phone light wasn't on."

"No, no, I was just muttering to myself, but thanks anyway," Bobby answered, feeling more like a prisoner responding to his jailer.

He settled down to prioritize the files with a fierce determination. A half hour later Bobby was deeply involved in preparing for the deposition of Giles vs. Powell. He worked through lunch, accepting a cold sandwich from Miss Lears. Bobby barely noticed when his co-workers went home. Miss Lears had her coat on as she stepped into his office to ask with a distinct tone of disapproval, "Is there anything else you need before I leave?"

"No, no thanks. I'm on a roll here and have to get as much done as I can while my juices are flowing. Thanks for everything, have a good evening," Bobby answered without looking up from his computer screen.

"Do you want me to order you some dinner? It wouldn't take but a minute." She persisted, always the hovering hawk though impersonating a dedicated secretary.

Bobby turned to her, trying to conceal his irritation. "No thank you, Miss Lears. I'll just grab a bite on my way home. I want to finish this file before I leave."

"But you must be hungry; I wouldn't mind at all…oh, I see you're working on the Giles vs. Powell case. Mr. McDowell has been looking for it. He'll be pleased. Now, what about some dinner?" She persisted.

It was becoming increasingly difficult for him to remain civil with this annoying busybody. "Miss Lears, I said *no* thank you."

"Well! Good night then, Mr. Malone." She slammed the door as she finally left the office.

Billing hours were the all-important gods to the bean counters upstairs. Bobby was earning a reputation as a maverick and had locked horns with this secretary since his first day at the law firm. He rarely arrived on time and burned the midnight oil. He completed more prep files than any of the other fifty lawyers, yet his billing hours for comparable volumes of work was twenty-five percent lower than his peers. His so-called secret was working late and avoiding the distractions of the daily office hubbub. He found it much more conducive to work at night…alone.

The ability to concentrate was a gift he unwittingly had inherited from his mother. He didn't think of her again until later that night…when Billy called.

When Bobby walked into his apartment about 11 p.m., the phone was ringing.

"Hey, it's Billy. Well, how did the weekend go with Mom?"

"You've got to go see her. She's phenomenal. We had a great time together. I feel like I met my mother, the person, for the first time." Bobby was suddenly alert again after the long hours at the office. So many stories to tell his brother. Then he remembered where Billy had spent the weekend. "So, how was Janie?"

"I don't know how to answer that. I have a feeling she's not doing very well but of course she won't admit it. I think you should spend a weekend with her and see what you think. I know she's very unhappy and disappointed with her life. I can't quite put my finger on it, but I'm worried about her. Liz and I both felt something just wasn't right."

"Do you think she's using again?" Bobby asked.

"I'm not sure but yes I think she might be," Billy answered in a faltering voice.

After a few seconds of brotherly silence, Billy continued, "She's skin and bones, so very, very thin with childlike mannerisms that no longer seem so cute, now just rather peculiar. She's barely making it, works as a waitress! She auditions a lot but has only landed a few commercials. I get the feeling Janie was used to a lot more help from Dad than the trust provides her. She's angry, confused and just...well, lost."

Bobby sighed. "Oh God help us, what are we going to do with this girl? I often wondered how she could really have been our sister. But since she is and Mom doesn't seem to have a clue that she is the lucky winner of an adult troubled child, we've inherited more than we counted on with Janie. Which reminds me, have you talked with 'fireball,' Jessica?"

Billy answered, "Not since the night we all received our tapes from Mom. She was pretty upset too but not the same as Janie. Jessica has always been very independent and focused. But equally angry at Mom."

Bobby replied, "Sisters."

Billy agreed, "Amen, brother! I'll talk to you in a couple days. Good night."

Bobby turned off the phone and opened the refrigerator, looking for a quick late night snack in lieu of dinner. His thoughts were skewed as he finally headed for bed.

JESSICA

Jessica checked her watch. Two more hours left of her shift. Tonight she was going home. First time since her father's funeral. Damn him anyway.... "Maybe I should have called Mom. No, I'll take my chances." Her thoughts were interrupted by a co-worker.

"Hey, Jess, could you cover for me this weekend?" Lou asked. "I hate to ask but I really need to go back home, it's Nancy's grandmother's seventieth birthday, they're having a big surprise party. It's kinda last minute but that's how her family operates. Whaddya say, Jess?"

Jess looked at him evenly. They had worked together for three years and this was only the third time he'd asked her to cover his shift. He was an okay sort of guy. Besides, it got her off the hook of going home again. She was dreading the thoughts of it and no one was expecting her anyway.

"Sure, Lou, but remember, you owe me one! Have fun and bring me a piece of the birthday cake."

That night she decided to call Billy. And Bobby. And Janie. And even Mom. This urge to call her family was very unfamiliar to Jessica. Maybe hearing Lou babble on about the fun he always had when his or his wife's families were together…or maybe it was just time to touch base.

Billy was pleasantly surprised to hear Jessica on the phone. After the usual pleasantries, he said, "Liz and I spent last weekend with Janie in the city."

"So how is our little movie star-to-be? Is she still clean?" Jess inquired.

He hesitated as he carefully answered, "I'm not sure, I have a gut feeling that she's not doing very well, she's bone thin, very restless and so, well…sad. I think part of it is Dad, but she's not getting acting jobs and she's working as a waitress…."

"Does Mom know? God! Something just doesn't feel right about this whole thing. How does she figure it anyway? Because we are all grown, she thinks she can just give notice of parental termination? Does that mean we'll have to take care of the clean up on Miss Janie, 'the fruit cake,' this time? Oh God. Why didn't Mom and Dad just tell her to get a real education and a real career rather than chasing after this stupid acting dream?" Jess always said what she thought; sometimes it was refreshing and other times just downright vexatious. Tonight it was somewhere in between.

She continued, "I was planning to visit Mom this weekend but something came up at work. Maybe next week. Guess I'll call her."

"I'm impressed, Jess," he teased. "I think Liz and I are driving over tomorrow morning. I have to call Mom tonight. We have Monday off, so that makes it much easier. Bobby was home last weekend and he had a great visit with Mom."

"He always has a great visit with Mom," she replied in a flat tone. "Are any of you thinking of contesting her plans for the estate? I mean, I live on what I earn. I've never taken a dime from the trust. I just roll the interest over and invest it in the market. And with my pension from work, I'm doing okay. I don't expect to ever marry. I saw what hell that was watching Mom and Dad. I wasn't as naive as she thought I was; I had to grow up fast. I've always known I'd have to take care of myself. All the men I meet turn out to be the same. Jerks! So, there you have it. But what about our rightful inheritance? Do we fight or just pretend it's okay? Unlike my sister, the actress, I've never been any good at pretending." Jessica's voice faltered. She was glad she was alone; she didn't want her brother to know tears were silently trickling down her cheeks.

"Jessica, I don't know what to say. First of all I don't know if we can convince her to change her mind or if the courts would accept a challenge to legal estate planning. Is that why you wanted to visit Mom for the weekend?" Billy asked his sister.

"Yes, partly that, and I'm just kinda curious about Mom. She sounds so undone. Don't you think so? How can anyone have a daughter like Janie and think she's just a 'volatile creative beauty'? Well, if she really believes that, then it does make it a little easier to understand how she managed to stay married to Dad all those years. I'd say it required 20/20 rose-colored vision. If it worked for Dad, maybe it works for Janie, too." Jessica surprised herself by saying so much. She was usually much more guarded when speaking to family members, even Billy.

"Maybe you ought to make a trip to the city and spend a couple days with Janie and see what you think. I'm worried about her; she seems so lost and vulnerable." He paused, uncertain of how to phrase the question without setting off his 'fireball' sister. "Well, how do you feel about that idea?"

"You know, I just might do it. Then I'd have something to talk to Mom about when I finally do go visit her. Guess I'll call the actress next. Thanks, Billy, I'll be in touch." Jessica put the phone down and somehow felt more connected to her roots than she had in a very long time.

JANIE

Janie smoothed her blonde silky hair and touched up her makeup as she waited for her turn at the soap opera audition. She was trying to practice the visual imagery her last shrink had tried to teach her. It was supposed to increase self-confidence and enhance goal achievement. But she looked around the room and eyed the competition with a seasoned wisdom. The actresses were getting younger and younger. Prettier and thinner, too. Here she was thirty years old and her claim to fame was a few commercials! Not where she had expected to be at thirty. She heard her name being called for the audition. She was reading for the part of Angie, a "strung-out has been" trying to win back the love of her former fiancé before he goes through with his imminent wedding plans....

"Doug, it's really you! How long has it been? Five years? You look wonderful. God, we had some times, didn't we? Are you still mad at me...it wasn't you. I just wasn't ready to settle down back then. Are you married?"...etc. Janie said the lines softly and with such affect that even the hardhearted director had tears in his eyes. After the reading, he sent for her to meet him in his office.

She'd met plenty like him before. The promises, the lies and *always* the betrayal. Janie told the bewildered aid, "Please tell Mr. Director to call my agent if he's interested in offering me the part. My agent's name and numbers are on my call sheet. I must go. I have another very important appointment."

Janie deliberately and dramatically threw her coat around her shoulders and left the studio with her head held high.

"Whew, what an exit! You've still got it...someday, kiddo." She sighed cynically. Janie frowned as she looked at her watch. "How could it be 5 p.m. already? I'm going to be late for work again...if the manager notices, I'm cooked. That's all there is to it."

She ran toward the first cab she saw. He mercifully stopped. She did a fast change in the backseat as the cabbie sped toward the uptown La Cuisine Restaurante.

She hastily paid the driver and ran in through the employee entrance, stuffed her bag in the locker and freshened her make up and hair. She was ready to make her entrance.

The head waiter, Phillip, pointed to his watch as he raised his eyebrows in disapproval when he saw her. Janie shuddered as she hurried out to the dimly lit already crowded dining room. She knew she really needed this job and she was on very thin ice with Phillip giving her that all-too-familiar look of disapproval.

"What does it take to get a little service around here?" A fashionably dressed middle-aged woman asked with a strained voice as she tapped the side of her water glass.

"So sorry for the delay, Madame, may I offer you a drink on the house for the inconvenience?" Janie used her sweetest and most sincere voice. She thought, now that was an academy award-winning performance! The old bat; thinks she's the only one in the whole world with a schedule to keep...and the damn free drink will come out of my pocket! On top of that, she'll probably not even leave a decent tip...great.

And so began another long night of serving people their dinners and drinks as they celebrated birthdays, engagements, anniversaries, graduations, promotions, friendships, etc. Janie, the model-thin waitress with the endless energy and bubbly smile, felt empty inside and so alone. Nothing to celebrate and no one to celebrate with.

When she finally walked into her apartment, the light was flashing steadily on her answering machine. First message was her agent, Gloria's thick Brooklyn-Italian accent. "Great news, doll, great news! They've offered you the part of Angie; it will be a regular role. It's prime time soap, millions of people watch this shit every day. This is what we've been waiting for, your big break! Hell, Demi Moore and Jessica Lange both got their starts on soaps...I always knew it was just a matter of time."

Janie stood there in shocked silence and rewound the tape. She listened to the message two more times and then sat down to relax with a coffee mug full of Zinfendel. "My God. My God. I can't believe it...." And she fell asleep on the sofa with the empty coffee mug still in her hand. The other messages would have to wait for another day....

Chapter Five

BARBARA

It had been a fun weekend with Bobby, he was such a genuine sweetheart. And then the surprise call from the always distant Jessica, and she hadn't been her usual unpleasant or testy self. Barbara shook her head and smiled as she settled down at the kitchen table with a cup of tea and her Spanish manuals preparing for the Peace Corps training course; so much to learn and only eight more weeks.

Her parents had reluctantly given their blessings about her two-year commitment to the Peace Corps. It gave her a sense of freedom and security to know they were still her number-one supporters. Also just knowing they'd be there for her children, offering unconditional love and a reminder of their roots.... She knew going to the mountains of Central America to help the less fortunate would somehow help heal the wounds of being Mrs. Billy Malone for so many years.

Her brother Eric and his family were stunned and began to act as if they had just met her and the teenage nephews and eleven-year-old niece were using the Internet to scope out all the details they could about Honduras. They wanted Auntie Barb to take a computer with her to e-mail but since that was not possible, they had promised to write every week. Barbara had promised to take lots of photos and send them descriptive letters about her adventure in the tropics.

Barbara's best friend Alice reasoned, argued and begged her not to go. She presented every negative rational argument and innuendo regarding Americans in Central America or Peace Corps tragedies anywhere in the world. This was very much out of character for Alice who never meddled or gossiped. Alice had never been outside the U.S. and seldom out of their home state of Pennsylvania. She paid close attention to current events and believed without a doubt everything as presented by the media. She freely admitted she was fearful for her friend's safety and very survival. However, they were best friends and Barbara was still going, despite six weeks of the ineffective barrage.

Barbara's mother-in-law was another story. The older Widow Malone was a proud and stoic woman. She had stood beside her ruthless husband and adored her son and grandchildren. She also adored her social position in the community, guaranteed by the wealth and power of her husband. Barbara had always been a bit peculiar in the eyes of her in-laws. The sudden death of Billy, followed by Barbara's announcement of joining the Peace Corps, had rocked the older Mrs. Malone's very foundation. She had aged markedly in the weeks following the funeral. Her personal attorney had visited Barbara to discuss some of the deep concerns expressed by her mother-in-law.

Mr. Bailey, the attorney, cleverly asked many questions in a thinly veiled disguise of concern while assessing Barbara's competency. He was impressed with her sincerity and clarity of thought, besides the fact that she had remained uncorrupted by the trappings of wealth while being part of the Malone family for so many years.

"Amazing," he muttered to himself as he trudged to his car after their two-hour visit. He dreaded reporting to the older widow Malone that there were absolutely no grounds for contesting her son's will or declaring her daughter-in-law incompetent.

Ever so reluctantly the older Mrs. Malone began to reach out to her son's widow. And this did breathe a bit of life into her shriveled soul. She could not fathom anyone giving up modern comforts to "help" the needy; after all, wasn't it their own fault they were poor, ignorant and sick and why did they keep having babies if they couldn't take care of the ones they already had? But Barbara's enthusiasm was genuine and somewhat contagious.

Now her grandchildren would need her more than ever. Sure they were grown up, but they would still need a place to call home. Everyone does. Each of them was so dear to her and so unique. Sweet Billy, charming Bobby, fiery Jessica and the beautiful, complicated Janie. It was good to think about the living rather than dwelling exclusively on the loss of her beloved son. Times like this she truly wished her William was still alive. Despite his faults, he had been her rock.

The older Mrs. Malone toasted Mr. Bailey. "When it's all said and done, the only thing that really matters is family and those young people are now my only family." She slowly and thoughtfully sipped her wine after he had informed her of his assessment of Barbara.

"I quite agree with you. I've been spending more time with Barbara and I have to admit there were moments that she even had me almost feel like joining the Peace Corps!" Mrs. Malone smiled reflectively and thanked Mr. Bailey for his assistance. She knew very well that she would receive a hefty bill for the "assistance."

Barbara methodically prioritized her lists of things to do before leaving for her training. She softly smiled to herself as she thought of the important people in her life and how they had ruefully come around to accept her decision. Even Mother Malone was asking questions that indicated more than just a casual interest and had even hinted at a possible vacation trip to Honduras.

Chapter Six

JANIE

Janie woke up at 10:15 a.m. and her brain felt a bit fuzzy, yet she knew her life was about to change. She called Gloria whose phone screening messages were always changing; today's was even more terse than usual. "Goddamn! I told you not to call me, if anything comes up, I'll call you. Leave your info after the tone...." As Janie started to speak, Gloria picked up and could hardly contain her excitement. "Listen, doll, we need to do lunch an' review the contract before we go for the formal contract signing at 2 p.m....*today*. Kuddos, Sweetie! You must've been real an' total dynamite to make them wanna sign you so fast. They want you to start on the set by Monday, that's only four days. What do ya say, Janie babe?"

Janie took a deep breath and sighed. She smiled as she'd listened to her agent's thick Brooklyn accent and her natural aggressive communication style. "Hey, Glo, I can't believe it!" Tears of relief and joy trickled down her cheeks and she softly said, "Yes, yes, this is what I've been waiting for."

Gloria told her she'd pick up something at a deli and be at Janie's by 12:30. "Listen, Janie, you be ready to roll when I get there, okay? We'll eat a quick bite, review the contract and be on our way. You're gonna knock 'em dead again today."

Before getting up to take a shower, she listened to her other phone messages. Wow! How long had it been since Bobby and Jessica had called her and both on the same day no less? She knew her family viewed her as something of a misfit or worse. Janie had thought they were probably right until last night. She stood up, stretched and decided to start the coffee before showering. She smiled to herself and looked at the street below her window, as if seeing it for the first time. Maybe New York wasn't such a bad place after all. It occurred to her that she hadn't really smiled for a very long time.

Janie sipped her coffee, relishing the strong distinct flavor as she carefully chose the perfect outfit for signing her first real contract. And to think she'd been on the verge of giving up on her dream.

Gloria arrived ten minutes early with her usual flair. "Oh God, doll, you look gorgeous! It's about time those castin' idiots get themselves a real actress. Let's eat an' then move. City's crowded today, a lot of those damn tourist types. An' we don't wanna be late."

Janie signed a generous one-year contract, renewable at the discretion of the studio. She felt like she was on cloud nine. "I wish my dad were still alive to see this! He was always my number-one fan."

Gloria looked at her, arched her eyebrows and with a softer tone than normal, said, "Hey, I keep forgettin' you're not really a tough New Yorker, you're always jus' gonna be a small-town kid from Pennsylvania. Ya know what though, I think your dad will know. I bet he's still your number-one fan. My dad died when I was ten. I had to be tough to look out for my kid brothers and sisters. My mom always was workin' after that, an' then she started hittin' the bottle at night. But I'd talk to my dad when I got scared, I knew Mom was only drinkin' cause she was so sad and lonesome for Dad. Hell, she was only 29 years old and had five kids under ten. I'd a drunk too if I'd a been in her shoes."

They walked on in silence. Finally Janie put her hand on Glo's arm and said, "Thanks for telling me about your dad, and your family. Where are they all now?"

"You know I really don't like to talk about my family much. Most of us New Yorkers don't and for good enough reasons. I'm forty-four years old. Divorced twice. No kids, thank God. I think I got my fill of takin' care of kids when I was growin' up. My brother Jimmy was killed ten years ago, innocent bystander in a drug bust gone bad. My other brother, Lou, joined the Air Force 21 years ago, got himself an education and a nice pension. Nice family, too, even has a couple grandchildren. My sisters have been divorced, Maria remarried a decent guy a few years back. She's doin' okay. Madeline jus' goes from bad to worse, always blames somebody else, nothin' is ever her fault. She's in the State Penitentiary again. Been down there two months this time. Her kids are eight and ten. They live with their father's parents. Mom died two years ago. But life goes on. No matter what, life goes on."

"Sorry about your troubles, Glo, but thanks for telling me. You really manage to take everything in your stride. I admire that."

They walked along enjoying their new sense of camaraderie. "How about a coffee to celebrate my new role? I have about two hours before my shift at La Cuisine Restaurante and I can't wait to give Phillip my two-week notice."

Gloria shrugged. "Sounds good. But no more talk about families. God that's a downer that I sure as hell don't need. How about a toast to your success on the small screen?"

Later that night when things started to slow down at the restaurant, Janie told Phillip her news. She was shocked at his reaction. He pulled out a bottle of good champagne, clanged on a glass to announce her new role and everyone sang "Auld Lang Syne." Staff from the kitchen, waiters, waitresses, management, restaurant patrons besieged her with congratulations and hugs, reminding her that they had known her when and not to get too big for her old friends. Wow. Another surprise to add to an already highly exceptional day.

To top it off, Phillip told her, "You really don't have to work out a two-week notice if you don't want to. And if you ever need to wait tables again, come see me because I can always find a place on the schedule for a classy competent waitress like you, Janie. Now you go knock 'em dead!"

Janie was stunned with everyone's reaction that night. It made her feel very special and yes, even happy. It was too late to call her family after her shift but tomorrow morning first thing, she had some calls to make. Strangely enough it never even occurred to her to smoke a joint or even have a nightcap. She arrived home exhausted, yet contented from the events of the day and slept in her bed without the aid of any chemicals. It was a good change for Janie.

By 9 a.m. the next morning she had showered, had a bagel and coffee, and made a list of people to call to share her good news. Starting with Jess, of course. Then Mom, Billy, Bobby, the "Grands" and finally Arnie. She really hadn't talked to that bum since he'd stiffed her when Billy and Liz were there two weekends ago but she had to share her good news with him; actors were always happy for each other when the struggles pay off and you get a shot at the big time. "Okay, so it's just a soap opera role but it's a year contract and it is on national network TV." She smiled to herself remembering how she had arrived in New York, age 21, right out of college, fully expecting to land a lead role on Broadway. "I just knew I'd never do commercials or daytime soaps. Cripes, I didn't have an agent and couldn't even get into an audition. But I learned the ropes and Gloria has been a godsend. So here I am."

Her family responded to her news in much the same way, only Jess expressed a hint of surprise or cynicism. But any other response from Jess would be out of character. Everyone else said they had been expecting this and wondered what was wrong with those New Yorkers that it took them so long to recognize talent and beauty when they saw it.

Arnie's response had been unexpected. "So, Janie, old girl, how many producers and directors did you have to lay for this role?" The tone of his voice was acidic.

Janie was startled by his words and tone. Yet she managed to respond with a civility she didn't feel. "Why, Arnie, I'd think you were jealous if I didn't know better! I don't expect you to believe me but I won this role on sheer talent. It was just the right part and the right time for me."

"Sure, babe, whatever. Hey, do you need something to celebrate? I could drop by your apartment in an hour or so." Arnie was always trying to supplement his meager acting income by providing his "friends" with their social drug of choice. He was proud of only dealing with "quality products."

"You know, Arnie, I don't think I'll need any for awhile. I want to stay clean. After all these years I finally have a chance and I really don't want to blow it. Hey, I'll talk to you later." Janie leaned back on the sofa.

"Yeah, right. You have my number when you want some good stuff. Oh yeah, and kuddos on your new job. I really mean that, Janie, it's your time to shine." Arnie then cut the connection.

Janie turned off her phone and murmured to herself, "What a jerk, and he's the first unmarried boyfriend I've had since coming to New York!" Janie reflected on the choices she'd made with her life and realized most of them had been made with little regard for consequences and perhaps, just maybe, some of her struggles had been a direct result of her impulsive decisions.

"Maybe it's time for me to thank God I've survived and ask him to show me the way from here on out. Maybe." Janie felt an unfamiliar sense of contentment and prayed, "And please, God, no more married, drug-dealing or mean-spirited boyfriends."

She smiled and somehow knew that her life was going to be different. "I'm going to call my own shots from now on. Sure it'll take my friends and family some time to accept and believe I've really changed but eventually they'll see."

JESSICA

Janie's phone call had been an extremely pleasant surprise. Janie sounded sane and truly happy, even...kind of grown up. "I hope this is the start of better times for my little sister," Jess whispered as she finished her morning chores. As she passed a mirror, she was stunned to see herself...smiling!

"This is probably as good a time as any to call Mom. Might as well get it over with." Jess found herself thinking out loud more and more often; seemed to be a rite of passage for the loners of this world. "No big deal, right?"

Jess called the familiar number, and her mother answered on the fourth ring. "Morning, Mom, how you doing?"

"Jessica, what a wonderful surprise to hear from you. How are you, dear?"

"I'm fine, Mom. Just had a happy call from Janie. Nice change getting a happy call from that one."

"I did, too. It's fantastic, isn't it? I'm so proud of all my children and so happy for Janie's long overdue break. I have a really good feeling about this part."

"Mom, your tape really set me on my ass, it was like right out of left field. I never knew you were entertaining such ideas. Anyway I wondered if you needed any help, I could take a few days off next week. I just want to see you and spend a little time with you before you go. We just lost Dad and now it feels like we're losing you. Oh God, I don't want to start sounding like some emotional...." Jessica's voice cracked as she fought the urge to cry.

"Jessica, honey, I'm only going away for a couple years. I will be back and you can come visit me while I'm in Honduras. It could be an adventure for all of us. And Jess, I can't think of anything I'd like better than to see you. I could use some help and your company would be a real going-away gift. I know how busy you are with your work and that makes your offer even more special. I love you, dear." Her mother's soft reassuring voice momentarily paralyzed Jess's emotions.

"I'll see you Wednesday evening, Mom."

A few minutes later Jess laid the phone down and soon her tears gave way to mournful sobs from deep in her heart. Jess, the strong one who hadn't cried one tear at her father's funeral a few months earlier. This time she didn't fight it as she collapsed on her freshly made bed and cried and cried...till there were no more tears.

BILLY

Billy felt an overwhelming sense of doom and panic as he entered the teachers lounge for an emergency phone call from his sister. This could only be bad news.

"Billy? It's me, Janie. Sorry to call you at work…but I just couldn't wait to tell you, I got a good role in a national daytime soap with a one-year contract. It's like a miracle, after all these years. I was almost ready to give up on New York and then this happened! I'm so happy, I just wanted to tell you, please tell Liz for me."

"Janie, I'm so proud of you. Kuddos! It's about time they chose some real talent. Thank you for calling. Knock 'em dead, little sister!"

"I'll call you at home soon. Billy, thanks for coming weekend before last. I know I wasn't good company but I'm glad I have you, big brother." Janie sighed and smiled as they ended the brief phone call.

Billy sat down, stunned with the flicker of a faint smile; after all these years it almost sounded like the real Janie was back. Her news was a welcome relief, yet he couldn't shake the lingering sense of doom he had felt for her last weekend. Billy was glad for a few moments of solitude in the teachers lounge.

He absentmindedly bit his lip and muttered, "I hope I'm just a pessimistic big brother," as he slowly walked back to his classroom.

BOBBY

Miss Lear informed Bobby immediately after his usual tardy arrival, "Your sister from New York called thirty minutes ago and wants you to call as soon as possible." She took special note of the color draining from his face upon receipt of this message.

He closed his office door and began to call when Miss Lear appeared with a cup of coffee. He immediately laid the phone in its cradle and thanked his lingering secretary for the coffee. Finally he stood up, walked to his office door and said, "Miss Lear, do you mind if I have a few minutes of privacy please? I do not want to be disturbed until I open this door again, understood?"

"Well, I never!" She huffed as she turned and went back to her desk.

Bobby sat at his desk with his face in his hands. "It already feels like a long day and I just got here," he thought. He made a note to call his supervisor to discuss a change in secretary.

He decided to use his cell phone to call Janie. What a relief to hear her happy news. She was delighted at the prospect of Bobby coming to visit the coming weekend. Plans were made and both anticipated their first "sister, brother" visit in years, only two days away.

Then he called Mr. McDowell and told him, "I think there might be a bit of a personality conflict between Miss Lear and me. She's a competent secretary but I was hoping to maybe have someone less overbearing traded into her position."

Bobby did not expect the response. McDowell howled with laughter. "You got balls, Bob Malone! It's a rare first-year lawyer who'd have the guts to ask for a different secretary. Let me tell you something, it's just not going to happen. She's part of your initiation to the legal world, helps us weed out the undesirables. Bide your time, kid, you're doing okay. Hey, I liked your work on Giles vs. Powell. You've got a great future. Oh and tell Miss Lear I said, 'Keep up the good work!'"

Bobby hung the phone up after a feeble attempt at a pleasant good-bye to his supervisor. He focused his growing frustration and anger with a vengeance on the next file on his agenda. He worked for four uninterrupted hours, never once opening the door to his office. Before he went out for a quick lunch, he assembled his desk with a tiny clear label between the top two papers, as a test of his office privacy. He only nodded to his "dear" Miss Lears as he walked out. Upon returning he was not surprised to find the tiny clear label under his chair. Other than the moved label, all the papers and files on his desk seemed to be exactly as he left them. Bobby silently decided, "That does it. Tomorrow I'll come early and install a new lock on my office door...."

Bobby worked as if in a trance and his superiors were increasingly impressed with his single-minded ability to produce results in the huge back-up of files they had dumped on him. As usual he worked until 11:30 p.m. and arrived late again on Thursday. However, he left by 7 p.m. and stopped at Home Depot on his way home. On Friday he arrived at the office at 5:30 a.m., his brief case loaded with necessary tools and the new doorknob and lock set. He bought one as close to the original as possible to avert immediate attention from the change in locks. Bobby had a premonition that this wouldn't sit well with the powers that be. He even brought his own handvac cleaner to clean up any residue that might accumulate as a result of his project. He carefully packed the old doorknob and his tools into his briefcase. With his mission completed, he made a fresh pot of coffee to welcome the rest of the staff.

He knew that a couple of his first-year counterparts were very close to resigning, the married ones appeared to be the most stressed. He vowed, "If

I'm ever in a position to offer young lawyers a start, I will treat them with dignity and respect, I would never use my position or power to try to break them."

Miss Lears arrived at 7:15 a.m. She was stunned to smell fresh coffee, hear the copy machine's gentle hum and to see Bob Malone already working in his small office.

When he heard her, he went out for a fresh coffee and said with exaggerated charm, "Good Morning, dear Miss Lears, how 'bout a cup of java?"

For once she was without words, except to say in a very strained voice, "Yes, that would be nice." It was clear she did not like someone, especially him, stealing her morning thunder.

"I must get back to work." Bobby smiled and nodded to her as he gave her a cup of coffee and sauntered back to his newly secure office.

Chapter Seven

JESSICA

Jess was flooded with ambivalent feelings as she prepared for the three days at home with her mother. She couldn't help but secretly wish she was six years old again. The world had made sense back then; there were no complications and she had felt safe and secure. "What happened to me? How did I change into this cynical angry old maid?"

She felt her teeth begin to grind as the bottled-up hostility took over again. Jess had arranged for one personal day and two vacation days, starting on Wednesday with an open weekend. She'd have the option of staying longer if she decided to.

Seeing the "grands" was definitely a positive and seeing Mom would be good. "I just wish I didn't have so many negative feelings about going home." Jess quickly packed her bag; it was easy to travel light when she didn't feel a need to impress anyone. She packed only a sweater, one extra pair of jeans and two shirts. "After all, Mom has a washer."

Jess scrubbed the gloom from her face and applied a light foundation and eye liner, stood back and couldn't help admire her trim figure. "At least I've never had a weight problem, I can be thankful for good genes. Oh yeah, but what about Dad's sudden heart attack? Guess the genes aren't exactly perfect." Jess had mastered loneliness by constantly chatting with herself, mostly silently. She had found over time that her own company was by far less annoying than anyone else's.

After driving four hours to get home, Jess decided to stop at Grandmother Malone's before going to Mom's. She always felt better after visiting the fiery old lady who loved her so completely and with absolutely no strings attached.

Grandmother loved to hear about Jess's life and laughed till she cried at some of her work stories.

Grandmother let down all her sophisticated ways, wiped her eyes and said, "You tell a story just the way your dear grandfather did. I love your visits and phone calls. Dear Jessie, how are you, darling? I miss you so much." And Grandmother reached across the table and squeezed her granddaughter's hand.

Jess felt reinvigorated after an hour with Grandmother Malone. Jess thought how much she would want grandchildren when she was old, but dreaded the husband part and having to balance children, marriage and work demands as a career woman in order to have grandchildren someday. She often saw the strain on the faces of her female co-workers, those married with children, and felt sympathy for them. A good book or relaxing bath was not something these women had had time for in years.

Onward to her childhood home; Jessica felt an overwhelming dread of the inevitable as the sprawling home came into view. She slowly turned her Honda into the driveway. She stood by the back door, bag in hand as a flood of happy memories brought an unexpected smile. The door opened. "Oh Jess, you're really here! I've missed you. We're going to have a wonderful time this week. Just wait and see." Her mother embraced her.

Jessica returned the hug. "I'm glad to be home again, Mom." And she meant it.

The next three days flew by, much to Jessica's surprise, and she decided to stay until Sunday afternoon. Being with the grands, Mormor and Morfar, as well as Grandmother Malone, was refreshingly sweet and fun. No wonder she had loved them so much as a child. And Mom; it was like meeting her for the first time. A new friend who accepted and loved her beyond reason. "Good thing this 'new friend' can't read minds or she'd know I'm not nearly as lovable as she thinks I am," Jess mumbled as she enjoyed the beautiful autumn day on the old wooden swing behind the house.

Her mother suddenly appeared with two tumblers of iced tea. "Want some company?"

"Thanks, Mom." Jess sipped the tea and the pleasant taste lingered. "No one can make tea like yours."

They sat in comfortable silence until Jessica hesitantly asked, "Mom, why the Peace Corps? Why Honduras? If you want to work, why not be a nurse here in Lewiston? I saw the newspaper classified; they need nurses right here."

Barbara reached over and gently took Jess's hand in hers. With a faraway look in her eyes, she looked at her daughter and then began to speak in a soft tone that gradually became animated as a new found glow of anticipation swept over her.... "Oh, Jessica, I hope I can help you understand. We all have so much here in America and I truly love our country. But I've volunteered at the hospital and I have many friends in nursing. Paper pushing is just not the kind of nursing I want to do. I want to help people who truly need help. It is astounding how little the mountain tribes have. How little they expect and how very much they need. They've been so appreciative of the Peace Corps efforts and the Corps' so pleased to have a bilingual nurse. Do you understand...just a little better now, Jess?"

Jessica was embarrassed to find herself tearful again and nodded. "Yeah, a little, but I still wish you weren't going." She choked back her tears and quietly said, "What if something happens to you?"

"Jess, my dear, 'something' could happen to me right here in Lewiston. Your father died on the golf course. Besides, I really need a change of scene. I have so many things to sort out in my mind. Helping those in need is one of the best ways to help oneself. I'm sure you see that in your work as a physical therapist." Barbara gently squeezed her daughter's hand and continued. "You know, I feel this is where I should be at this time in my life. When we are open to going and doing what God wants us to do, we can feel a sense of peace that is unsurpassed in this world."

They sat together in a peaceful silence enjoying the fall colors and the gentle afternoon breeze.

"Mom, there is something else that really bothers me. What about giving Dad's estate to charity, I...well, I just don't think that's fair to us." Jess sighed and stared at the ground as she thought, "At least I managed to say it."

"Having money is a big responsibility; it can be a curse as well as a blessing. In talking with your grandparents and the attorney, I've decided to leave everything as it is until I return in two years. It's invested in secure trusts for now. Uncle Eric and Morfar will monitor financial reports while I'm away." After a somewhat uncomfortable minute of silence, Barbara continued, "Does that make you feel any better, Jess? I'd never cheat my children; I hope you realize that, dear."

Sunday afternoon came too quickly. All three grands came to bid her farewell and inform her of her need to come home more often. Jess knew they were right. Her final hug was for her mother. "I promise I'll be home one more weekend before you leave, Mom."

The cynical Jessica found tears on her cheeks again, but this time they were caused by a sense of peace, a new feeling of connectedness with her family that somehow made her feel less alone in the world.

BOBBY

The long drive to Janie's had been uneventful. It seemed the heavy traffic was going out of the city so he had made good time. Janie had sounded good on the phone but he couldn't help fearing it was just another of her many phases. But then this was her first real chance at breaking into her chosen field of work. He wanted to believe she would make it….

Janie was thrilled to see Bobby and made no effort to hide her excitement. She had picked up Chinese dinners, which they enjoyed with leisurely glasses of wine. Catching up was always fun when Janie was in a good mood. And Bobby had never seen her happier.

She confessed with a great deal of self-depreciating humor about her bankrupt love life. "No more married men, drug dealers or mean-spirited boyfriends for me. But the hard part is the initial screening. Not one of those jerks told me about their secrets until we were on second base, heading for third. By then it's always a bit complicated. I just broke off with a guy named Arnie. In New York City there are so many phonies. He's a struggling actor, supplements his income as a 'social drug provider.' So many people use; well, I've been clean for a week now and I don't plan to use anymore. Do you know what that bastard said to me when I told him about the new role? He says, 'So how many directors and producers did you have to lay for this part?' Never a congrats, nothing but bitterness and resentment. I think he was jealous that I finally got a break. And, Bobby, this time I gave no favors to anyone at the studio. I was one cold bitch and they gave me the part. Oh God, I'm so happy, I can hardly believe it. Did you know I was on the verge of throwing in the towel and giving up on acting? But I thought okay, one more audition and boom, it happened." She leaned back on the sofa and smiled as she raised her glass. "To my brother, the sassy lawyer!"

Bobby smiled in return and toasted Janie. "To my sister, the gorgeous big-city actress!"

As their glasses met, they laughed and said together, "To the Malones!"

"So, tell me about your life, any special lady I should know about? Come on, Bobby, spill the beans!" Janie always wanted to know about everyone's love life. She considered it much more interesting and unpredictable than work news.

"Work takes up all my time, Janie. It's grueling, boring and leaves no time for any social life. Guess you could say I'm paying my dues. It certainly is not what I expected when I started law school. Paper shuffling. But enough of that, I'm tired and we need some rest if we're going to do the town tomorrow." With that, Bobby carried his empty glass to the tiny kitchen.

The weekend sped by: shopping, museums, theater and a late dinner at La Cuisine Restaurante where Janie proudly introduced her brother to her former co-workers. Bobby was pleased to see Janie had been working in a classy place with great food.

On Sunday they enjoyed an unhurried brunch at a small café near Central Park and then a pleasant walk through the park, which was at its height of autumn glory. They talked about their mother's plans to work in Honduras with the Peace Corps. Bobby told her about his visit home two weeks ago and, "I hope to spend one more weekend with Mom before she leaves. In many ways it was like I was meeting her for the first time. We're lucky to have such a courageous woman as our mother. I don't know anyone else whose *mother* has joined the Peace Corps! Do you?"

"Well, no, I don't think I do. But doesn't that in itself seem just a little kooky?" Janie stared straight ahead, deep in thought.

Bobby smiled softly to himself, hoping Janie wouldn't notice. He thought, "Man, that's like the pot calling the kettle black." After a few seconds, he said, "You know, Janie, you really ought to go see Mom for a day or two before she leaves, I know it would help you understand. I think Jess went home this weekend."

Janie looked at him in surprise. "She did? How did that come about? She and Mom always seemed to mix like oil and water. I hope they both survive the weekend."

"You know, I think they will be fine. It's time to bury the old grudges and move on. What do you say, want to plan a weekend home?" Bobby persisted.

"I don't know. I'll have to think about it. There're so many ghosts in that house and all around Lewiston. I just don't know if I'm ready for that yet," Janie answered flatly.

As he prepared to leave he gave his little sister a warm hug and wished her well for her first day on the set. He made a mental note to send her a dozen red roses with a note, "Break a leg!" First thing tomorrow.

Bobby felt lucky again, to be driving against the flow of heavy traffic as he started the long drive home. Yes, he was glad he had come and he felt much better about Janie. He wasn't much of a praying man but couldn't help whispering a little prayer asking God to somehow keep his little sister safe.

Chapter Eight

BARBARA

So little time and so much to do. All magazines had been cancelled. Newspaper cancelled. Cable cancelled. Phone service would be discontinued in three weeks. All valuables had been carefully packed and placed in the large safety deposit box at the bank. Rugs had been rolled and placed in the storage room at her parents'. The few good paintings were placed in an extra upstairs room at Mother Malone's. She had three weeks to tie up any forgotten loose ends. Barbara made a quick note to contact utility companies; she'd have water and sewage turned off, and leave electric on for the automatic timers and gas on to keep minimum heat in the house. Barbara made a note to talk to her father and sons about the stereo system, televisions and computer. Might not be a good idea to leave them in an empty house…no sense making it easy for thieves.

Barbara looked at the calendar and sighed. "Oh yes, today I'm having lunch with Alice. She's had a hard time adjusting to the idea of me going. At least she's given up trying to talk me out of it, but makes it quite obvious she is not a happy camper about it."

Next thing on her list was to choose the right clothing, several pairs of khaki slacks, one travel dress, one pair of sandals, two pairs of good walking shoes, a few pairs of khaki shorts, tee shirts, two cotton blouses, one sweater, one all-weather jacket, socks, underwear, two lightweight pajamas, toiletries, two flashlights, extra batteries, camera, extra film, stationery, pens…her list seemed to be complete. There was still plenty of time to recheck her supply list. Sometimes Barbara did feel a little uneasy about her decision. She'd hardly ever traveled out of Lewiston, let alone live anywhere else. Here she was, a middle-aged widow...yet on the other hand she truly believed this is what she should do. It was her chance to make a personal contribution to a worthy cause. She smiled ruefully to herself. "I've been talking the talk, now it's time to see if I can walk the walk."

Lunch with Alice was surprisingly light and uplifting, just as it had been before the "changes."

"So, tell me how did the weekend with Jessica go? Is she still upset about you going away?"

Barbara's radiant smile answered the question before she even started to speak. "It was by far the best time I've had with Jessica since she was a young girl. I think she might even come visit me in Honduras and she wants to come home for another visit before I leave. The weekend was simply amazing!"

Barbara informed Alice as they casually window shopped after lunch, "You do realize I expect you to visit me after I'm settled and get my bearings. It will be an adventure for both of us."

"I don't know. I won't make any promises. I know I'm really going to miss you," Alice answered quietly as they walked arm-in-arm. She thought, "I'm so glad to have Gwen and the grandchildren living in town. Not to mention Jimmy, my husband and friend for thirty-four years. Sure, he's not rich like Barbara's Bill and thank God he wasn't the cheat Bill had been. If Barbara wants to do this Peace Corps thing, then so be it. Maybe she'll find 'peace.' She deserves whatever she wants after all those years of putting up with wild Bill."

"Well, at least that's almost a yes." Barbara happily squeezed her friend's hand as if extracting a solemn promise of a visit to Honduras.

That night she received phone calls from Jessica, Billy and Bobby. Billy and Liz were planning to come home next weekend. Bobby told her about his weekend with Janie in the city, and Jessica just called to thank her for a wonderful weekend and say, "I love you, Mom."

Barbara called Janie to inquire about her first day on the set, to see when her part would start on television and wish her luck. "I'm so proud of you, Janie."

After an unusually pleasant and short conversation with Janie, she hung up the phone feeling satisfied and happy. Life truly was good. As she turned out the light, her last thoughts were of her children and how very much she loved them and always would. Having them made everything worthwhile....

Chapter Nine

BILLY

Billy was clearly relieved after talking to Bobby about his weekend visit with Janie. The new role certainly seemed to have perked her up and maybe even served as a wake-up call. She sounded much different than when he and Liz visited two weeks earlier. Whatever caused it, he hoped it would be a permanent change. "Break a leg, Janie," he thought with a weary smile.

Next he hesitantly called Jessica, never knowing what to expect. Especially after her dreaded weekend home. Billy was stunned at the difference in her attitude towards their mother. It was definitely a much less bitter Jessica. Again he hoped it would be a lasting transformation of his far-too-cynical sister.

Finally he called his mother and she was delighted to hear Liz and Billy were coming for a weekend. Billy was pleasantly surprised when she told him about the peace and joy she had experienced during Jessica's visit. He ended the long conversation with mounting anticipation for the coming weekend. "We should arrive around ten on Friday evening. See you then."

"Mom seemed really happy that we're coming for a visit. I can't help being curious about Jessica's transformation. Incredible." He told Liz about the latest family news.

Hectic teaching schedules quickly brought Friday to Liz and Billy. They put their weekend bags in the car before leaving for school and left for Lewiston as soon as the final bell rang. Heavy rain and traffic slowed them down considerably; they didn't arrive until 11:30 p.m.

Barbara had a pot of tea, sandwiches and Billy's favorite chocolate chip cookies waiting for them. They talked till 1 a.m. "It's good to be home again," Billy said to his mother as he kissed her good night.

"Oh Billy, it's so good to have you and Liz here. We're going to have a grand weekend. Sleep well, my dears." With that, Barbara walked down the hall to her bedroom.

Liz smiled at Billy as she wrapped her arms around him. "You know I've always liked your mom. Though invariably, I felt her smiles were an effort at camouflaging a deep unhappiness...but I've never seen her looking more radiant or contented than she was tonight."

The next day after a late breakfast, Barbara, Liz and Billy visited Mormor and Morfar Olson. They were a little older than he remembered them but just as active and full of energy. They talked in solemn guarded tones about their daughter's frightening decision to go to a foreign tropical country to work as a nurse. Barbara had laughed and reassured them *again*, "I'll be fine...you'll see when you come to visit that it's just about helping and teaching the less fortunate."

Before leaving, Morfar pulled Billy aside and asked him man to man, "Liz is a real sweetheart. When're you going to marry her, boy? Don't you think it's time you make an honest woman out of her? What kind of an example are you setting for your students? Living in fornication! It's time you settle down and make a commitment to this girl. Have a family."

Billy squirmed but admired his grandfather's boldness. "Yes, sir, Morfar, I'll talk to Liz. You'll be the first to know." He had always enjoyed an especially close relationship with Morfar and hated the disappointed look on his grandfather's face. Maybe it really was time to get married. He decided to talk to Liz. Billy knew beyond a doubt that she was the woman for him.

Grandmother Malone was waiting for them with afternoon tea. Liz liked all of his grands but enjoyed this one the most. She was in rare form, candid about the conflict she had felt about his mother's decision to join the Peace Corps and how doubtful she had been about Barbara's. But she'd come to accept the inevitable.

Barbara chuckled as she teased her mother-in-law and told Billy and Liz about the attorney Grandmother Malone had sent to evaluate her ability to make rational decisions.

Sunday afternoon rolled around way too quickly. All the grands came over to see them off; it had been a good weekend home for Liz and Billy. Barbara gave them their final hugs goodbye.

They drove in silence until they reached the main highway, comfortably holding hands. Billy kissed Liz's hand and thanked her for coming home with him for the weekend. She gave him a puzzled look and asked, "What did you expect me to do, send you off alone? Hey, we're a team, remember?"

Billy swallowed hard, pulled the car to the side of the highway, gently framed her face with his hands and whispered, "Liz, my love, will you marry me? We could make our 'team' official, what do you think? Will you?"

Liz was stunned! Tears slowly welled up in her eyes, her left hand covered his and her right hand gently stroked his face. "Yes, Billy, yes."

They sealed their big decision with a slow sweet kiss, and drove an hour without talking, just holding hands in a state of blissful rare contentment.

She silently kissed his hand and asked, "When do you want to do it? We've talked about it in the abstract before. I said I didn't want a big wedding and I meant it; it'd be too much stress and too much hoopla for me. What do you think?"

Billy grinned at her and agreed. "I don't want a big wedding either. I just want us to be married. What about this week? We could apply for our license tomorrow after school and take personal days on Thursday and Friday and be married by next weekend. What do you think?"

"I think I like your style, Billy Malone! Let's do it. We can call our families after it's all said and done and tell them the news. I'll bet they'll protest but secretly be relieved that no one had to deal with the big wedding blues."

Later that night he told her about Morfar's stern words on responsibility and Liz laughed and said, "Bless the dear man! It's about time. Maybe in two weeks we could get all your family together for a wedding dinner, our treat. Do you think Jessica, Janie and Bobby would come? Of course, we want your mom and the grands, too."

"I think so. Everyone wants to see Mom one more time before she leaves anyway. The way I see it, if my mother can join the Peace Corps without consulting the family, then I can marry the best girl I'll ever know and tell them about it after the fact. Besides they all love you and have been waiting for an announcement, invitation or something ever since they met you."

Thursday they shopped for wedding rings. Liz decided she wanted a new dress and new sheets for the bed they'd shared for the past two years. They'd decided it would be silly to stay in a hotel on their wedding night since they weren't going anywhere. So they used that money plus some more to buy truly exquisite new bedding for their wedding night. They also bought a few fresh flowers for the apartment, a bouquet of baby pink roses for Liz and a matching boutonnière for Billy.

They decided on a Friday afternoon wedding at a neighborhood Protestant church they had visited a few times. The pastor was enthusiastic; his wife agreed to be a witness as did the church secretary. The organist provided traditional background wedding music. Liz looked gorgeous in her new ivory satin tea length dress. Liz and Bobby thought their wedding was perfect in every way.

Mr. and Mrs. William Malone were radiant and had no regrets about not having a large wedding or reception. They simply felt lucky to have found each other and to have had the courage finally...so be it with a little nudge from Morfar Olson, to have made the formal commitment. They stopped at the photographer for a few formal wedding photos. Later the newlyweds enjoyed a quiet candlelight dinner with soft romantic music, champagne and their favorite Chinese take-out. That night on their beautiful new sheets and bedding, they discovered there was nothing more precious than love with someone who loved you enough to make a commitment. They laughed remembering their pre-wedding jitters. Liz and Billy fell asleep contently.

Both of them came from unhappily married parents; having separate small wedding parties would make it much easier for Liz. Her mother and father had bitterly divorced when she was ten years old. Both parents still threw verbal darts at each other every time she talked with them. After seventeen years of listening to their foolish pain, Liz coped best by avoiding them as much as possible. She loved the fact Billy had sisters and a brother. She had been a lonely only child and the brunt of her parents' ongoing battle. Her grandparents had all died before her sixteenth birthday.

Late Saturday morning they began calling family to notify them of their marriage. Liz saved her parents for last. They called Barbara first. She was stunned but very happy. She insisted on hosting a small wedding dinner for them in Lewiston in two weeks, five days before she'd leave. His mother promised not to call anyone about the dinner party until later that afternoon. That would give Liz and Bill time to share their happy news with the family.

Then they called Mormor and Morfar Olson first and the old man cried; he was so happy. He was pleased they'd be coming home again so soon to celebrate their marriage.

Mormor was ecstatic and could hardly wait to call Barbara to help start planning the celebration. "Surely this will be worthy of all the grandchildren coming home, including Eric and his family from California," she thought with happiness and anticipation.

Next was Grandmother Malone. Billy enjoyed this grandmother but never knew quite what to expect. She was as unpredictable as the other grandparents were predictable. After listening to their news and then to their reasons for the short simple wedding, Billy was concerned about her silence.

One thing Grandmother Malone always had plenty of was words. Finally he asked, "Are you all right, Grandmother?"

"Well. My God in heaven! Of course, I'm all right. Not that you'd likely care. You didn't even invite me to your wedding!" Grandmother retorted. Billy smiled at Liz and gave her a thumbs-up sign.

Billy was startled when Grandmother started to laugh. "Actually I'm thrilled for you both and I don't blame you a bit for not wanting to go through all the headaches of a big catered affair. Bless you and be happy. Stay best friends. And I'm so glad you'll be home in two weeks to allow us to congratulate you both for your good taste and celebrate your marriage."

"Wow. That old girl is always a trip. That's four down and three for me to go and two for you. I'm glad we decided to print up our own announcement and scan a wedding photo on each." Billy looked at his new wife admiringly and asked, "Would you like a coke, coffee or tea?"

"Me too. And it's good that the photographer will have our pictures ready for us by next Wednesday. I'll go ahead and preprint up all the envelopes this afternoon. I'll write the announcements too and leave room for the photo. Then next Wednesday evening we can print them up and get them in the mail Thursday. Oh, no thanks, I'm not thirsty yet," Liz answered him while concentrating on her to-do list.

Billy smiled and leaned over to kiss his wife's cheek. Then he called Bobby, only to get the answering machine. He left a brief but bold message and knew it would merit a speedy response.

Jessica answered her phone on the second ring, and started to chatter immediately about her weekend home. Billy couldn't remember the last time he had heard her sound positive about anything, especially home or Mom. Finally he took the initiative to tell her he'd called with big news. Her reaction reminded him of Grandmother Malone's, first a negative self-centered rebuke followed by joy and excitement. It helped that everyone had known Liz for the last two years and they all loved her. He was a lucky man indeed.

Next he called Janie. She was excited to hear from him, she sounded good. Sounded clean. Her first week of work as a soap opera actress had been even better than she'd expected.

Finally she asked, "What's new with you?"

He told her. She immediately started to scream with joy. "I'm so happy for you both. Liz is great. Oh, Billy, you devil, you! You're both so lucky…I hope some day I'll find a soul mate. This is fantastic news!"

"Thanks, Janie. Hey, what happened with your friend Arnie? He seemed like a nice enough sort," Billy forced himself to ask.

"Let's just say he's history and I'm damn lucky for it. He was not a nice sort. Of course at the beginning he seemed like he might be different than the others. I've had the worst luck with men. Oh well, I'm just sooo happy for you and Liz," Janie answered.

He mentioned the wedding dinner Mom was having in two weeks and even Janie said she'd be there. "It's not every day my big brother gets married!"

Liz deftly handled the calls to her parents. She scheduled them for two different weekends and promised to make them each (with their current paramours) reservations at the local Marriott Hotel. At times like this Liz was very thankful for a small apartment.

Just as they were about to leave for an afternoon walk, the phone rang. Billy looked at Liz and asked, "Well, Mrs. Malone, do you think we should answer that or let the machine pick it up?"

Liz looked at him and then the phone. The ringing was very persistent. She smiled coyly. "Maybe you should answer it. Then we'll go for a walk."

Billy turned the speaker phone on and said, "Hello."

Bobby replied, "So tell me your big news, big brother!"

Billy told him about their wedding, about Morfar's chiding on their visit home and about the wedding dinner in two weeks in Lewiston...which would also be a farewell dinner for Mom.

"Well. Congratulations. Whew, it's not often I'm at a loss for words. You blindsided me. I just didn't see it coming. I mean, Liz is a heck of a girl and you two are great together. I guess I was expecting to be your best man someday...oh, hell, what's the matter with me? This is great news. You bet I'll be there for the celebration," Bobby answered. He obviously preferred control to surprises. But when he came around, his approval was one hundred percent. He had always relied on his older brother for moral support. Despite his mother's efforts, growing up unscathed in the Malone home had been impossible. After a few minutes of pleasantries, they said good-bye and the newlyweds went for their walk.

Billy gently squeezed her hand and whispered, "What a week, Liz. I'm really glad we did it, though. How about you?"

Liz squeezed his hand and laid her head on his shoulder as they continued their walk down Chestnut Street. "You know I am. Quiet and simple is the only way to get married as far as I'm concerned. Ours was the most romantic wedding I've ever seen."

At the corner while waiting for traffic, they tenderly embraced and kissed. For them life was perfect right there on the corner of Chestnut Street and Laurel Avenue.

JANIE

"Well, now there's no choice, I'm going home. I have to be there for Billy and Liz. And Mom. It'll be easier with everyone around. Not like I have to spend time with her alone. I know none of the shit was really her fault. I just feel like I've had to prostitute myself for too many years. I hate to admit it, but it's really pretty neat that Mom is going off with the Peace Corps. Who knows, maybe I'll do the same thing someday." Janie continued, "Thinking aloud, a common habit or is it a curse for singles? Oh shit, who cares?" She smiled. "Only four days on the show and already I've been recognized by a few soap fans. At least I'll have a small claim to fame when I go home in two weeks. Maybe they'll look at me with a little respect instead of all that damn pity and concern."

Her thoughts were interrupted by the phone. She wasn't surprised to hear her mother on the line. "Yes, Mom, I talked to the newlyweds, they sound so happy. Of course I want to come to their wedding dinner. How are you, Mom? I've wanted to call...just been so busy."

"Janie, it's so good to hear your voice. We've all been watching you on the soap. You steal the show with your radiance; you simply glow! Sometimes it's embarrassing...we feel like we're eavesdropping on someone. You don't seem to be acting. You make it seem so real."

Janie was thrilled with her mother's review of her work. "Hey, Mom, you don't think you could be just a little prejudiced with your opinion? But I really do appreciate your vote of confidence. Would you believe, I was just ready to give up on acting when I finally got a break."

"You deserve it, dear. You've worked and struggled a long time and you are very talented. Your grandparents and old friends in town are so proud and excited for you. Your father would have been ecstatic...." Barbara's words seemed to just hang in mid air.

Finally Janie replied, "Not to change the subject, but I don't have a clue what to give Billy and Liz as a wedding gift. Any ideas?"

"Gosh, it's hard to know what would be best. Maybe theater tickets and a weekend in the city. They love live theater. Maybe a gift certificate from

Macy's. You'll have to decide, but I'm sure whatever you do, they'd love it because it came from you," Barbara reassured her daughter.

After a few more minutes of small talk, and promises from Janie to be home before midnight on Friday, just twelve more days, they said good-bye.

Janie was surprised at how good she felt after talking to her mother whom she had carefully avoided as much as possible for the past fourteen years. She shook her head and muttered with a wry smile, "Ain't life strange?"

Chapter Ten

BARBARA

Barbara's to-do list had suddenly grown even longer. But it was a healthy and positive growth. She had talked with all the children and everyone had agreed to come home for the wedding dinner in two weeks. Eric and his family were flying in from California for five days, Thursday through Monday. Katie's children, the North Carolina cousins, were even coming. Her parents and Mother Malone were as excited as she was, maybe more so. They'd all agreed it would be catered in the large private dining room at the Lewiston Country Club. Wedding decorations, cake and music were part of the package. They felt very lucky the date had been available at the last minute. The club manager had said, "Thank goodness for cancellations."

Barbara whispered, "Amen!" It certainly simplified the party planning. Barbara insisted she'd pick up the tab over protests from her parents, Mother Malone and the newlyweds. They were all a bit baffled with Barbara's new streak of boldness.

She went to the best gift shop in town and carefully chose an eleven-by-fourteen silver picture frame, to be engraved with Mr. and Mrs. William Malone, and their wedding date. Next she went to the bank and cashed a ten-thousand-dollar CD and had a cashier's check printed by the bank for the newlyweds. She was relieved to have accomplished so much in one morning.

Barbara called Alice, told her the big news, and invited her and the family to the celebration. Next a couple of Billy's close childhood friends who still lived in the area. Mother Malone insisted on inviting Charlie since he and Bill had grown up together as had their children. Still it would be a relatively small affair.

Of course, Barbara realized that many of the guests would also be attending to bid her farewell as she would be leaving the following Wednesday to officially begin her training for the Peace Corps.

Everything seemed to be falling into place as she completed last-minute details on her party "to do" list as well as her Peace Corps "to do" list. One morning she called Jessica to chat and felt so grateful to finally have a warm and gratifying relationship with a daughter. She told her about Eric and his family flying in from California. They'd be staying with the Olson grandparents. The North Carolina cousins had booked rooms at the local Holiday Inn; they liked the idea of an indoor swimming pool.

Sleeping arrangements had to be reorganized to comfortably accommodate the newlyweds for the upcoming weekend. Barbara hesitantly asked, "I know how close you and Grandmother Malone are. She will feel more involved in everything if you are with her. She lives close by, so you'll be able to spend as much time with us as you'd like. What do you think, Jessica? Is it okay with you?"

"Sure, Mom, no problem. Will my old room be the honeymoon suite? Ooo, la, la!" Jessica couldn't resist a bit of teasing. She knew her mom never liked to reference anything even slightly sexual. That's just the way she was.

Barbara ignored the remark just as Jessica had expected. "Thanks, Jess. I knew I could count on you. See you Friday evening."

Jessica mumbled as she walked away from the phone, "And then she signs up to go off to the tropical jungles. According to the National Geographic and Discovery channel, some of those primitive mountain tribes can be pretty uninhibited about their sexual activities. Boy, I hope you know what you're doing, Mom."

Barbara smiled and shook her head as she marked another check on her list. "Jessica *always* had something off the cuff to say! But I'd like her even if she wasn't my daughter." She laid the pen down, sipped her lukewarm tea and reflected on her life. "It really wasn't so bad. I actually have connections to four young people whom I like and respect, not just because I'm their mother. I have had wonderful parents who are still active and in good health as well as a very unique and devoted mother-in-law. I have no financial worries, an education, good health and a future. So, I had a lousy marriage, life isn't perfect. Somehow, today I feel like a winner."

Barbara called the florist to have fresh bouquets ordered for each grandparent's home and three for hers, one for the "honeymoon suite," one for the living room, and one for the dining room. Things were looking a bit Spartan with so much already locked up in the bank vault or in storage.

She decided to spend the afternoon reviewing her Spanish language tapes to refresh her memory since she seldom had a chance to use the language and it would be her primary communication all too soon. As the date drew closer, Barbara couldn't help feeling a little apprehensive about her decision. It wasn't that she was sorry about her choice, just a free-floating ambivalence about the unknown.

Eric and family's flight had arrived on time Thursday afternoon. Barbara had made the two-hour drive to the airport to save her parents the hassle and also for the chance to have her brother, Joanne and the children to herself for a few hours. The children had kept a steady barrage of questions going her way. Twelve-year-old Erica seemed to think her Aunt Barbara was the absolute most interesting person on earth. Joanne told Barbara, "The girl hardly talks of anything else except you, the Peace Corps and Honduras."

Barbara smiled at her niece and found a young lady who overwhelmingly reminded her of herself so many years ago.

Katie's adult children arrived Friday afternoon. Mormor and Morfar were thrilled to see them again, the living links to their Katie.

All the Malone children had arrived between eight o'clock and midnight on Friday night. This was a much happier reunion than the one a few months earlier when they'd all come home for their father's funeral.

Liz and Billy radiated such happiness and love. For the past two and a half years they had complemented each other and proved to be very compatible, but this new glow seemed the result of finally getting off the fence and officially committing their lives to each other, despite their mutual exposure to growing up in atmospheres lacking marital harmony.

Saturday the weather was cool and clear. The wedding party was perfect. Liz was lovely in her ivory satin wedding dress.

The photographer, Jim Campbell, captured candid shots where everyone looked just as happy as in the posed family portraits. Jim commented to Morfar, "This is how everyone oughta get married. Hell of a lot less pressure on the bride and groom and everyone else in the family. And it does the job just as good as those big fancy weddings. You wouldn't believe the fightin' and carryin' on some families put themselves through. And then half of them are divorced before they even been married five years. Hell, it took me longer than that to figure out how to get along with my woman. Once we got each other figured out, it's been fairly smooth sailin', know what I mean?"

Morfar Olson smiled and nodded. "Sure do, Jim. Takes time and patience. I wouldn't be half the man I am without my missus. We've made a damn good team for goin' on fifty-five years now."

Liz and Billy were stunned with the generosity and thought their family had put into choosing their gifts. The handmaid quilt from Mormor Olson was the perfect color for their bedroom. She'd even embroidered their wedding date and names on it. Liz was bewildered. "How could you have possibly completed a quilt in the short time since our wedding."

Mormor's eyes twinkled as she smiled. "Honey, I've had it all done for more than a year and was just waitin' to add the date. I knew you two would be marryin' one of these days."

Everyone enjoyed Mormor's candor. She'd always had a talent for insightful perceptions and rarely missed the mark. She easily qualified for a PhD in common sense.

Liz and Billy were touched with Janie's gift of four theater tickets and a weekend alone in her apartment. Janie winked as she smiled and said, "I thought I'd make a trip home and see the grands for a weekend while you two paint the town."

Jessica gave them an exquisite Dave Hodge bronze horse statue, a collector item for sure. Just looking at it brought back happy memories of horseback riding with his sisters and Bobby at the stable near Lewiston. "Thanks, Jess, it's perfect. It really is. Thank you."

Bobby gave them a generous gift certificate for Macy's. "You can use it the weekend you go to the theater. Buy yourselves new dishes or whatever else you might need to start your married life together."

Grandmother Malone gave them a beautiful white leather Wedding Memories album with their names and wedding date imprinted in gold letters on the front. Inside they found a beautiful card with a gift certificate for five thousand dollars, issued by a local travel agent. "You deserve a proper honeymoon trip. You must go within the next year, destination and date...your choice, of course." (And several days later they found a cashier's check for five thousand dollars, payable to Mr. and Mrs. Bill Malone, tucked carefully into the middle of the photo album from Grandmother Malone.)

Barbara's silver engraved picture frame was gratefully accepted. She had placed the cashier's check inside the papers of the frame where they'd not find it until they put a photo in the frame. Barbara avoided embarrassing them, the dinner guests or herself with the amount of the gift. (Three weeks later when they finally received their entire wedding photo order, they chose just the right wedding portrait and were astounded to see the cashier's check for ten thousand dollars when they put their portrait in the silver frame.)

They opened several more wedding gifts before everyone took to the dance floor. The band played a nice mix of contemporary and nostalgic numbers. Barbara enjoyed a dance with each of her sons. She felt like the luckiest woman in the world.

Grandmother Malone beamed as she danced with Bobby. Soon she had Jessica and Janie dancing. Grandmother's vivacity was contagious. Before long they were all having so much fun that they simply forgot about the time. Any semblance of sophisticated reserve was checked at the door. Grandmother Malone was enjoying her family and life. "To hell with anyone who has a problem with that."

No one left before one a.m. The small group of wedding guests appeared to have a genuinely good time. It seemed Charlie was the only one who openly missed Bill as he downed drink after drink.

It was a relief for Barbara to celebrate without the noise, heavy drinking and unpredictable behavior she'd tolerated all her life with Bill.

The family gathered at Barbara's for a late brunch on Sunday. The Malones enjoyed Uncle Eric and his family. The much younger Olson cousins seemed to be getting closer their ages. Funny how that happens…they were witty, bright and sooo California. They all vowed to stay in closer touch and to make efforts to visit regularly. The North Carolina cousins were fun loving and bright with a charming Southern wit. Their presence made Mormor and Morfar Olson bask in the glow of having their whole family together, even though it was for such a short visit.

Eric surprised them as he opened a bottle of champagne, poured small Dixie cups half full for everyone, then offered a toast. "To my sister, Barbara Ann Olson Malone, there's no one like her," and looked directly into Barbara's blue eyes, "and no one could ever take your place. You be careful, take good care of yourself. You're leaving a hell of a hole in this family, going away like this, sis." Eric hesitated, his voice choked and his eyes filled with tears. "But you're probably going to help tourism flourish in Honduras when we all start coming down to visit our one and only Barbie."

The room was filled with a chorus of "Cheers." Most eyes were at least misty. Awkward silences slowly were replaced with quiet conversations until the dining room was once again full of life and hope.

Grandmother Malone found her way to Barbara, uncharacteristically took the teacup out of Barbara's hand, set it aside and gave her an affectionate hug. In stifled sobs, she said, "Thank you, Barbara, for being such a special daughter to me and always making room in your family for me. You and the children are all that really matter to me. Sure, I still have my bridge friends at the country club, but that's just a way of passing the time until I can be with the family again. Marrying you was the smartest thing my son ever did. I love you, dear."

Barbara quietly led her mother-in-law into the family room, holding her hand all the while. "I've always felt blessed to have you as my second mother. I loved your son the best I could. I adore our children and if it wasn't for Bill and me being together, they wouldn't exist. Remember I'm only going away for two years. You'll just have to make a trip with Jessica to visit me. I'm going to miss you, too. You've been more than just my mother-in-law, you've been a dear friend."

They sat in silence for a few minutes just holding hands as a few tears trickled down their cheeks. At the same time they turned to each other, wiped the tears, gently squeezed each other's hands and with weak smiles, said simultaneously, "Better get back to the guests now."

Later that evening, after the guests were gone, Janie was looking at old photo albums in the family room. "Hi, sweetheart, we still have three hours before we leave for the airport, would you like a cup of tea or anything?"

"No thanks, Mom, maybe later. These pictures are great, so many long-forgotten memories in these pages." Janie sat there with a sweet smile as she relived some mostly happy times from long ago. "I do miss Daddy; he'd have been happy for Billy, and this weekend's celebrations, don't you think?"

"Yes, I think he would've. Maybe he'd have wanted a bit bigger affair. But he'd have been so proud and happy to see you all together and having such a good time too," Barbara answered her daughter. After a few minutes of comfortable silence, she asked, "Janie, it'll be daylight for another hour, there's a chill in the air but if we bundle, we could take a nice walk to the park and back. Are you up for it?"

"Mother, really, you're talking to a New York City girl. What I do is walk. Let's go. Haven't walked the old neighborhood or seen the park in years."

An hour later it was almost dusk as they returned to the Malone home. Conversation had been superficially light and pleasant until Janie asked, "Did you know that most people had written me off as a strung-out failure has-been that never was? That this role came just in time, I was on the verge of giving up my dreams?"

They kept walking; Barbara unlocked the door and announced, "It's tea time now, how about a little sandwich?" Janie agreed.

Across the small kitchen table from each other, Barbara looked into Janie's beautiful blue eyes. "Now to answer your questions, I never listen to gossips. They only think they know what goes on in other people's lives. I've always been so proud of you. You knew what you wanted and had the courage to pursue your dreams.

"It's probably to your advantage that success eluded you the first few years. During that time you were able to gain real-life experience and that can only make you a better artist."

Janie listened closely as she sipped her tea and ate her sandwich.

Her mother continued, "I was privy to inside information that no one else had. I knew the real you. I knew you as a child. You had a natural coyness and sweet charm that enabled you to get what you wanted, not just with family but with everyone in town and at college. Combining that with your innate beauty and most importantly with that strong streak of Olson obstinacy, I knew it was only a matter of time till you would achieve success."

Janie stared at her mother in disbelief. "You really always believed in me? I thought Daddy was the only one who did and after he died I just felt abandoned, so alone. You really believed in me?" Janie shook her head in shock. "So why didn't you ever tell me?"

Barbara lightly stroked Janie's cheek and replied softly, "I did but you weren't ready to hear me. I became the piranha of your rebellion and your life. I just bided my time. I knew someday you'd see I was not the enemy but rather one of the best friends you'd ever have. I just waited and knew you'd be a great success and you'd someday come back to the one who knew you first and knows you best."

Janie's eyes burned as her pent-up tears slowly overflowed. "Geez, Mom, I never knew you were that smart. You've had everything figured out for a long time. I'm sorry, I really am. And thanks for believing in me…even when I didn't.

"Mom, I've done some things that I'm not proud of, things you'd be shocked at. Maybe you don't know me as well as you think."

"Enough, Janie, none of that matters. I know the real you and you are a gifted actress, a wonderful daughter, sister and friend. If you've made choices that later proved to be mistakes, you've learned and become stronger." Barbara held Janie's hands in hers. Mother and daughter never felt closer than that moment.

The next few days flew by and Barbara found herself, feeling ambivalent, standing in the airport with her parents and Mother Malone. It was the last call for her flight to Washington, D.C. She hastily hugged and kissed them and ran for her gate. "I love you, guys. Stay well. I'll call."

Chapter Eleven

BARBARA

Barbara's apprehension soared as she arrived in Washington, D.C. for the Peace Corps' two day "staging seminar" (a.k.a. orientation). She looked around the crowded, austere hotel lobby; her fellow volunteers were also nervously checking each other out. The trainers were the ones with the large trainer ID badges. At first glance they all looked alike, very young, but on second look…so different. The trainers were not nervous; they looked like they knew what they were doing and loved it.

She couldn't help thinking, *What a misfit I am. Everyone is so young, even the trainers! If I had a predisposition to panic attacks…I'd have one right now.*

Barbara listened closely to instructions on the time to report to the Peace Corps Assembly Room for the first in a series of staging meetings. She signed in and received her room key. There were no bellboys to help. "Thank God for wheeled luggage," she thought as she struggled toward the elevator.

The elevator was packed on the way to the sixth floor. A pleasant young man with twinkling blue eyes and only one large backpack remarked teasingly, "I see we're all traveling light today!"

Barbara and the eight others who were burdened with equally bulky pieces of luggage could only stare at their possessions with embarrassment. Each felt relief when the elevator doors opened for their escape to individually assigned rooms.

Minutes later as Barbara approached Room 628, she heard lively Reggae music. She slowly opened the door to face an attractive young black woman, corn row hair pulled back to a thick multi-braid pony tail, moving rhythmically to the beat of Bob Marley. Barbara smiled and extended her hand. "Hi. I guess we're going to be roommates. I'm Barbara Malone."

Her roommate cocked her head to the right and put her hands on her hips. Then she smiled the most beautiful smile Barbara had ever seen. "I'm Alvira Novak; everyone calls me Alvie. Hey, we're gonna have a blast." And she shook hands with Barbara. Then suddenly, she dropped Barbara's hand and gave her a gigantic bear hug, explaining, "We might as well; cause, honey, for the next two years, we are family."

Barbara couldn't help laughing or liking her roommate. "It's nice to meet you, Alvie."

Alvie turned the radio volume down as they chatted before returning to their first staging seminar. Alvie had graduated from college two years ago as a certified English teacher but had only been able to find substitute teaching positions, which left her feeling frustrated and unfulfilled. She was fluent in Spanish and was on her way to teach in a village in Honduras. Her positive attitude and enthusiasm had a calming effect on Barbara.

Alvie laughed after Barbara had told her a little about her family. "I can't believe it, my roommate has four children, all older than me! And you don't look old enough for that to even be physically possible. Isn't life funny how we get to meet so many different kinds of people when we venture out of our safe little caves?"

There appeared to be about forty volunteers, a diverse group from all walks of life, and most of them appeared to be in their twenties. Barbara's apprehension started to give way to anticipation. "I'm really in the right place at the right time and that's a damn good feeling."

Each person was given a curriculum packet for Honduran culture, another packet for language review and another for their professional domain. The room was full of curious glances among the volunteers. Yet, there was a silent respect among them already because every person there was aware of the stringent screening process they had endured just to make it to training. The lead trainer repeatedly tapped a glass to silence the murmurings before starting. "Okay, volunteers. Heads up and welcome to the Peace Corps! This will be the toughest job you'll ever love! Now, everyone, I'd like us to get to know each other. I'm Peter Blair, you'll see a lot of me the next two days. But first, please, introduce yourselves, one at a time, of course. Name, home state, assigned country, area of expertise and briefly share why you joined the Peace Corps."

Automatic groans filled the room as the volunteers expressed their aversion to the introduction process...until a white-haired feisty lady stood up and began. "Well, I guess someone has to start this ball rolling, so why not me? My name is Ethel Yeaney. If I look old to you, it's because I am. I worked for forty-five years as an RN. I raised four sons and buried two husbands. I have twelve grandchildren, the youngest is now eleven and the oldest is twenty-five. Great kids but too busy to spend much time with Granny anymore. I'm only seventy-five and I detest hanging out at the Senior Center. I don't know if I'll ever get old enough for that! God has blessed me with good health and knowledge; I still have more to give to help my fellow man. I say let's do all we can to make Honduras a better place for its citizens."

Silence filled the room when Ethel sat down. Slowly at first some of the volunteers applauded. Soon the entire room was giving her a standing ovation. Ethel blushed, then stood and bowed mockingly, and said, "Enough already, let's hear from some of you young folks."

Barbara observed Alvie in action as her natural humor and enthusiasm melted apprehensive jitters away for many in the group. She started her self introduction by standing up immediately after Ethel, stating, "Man, that is one tough act to follow."

During the next two hours laughter frequently filled the room. The odd looking group of strangers was beginning what would be lifelong friendships for many of them.

They were pleasantly surprised to learn Honduras had the largest contingency of Peace Corps volunteers in the world, with over two hundred on assignment throughout the country at any given time.

Each volunteer was issued a special Peace Corps passport and their immunization records were closely scrutinized. The Corps was emphatic that all requirements be precisely upheld.

Two days later they were boarding a direct flight for the capital and largest city in Honduras, Tegucigalpa.

Barbara had traveled very little, never before to Central America. There had been the fateful honeymoon trip to the Bahamas, family trips with Bill and the children to England and another to Hawaii. Last year she had traveled to California with her parents to visit Eric and his family. And that was it.

She was impressed with the bright green hills as the plane descended, and the simplicity of the whitewashed stucco buildings near the airport. As the plane made a smooth landing, she was surprised to see all the Central Americans on board applaud and cheer the pilot for a job well done. This was the first of many new and unique experiences for Barbara as she bravely entered a different culture.

The heat was the first thing she noticed when disembarking onto the airport runway where the passengers and crew were transported to the main terminal in an open window shuttle bus, comparable in size to a large mini van. She suddenly felt nauseous with the extreme heat after so many hours in the carefully controlled air-conditioned environment of the airplane. The terminal had many huge ceiling fans and open windows to circulate the thick hot air. It was clean and cheerful. Most of the airport decorating was intricately handmade Honduran art work. The many posters promoted each region's attributes of minerals, agricultural, forestry and government development, while the military presence of young men in shiny black boots with machine guns reminded her she was no longer in Pennsylvania. Never before had she experienced 110 degrees F and 98% humidity under a scorching relentless sun and it was only 10 a.m.

Barbara noticed Alvie wiping perspiration from her forehead as she stood in line. "I don't know if I'll be able to take this heat, Alvie," a worried Barbara confided to her new friend.

Alvie looked worried too, but couldn't help laughing at her roommate. "You know what, Barbie, you don't care if I call you Barbie, do you?"

Barbara shook her head to indicate it was okay.

Alvie continued, "The way I see it, if the Hondurans can exist in this heat, we can learn to adapt to it too. You and me, we're survivors. Right?"

Barbara smiled and gave Alvie the thumbs up. "We will survive!"

She couldn't help notice the curious stares from passersby as the odd bunch of khaki-denim clad Peace Corps "ambassador-volunteers" waited for transport to the training facility.

Each of the thirty-eight volunteers was assigned to live with a local family to sharpen their language skills and become accustomed to life in Honduras. By day they'd have intensive training at Honduran Peace Corps Training Headquarters. Standards were very high. By night they'd live with the Hondurans.

Barbara's host family was Maria and Jose Gonzales; they did not have a phone in their home. Maria explained the absence of telephone. "What for we need *teléfono*? Everyone we love right here. We tell them in da face!" Her wrinkled brown hands waved about comically reinforcing her words as she spoke.

Ironically Barbara spoke only Spanish to the Gonzales family and they tried to speak only English to her. When she tried to convey ideas or questions to them, they'd often chuckle and try not to be disrespectful to their guest.

"My Spanish is probably no better than their attempts at English," she thought ruefully.

There was a bank of five phones in the lobby of the training facility that all trainee volunteers had to share during their limited "free time."

The weeks flew by at the training center. Barbara called home once a week and even that took a major effort. She alternated calls between her parents and Mother Malone. Each would faithfully call the other, the children, and Alice to report her latest news. They also kept her posted on family and local Lewiston news. It was better than no communication but not the same as personal contact. Adjusting to minimal communication back home was difficult for Barbara. She sighed. *Somehow I feel emotionally distant from the goings on of Lewiston. It sort of seems, I don't know, irrelevant now. But, oh God, how I miss the family. I knew this would be hard, but that doesn't make it any easier right now.*

Life in the Gonzales home was very pleasant. There were six handsome children at home, a young married daughter with a bambino who visited several times a week. Jose was a security guard at a large bank downtown, the children were good students at the convent school, and Maria worked as a seamstress in a dress shop near their neighborhood. They ran a tight ship and all the children helped with chores. The house was small by U.S. standards with three small bedrooms, one for *madre* and *padre*, one for the boys and one for the girls, a busy kitchen, crowded dining and living rooms. A small enclosed porch had been converted to a bedroom and rented to Peace Corps *gringos* for the past three years.

They had never had a car. None of their neighbors had either. They did not feel at all deprived. The Gonzaleses were warm, hardworking, generous and proud people. They opened their home and their hearts to Barbara. She quickly grew to care about each one of them and learned volumes first-hand about emotional intelligence. Yet, between the long hours of training and the family, the reality of having so little personal time became overwhelming at times.

Barbara appreciated Alvie's optimistic nature. A few of the others were becoming down-right unpleasant and full of complaints. While some were grumbling about the food, phone service, grueling schedules and even their host families, Alvie would grin and say, "Early to bed and early to rise makes Alvie alert and set for the prize!"

Barbara smiled at her and said, "I've never heard you complain, not once. What's your secret? Some of the nurse trainees are so bitter and angry, it's kind of like a venomous cloud over some of our sessions."

Then she added as if an afterthought, "Ethel is the one lady in our nurse training group that keeps everyone grounded. She's so full of energy and common sense. She's really great, sharp and funny, too." Barbara smiled with admiration as she described her to Alvie.

"She always reminds me of a grandmother who ought to be home making cookies or something. She's a dynamo and will be a great asset to the Corps. Can you imagine doing this at her age?" Alvie hesitated as if deep in thought, then tentatively replied, "Sorry to hear about your complainers, Barbara. We have a couple in our teacher sessions too. My grandaddy used to say, 'You can't please all o' the people all o' the time and you can't please some o' the people any time. Hell, some folks would complain if ya hung 'em with a new rope!' I wasn't expecting a vacation when I came here. We best learn all we can, 'cause, honey, we're going to be mostly on our own when we get to our assignments. We better know how to handle ourselves with limited resources."

Barbara listened closely to her words. She admired Alvie and teased her. "You are so wise for your years, organized and focused. Even when you have time to relax a few minutes, you see what needs to be done and do it. Your family must be very proud of you."

Alvie smiled at Barbara but there was a sad faraway look in her eyes. "My family thinks my brain malfunctioned or else I'd never have joined the Peace Corps. I figure they'll get over it someday. To be a good Peace Corps volunteer we simply have to be as wise, resourceful and organized as we possibly can, don't you think?"

"Alvie, you are a lifesaver for me. I didn't expect a vacation either but this is tougher than I thought it would be. You're a good buffer after spending hours with the grumblers."

"You know, I feel pretty lucky to have met you too. Who'd ever have believed you and I would get along so great? I bet we'll stay friends for all our lives. Someday I'll meet your whole family. And you'll meet mine. You'll have to come to my wedding, if I ever get married, that is." Alvie stared out across the plaza as she sipped her coffee at the small sidewalk café, then turned to Barbara with a wink as that glorious Alvie smile erased the worried preoccupation.

Barbara smiled as she watched Alvie closely, then quietly asked, "Is there anyone special back home waiting for you at the altar?"

"Hell, no. That's why I don't know if there'll ever be a wedding!" and she laughed irreverently.

"You're too much, Alvie! Of course, I want to stay friends whether or not there's a wedding to attend. Hard to believe we only have four more weeks of training left. I hope we'll all be ready when it's time to go. There's so much to learn."

"Hey, Barbie, you bet we'll be ready. Come on, let's head 'home' before it is totally dark."

Alvie was staying with two elderly widows whose home was on the same block as the Gonzales family. Barbara gave Alvie an impromptu hug and whispered, "Good night, sweet child, sleep well." She walked toward the front door and stood there watching to be sure Alvie made it to the widows' home. Barbara went in to exchange quick pleasantries with her host family. She felt tired and went to bed early. She smiled as she settled in her narrow bed for the night. "Exhaustion can also be a friend." Despite the noise of the lively household, she slept for eight uninterrupted hours.

There was an assembly meeting the next day after breakfast. They had not really been tested yet on any of the material they had gone over during the last eight weeks. The speaker explained, "You've all been accepted as qualified experts in your chosen fields. Our training has been intense and exhaustive. This was to prepare you for field work. I've heard some rumblings of discontent within your ranks. A positive attitude is essential to move onto the final phase of training. This is the testing phase. Verbal as well as written. Good luck, everyone. But before you all go to your assigned groups, I urge you to search your hearts. Ask yourselves, 'Is this what I really want to do with the next two years of my life?' If for any reason you doubt, please make an appointment to talk to me as soon as possible. There is no shame in quitting."

Barbara wondered as she walked to her first session, "Do they have to give a speech like that to every class or did we just get lucky with too many complainers? Oh well." She smiled in a dreamy way as she considered changing her mind and thought, "Not a chance. I've had my moments but I feel good about this. It's finally my chance to give back and I'm going to do it without regrets."

She slipped into her seat just before Jeremy, their favorite nursing trainer, entered the room. Ethel looked at her and laughed quietly. "Girl, I'd like to know what you're on. You look too happy, remind me o' the story o' the cat that swallowed the mouse, what have you been up to?"

Barbara whispered with a finger to her lip to encourage her chatty seventy-five-year-old friend to be quiet. "A good night's sleep does wonders for one's disposition."

They were given a final exam schedule. There were familiar audible groans from the back of the room. "Nurses, you surely recognize this is an essential part of your preparation. Many of you will be working in remote areas. You may be the only medical person for a whole village with a doctor visiting maybe once a month. This kind of autonomy requires most of you to perform independent procedures that would never be heard of in the States. We want you to show us your current level of clinical skills and we'll test your overall knowledge of pathology and treatment. In some cases we will teach you a few basic skills. Any questions?"

The trainer handled the barrage of queries in a professional manner. Three of the angry nurses stomped out of the room in unison. Barbara expected they were on their way to resign from the Peace Corps. She'd seen it coming for weeks. What was so baffling was why on earth they had ever considered joining in the first place.

Ethel asked in a shaky voice, "Will this be like taking boards again? It's been more than fifty-five years since I've taken that test. I worked for forty-five years, I know how to do nursing but I don't know if I can pass your tests. Oh Lord, if I flunk outta the Peace Corps, how will I ever face my grandchildren?"

Poor Ethel looked like she was about to cry. Jeremy smiled and reassured her. "Ethel, I'm sure you could teach us all anything and everything we'd ever want to know about clinical skills. And to be a professional as you have for more than fifty years, I know you've got the theories of pathology and treatment down pat. You won't flunk out, trust me."

The Spanish classes were even more grueling. Barbara and most of the others had mastered reading and speaking Spanish, slowly with each other as well as with their host families. But the real test was speaking with Latinos in their normal rapid-fire speech. Everyone struggled except the two Puerto Rican volunteers who were especially helpful to their classmates. The first few weeks they had begun to feel just slightly self-confident regarding their language skills. By the beginning of the last week, everyone was considerably more proficient in Spanish.

During their last week of training, Barbara, Alvie, Ethel and another volunteer teacher, Janice, decided to have dinner at a downtown restaurant. They laughed and talked for hours, barely making it to the theater in time for the Spanish-speaking film. The challenge of the Honduran taxi ride back to their host families strengthened their bond of friendship and reminded them why they had chosen to walk during their weeks of training. By midnight they were deposited at their designated homes feeling lucky (to have survived the taxi ride!), happy and totally relaxed.

The next morning came way too soon, but they dragged themselves to the Center in time for their first sessions. Somehow feeling refreshed on four hours of sleep, Alvie met Ethel in the hall and smiled. "Hey, girl, give me a high five!"

Ethel laughed and wagged her finger at her. "I'll high five you, you naughty little girl, trying to get this old granny into trouble."

"Wait a minute, Miss Ethel, you didn't need any help. I have a feeling you can find all the trouble you can handle without a speck of help from me!" With that, a smiling Alvie hustled off to her first session of the day.

The testing had begun and everyone was pleasantly surprised at their own level of proficiency and as they began to get positive feedback and passing scores, their anxiety began to dissipate. Relaxing smiles replaced the worried scowls. Only two more days before they'd move on to their various destinations. Everyone knew this would be the last time they'd all be together again, and they felt a sense of connectedness after twelve intense weeks of training. Only four of their group of thirty-eight had dropped out.

Each one of the new volunteers anticipated changing the world for the better and were anxious to get started at what the Peace Corps trainers repeatedly told them would be "the toughest job you'll ever love." Location assignments were distributed. Alvie, Ethel and Barbara quickly found each other to check out distances between their villages. They were ecstatic to learn they'd be within a hundred miles of each other. They'd soon learn a hundred dirt road mountain miles was much farther than the same distance on paved flat country highways in the U.S.

Maria prepared Barbara a delicious hot breakfast; all the children lined up respectfully to tell their house guest "*Adiós*." After the children had gone to school and Jose to work, Maria hugged Barbara and cried, begging her to write letters and come see them again. Barbara thanked her for the gracious hospitality during the last three months, promised to write and hugged her back. She looked at her watch and rushed down the street, dragging her luggage, to meet the bus that would take her to her new village home.

Chapter Twelve

The volunteers gathered with their belongings on the training center veranda by seven a.m. Friday morning, waiting for transportation to the bus terminal for various destinations all over Honduras. Hugs, tears, promises to stay in touch, as well as good luck wishes were vibrating through the excited though apprehensive group.

A modern shiny metallic blue and gray passenger bus arrived thirty minutes late to transport their group to the Centralia Bus Station. As the new volunteers made their way on board, they were busy trying to find their assigned posts on their Honduras pocket maps. As they looked at the armed guard on board the bus, an air of uneasiness swept through the group.

Barbara and Alvie had villages in the Montanas De Colon of southern Honduras. Ethel's was at the foothills of the Colons. In Puerto Pelon, they transferred to a smaller, crowded, dirty and rickety older bus. Three peasant women sat stoically staring out the dirty bus windows as noisy chickens cackled in the large rustic wooden boxes they held securely on their laps.

There was also an armed guard on board, as well as a few bullet holes in the windows. A local passenger cautioned the three women in Spanish. "The guard is to protect us from armed robbers. But if anyone does get past the guards...give them what they want, do not resist. They will kill for the thrill of killing, they love to see the blood."

Barbara, Alvie and Ethel exchanged quick glances and sighed. Barbara murmured, "How in the world did we end up in a place like this?"

After a long, hot, bumpy and crowded journey, the bus finally arrived at Valencia at seven p.m. They were tired, hot and dirty. This was Ethel's town. A pleasant young woman held a Peace Corps sign to help the new volunteer identify her, while two young soldiers stood nearby. There were dozens of shy barefoot children staring at the volunteers with curiosity. The brightly colored stucco buildings added a festive flavor to the town. The temperature was still in the upper nineties and very humid.

Valencia had a well-established and larger clinic. Ethel laughed and said, "I'm sure they didn't think I could hack two years in the mountains so they put me in town with all the conveniences of home."

Barbara and Alvie left the bus to stretch their legs and find a public restroom. When they returned to the main station, they found Ethel prepared to leave and gave her a final good-bye hug. Barbara whispered, "We just used their modern toilets. Trust me; you do not have all the conveniences of home. Now take good care of yourself!"

They watched her load her luggage into the back of a rusted old Jeep and climb in the back seat with the young woman. A local driver and an armed guard rode in the front seat. Barbara and Alvie waved as Ethel was driven away.

Alvie and Barbara returned to the bus to find the driver in a heated argument with the bus station man who wore an ill-fitting deep blue bus company uniform. Soon the driver threw their luggage out of the bus in heaps near where the volunteers were standing. And with no explanation, the driver closed the rusty door and roared out of sight in the rickety bus.

Alvie immediately approached the bus station man to ask what the problem was. He looked embarrassed at first, though quite pleased that the strange women spoke his language. He smiled and disarmed them with his sparkling brown eyes and gallant Latin charm. "My name is Juan. Please to meet you, *señoritas*. Would you like drink? Come, please, rest in de shade."

They followed him to a rustic bench on the veranda of the station platform. "We must get to our villages today. They are expecting us. Can you help us? Why did the driver get angry and leave us here?" Barbara asked in her very best Spanish.

"Yes, yes. I will help you to find new bus. It will not be fancy like de old bus. Driver refused to take his good bus on de mountain roads; too hard on bus, he says. You wait here. Juan get *señoritas* a bus." He returned a few minutes later with two cans of cold orange-flavored soda.

"You drink and rest in shade. Now Juan get *señoritas* a bus." And he was gone.

They were left alone on the station platform with the two young soldiers in their shiny black boots and machine guns.

Alvie whispered to Barbara, "I think they're supposed to make us feel safer, but it's not working. Can you imagine what kind of bus we're going to get into next if that last one was a *good* one?"

The curious children's giggles could be heard from the bushes and trees they were huddled around. One little girl shyly walked over to Barbara and Alvie to give each of them a small bouquet of wildflowers. Her faded plaid dress did not conceal her innocent beauty as she smiled, bowed her head slightly, thick long eyelashes fluttered briefly and she softly said, "*Hola, señoritas. Bienvenido.*"

They happily accepted the flowers, smiling at the child as they replied, "*Gracias. Cómo se llama?*"

The child answered timidly, "*Me llama es Rosa.*"

Alvie slid to the floor to be eye level with Rosa and soon the little girl was giggling as Alvie used her charms in Spanish. Rosa turned and waved for her friends to come. Barbara and Alvie found themselves surrounded by dozens of children. Alvie taught them two songs and soon the air was filled with the sounds of their sweet voices as they clapped their hands and tapped their feet in time to their lively new songs.

An hour later they heard a motor clattering. It stopped directly in front of them: an ancient muddy Volkswagen van, original color unknown. Juan slid out from the driver's seat, beaming. "See, Juan find bus for *señoritas*! Big one. Two *señoritas* in back, one guard and one driver in front."

"*Gracias*, Juan, but do you think it is reliable?" Alvie asked.

Juan smiled with pride. "*Sí, señoritas*! This is good bus."

Alvie and Barbara looked at each other apprehensively and whispered, "Did we daydream through this situation in training or did they neglect to tell us about bus driver hang ups?"

Alvie hesitantly answered, "Honey, this was no way covered an' we aren't even there yet!"

They turned back to the children. "*Adiós, amigos. Gracias. Gracias.*"

An hour later, as dusk and a slightly more comfortable temperature was settling around them, Juan and a guard loaded their bags and they climbed into the back seat. The lumpy upholstery was covered with colorful woven blankets. The back window had plastic taped over to prevent weather damage since the glass was long gone.

Juan announced, "Tonight you stay at Peace Corps house. We come in the bus at eight a.m. *mañana*. Then we go to the mountain villages. Too late tonight. Already dark."

They rode on in a stunned silence. Barbara said, "Good news and bad news. Guess we'll see Ethel again before we expected to. Hope no one in the villages will be too upset about our tardiness."

Alvie nodded. "I'm thinking maybe in this country they just don't get so excited about time. Maybe they just kinda take life as it comes along. Just go with the flow."

Juan's bus shook when he stopped in front of the Peace Corps house, a neat and very long stucco bungalow. Soft warm lights glowed from the windows. Barbara and Alvie climbed out of the van, retrieved their bags and thanked Juan and the guard as they walked across the courtyard to Ethel's new home. Juan reminded them, "I be here eight o'clock *mañana*."

They waved good-bye to their new self-appointed guardians and knocked on the door. The young woman who had met Ethel opened cautiously with a thick chain securely connecting the door to the heavy frame. They explained their predicament to her. She smiled and immediately opened the door and ushered them into the house. Barbara noticed she re-locked the door securely before she even introduced herself.

"Welcome to our humble home. My name is Sharon. We have these three private quarter rooms. This building also doubles as our Outreach Clinic and school. Please sit down and make yourselves comfortable. I'll tell Ethel you're here." The petite blue-eyed blonde left them alone.

Ethel came out looking like the grandmother she was, ready for bed wearing a long cotton nightgown. "You really did miss me! I thought maybe Sharon was just teasing me." She gave them each a hug.

Sharon brought Barbara and Alvie sandwiches and water. "I'm pretty sure you didn't have a chance to get any food tonight."

Barbara and Alvie declared in unison with their mouths full, "The best peanut butter sandwiches I ever had." Then they started to giggle like tired school girls with bits of peanut butter sticking to their teeth.

Ethel pointed her finger at the two visitors as if to scold, looked at Sharon, shrugged and joined their laughter as she explained, "If I appear silly at times, just remember I trained with these bumpkins and I just can't help myself if they led me astray."

Sharon sat on a large pillow with her back to the front door, relaxed and laughed with the volunteers. "I really mean it, *welcome* to Montanas De Colon. To my new house mate Ethel and it's going to be fun having Barbara as our neighbor. The locals are warm, wonderfully kind, generous people. But still, we are outsiders and sometimes it gets a little lonely." She slid a box out from behind the sofa, pulling out a bottle of white wine.

She quickly retrieved four paper cups and a wine opener from the tiny kitchen and poured them all a cup of the Honduran wine. "To our new friendships and the Peace Corps!"

They all joined the toast and turned their cups bottoms up. The bottle was still half full. Sharon informed them, "It won't fit in our small refrigerator, so everyone must have a refill."

No arguments were offered as they held their cups out for a final nightcap. Sharon and Ethel cleared space on the small living room floor for them to sleep and gave them each a sleeping bag and a pillow. Sharon explained, "This isn't the first time we've had stranded volunteers so we just keep these sleeping bags for our homeless friends as they pass through. Sleep well, girls."

They took turns using the small primitive bathroom and slept like logs.

At seven a.m., Ethel nudged them to wake up. They could smell fresh coffee from the kitchen. Barbara forced herself up and quickly used the bathroom to freshen and prepare for her day of mountain traveling. Then Alvie did the same. They enjoyed Sharon's wonderful coffee and local bread. Surprisingly Juan was knocking on the door by eight fifteen a.m. They thanked their hosts for the hospitality and hugged them goodbye.

"*Buenos días*, Juan," they said together.

"*Buenos días, señoritas*," he answered. "This is your guard, Louis." He was a young man, barely twenty, with darting watchful eyes, dressed in threadbare faded jeans and cotton plaid shirt with only two buttons remaining to hold it shut. He also had a semi-automatic gun on a belt carefully hanging across his left shoulder.

Both women smiled politely and said, "Nice to meet you. Thank you for helping us."

"Thank you for coming to Honduras to help us, *señoritas*. It is my honor to help you." With that Louis nodded to show them respect.

Alvie said in near perfect Spanish (well at least near perfect to Barbara's ears), "It is our high honor to help the people of your beautiful Honduras."

Juan loaded their luggage and they climbed in the back seat of the old Volkswagen bus. It looked even worse in the bright early morning sunshine.

Just as they were about to leave, Sharon came running out of the house with a large paper bag. She quickly reached through the open window to give Alvie the bag. "Lunch for the travelers. Have a safe trip...please keep in touch."

Alvie peeked into the bag...several bottles of water, bananas and, "Peanut butter sandwiches. Bless you!"

She and Barbara smiled and waved. "Thanks again for everything."

Sharon grinned and shrugged. "Hey, they won't spoil in the heat. And warm safe water can quench your thirst even if it's not as refreshing as cold drinks. Welcome to the real world of the Peace Corps."

Ethel hurried out to wave good-bye again. "Be careful and stay well, my darlin' children."

As Juan drove out of the town, the bus's motor sputtered and banged. Alvie and Barbara glanced at each other with a look of uncertainty as they silently prayed for safe arrival at their destinations

Four hours later they pulled into a roadside service area for *petro*. Alvie and Barbara climbed out to stretch their legs and to hopefully find a restroom. They did. But then decided they really didn't need a restroom yet. This one made the restroom at the bus station in El Progeso look modern and clean. It had been neither.

Back on the bumpy road again, they shared sandwiches, water and bananas with Juan and Louis.

The dirt road was becoming increasingly narrow and traffic seemed to be limited to only their bus. They saw occasional pedestrians dressed in colorful native garb, always wearing large straw hats to protect them from the fierce sun. As the bus slowly climbed the winding mountain road, the temperature was gradually becoming more bearable. As the jungle growth became thicker, the sun was blocked out more and more. The piercing sounds of tropical birds alarmed Alvie and Barbara until Juan reassured them, "You not be frightened for long. Jungle sound beautiful, it is God's special music. You wait. It true."

By one in the afternoon, Juan announced, "We will arrive at first village, Cabela, very soon. Pretty village. You will like."

Alvie was delighted. "That's my village. Oh God, I can hardly wait!"

An hour later they arrived in Cabela, a small village of stucco buildings. The whitewashed Catholic Church with the bell tower was the most impressive building, located in the village square. There were a few small open-air cafés, a newspaper stand, open-air booths for shoes, clothing, bedding and fresh produce. Two small shops had signs advertising milk, cheeses, eggs, meats and ice cream. There was even a movie theater; the marquee announced *Rocky II*, playing each evening at six p.m. All the booths were colorful but the plaza was nearly empty since it was *siesta* time.

They located a *petro* station first. Juan explained, "We must not let *petro* get too little in de bus, because then bus would really chug chug." He was quite serious without a trace of humor on his face.

"Next stop will be de Peace Corps house of Cabela. They need new teacher in de school for long time now. They be happy to see you, *Señorita* Alvie."

"Thank you, Juan. Louis, where are you from? How did you become a guard?" Alvie asked.

Louis answered in broken English, "I come from El Pariso. I guard to help people, safe from *banditos*. Peace Corps help Honduras. Louis love Honduras."

Alvie nodded appreciatively. "I love Honduras too! I'm so happy to be here. Is El Pariso far from here?"

Louis stared at her for several seconds before answering very slowly and with an almost paranoid guardedness, "*Sí*, my village far from here. No family left in village, so I come where I find work."

Alvie nodded, then smiled and quietly replied, "Well, thank you for all your help, Louis."

The bus lurched to a stop in front of a small white stucco compound of three buildings inside a three-foot-high white stucco fence. The Peace Corps insignia was displayed at the entrance to the compound. Everyone climbed out to stretch and say good-byes. Barbara smiled at Alvie, even as she blinked back tears. "Well, this is it, you're finally here and it looks like this is where we go our separate ways. I'm going to miss you, kiddo."

Alvie wiped her tears away with her shirt sleeve. "Hey, girl, we're gonna be neighbors, it's not really good-bye, more like see you later, pal. Right?"

They were interrupted by Juan and Louis who had been talking to a villager. "*Señoritas*, so sorry, but there is small problem. We stay here tonight, too many *banditos* and attacks on travelers on the mountain roads at sundown and night. *Banditos* mean and greedy. No respect for persons, very bad. Very bad. We stay here and leave at eight a.m. *mañana*. This will be safer." Juan informed them firmly of the change of plans.

All the while Juan talked, Louis stood there with his eyes darting continuously about the visible area. Barbara thought, "This guy has had some very intense guard training...somewhere. Or else he's one heck of a nervous paranoid."

Juan and Louis carried their luggage to the Peace Corps house. Just as Alvie was ready to knock on the door, it was opened by a tall thin young man wearing wire-framed glasses, which magnified his intense blue eyes. He smiled broadly. "Hi, ladies, Juan and Louis. I'm Patrick Sherwin, call me Pat. Please come in; lavatory is down the hall. Let me get you a cool drink."

This house was newer and roomier than Ethel's back in El Progreso. Pat was back a few minutes later, carrying a tray with five tall glasses of iced tea and a plate of English tea cookies. The refreshments were a welcome treat for the weary group of travelers. Barbara said, "I believe this is the best tea I've ever tasted."

Pat smiled as he shrugged and replied, "I doubt that, you're just tired and thirsty and I'm the only show in town, but thanks anyway."

Juan explained the need to stay overnight due to the recent increase in "highway robberies."

Pat smiled graciously and said, "No problem. Do you guys need a place to stay too?"

Louis declined, "No, thanks, I stay friend's house in de other side of de town."

Juan said, "I stay with Aunt Gloria, she be insulted if I not stay her house. Thanks anyway, *amigo*."

Barbara helped Patrick carry the glasses back to the kitchen. "Thanks for the warm hospitality. Sometimes I can't believe I'm really here. How long have you been in-country, Pat?"

Alvie walked into the small kitchen as Pat answered, "Eighteen months; I'll be going back to the states the end of March. Time goes so quickly here, it's hard to believe my two years are almost completed."

Pat looked at his watch and asked, "Hey, it's only five p.m., would you lucky ladies like a tour of the town before dark?"

Alvie and Barbara grinned and answered enthusiastically, "We'd love to!"

Alvie's excitement was almost palpable. "I want to see everything. Please tell us all you can about serving in this village, Honduras, and the Peace Corps."

Pat laughed. "Whoa, Alvie! That may take more than one evening. Let's go. Geez, I hate to ask, but do either of you have money? If you do, don't leave it in the house when you are out. And carry it discreetly; I'm sure they must have talked to you about this in training. It's always better to err on the side of safety."

Pat locked the house as they left. Barbara thought, "There's something odd about all this, I feel a sort of ominous discomfort with these seemingly extraordinary security efforts...the armed guards and their less than subtle warnings, now locking the house securely while being cautioned about leaving any valuables while going for a simple walk. Just feels sorta strange."

As they walked the three blocks to the plaza, he told them about the Peace Corps clinic located in the compound. "It's closed for three weeks while Carolyn, a really terrific nurse, went home for a family emergency. Twice a week Honduran volunteers trained in first aid by Carolyn open the clinic and do the best they can, offering therapeutic maintenance care to those in need. Carolyn's a real Georgia peach. I'm sure you'll like working with her, Alvie."

Pat appeared to be well-liked in his neighborhood. Everyone they passed waved and shouted, "*Buenas tardes, hola, Señor* Pat."

When they reached the village center, Pat's eyes twinkled mischievously as he grinned and bowed, while extending his right arm toward the now crowded plaza. "Welcome to Plaza de Cabela, my home away from home."

Alvie and Barbara were surprised to see so much activity; the plaza seemed to be bursting with life. Now there were many people milling about where it had been nearly empty when they arrived in town a couple of hours earlier. A Maraji band serenaded in the plaza, the cafés provided single singing guitar players and one had a trio. Latin beats and melodic voices filled the air.

Barbara asked, "Is this some kind of festival?"

Pat smiled. "Nope. This is just a normal Saturday evening in Cabela. The locals are basically happy, friendly and good-natured people. There are very few radios, so they go out and socialize to relax. They love their marajis. If you think this is festive, just wait for the real festivals."

He continued in a serious tone, "Sometimes I feel like they should send volunteers to the States to help us learn how to really live. I remember growing up with lots of rushing to get to all the activities, pressure to achieve, competition and my folks bickering about money just trying to keep up with the neighbors...but I don't remember the joy of living I see in these people who mostly live way below the poverty level by U.S. standards."

They walked on in reflective silence, each one of them reminiscing about life back in the U.S. and comparing it to what they were witnessing here in Cabela. Alvie and Barbara were a bit surprised by Pat's candid comments. But they couldn't help making the same comparisons themselves.

Barbara broke the silence. "Pat, if you like it so much, have you considered volunteering for another two years or maybe making the Peace Corps your career?"

"Well, actually I have considered both options. Nothing is certain yet, I still have time. Somehow my expectations of teaching in Honduras inverted the educational process and I, the teacher, became the student."

He continued, "Alvie, I'm sure you'll love it here. The Hondurans love their families and are gracious and kind hosts to the Peace Corps volunteers. It's just an amazing land. They encourage and respect education for their children."

As Alvie and Pat talked about life in Cabela, Barbara was flooded with memories of home and family. There was just something about Pat, this intense young volunteer. He reminded her of Billy. She silently prayed, "Oh God, please be with my Billy tonight. I pray that he and Liz are happy together and will have the life they both deserve. I also pray that you will guide Bobby and protect him from himself when need be. I pray the same for Jessica and Janie. Please be with Mother and Father as well as Mother Malone. Also bless Eric, his family, Alice and her family. Thank you, dear Lord."

All of a sudden Barbara felt a tug on her sleeve. A concerned Alvie asked, "Hey, girl, are you all right? You look like you're a thousand miles away."

"Sorry, it's just so beautiful here, it reminded me of something back home...." Barbara forced a smile.

Alvie raised her eyebrows skeptically and sighed. "Later, girl, you and me are gonna talk!"

Pat interjected awkwardly, "Hey, ah...there's a little café that serves great safe food, anybody hungry? My treat."

Barbara smiled, and this time it was a real one. "Sounds wonderful. I hope your café has maraji music, too."

"It does, indeed. I recommend spicy food but no salad when out. Buy your vegetables and fix your salads at home after washing with proper water," he answered.

The food was deliciously hot and spicy and the music provided a light fun touch to the evening. Two hours later they walked back to the Peace Corps compound. The local night guard smiled and reassured them, "Everything okay, *Señor* Pat. *Buenas noches.*"

They enjoyed a late cup of tea and settled down for the night. Alvie was pleased with her small Spartan bedroom. She beamed, "It's clean and big enough. I have arrived!"

It had been a pleasure to take a shower in the makeshift modern convenience of the spacious new building. Barbara was given Carolyn's bedroom. Pat slept on the sofa, which he insisted proved to be quite comfortable. At seven a.m., the smell of fresh coffee was a pleasant wake-up call. She quickly prepared for another day of travel and tidied up her bedroom for her host.

As they finished a breakfast of fruit, bread and coffee, a persistent tapping on the front door announced the arrival of Juan and Louis. It was eight a.m. They declined Pat's offer of coffee. Juan stated, "We go now when *señorita* ready."

Pat quickly prepared sandwiches (peanut butter, of course), fruit and bottled water for the travelers. Barbara gave her luggage to Juan to load in the bus, and turned to Pat. "Thank you for your hospitality and insight about the Peace Corps. I wish you well and I know you will make the right choices for your future." She hesitated, then smiled. "And thanks for the lunch, Pat. You know, there's just something about you that reminds me of my oldest son, Billy. He's a teacher too. Oh, and please take that as a compliment."

Pat looked surprised and couldn't think of anything to say but, "Thank you, Barbara. Good luck."

Barbara and Alvie stood on the small veranda blinking back tears as they shared a quick good-bye hug. "Alvira, you take care of yourself and no crying either! We will see each other as often as possible; after all this is what we trained for, right? Geez, I'm really gonna miss you, sweet child! Do be careful." And she hurried down the pathway to the waiting bus.

As they traveled along the bumpy dirt road, the jungle overgrowth became thicker and thicker. Little sunlight made it through the dense green jungle ceiling. The sounds of exotic birds and insects filled the air. Now and then they'd hear an almost human cry of a not-too-distant monkey. A light-weight long-sleeved shirt felt just right in the considerably cooler mountain air. The humidity remained constant. Barbara decided, "I'll not even try to wear any make up while I'm here, it would just be a waste. The humidity would have it washed off and smeared on my clothes within minutes anyway. I'm glad my hair is cut short, I'll definitely have to keep it in a wash-and-wear style for the next two years."

About two hours later, Barbara asked Juan and Louis, "When do you think we will get to Rebita?"

Juan answered, "Maybe two hours, maybe three. We will see."

Barbara couldn't help it, she was getting excited and anxious to see her village. "Would you like a bottle of water?"

Both young men accepted the offer with, "*Sí. Gracias, señora.*"

Despite the bumps, Barbara fell asleep for a short time in the stuffy humid bus. About an hour later, she offered the men sandwiches and fruit. Again they accepted with gratitude.

They did not stop the entire drive. Five hours after leaving Cabela they arrived in the village of Rebita.

Barbara felt like a child on Christmas morning. They arrived at one p.m., arriving during *siesta* to an almost-empty town plaza again. It was a very small village compared to Cabela but nonetheless charming, despite the obvious poverty.

Louis glanced at Barbara. "You wait, after *siesta mucho* people fill de plaza. *Siesta* is good for de people."

They drove slowly around the square to a side street called Avenue de Angelos and stopped in front of a small whitewashed stucco bungalow, surrounded by a three-foot-high matching fence displaying a Peace Corps insignia near the gate. Inside the compound beside the small house was another whitewashed slightly larger building with a Peace Corps insignia and a Red Cross signifying availability of medical care.

A smiling Barbara slid out of the bus and stretched. "It's beautiful! *Gracias*, Juan and Louis. *Gracias*."

They carried her luggage to the tiny veranda. Juan announced they would be driving back to Cabela immediately after refueling. Juan said, "We go to Cabela in de sunlight."

Barbara shook hands with Juan and then Louis, thanking them again for their kindness and service to her and the Peace Corps. She gave them each a tip, knowing they would be reimbursed for their services by the Peace Corps.

She turned and knocked lightly. The door opened with the chain guard firmly in place, a tired looking young woman with dark brown eyes and a dish water blonde pony tail peered out. Barbara smiled. "Hello. I'm Barbara, the new volunteer." She showed her Peace Corps passport as identification to the face peering out from inside.

The door opened wide. "Please come in. My name's Anita Pettinato. Welcome to your new home." Anita quickly locked the door again and then turned to Barbara and smiled warmly. "I know you'll like it here, I certainly have. My two years will be up in four weeks. It's good we have some overlap, makes the transition a little smoother. How about a glass of iced tea? Here, let me help you with your bags. This is your room." She motioned for Barbara to follow her across the small tidy living area to a cheerful room across the hallway from the bathroom.

After depositing her belongings in the bedroom, Barbara gladly accepted the offer of a cold drink. She looked around the tiny living room and admired the way Anita had arranged it. The house was cozy, a living room, bedroom, bath and eat-in kitchen. Anita had created a welcoming sense of warmth and order in the small home.

She talked fast like a harried New Yorker. "Yeah, I'm from Brooklyn. It's hard to slow down and smell the roses when you've been pushin' and shovin' all your life. But believe it or not, I've slowed down and relaxed during my time here in Rebita. More about that later. Let's get you settled. I moved my things in to the hall closet. I'll sleep on the sofa till I leave."

Barbara started to protest, but was abruptly interrupted by Anita. "Listen, honey, it's already said and done, so can it. You're movin' right into the bedroom. The bedding is washed fresh for you. Make yourself at home. After you get settled in, I'll show you around."

Barbara swallowed hard. Anita was very generous but brash. She went into the bedroom. The walls were whitewashed and the curtains and bedspread were a cheerful yellow. There was even a yellow area rug beside the bed. It didn't take long to unpack and organize her things.

Barbara rejoined Anita in the living room. "The bedroom is so cheerful and pretty, I appreciate you giving it up early for me. That's very kind of you."

Anita grinned and waved a hand as if to dismiss a student. "It's like this, when I arrived here twenty-three months ago, my time was overlapping with a selfish major slob. I had to share this house with that guy for one month. The Peace Corps wanted me to orient to the clinic and learn a few of the ins and outs of Rebita before being on my own here. He taught me some very important procedures for the clinic and about local cultural customs. Inadvertently, I learned how not to host a new volunteer."

"He not only kept the bedroom, but also laid claim to the rest of the house. I was only entitled to sleep on the sofa after he decided he was ready to go to bed at night. The place was filthy despite the fact he hired a local cleaner twice per week, there was no organization and little air circulation. I swear that man couldn't possibly have noticed if he'd a been robbed."

Barbara sympathized. "Sounds terrible. Didn't you feel like just turning around and going back home?"

Anita shook her head emphatically. "Hell no! I just did what had to be done, I staked out my territory and let that idiot know he had better not get on the bad side of a Brooklyn woman with a chip on her shoulders.

"By the end of the first week, we had reached a few compromises. He stayed in his room until the day he left. And then I had to air it out for three days, whitewash the walls and clean all the bedding before I'd even consider calling it my bedroom."

Barbara realized the considerate and generous gesture Anita had made. "Thank you for making my transition from trainee to volunteer as smooth as possible. It sounds like it was somewhat of a nightmare when you first came."

"Yeah, it really was, but it passed and I learned from it. Let me show you the clinic while we still have some daylight." They stood up and walked toward the back door.

Suddenly Anita stopped and continued, "Oh yeah, I forgot to tell you, we have two locals who work as guards here at the compound. Peace Corps pays them. Pablo works the day shift and Miguel works at night. Armondo is our handyman and groundskeeper; he can fix anything. The Peace Corps pays him too. Karena is our cleaner, twice per week at the house and five days a week at the clinic after it closes. Peace Corps pays for the clinic cleaning and we have to pay out-of-pocket for the house. I've made you a notebook to help you with the details of transition. I'll give it to you later. I call it, 'Rebita's Trivial but Necessary Survival Information for Peace Corps Volunteers.' Come on, let's take a quick peek at the clinic."

As they were leaving the back door, safely inside the compound, Anita turned back to the door with her key and announced, "First rule. Always lock doors. Second rule. Never flaunt jewelry. Hopefully you haven't brought any with you. That's another story."

A few steps across the compound and Anita was unlocking the clinic doors. It was like stepping back in time for Barbara as she looked around the sparkling clean clinic. She said, "This reminds me of the doctors' offices my mother took me to when I was a child."

Anita grinned. "Yeah, we've come a long way to bring jungle mountain health services into the twentieth century!"

There were two treatment rooms. The one waiting area had a small desk for a receptionist/office worker and fourteen chairs placed around the exterior walls. There were a few magazines on a table to help patients pass the time as they waited their turn for medical care. Outside the building, rustic wooden benches were sturdily built against the walls. Anita said, "That's where our overflow patients wait."

"You really work here alone? How do you manage? I just can't imagine...." Barbara suddenly felt uncertain about her own capabilities.

"Listen, it's really not so bad. I have trained a young woman from the village, Gabriela, to be my assistant. She knows symptoms, medications, makes appointments and handles triage classification when the waiting room fills up with sick people. I'd like to have trained more of the locals to the level of Gabriela...." Anita stopped in the middle of her sentence, obviously preoccupied with the reality of leaving Rebita so soon.

As they walked back to the house, Barbara said, "I'm really impressed with your clinic. How many patients do you see on a normal day?"

"It varies. Sometimes only ten and there were plenty of days we treated fifty. Mostly infections from the water like scabies, lice and parasites. Lots of education needed to help the people learn how to avoid some of their illnesses. The time has passed so quickly, it's hard to believe."

"I admire the work you've done here, Anita. I'm sure the villagers are going to miss you very much. Yours will not be easy shoes to fill. What's next for your career when you're back in the States?" Barbara asked.

As they returned to the house, Anita answered, "I've been thinking a lot about that and I'm pretty sure I'll take advantage of the Peace Corps tuition scholarship program. I loved the medical independence I've experienced here. I bounced around between becoming a doctor or a nurse practitioner. I want to work and make a difference. I love helping people, real hands-on medicine. I'm pretty certain I'll go for the nurse practitioner education. It can be accomplished in two years and I can also earn a master's degree in nursing at the same time. I know a medical degree would take me at least seven more years and mega bucks more than the scholarship will pay. Besides, nurse practitioners spend more quality time with patients. That's important to me. Yeah, I know doctors make a lot more money. But I can live well enough to suit me on a nurse practitioner's salary."

Barbara smiled at the petite young woman in the kitchen of the small Honduran mountain village of Rebita. "You certainly seem to know exactly what you want and I'm sure your patients will be the big winners. Did you always know you'd be a nurse?"

Anita shook her head. "No way. I got pregnant, quit high school, married my boyfriend, headed out west. Both our families acted like we'd committed the crime o' the century. Had a miscarriage in Kansas, got divorced in Nevada, made my way back to Brooklyn, made up my lost classes in summer school and graduated with my class the following June. Then I went for a two-year associate's degree in nursing, worked nights in ICU and two years later earned a BS in nursing from City College. I worked another two years, paid off my loans, socked some money away and joined the Peace Corps. You know the rest of the story. Hey, how about a drink of iced tea?"

"Sure, thanks, it's delicious. I have to say, I admire your spunk. Your folks must be very proud of you," Barbara replied.

"I seriously doubt that. They never got over the shame of my pregnancy. I think they were relieved to have me outa the way for a couple years. I'll stay with them for three days or so when I return. Then I'll be off to find a new life for myself." Anita sipped her tea and smiled softly as she anticipated her imminent family reunion.

"Do you have any siblings? A boyfriend?" Barbara asked, intrigued with her newest Peace Corps acquaintance.

"No sisters, three little brothers, nice kids but so much younger than me, nothing in common really. One is still in grammar school and two are in junior high school. Thank God, *no*, no boyfriend, not since my divorce eight years ago. I say who needs it, lies and broken promises!" With that Anita finished her iced tea and said, "Enough of that! Wanna see the village on a Sunday evening?"

Barbara nodded affirmatively and gulped the last of her tea. "Let's go!"

And they were off for a walking tour of Rebita. Anita cautioned her about life in the mountain village. "It's good to mingle with the local folks in the plaza several times a week. Chat them up, you know, smile and make a few friendly inquiries about their families. But do not eat the food sold there. Buy fresh fruits and vegetables. Get all the bottled water you can. When you can't get bottled water, boil, boil, boil! We *gringos* have no natural immunities to the bacteria in their water supply. You can drink bottled sodas, but don't take any coffee or teas while in the plaza. Since it's so warm, it's not hard for the venders to understand why we always want cold Coca Cola. I swear, they think Coca Cola and Peace Corps volunteer is a given equation! But that's okay, really. I always accept food gifts but I never eat them. Usually give it to one of the workers in the compound to take home or give it to a neighbor. That way it's not wasted and I don't get sick."

"It sounds like your dietary advice is from experience. Have you been sick?" Barbara asked.

"Yeah, I was terribly sick for almost two weeks in Tegucigalpa when I was in training. They almost had to send me back to the States. I made the mistake of going out to eat with some friends and hit the salad bars real hard. Well, to make a long story short, we later learned the salads had been washed in the local water. My GI system couldn't tolerate whatever their little bugs were. I do all my own food preparations here, except when I get a short holiday and get together with some of the other volunteers in this region. I've lost twenty pounds since I've been here but that's good news. I hope to maintain this weight when I go back. Geez, sorry I'm so long winded this evening. Well, here we are…what do you think of Plaza de Rebita?" Anita asked.

Barbara sighed and smiled. "It's charming, enchanting even. I'll never forget the way this plaza looks right now as long as I live. Is this a typical evening?"

"Yes and no. Yes, a typical Sunday evening but fewer venders than on the other nights of the week. This is the gathering place where people come to socialize, buy and sell, make business deals and even marriage matches are arranged here. Every night there's at least one maraji band playing. So many of the locals are musically talented, it's really quite amazing. Most of the people do not have high expectations from life. Therefore, there's a low level of disappointment and a higher level of life satisfaction. Well, at least that's what I think. These people are very poor but they are genuinely kind, generous and fun loving. They often sing and dance till midnight and worry about *mañana* when it comes," Anita explained.

As they slowly walked around the plaza, many of the locals spoke and waved. "*Hola,* Nurse Anita."

Barbara loved the way they pronounced Anita's name. A lovely young Honduran girl approached them and spoke in broken English, "*Hola,* Anita. Did you have good day free from work? Who es your new *amigo?*"

"*Hola,* Gabriela, yes, I had a good day. This is the new Peace Corps nurse. I told you she'd be here soon. Gabriela, this is Barbara."

Barbara smiled warmly and extended her hand. "*Hola,* Gabriela, very nice to meet you. I look forward to working with you in the clinic. I hear you are an extra special helper there."

Gabriela blushed. "*Gracias, señora.* Good to meet you." Then she turned to Anita and said, "I see you *mañana. Buenas tardes.*"

"What a sweet girl and she's so pretty. I'll look forward to working with her. Maybe you can help me plan a way to train more locals in basic first aid training and safe care-giving skills. What do you think?" Barbara asked hesitantly.

"I like that idea. We'll talk about it with Gabriela tomorrow. She may even have suggestions as to whom we should include in the class," Anita replied.

Barbara had noticed only one vehicle in the plaza, an old Suburban that was freshly painted orange and lime green. It had a red light on top and a star painted on the driver's door. Anita explained that it was the official village car, driven by the village *policía.* The entire *Policía* Department was one policeman, Arturo, who lived in a small apartment with his wife and children attached to the back of the police station.

They walked back to the compound by the lights of the street torches. Barbara helped Anita prepare a simple dinner. They ended the evening with a glass of wine.

Barbara said, "I'm really tired, but I have one last question for you. If the locals are so nice and generous, etc., then why so much security and so many security guards everywhere. I find it a bit confusing."

"I'm sure I wondered about that, too, when I first arrived. You see there's a small element in this society who are greedy and prefer not to work. They've been able to acquire powerful weapons and seem to operate without a conscience. All the villagers are afraid of these angry ruthless men. It's rumored they are involved in drug trafficking," answered Anita.

"Ah…I see. That's why Juan and Julio were so anxious to head back down the mountain today. Julio was determined they'd not travel in darkness." Barbara continued, "Well, good night, Anita and thank you for everything. It's been an eye-opening day. Sleep tight, my dear."

"Good night to you. It's great to have you here, Barbara."

The next day flew by. Gabriela's clinical skills were superior and she had a kind and persuasive manner of interacting with the local people, which was a tremendous help. Thirty patients went through the clinic on Barbara's first day. The waiting room was always full. Barbara assisted Anita in setting a young boy's broken arm and applying a cast. A young woman in labor came in accompanied by her frightened young husband…Barbara assisted Anita in delivering a healthy baby girl. Four hours after delivery, the orange and green Suburban pulled into the compound and with great fanfare, the villagers and family of the young mother carried her and the new baby to the Suburban and laid her on the back seat for a short ride to her home to continue her postpartum recovery. Two guitarists provided chords as two dozen family members and friends sang and clapped their hands in joy walking alongside the Suburban as it trekked slowly toward the home of the new parents. Several carried bouquets of fresh wildflowers.

And it had only been a routine day with common complaints from the patients according to Anita and Gabriela. Barbara was stunned at the constant pace and variety of medical problems she'd been exposed to her first day on the job.

The barefoot villagers of Rebita were short in stature with dark skin, penetrating dark brown eyes and shiny straight raven hair. Barbara had been accustomed to a more diversified population volunteering in the Wellness Clinic in Lewiston, one of those good old U.S.A. melting pot communities. But what impressed Barbara most was the villagers' genuine kindness and friendliness. Barbara found her open-back Birkenstock sandals were perfect shoes for the long, hot days in the village clinic. A few of the villagers made their own sandals using jungle vines, bark, large leaves and a few pieces of leather. These were mostly men who hunted or traveled outside the village perimeters. Most were perfectly happy without shoes. Arturo, the policeman, had a pair of shoes he took with him when he made his weekly trips down the mountain in the official Rebita green and orange Suburban for supplies and mail. He wore them only while in the "more sophisticated" village. This way his shoes would not wear out so soon. The village priest wore handmade leather sandals purchased in one of the larger towns of Honduras.

Before leaving the clinic, Anita told Gabriela about Barbara's idea to train more villagers in basic first aid and Gabriela's pretty face clouded over with an angry scowl. "What for you do that? You no more want Gabriela? I not good enough? Why? Why?" And then she cried as if her heart was breaking.

Barbara looked at Anita helplessly. Anita rolled her eyes, spoke in rapid fire Spanish as she walked to the sobbing girl. "Good God, Gabriela! Are you loco? We always want you. You are the best nurse helper we could ever find. We couldn't get along without you. We just thought it might be good to show village mothers how to take care of little hurts and help big hurts heal faster without complications. Do you understand, Gabriela? You stay, you help us to teach others. Okay?"

The sobbing slowly stopped, and Gabriela wiped her eyes with the edge of her long floral skirt. She looked at Anita and Barbara. "Really, you want me help teach de class? You want keep Gabriela in clinic as nurse helper?"

Both volunteers walked across the small office and put their arms around the insecure young Honduran girl and Anita said, "Of course, we want you to stay and help us. How would we run this place without you?"

Barbara added, "Gabriela, I'm sorry you thought we'd try to replace you. Never, never. Please stay! I really need you, dear girl."

Gabriela smiled sheepishly. "I stay. I help. I sorry I cry. I not want lose my job."

Then they brain stormed and decided Wednesday nights would be a good time to offer the class. They agreed six students per class was the maximum they could handle. That night Anita and Barbara sat down and planned the curriculum.

Depending on class response, aptitude and participation, it would probably take between six and eight weeks to complete the basic first aid course.

The busy days in the clinic flew by. Barbara was shocked to realize a week had gone by and it was Sunday again. "Is there a church I could attend today?"

"Well, there's only one church in town. Do you remember the largest white stucco building on the plaza, the one with the tall steeple? That's it. I believe services start at nine a.m.," Anita responded.

Barbara enjoyed the Catholic service, even though she was not Catholic. Since it was the only church in the village, she decided to attend each week. Somehow it made her feel grounded and reinvigorated to tackle another busy week.

The clinic was open for eight hours Monday through Friday and four hours on Saturday. The second and third weeks went by just as quickly. Barbara used Saturday afternoons to write letters to the family and Alice. She also wrote to Alvie and Ethel.

"Anita, I'm really going to miss you. It's hard to believe you'll be gone in only one more week. When you go, would you post my letters for me at the airport?"

"Sure, no problem; just put them on top of my luggage in the closet."

Now when Barbara walked about the village, she'd hear the locals greet her. "*Hola,* Nurse Barbarra. *Cómo está usted?*"

Anita teased her. "Barbara, you're famous already! Keep up the good work."

Barbara was happy; she liked the way the locals pronounced "Barbara." She felt her life was making a difference and felt a new sense of confidence in herself. She asked, "Anita, you mentioned that sometimes you'd get together with other volunteers in the region…how often does that happen and where do you meet?"

"We have annual Peace Corps meetings in Tegucigalpa. They're recommended but not mandatory. It's kind of fun to see all the other volunteers, but as you know from your trip here, traveling can be a hardship, especially from such remote locations as this. Then we're all entitled to four weeks vacation per year. Last year a group of us from this region went to Cabo Falso for ten days. It was great! A few months before that, some of us spent a long weekend in Valencia at the Peace Corps house. We had such a good time. That's when we planned the beach trip. Keep in touch with your cohorts and it will all fall into place, you'll see."

During Anita's last week, the clinic's medical doctor was scheduled for his monthly day and half rotation on Tuesday. By nine a.m. the compound was already overflowing with families waiting their turn to see the doctor. The waiting room had filled almost immediately when they opened the clinic at eight a.m. Gabriela and her assistants had everyone registered to be seen by either the doctor or one of them.

"There is a method of organization in what first appears to be total chaos, just wait. You'll see; it really does come together," Anita assured Barbara. Anita's voice changed to a lower, more serious tone as she warned Barbara. "Dr. Kane's a moody old man. He's mostly gruff and testy with Peace Corps volunteers. I guess he was a Peace Corps volunteer himself back in the sixties. Then a few years ago after he retired in the States, he worked out an agreement with Peace Corps administration to provide contractual medical services to this region. He lives somewhere near these mountains. He's quite a character and a very competent doctor. The Hondurans love him and he's fluent in Spanish. You seem like a sensitive and nice lady, just don't take any of his bullshit personally. Okay?"

"Thanks for the warning, Anita. I won't let him get to me, I promise," Barbara replied. Remembering the years of insults and putdowns from Bill, she thought, "Yeah, I can handle a grumpy doctor once a month, no problem!"

"Well, don't say I didn't warn you..." Anita was interrupted by the sounds of an approaching...army? That's what it sounded like while in reality Barbara soon realized it was only Dr. Kane's SUV approaching.

Pablo, the day guard, quickly opened the compound gate and saluted Dr. Kane, who returned the salute. He stopped the jeep with a jerk on the far side of the clinic. A well-dressed and equally well-armed security guard jumped out of the passenger side and quickly circled the jeep to open the driver's door. Out stepped a giant of a man, wearing wrinkled khaki slacks, a short-sleeved brown camouflage shirt and thick-soled sandals. A faded NY Yankees cap covered his long gray hair, which was pulled back in a ponytail. His face had full beard and mustache. The security guard saluted and the giant saluted back.

The waiting villagers suddenly stood quietly in awe, as if God himself had appeared.

When Gabriela heard him, she ran out to greet him, shouting, "*Bienvenido*, Dr. Kane!"

"Oh look at you, my little Gabriela!" The animated giant picked the young girl up and swung her around. "Have you been a good girl? Learning how to be a good nurse, Gabriela?"

"*Sí*, Doctor, I will help new Nurse Barbara teach the village *madres* first aid," she told him proudly.

"You don't say. Well that's great, you better get back to work now. I have to go see the PCVs now. *Adiós*, Gabriela." With that, the giant turned to come inside the clinic.

Barbara quietly asked Anita, "What's a PCV?"

Anita whispered, "We are!" just before he entered the room. Anita refused the salute routine that Dr. Kane craved. She had told him bluntly from her first day, "Sir, I am not part of the military. I do not salute." Today she simply said, "Good morning, Dr. Kane. You appear to be in good form this morning. Doctor, this is Barbara Malone, she's the new volunteer for the clinic. I'll be leaving this weekend. It's been fun, Doc."

Dr. Kane said, "Hi" to Anita and then ignored her. She shrugged her shoulders and smiled as she went back to work.

Barbara walked across the room to the doctor and extended her hand. "Hello, Dr. Kane, it is nice to meet you. I'm Barbara."

He ignored her hand, quickly looked at her and then shouted to Anita, "Good God, they're sending AARP members down here now. Holy shit, what next?"

"Sorry, Doc, I'm busy, Gabriela has your list of patients for today!" Anita shouted back at him.

As he turned to walk away, Barbara said in a firm clear voice, "Excuse me, Doctor, but you look like you're only about one foot outa the grave yourself, so what's the big deal if I'm not a young chick? I'm a damn good nurse and that's why I'm here."

He stopped cold; Barbara suddenly didn't feel quite so bold. He slowly turned around and it felt like his dark brown eyes stared into her soul. She stood her ground and stared right back at him.

Then he smiled and extended his hand. "Pleased to meet you, Barbara, I'm Mike Kane. You're a feisty one, aren't you?"

Barbara shook his hand briefly and answered his question. "Only when I have to be. I must get back to work now." She turned and walked away.

Dr. Mike Kane didn't know quite what hit him.

Barbara was seething but had to admit Anita had tried to warn her. She shook her head and smiled as she muttered, "What a character!"

Chapter Thirteen

BOBBY

Bobby was the first one to arrive at the office that Tuesday morning. He was surprised to see a large white envelope had been slid under his office door. He immediately opened it, handwritten on official firm letterhead stationary. The writing was not easy to decipher at first, then slowly he realized it was from Mr. McDowell, the managing partner of the Holbrook, Newcomb and McDowell Law Firm. It was obviously not a friendly letter, nor was it threatening. Bobby still had his job but the letter had an ominously vague tone that gave him an uneasy feeling. "...defacing the firms' property, secretive suspicious behaviors...it'd be a shame to jeopardize such a potentially bright future in law..." It ended with a request for Bobby to call his boss for a personal meeting as soon as possible.

He thought, "McDowell's ticked off about the new door lock. I wondered how long till they realized their key no longer opened my office door. I'm sure dear Miss Lears reported it. For some reason, they want constant access to my office. They are so damn petty. God! I hate this job. I hope this is not the typical office ethics of the legal profession. If it is, then I'm definitely in need of a career change."

He closed his office door, called McDowell and left a message on his voice mail. Bobby quickly assessed the files stacked on his desk, prioritizing them according to brief summaries including dates due attached to each file.

An hour later Miss Lears opened his door, her eyes seemed to be searching his desk as she crisply said, "Good Morning, Mr. Malone. How are you today? Would you like a fresh cup of coffee?"

He answered her without looking up from his work. "Good morning to you, my lady. I'm feeling great and how are you today? Oh…ah, no thanks on the coffee."

She hesitated before leaving. "Is there anything else I can do for you before I go?"

Bobby finally looked at her and faked his most sincere smile. "No thanks, I'm all set, already into the research on the Ruiz case. Is there anything else? If not I'll just get back to work."

An hour later, Miss Lears buzzed him, "Mr. Malone, you have a call on line one. It's Mr. McDowell."

Bobby picked up. "Malone here. How're you, Mr. McDowell?"

McDowell answered, "I think we should talk face to face. Be in my office in five minutes." Click.

"Great phone manners, McDowell! Your momma should've spent a little more time with you when you were a kid," he muttered under his breath. "I might as well get this over with." He stood up, combed his hair, put *the* letter in his jacket pocket and walked to the door. Bobby discreetly locked his office door as he was leaving.

Miss Lears peeked over the top of her glasses, the ones she only wore when she needed to see. "Going somewhere, Mr. Malone?"

"Yes, I'll be out for a short meeting. I should be back before lunch," he answered.

Bobby walked up three flights of stairs and entered McDowell's office suite. His secretary smiled like she was really glad to see him. Bobby knew it was a practiced professional smile, but it worked for him. He thought, "She's gorgeous, she could be a model or a movie star and she's McDowell's secretary. Meanwhile I'm stuck with Miss Lears. Life is not fair!"

She broke into his train of thought with the voice of an angel. "Good morning. May I help you?"

He was enchanted. "I'm Bob Malone, I have an appointment with Mr. McDowell."

She looked at her boss's daily schedule, and back to Bobby. "You said Malone? I can't seem to find your name on today's agenda. Excuse me till I check with Mr. McDowell." She buzzed the inner office and a few seconds later turned to Bobby with *that* smile and said, "Please, go right in. He's expecting you."

Bobby thanked her and started to the inner office door. Then he turned back to the young woman and asked, "Have you been with the firm long? I don't remember seeing you here before. And I would've remembered *you*."

She smiled again. Bobby thought, "I'm in love. This is insane but I really think I could spend my life with this girl. She's so beautiful and that smile, the voice...." His trance was interrupted by the secretary tapping her watch and pointing at McDowell's office door with perfectly manicured nails, of course.

She whispered, "My name is Ashley. I'll talk to you after your meeting. Go!"

Bobby walked into the spacious dark cherry office. Two walls were lined floor to the ceiling with dark leather-bound books. It was an ornate masculine office intended to impress visitors and it did. The bulky graying McDowell stood up and shook hands with him. Bobby thought, "Well, not a bad beginning."

McDowell started, "Please, sit down." He indicated a comfortable leather side chair. "I like you, Malone. You stand apart from the crowd. That's good. But sometimes your kind of individualism can cause a few problems for successful team work. Around here, we like to think of ourselves as a team. You've got to ask yourself if you *really* want to be part of our team."

Bobby thought, "Whew going downhill fast. Brief, clear and to the point. I like that." However he carefully answered, "I'd just like to clarify what we're talking about here. Is it this letter?" Bobby pulled it out of his jacket.

McDowell cleared his throat and grinned as he shook his head. "Is it really that bad for you to work with Alice Lears? She's been with the firm for thirty years. That's five years longer than I've been here. She's only trying to do her job. You, young man, have proven to be a real challenge for her. The firm is her life. Why don't you just ignore her annoying habits and simply do your work?"

"I'll try, but I'd appreciate you telling me just what her job description covers," Bobby replied.

"It's a little complicated. But let's just leave it at this. She's our radar, our conscience, and if you want to play on this team, she's the captain's assistant. She can make you or break you. The ball's in your court, Malone."

"Mr. McDowell, does this mean you want me to put the old lock back on the office door?"

McDowell suddenly roared with laughter. "Malone, you've got grit. You crack me up! Hell no, just give me an extra key to your office and I'll see that Alice Lears gets a copy. That way you don't have to let on to her that you know that she knows you changed the lock in the first place. Got it?"

"Yes, sir." Bobby stood up to leave and laid the extra key to his office on the boss's desk. "Is that all for today, Mr. McDowell?"

"I must ask you what is such a big secret about your work that you felt compelled to change the lock on your office door? I suggest you do not bring personal things to the office and if you do, *never* leave anything there when you go home. Oh yes, just a reminder, all legal files are confidential property of Holbrook, Newcomb and McDowell Law Firm."

"Sir, it was just a matter of principle for me. I've had no personal belongings at the office. I realize I was out of line. It won't happen again." Bobby stared at the floor, in an effort to appear humiliated.

"I believe that covers my concerns, son. You're doing a good job for us and we see great things for your future here at the firm."

"Thank you, Mr. McDowell. I'll do my best." Bobby started to leave then turned and said, "Sir, there is one other thing. I think there are unnecessary communication issues in the offices that cause morale problems and staff turnover. Well, that's my opinion based on nine months of on-sight observations, sir."

McDowell stared at the young attorney, astonished at his relentless badgering. He replied, "I'll keep that in mind. Didn't realize we had a morale problem, I'll have to get out on the floor more often and get a feel for the staff's attitudes. Thanks for pointing that out to me." Even though he answered the young lawyer with apparent good humor and civility, McDowell seethed inside. "You little son of a bitch. Who do you think you are? Coming in here and telling me how to run my business? You better watch your back, buddy, 'cause you can be replaced very easily."

Bobby closed the office door and took a deep breath.

Ashley looked up from her work when she heard the door close. "That bad, huh?"

Bobby answered with a shrug as he tried to smile. "Could've been worse, I've never liked double talk conferences. At least I still have a job."

Her smile looked so damn sincere. "I'm sorry he was rough on you. But that's the way it is. You look like you need a friendly break. Could I take you to lunch? My break starts in five minutes."

Bobby felt like a bowl of melting Jell-O. "Lunch? Me and…you? Whew…ah, well, yes! Sounds great, I'll meet you in the lobby in five."

He felt like he was walking on air when he entered the office suite he shared with seven other rookie associates and a pool of six secretaries and two paralegals. Miss Lears was the office manager and didn't want anyone on the staff to ever forget it.

She looked up as he floated through the door with a goofy grin on his face. "How did the meeting go, Mr. Malone?"

He looked at her with a tinge of sympathy and thought, "It truly is a sad thing when a person's job becomes their entire life. I definitely will try to be kinder to this lonely cold-hearted woman." While he said, "The meeting was great, thanks for asking. Did I have any calls? Oh, I'll be going to lunch, should be back in an hour or so."

Miss Lears couldn't help but notice the difference in his demeanor. It was not what she expected from a rookie associate, especially not Bob Malone, after a confrontational meeting with the managing partner of the law firm.

She silently watched him unlock his office door. He grabbed his jacket and told her as he was leaving, "I'll be leaving my office unlocked today, in case you need something while I'm out. See you later."

"Have a nice lunch, Mr. Malone."

"Now that wasn't so hard, was it?" he thought as he ran down the flight of steps to the lobby. Ashley stood there like a goddess. When she saw him, she waved and smiled that smile again.

"Thanks for having lunch with me today," she said. "I really needed to get away from the office for awhile. Sometimes it gets pretty tense up there."

"Trust me, Ashley, it's my pleasure. Going to lunch with you makes me feel like I won the lottery! Where shall we eat? Any favorite restaurants?" he asked, while thinking, *This is scary. I think I'm falling in love.*

"Do you often ask black sheep attorneys out to lunch, Ashley?"

She blushed slightly and answered, "You're the first."

Ashley and Bobby talked amiably like old friends as they walked down the street in the brilliant noon sunshine. They ate at a small café two blocks from the office.

He was relieved to learn she worked for a temp service and had turned down a lucrative job offer from McDowell. He was not surprised when she told him she did do part-time modeling.

She explained, "I like to see new faces and meet new people. I don't want to be tied down to a five-day-a-week, nine-to-five job, doing the same thing day after day. Maybe I sound like a restless soul, but I don't think I am. I just like some flexibility and freedom. I don't need a lot of money to live life the way I want to. Most of my entertainment comes from the books I read through the public library. I've been blessed with good health and have minimal expense maintaining my appearance. I shop mostly through resale shops and manage to put together some great outfits. Now, please tell me about Bob Malone, the best looking and quite possibly the most human lawyer I've had the pleasure of meeting."

Bobby could feel his face blush. "Well, this is my first job out of law school, I graduated last spring. I hate to say this but I really hate my work most of the time. I'm embarrassed to admit it. You seem to have figured out what you want and live a contented life. I admire you for that. How can you be so wise so young?"

Ashley laughed. "I never thought of myself as wise. My father thinks I'm a bit lazy. I watched my paternal grandparents work so hard and save for their dreams until they retired. Between cancer, arthritis and heart disease…well, I only have my maternal grandmother left. She told me a few weeks after my grandfather's funeral, 'Ash, don't wait till you're old to live your dreams. Find a way to live each day as if it could be your last. We have no guarantees in this life.' So, I reevaluated my priorities and decided to make some changes. I quit my job as an accountant, I dropped out of the rat race and I've worked for the temp agency for a year now. It pays the bills and I set my own pace. It's right for me."

They barely touched their food over lunch and were stunned when they checked the time. Their lunch had lasted two hours. Bobby quickly paid for lunch, over Ashley's protest. "Hey, I invited you to lunch, I want to pay!"

"Not this time, it's my treat; I was going to ask you anyway. We better hustle."

Before entering the Holbrook, Newcomb and McDowell Law offices, as casually as possible, Bobby touched her hand, and asked, "Ashley, I loved being with you for lunch. Would you consider dinner, a movie? What I mean is could I see you again?"

She squeezed his hand gently and smiled. "I was hoping you'd ask because there's absolutely nothing I'd rather do." She pulled one of the temp services business cards from her purse and quickly wrote her number on the back. "See you soon, Bob." And she hurried off to McDowell's office.

Bobby forced himself to concentrate and by seven p.m. called it a day. He was pleased to see a thick envelope from Honduras when he picked up his mail. Over a frozen chicken entree and a glass of wine, he read his mother's descriptive nine-page letter. He could visualize the village and the locals as well as understand why she felt it was where she ought to be at this time in her life. An hour later he reached in his pocket and found Ashley's number but just as he was about to call her, the phone rang. It was Jessica. "Hey, sis, long time no talk! How are you?"

JESSICA

Since her mother had left for the Peace Corps six months ago, Jessica had been home once every month to visit the grandparents. She told herself, "Someone has to look out for them." But in reality she knew she benefited more than they did from the visits. Grandmother Malone had even started to send and save classified ads in a less than subtle hint that Jess might consider moving back to Lewiston. To Jessica's cynical side, this was a horrific thought. But deep in her heart, she was shocked to realize that maybe, just maybe, this is what she really wanted to do.

The fact that Michael Bleem, an old and still single friend from high school, had relocated back to Lewiston to teach at the community college made thoughts of moving home even more tempting. Jess had been home six weekends since literally bumping into him at the park four months ago. He called her almost every night and encouraged her to move back to Lewiston. Michael had also driven to visit her three times.

It was a relief to get the sketchy reports from the grands each week about her mother's status and experiences in the Peace Corps. When she finally received a long letter from her mother two months ago, it had been a welcome relief for her worries. The letter was ten pages long and full of descriptive anecdotes about her life in the Honduran mountains. After reading it the third time, Jessica had smiled and thought, "The Peace Corps should really be using that woman for public relations. She loves it and seems to be more animated and alive than I ever knew her to be. From what she writes, she's so busy that we're lucky she takes the time to write any letters at all. I just hope she stays safe."

Jessica sat down, propped up her feet and decided to call Bobby for some brotherly advice.

"Hi, Bobby, it's good to hear your voice. Am I calling you at a bad time? How have you been, anyway?"

"I just finished reading my first long letter from Mom. She wants me to make copies and send to the grands, you, Janie and Billy. I'll take care of that tomorrow. She sounds great. Even makes me want to run off and join the Peace Corps! But don't worry; it's a fleeting desire. I'm glad it's worked out so well for Mom. If she hadn't gone, she'd have always wondered, 'What if?' Now regardless of what the future holds, she'll have this experience and be a stronger and better person for it. Now I'm glad she refused to be talked out of going."

Jessica smiled as she listened to Bobby. "Me, too. So what's new? How's work going? You know you sound like a lawyer when you start talking..."

"Okay, smarty, maybe I sound like a lawyer because I am a lawyer! Work is work. I don't like it any better than I did before but I'm still there."

"Do I detect a little testiness about your job, brother of mine? What is it you dislike so much about your job anyway? Are you looking for another position or do you just like to complain?"

Bobby counted to ten under his breath; Jessica always managed to touch a nerve. He finally answered her, "You're without mercy, Jess. No, I don't like to complain and no, I haven't started to look for another position yet. I'm anticipating working for this firm for at least a year so my work record won't look like a restless job hopper. That doesn't make it any easier day to day, but I'm hanging in there. How about you? What have you been up to?"

"Well, are you sitting down?" Jessica teased.

"Yes. What's up?" He was suddenly very attentive.

"Did you know I've been going back to Lewiston every third weekend since Mom left? I stay with Grandmother Malone but see Mormor and Morfar a lot too. At first I did it out of sympathy and obligation. Then slowly our relationships began to change. I saw each of them for the individuals they are instead of just the 'grands.'

"They all have totally different ways of making me feel very special. I know that sounds self-centered and immature. I really don't think either description could be accurately applied to me. I know lots of other words that could. Like...oh, maybe sarcastic, bitchy, honest, well, you get the picture." Jessica hesitated trying to decide how much and what to tell him next.

"So, ah...what are you trying to tell me, Jess? No, I didn't know you were going home so often. Glad to hear the grands are doing well. But I don't see where this is heading," queried a puzzled Bobby.

"About four months ago I was walking in the park near our old neighborhood and I ran into Michael Bleem. Do you remember him from back in high school? Anyway we started talking and we really hit it off. I never expected anything like this to ever happen to me. We were on the debate team together in high school. We even went to one homecoming dance together. We were just good friends back then. Now he's back in town teaching at Lewiston Community College. We've been dating. He's met the grands. I want him to meet you, Billy, Liz and Janie. Bobby, he calls me almost every night and he wants me to move back to Lewiston. I have an interview for the Physical Therapy Manager position at the Lewiston Hospital

Rehabilitation Center Friday morning. Wish me luck! The grands like Michael and Grandmother Malone was the one who gave me the classified section about this position. Are you in shock? Any comments?"

"Wow! You've double blind sided me with this. It sounds like you're in love. I only vaguely remember Michael from high school. I followed the football team a lot closer than the debate team. What about your present job? I thought you liked it," Bobby asked Jessica.

"I love my work. Sure I'll miss my coworkers and my patients; but after work my life here is really empty. If a person doesn't do the bar scene, and I don't, well it makes for too many long quiet nights. Maybe that's why I like going home so much; the grands make me feel connected in a way that just doesn't happen when I'm alone in my apartment night after night," Jessica answered in a soft strained voice.

"Are you okay, Jess? You don't sound like yourself."

"Yeah, I'm fine. It's just such a big step, I mean the Michael part. I'm sorta scared. I don't want to make a mistake. I don't want to live my mother's life…oh, Bobby, what should I do?"

"Get the job, make the move and take some time getting to know Michael. See how compatible you really are. Remember the tape Mom sent us? She doesn't regret her marriage to Dad. She didn't pretend that it was a good marriage either. She said having us children made everything worthwhile. Mom always told us life wouldn't be perfect, and when we get stuck with lemons, make lemonade," he reminded his sister.

"I know you're right, Bobby, it's just so damn hard for me to make such a big change. I always said I'd never in a million years live in Lewiston, but going away to college and then working here…you know what I found? What I disliked about Lewiston most must've been me because I've never been truly content or happy. Guess I've unknowingly had an attitude problem. Anyway the closest I've been to happiness has been since I went home for that weekend with Mom last September. I don't understand why. Maybe it's just natural maturation, what do you think?"

"I think the timing was right and maturity is a factor. Dad's death and then Mom going off to the Peace Corps…these were wake-up calls for all of us to stop taking our parents for granted. Suddenly we were forced to realize we're all adults. That's not easy. Sure we've demanded and fought for adult privileges since we were in high school but we didn't want the responsibilities that go hand in hand with it. Now we can't call or go running home anymore. It's a big change for all of us. Don't be so hard on yourself, Jess."

"Yeah, I see what you mean. I've been taking notes on your pep talk. It may help the next time I'm hit in the face with doubts and fear of change. How did my little brother get so smart? Do they teach you all this in law school?"

"Hang in there, Jess. You'll be okay no matter what. You're a survivor, right?" Then Bobby changed the subject. "Have you talked to our newlyweds or Janie lately? I haven't for at least six weeks, I've been meaning to, but work is so damn demanding. I know that's a rotten excuse, maybe I'm just lazy. Well, they could call me, too. I tape that soap Janie's on and watch it on weekends. She's really good. And to think some of us were about ready to give up on her. Poor kid, it took her awhile but she's made it. Looks like Mom's been right about her all along."

"No, I haven't talked to either for awhile. Now that I have a 'friend,' he takes up a lot of my free time."

"I beg to differ with you, sis, but I'd say you have a bona fide boyfriend. I don't think friend quite covers it," Bobby teased.

Jessica smiled. "I kind of like the sound of that, my boyfriend. I hadn't even had a date in more than three years, let alone a boyfriend. I think it's safe to say, Bobby, I'm excited!"

"And I'm truly happy for you, Jessica, you deserve a chance at happiness. I think Michael is one lucky guy."

"Geez, Bobby, if I'd have known talking to you would've made me feel this good, I'd have called you weeks ago! What's new with you? Are you seeing anyone special?"

"Well, maybe…I just met her today. We had a two-hour lunch and she seems almost too good to be true. I know Morfar always said, 'If it seems too good to be true, it is.' But you'd like her. She's beautiful and down to earth. I hate to get my hopes up, but if there is such a thing as love at first sight…this is it. I'll keep you posted."

"Whew, Bobby, sounds like Cupid has zapped you hard! You've had some girlfriends for a year and never mentioned them till they were history. Good luck. I hope she proves to be even better than your first impression led you to believe. Well, I really need to go; I want to call Janie and Billy before it gets too late. It's been great talking to you, brother."

"Good talking to you, Jess. Thanks for calling and good luck. Stay in touch, I want to know what's happening in your life. Remember, you gotta friend in brother Bob. Oh, ah, please tell Janie and Billy I said hi, okay?"

Jess laid the phone down and walked to her tiny kitchen in her sock feet to get a drink of apple cider. Then she called Janie. No answer; left a message.

Jess shook her head. Knowing Janie it would be at least three days before she'd bother to return her phone call. She looked at the clock, ten fifteen p.m., and decided maybe it was getting a bit late for phone calls. She wrote, "call Billy," at the top of her things-to-do list for tomorrow after work.

Just as she was about to go to sleep, the phone rang. It was Michael. She felt warm all over as she cuddled in her down comforter and listened to sweet words, words she'd been so sure only existed in romance stories, from someone she respected, trusted and...yes, loved. And Michael was saying those precious sweet words to her. Life was good. After telling him good night and hanging up the phone, Jessica fell asleep with a contented smile on her face.

JANIE

"At first it made me feel important to be recognized and have strangers ask me for my autograph. But when the fat lady from Dallas yelled at me because I had signed my own name and not my TV character's name, well I decided, enough is enough." Janie explained the long rain coat, hat and sunglasses to Gloria over a Saturday brunch in a small Manhattan café that was rarely frequented by tourists.

Gloria's Brooklyn accent and her rapid fire speech always made Janie pay close attention to her every word. "Honey, a year ago you were 'bout ready to sell your soul just hopin' for somebody, anybody, to ask you for an autograph! It's funny how success changes things. Hey, doll, I gotta tell ya though, you're pure dynamite. I just had a call from a Movie of the Week producer. They been watchin' you on the soap and they want you to test for a co-staring role on a made-for-TV movie about two thirty-somethin' sisters copin' after the sudden death of their parents. One sister is cold and distant but carin' in her own way. The other is mentally fragile and in and out of psychiatric inpatient care. They want you to play the sick one. Interested?"

"You bet I am! Now, finally after all the years of trying to get my foot in the door, offers coming to me! It's my dream come true. Thanks, Gloria. I'd never have made it this far without all your help."

Gloria lifted her coffee cup and said, "Here's to you, kid. You're the one with the talent. I'd a dropped you like a hot potato if I hadn't believed in you."

They munched their bagels in silence for a few minutes. Then Gloria looked at Janie and asked, "How's your mother? I don't know anyone else who has a mother in the Peace Corps...in the Central American mountain jungles, no less."

Janie smiled and answered, "She calls the grandparents every week and relays messages through them to us. I've had two long letters from her. She always asks that I copy them and give copies to the family. She sounds happy and very busy. She had to assist another nurse deliver a baby and set a cast on a child's broken arm and that was just her first day on the job. She'll be working almost independently since the doctor only visits the village one and a half days per month. I felt lucky that she had time to write at all. She seems to love the Peace Corps and feels needed. That's important for her; well, maybe it is for everyone."

"I'd really like to meet your mom someday. She sounds neat, a real one-of-a-kind sorta lady. Ya must really be proud of her."

"It's safe to say that I am. But sad to admit that I didn't even really know her until just before she left. I always took her for granted and had far too little respect for her while I was growing up. After Daddy died, well, everything changed so fast."

"Yeah, I know what ya mean about takin' people for granted and not respectin' them like we oughta. Better late than never. You know some people never get a second chance...."

They sipped their coffee silently for a few minutes, each lost to her own thoughts. Finally Gloria looked at her watch. "Ah shit! I'm late for an appointment. They'll be pissed, great way to start out a meetin'...oh, here's your call card for the audition, hope you can handle the time with your soap schedule. Good luck, sweetie. Knock 'em dead!"

Janie jumped up and kissed Gloria's cheek. "Thanks for everything, Glo, you really saved my life."

Gloria raised her finger to her lips and shook her head vehemently. "Enough of that talk. You're the one with the talent, I couldn't make anything happen if you didn't have what it takes, and, honey, you got it. See ya, kid."

Janie paid the check, put on her sunglasses, coat and hat, and walked home with a jaunty step to her gait. "Life is beautiful, yes it is."

She was pleasantly surprised to hear Jessica's voice on the answering machine. "I better return Jessica's call."

Janie was stunned as Jess reported all her news. Janie could only vaguely remember Michael from high school.

When Janie finally found her voice, she half teased, "Oh my God! Is this my sister, Jessica Michele Monroe, the *real* Jessica who emphatically insisted she would never ever in a million years ever live in Lewiston after the age of eighteen? Have you lost your mind?"

Jessica took a deep breath and smiled. "Okay, I guess I deserved that, me and my big mouth. I don't know what to say except that people sometimes change. I know I have. When I was a teenager, the grass always looked greener on the other side of the fence. Now that I've tried the other side of the fence, well…I'll just say it's maybe not even as green as in Lewiston. Of course, it helps with the grands there and now Michael. I'm sort of scared about such a big change but it's so nice to have someone to talk to, late at night…and to feel loved. I hadn't even had a date in three years. I'd pretty much resigned myself to a single life and now I feel like I've found my soul mate."

"Jess, all I have to say is, he better be good to my sister or he'll have the wrath of the Malones on him so fast, he won't know what hit him! Have you told the grands? How about Mom? Bobby? Billy? Here I was convinced you were a confirmed single. You just never know." Janie was sitting on her sofa, smiling as she shook her head…trying to digest all the implications of her sister's news.

"I've started a long letter to Mom; I'm waiting till after my interview on Friday to finish it, so I can tell her *everything* in one letter. She'll be surprised and I think very happy for me," Jessica answered.

"Do you want to live in the house when you move back? I bet Mom wouldn't mind if you did," Janie added.

"Heavens no, the house is way too big for me and I don't want to ask for it anyway. Yes, I talked to Bobby last night; he's very excited for me. And of course the grands know. They've been so supportive and kind. I'm going to call Billy when we finish talking. Oh Lord, sister, I think I'm in *love*!" Jessica felt her smiling face blush as she said the big four-letter word.

Janie shared her news about an invitation to audition for a lead role in a Movie of the Week. Jessica screamed with delight for her sister. The sisters talked awhile longer until they finally said, "Good bye and good luck, Miss J. Malone."

Janie decided to start a letter to her mother and finish it after the audition. She tried as hard as she could to visualize what Rebita, Honduras, looked like. Since her mother had left, she had checked out several Honduras books from the library. "The small villages looked so primitive, whereas the cities looked much like cities anywhere. I wish Mom had a phone…but when she did I rarely called her anyway. Guess just knowing I could was a source of security. Boy what a dipstick I've been! I disdained her for so long…and all that time she knew. Still she just took it and never gave up on me. What a fool I was."

Janie sat in silent reflection; evening came and darkness filled the room. "I just miss her so much, sometimes I feel like an orphan." Hot tears fell intermittently. The lunch with Gloria had left her with no appetite. Janie finally pushed herself to go to bed. Mornings come early for a working actress.

BILLY

The phone was ringing as Liz and Billy returned from the local cinema. They'd both enjoyed the comedy romance. Billy was pleasantly surprised to hear Jessica's voice when he answered. She sounded happy. Liz was dying of curiosity from hearing Billy's end of the conversation.

"I can hardly believe it, Jess, that's fantastic." Silence for Liz.

"Oh, my God, why didn't you call us sooner?" Silence for Liz again.

"When's the big 'M' day?" Silence again.

"Have you told Mom, Janie, and Bobby? Do you want some help when you do it?" And more silence.

"Wow, well, thanks for calling and keep us posted. If you decide you need more help, let me know. Okay?" Billy slowly laid the phone down. Stunned, he sat quietly until a smile of relief replaced his perplexed facial expression.

Liz sat down beside him and asked, "What's happened? Who was that?"

He told her about Michael, the job change and Jessica's plan to move back to Lewiston. The biggest change was Jessica's disposition.

Liz laid her head on Billy's shoulder. "I'm happy for Jessica. You know, I've always thought Lewiston was a very nice town, from the first time I went with you. It will be great for your grandparents to have family closer. They must be thrilled."

Billy held Liz's delicate hand tenderly, as they reflected on Jessica's imminent life changes. He finally said, "I hope she's not moving too fast on this. I mean the Michael part. I'm sure the Lewiston part is for the better. I hope she'll be as lucky as we've been."

Liz nodded softly. "Me too."

A few minutes later she broke the comfortable tranquility. "Billy, do you remember the nightmare weekends when my parents came to celebrate our 'union'?" She shuddered as unhappy memories clamored to the forefront of her conscience. "I hope our relationship never deteriorates to a 'Cold War'...do you think there are people who would honestly be better if they stayed single?"

"Yeah, sure." He smiled ruefully. "I think I've known a few, maybe my dad was one of them. I don't know. But I truly believe most of us are healthier and happier when we're married…to the right person." He squeezed her gently to emphasize his words and kissed her salty wet cheek. "Ah, Liz, honey, please don't cry. We've got each other and we'll never end up like them."

"Sorry. Sometimes I just can't help it." She wiped her eyes with her sweater sleeve. "You were lucky to have your mother, grandparents, sisters and brother when you were growing up. Every kid needs someone. All I could count on was constant bickering and fighting, even *after* their divorce. And then the constant flow of meeting new stepparents. Geez, you saw what they were like! Already I feel like I'm more their parent than they are mine!"

Liz held his hand so tightly that he could have pulled her to safety from a sinking ship. He smiled softly as he kissed her hair and thought, "Maybe that's actually what I'm doing." Then he told her again, "Liz, I love you now and I'll never stop lovin' you. You can count on me. Without you, I'd be lost."

JESSICA

Jessica sailed through the interview. She was asked to wait in the outer room while the Physical Therapist Supervisor, Sue Connors, and the Human Resource Manager, Kevin Smathers, conferred. They made a quick reference check with her present supervisor as a precaution.

The fact that Grandmother Malone was a Hospital Board member and her Olson grandparents were active Hospital Auxiliary volunteers didn't hurt. Of course, they remembered her mother's years of volunteer contributions and were impressed with her current Peace Corps position. Kevin Smathers had said, "…and at her age," like she was some ancient geriatric! Jessica had felt somewhat uncomfortable with the small-town assumption that everyone's business was everyone's business. They knew all about her just by seeing her name and college information on her resume. Jessica had graduated from high school with Sue Connor's younger sister.

Also their immediate need for a qualified experienced physical therapist was definitely in her favor. Jess thought it strange to be asked to wait a "few minutes" after the interview…an hour and a half later a secretary asked her to please return to the interview room.

"We're pleased and proud to offer you a full-time position as a physical therapist, Jessica." Details included full benefits, a generous moving allowance, and a five-thousand-dollar-a-year salary increase.

Jessica took a deep breath, astounded to be offered the position so quickly. "Could I please have a drink of water? I have to let this sink in. Wow! I can't quite believe it. Oh, thanks, Sue." She carefully swallowed the ice cold water Sue gave her.

Kevin fidgeted. "Well, I'll let you two girls talk about the PT Department. I have another appointment in five minutes. I'll need to see you before you leave, Jessica, if you decide to accept our offer. Good talking with you. It was great to finally meet one of the famous Malones! I hope you decide to come on board. I think you'd be an excellent asset to our Lewiston Hospital Treatment Team."

Jessica swallowed another drink of water. "Since the interview is over, could I ask you a few questions? Do you like working here, Sue?"

Sue smiled. "Yes, I really do. We get a good variety of clients and have maintained a proficient PT staff with a strong team spirit, dedicated to providing quality service to our clients as well as support to one another."

"How long have you worked here?"

Sue continued to smile. "Let me see, I graduated when I was twenty-three," she mumbled to herself as she calculated, "and since I worked for two years in Pittsburgh before moving back to Lewiston, I've been here seventeen years. It's a good place to work, Jessica. I know it must be a tough decision for you to move back home after living away so long. I know it was for me. And you know, I've never regretted it for a minute."

Jessica appreciated Sue's candor. "Just one more question, how is the staff morale? I didn't really get great vibes from Mr. Kevin. And *how* famous are the Malones anyway?!"

Sue laughed; she was one of those rare people with a natural sparkle. "Jessica, you're funny! I like you. Kevin is stuck in administration and we rarely see him. Sure he sends us occasional memos, which, between you and me, those memos are mostly disregarded anyway. He is not a Lewiston native and tries too hard to fit in sometimes. But really he's okay. Just a bit of a bumpkin but really quite harmless.

"Oh, yes, our staff morale…it's pretty healthy. I make it a policy to never hire anyone who does not have laugh lines. We try to avoid grumps!"

Jessica felt more relaxed; Sue's upbeat personality allayed her anxieties. "Has staff turnover been a problem for your department? How long do most people stay?"

"Good question. We have five full-time and four part-time therapists, plus me. Vera is retiring in six weeks. She's been here twenty-five years. She started to work on a flex schedule when her children were younger and came on full-time twenty years ago. Lauren is on an indefinite sick leave due to prenatal complications. Everyone is great to help pick up the slack when we're short-staffed. Vera even said she'd postpone retirement until we found a new therapist or until Lauren is able to come back to work. I'm happy to tell you we have a great team in the PT Department. Our newest therapist has been with us for five years. Any other questions?"

"Sounds good. You must be very proud of your department. Do I get a tour?"

"Yes, I am proud, but I'm only part of the picture. It's a great team spirit. Let's do that tour now."

Thirty minutes later with the mini tour completed, they returned to Kevin's office. He welcomed them and inquired, "So what do you think, Jessica? Will you accept the offer?"

"Yes, I think I'll enjoy working here and it'll be nice to be back home again. I'm required to give at least a one-month notice to my present employer."

He smiled and said, "Great! Of course, we expected you'd need to give an ample notice. Let's get some preliminary paperwork done before you leave today and we'll give you a start date for Lewiston PT."

Jessica left the hospital four hours after entering. "I can hardly believe I'm really doing this!" She sat quietly in her car and gradually relaxed, smiling as she called Michael on her cell phone. After leaving a message for him, she decided to visit Grandmother Malone to tell her the big news.

"Jessica, I'm so thrilled! *Finally*, you're coming home. I've prayed and hoped for this day ever since you went away to college. Oh, Jess, darling, I'm so happy!" Tears of joy filled the older Malone eyes as she hugged her Jessica.

"Grandmother, I'm happy to be coming home too. It's time."

"Being hired on the spot is quite exceptional, isn't it? Certainly speaks well of you, my dear. Where will you live? You are welcome to stay here until you find a place."

"Thanks. I don't know yet...I didn't expect it to happen so fast. Wouldn't Mom and Dad be amazed with this news? I know Billy, Bobby and Janie were. They were supportive but thought I was a little daffy. Wow, I start in five weeks. I'll have to give notice as soon as I go back to work Monday."

Jessica called her maternal grandparents and they were equally pleased with the news. She promised to visit them before leaving the next day. Michael called and insisted on taking her out to celebrate the new job that evening. When he popped the big "M" question, Jessica was puzzled by her sudden strong ambivalent feelings....

Chapter Fourteen

BARBARA

Barbara had been working on her own for four months and had just completed the monthly medication inventory. Gabriela and a first aid student handled the routine patients in the clinic while Barbara finished up the order forms. Antibiotics, antidiarrhea medications, and Tylenol were her gold standards, as well as basic first aid dressings, syringes, snake bite antidotes, etc. All supplies were getting low and since it took at least two weeks to receive a shipment, she completed the required paper work to reorder from the Honduras Peace Corps National Office before taking a break for lunch.

For the first time in three weeks she received a bundle of mail. There were letters from all the children, her parents, Mother Malone, Alice, Ethel, Alvie and Anita. She smiled. "Wow, I've hit the jackpot today!" She laid them on her kitchen counter, eagerly anticipating reading them after the clinic closed for the day.

Experience had already taught her not to skip lunch. She hastily ate a peanut butter sandwich. Afternoons were too long and hot to go without food. Her clothes were already becoming baggy. She followed the schedule established by Anita and closed from noon till one forty-five p.m. each day, and kept the clinic open until seven p.m. Monday, Tuesday, Thursday and Friday. Wednesday closed at six p. m. to accommodate the first aid training classes, which were proving very successful and popular. Barbara found the *siesta* provided her with the energy boost she needed to get through the long and busy afternoons. She kept the shutters closed and the ceiling fans running almost nonstop in the little house; well, at least when the generator was working. It was still hot by Pennsylvania standards but tolerable and even pleasant by tropical standards due to their altitude. She set the alarm for 60 minutes and relaxed on the sofa contentedly, dropping off to sleep almost immediately.

She was awakened by a commotion in the courtyard twenty minutes before her alarm was set to ring. Barbara opened the shutter slightly to see what was happening. There were a half dozen heavily armed military men, two commando-type jeeps, much shouting at the waiting patients and Pablo appeared dazed as blood trickled down the right side of his face.

A closer look revealed two bloody young men lying in makeshift stretchers, one in the back of each jeep. Barbara took a deep breath and prayed, "Oh God, please help me do the right thing." Then she opened the back door, locked it securely behind her and walked into the courtyard.

She approached the man who appeared to be their leader. "*Buenas tardes, señor.* I am Nurse Barbara. This is a Peace Corps clinic. What can I do for you?"

He was obviously only in his twenties, but a young man who carried the weight of the world in his frightened eyes. "I am Cergio, my *amigos* hurt, they bleed too much. Bad fight down the mountain. *Por favor, Señora* Nurse, help my *amigos*!"

Gabriela at her side, they had both injured men brought into the clinic treatment rooms. One appeared to have superficial stab wounds to the left shoulder and right thigh. The other had a bullet wound to the right shoulder. Both were losing too much blood.

Barbara told Armondo to send a waiting patient into the village to ask for four of the first aid students to come to the clinic as soon as possible to help. Gabriela began working on the stab wounds immediately. "I will ask a first aid student to check Pablo as soon as they arrive."

"Good. When you're done, please come back to the exam room and give me a hand with this one. Oh, and please ask one of the first aid students to assess the patients and send home as many as possible."

After cutting the blood-soaked shirt away from the wound, Barbara felt frightened at the severity and potential damage. "He needs to be in a hospital."

Cergio glared at her. "No hospital, you fix, you are nurse!"

She checked the bleeder's pulse, weak and thready. He was already slipping in and out of consciousness. His blood pressure was dropping fast. Respirations were raspy and weak.

"Julio is my little brother. I promise my *madre* I take care of him. You cannot let him die, Nurse Barbara." Cergio stood rigidly by his brother's bedside in the larger treatment room. His frightened tear-stained face did not fit Barbara's preconceived image of a rebel or drug runner, whatever this gang had been up to. Something about these two young men reminded her of her own two sons, her boys born in a land and to a family where opportunities were taken for granted and violence was not part of their lives.

She quickly prepared the sparse surgical supplies available in the clinic and said, "Cergio, go over there, wash your hands all the way up to your elbow. You'll have to help me. I have no one else. This is your brother. We've got to remove that bullet now, before he loses any more blood." A tearful Cergio stood still, shocked and frightened.

Barbara shouted, "NOW!" and pointed to a small sink in the corner.

Inside she was shaking like a leaf and prayed for God's help to save the young man's life…and that Cergio would not know how scared *she* was. The procedure was over in about thirty minutes; she had found the bullet with little difficulty and proceeded to stitch him up.

She had minimal supplies to help him post-op. Barbara explained, "The next four hours are crucial. If Julio can hold on, he'll have a chance of recovery. I did my best for him, Cergio. I'm not a surgeon. I never removed a bullet or stitched up an open wound before. Gabriela and I will stay with your brother all night. Please pray for Julio."

Gabriela's stab wound patient was resting quietly in the small treatment room. Pablo had a headache, a large swollen bruise and superficial cut from the butt of a rifle hitting him on the head when he denied Cergio's group entrance to the Peace Corps compound. Miguel, the night guard, came in early and Pablo had gone home after his wound had been attended.

It had proven to be Barbara's busiest day so far, as well as the hottest. The temperature was the highest since she'd arrived in Rebita. The other members of Cergio's group had set up camp in the center of the courtyard, in the shade of a cluster of mango and orange trees.

Barbara didn't like the fact they were there, but neither did she have the fire power to throw them out or a strong desire to do so. She went into her tiny kitchen and prepared a large plate of the good old standby, peanut butter sandwiches. She also grabbed a large pitcher of iced tea and mugs, which she promptly carried to the courtyard and clinic to offer drinks to her mysterious visitors.

Throughout the night, she and Gabriela took two-hour shifts attending to Julio and praying for a miracle recovery. Gabriela used the sofa in Barbara's living room for naps when Barbara took her two-hour shifts at the clinic. By morning Julio's vital signs were becoming slightly more stable.

Barbara asked Cergio to try to get some rest. He refused to leave Julio's bedside. However, he reluctantly agreed to use an old armchair as he waited for the recovery.

At seven a.m., Arturo, the village police chief, abruptly knocked on her cottage door as Barbara was about to swallow her last sip of tea. He declined the offer of tea and inquired about the safety of the compound. She reassured him the situation was stressful but under control. Behind him, she noticed there was already a slow steady stream of patients filtering into the courtyard. She asked, "Officer Arturo, please urge all the first aid students in the village to come help at the clinic today. I can see already we will need extra help. *Gracias*."

Barbara locked the front door and quickly splashed cold water on her face to feel awake, stripped off her dirty clothes from the day before and put on a fresh set of baggy khakis and white shirt. She brushed her hair and was heading out the door as she noticed her unopened letters on the counter. "Hopefully tonight I'll have time to read those." She locked the back door and hurried over to the clinic. A few minutes later she met a frazzled Gabriela in the clinic's reception area.

"*Buenos días*, Gabriela. How're the patients this morning?"

"Stab wound, strong vital signs, no bleeding. I change dressing this morning. Julio, I don't know. You better check him. Vital signs steady but not strong. Some bleeding through on dressing and I did not change that one." Gabriela sounded exhausted.

"Gabriela, I want you to go home, rest for an hour and freshen up. Do you think you could come back and work all day then, with so little sleep?"

"Will you work today, Nurse Barbara? If you can do it, you know I can because I strong and much younger than you!" Gabriela replied with a teasing hint of laughter in her voice.

"Well, when you put it like that, I guess it's all right to ask you to help me prepare the waiting room as a treatment room for today. Let's slide this desk out to the portico. I asked Police Officer Arturo to send all the first aid students in to help us today," Barbara informed the good-natured young Honduran girl without whom she'd have been totally lost at the clinic.

"That is good. We could use more help today. I will be back soon. *Adiós*."

Barbara checked on Julio. His dressing indicated minimal fresh drainage, so she decided to teach him a few deep-breathing exercises before changing the dressing. Cergio watched intently as he stood by the window facing the courtyard. She secretly wished there was some way to get a doctor in to evaluate him. His vitals continued to be steady but weak. Respirations were shallow. "*Buenos días*, Julio. How're you feeling this morning? Okay, now, I need you to start a few deep-breathing exercises for me. We'll hold this small blanket roll gently over your wound and on the count of three, I want you to breathe in as hard as you can and then slowly blow it out."

She continued to encourage him and he tried hard to comply despite his discomfort. Cergio sat quietly watching. When she finished, he followed her out of the room.

"Nurse Barbara, *gracias*! You save my brother's life. *Gracias*!"

"Cergio, your brother remains in very serious condition. He must rest quietly for at least a week."

"I can not stay here so long." A perplexed expression covered his face. Cergio walked back to his brother's bedside. His facial expression melted into one of utter devotion and tenderness as he watched his injured brother sleep. He silently prayed and made the sign of the cross, then turned and walked out of the makeshift treatment room.

"Nurse Barbara, I leave Julio with you. I know you take good care of him. I will come back in one week. I pay you for your work. Not worry. But tell all villagers, all soldiers gone. Keep Julio a secret, *por favor*." He turned and walked out of the clinic.

Barbara stood there as if hit by a stun gun. Soon she heard the two jeeps start and she hurried out to catch Cergio. He saluted her gallantly. "*Adiós, señora*!" The stab wound soldier lay in the back seat of Cergio's jeep as it bounced out of the compound. Barbara quickly ran to the jeeps and gave Cergio a package of clean dressings, supplies and orders to take care of his friend's wounds.

"Oh, my God," Barbara murmured as she shook her head from side to side and warm tears trickled down her cheeks. "It's too soon to move the boy like that. The wound hasn't had enough time to heal; he'll bleed."

She felt a hand on her shoulder and was startled to see Gabriela back so soon.

"Come inside with me, Miss Barbara." They made it just inside the door when Barbara collapsed on the closest chair, sobbing as she worried about the stabbed young man.

"Maybe they go slow and maybe not too far and they will let him rest until he better. Maybe, Miss Barbara, we must have hope. Right?" Gabriela had been a very good student and within a few minutes Barbara was composed enough to get back to work.

Five first aid students had shown up to help. Two of them cleaned the treatment room in which the stab wound had been treated. Gabriela agreed to stay with Julio throughout the day, encouraging deep breathing and monitoring vital signs. They kept that door locked and the first aid students busy in the clinic.

They had divided the waiting patients into groups according to the nature of the complaints. There seemed to be a new scabies outbreak in the village. There were also the standard GI complaints of diarrhea as well as a few hacking coughs of the respiratory distressed patients. Barbara praised the first aid students and was very grateful for their assistance. Each of them had a chance to clean cuts or serious skin scraps as well as apply dressings and ointments using their newly acquired sterile technique. By the end of the day, forty-five patients, not counting Julio or the stabbed patient, had gone through the clinic. All the students were tired, but none more tired than Barbara and Gabriela.

Julio was holding his own; he was in and out of consciousness but in more than out. He was determined and compliant with his deep-breathing exercises. His vital signs continued to get stronger. Barbara decided to start him on a full liquid diet. Walking out with Gabriela, Barbara said, "We won't be able to keep him a secret in the clinic. I think we'll have to move him to my house tonight, after dark. We could ask Miguel to help. Could you come back to help? Then we'll have to give the treatment room a good once over. I'll take a set of clinic sheets to put on my bed." They reassured Julio they'd be back soon and locked the treatment room door.

Karena smiled as they walked by. They told her not to worry about cleaning the locked treatment room and since it was so hot, to take a week off with pay from cleaning Barbara's house. Karena's smile grew even wider.

Barbara set her timer to ring in ninety minutes and flopped wearily onto the sofa.

When the timer rang, she jumped up and hurried to the clinic to check Julio. He sipped a half glass of water and volunteered to do his deep-breathing exercise. "Julio, does it hurt when you deep breathe?"

He answered in a weak voice with a slight grin, "Only when I think about it, today I think about getting better and going home."

Barbara patted his arm and reassured him, "I'll be back soon." She carefully locked the door as she left.

She hurried back to change the bedding and prepare her bedroom for her unexpected *guest*. Barbara put almost all her personal things in the hall closet. Then she prepared some broth and fruit juice for Julio. He tried to swallow the liquids Barbara had prepared but found his will was stronger than his ability. He laid there perspiring heavily. The room was very hot, but he had over exerted himself. Julio tried to smile. "Tomorrow I will do better."

Barbara concealed her concern as she reassured him, "Yes, you will. Tonight we'll just stay with water."

As dusk was settling in, she walked across to the courtyard to talk to Miguel. "*Buenas noches*, Nurse Barbara. How are you?" He stood up, took off his hat and bowed with respect.

Despite her fatigue, his respectful manners never failed to make her smile. "*Muy bien*, Miguel. And how are you? Have you heard, how is Pablo?

"*Sí*. Pablo is good. He will be back to work tomorrow." Miguel spoke softly and never stopped watching for unexpected trouble.

"Miguel, I need you to help me with a secret. You can never tell anyone. Not Pablo, not *Señora* Miguel…it must be our secret and stay our secret. Gabriela will be here soon to help us. Can I count on you to keep a big secret?" Barbara watched him closely. He was quiet while thinking over the implications.

"If Gabriela and you want me to share your secret, you can trust me and I will help," Miguel answered with a twinge of pride in his voice.

As they waited for Gabriela, Barbara looked at the sky. It was a half-moon night, not a cloud, and the stars looked so close on their mountain top that it seemed if she had climbed a tree to get just a little closer, she could have reached out and grabbed a handful of stars.

A few minutes later Gabriela walked casually up to the gate. "Are you ready?"

Barbara and Miguel nodded their heads, then he turned to the women and asked, "Ready for what? You not tell me what is secret."

"You will see soon enough," Gabriela replied.

"The gate will have to be left unattended for a few minutes, Miguel. Let's go."

When they entered Julio's room, it was stifling and he was still perspiring heavily. Barbara opened a window for ventilation. She unlocked the wheels on the exam table and they wheeled him to the exit nearest the cottage.

Miguel was shocked. He stood off by himself repetitively muttering, "Holy Mother of Jesus," while making the sign of the cross.

After they had successfully transferred Julio to Barbara's bed, they enjoyed a cup of conspiratorial tea and almost fresh muffins, which weren't too bad when dunked in tea. It was the first thing Barbara had eaten all day and tasted amazingly good to her ignored but ravenous appetite.

She sent Gabriela home and Miguel back to his night watch with many thanks. Then she checked on Julio who seemed to be resting more comfortably. Next Barbara went to the clinic to clean Julio's treatment room so it could be used tomorrow, leaving the window open for a little ventilation. An hour later, everything was in order for the next day. Julio was awake and complied with sips of water, deep-breathing exercises and using a homemade urinal as needed. She told him to bang a spoon against a small metal can if he needed her during the night.

Barbara fixed her bed on the sofa and took a quick shower. She collapsed into a deep sleep immediately after laying down.

The first thing the next morning, she rushed to check on Julio. He smiled and with a weak voice said, "*Buenos días*, Nurse." He reassured her he hadn't tried to call her once during the night.

Barbara was relieved to see minimal drainage on the dressing as she prepared to clean the wound and apply a new sterile dressing. "Julio, please do not try to get out of bed for any reason. I want you to do deep-breathing exercises every hour; you can see this clock from the bed, can't you?"

"*Sí*, I see clock good from here. I stay in bed. No problem," Julio answered.

"Here is some fresh tea and also a glass of water. Keep drinking but go a little slow. Okay? I have to work in the clinic today. Gabriela or I will come over to check on you every hour. You will be safe here. Just stay in bed and keep deep breathing. *Adiós*, Julio."

Barbara fixed herself a light breakfast. The sun was pouring in around the shutters and it looked like it would be another scorcher. As she finished her shower, she heard someone at the back door. "I'll be there in a minute!" she shouted. After getting dressed in near record time, she ducked in to Julio and apologized for the noise, then hurried to the back door.

It was a refreshed Gabriela. "*Buenos días*, Barbara, how is our Julio today?"

"I think he's doing a little better. He rested quietly all night, he does his breathing exercises and says it only hurts when he thinks about it!"

"This is good news, very good news. His brother, Cergio, will be happy when he hears this," Gabriela replied.

Barbara looked at Gabriela curiously. "Did you know Cergio and Julio before?"

"Nurse Barbara, this is a small village. We don't receive many visitors. Yes, I knew who they were. Everybody they hate or help is something special to somebody else. I wish they would just stop the fight. But they will not. Some people support them because they offer money, gifts and special scholarships to help our people."

"Why didn't you tell me two days ago when they first came?" Barbara asked, feeling a bit annoyed with Gabriela.

Gabriela turned to Barbara, her hands on her hips, and stated with a defiant air, "Did you ask me? What it matter anyway? Hurting person is a patient for nurse if a stranger, enemy or friend, right? Is that not what you teach us of Florencia Nightingale?"

Barbara sighed. "We have to open the clinic. Here's the extra key to my house. Please lock each time you leave. One of us will check Julio each hour. I will do even hours; you will check him on odd hours, starting at eight a.m. I will do your noon and two p.m. since I will be there for *siesta* anyway. Understand?"

"I no understand, what is this odd and even hour thing, Nurse Barbara?" Gabriela asked softly as she stared at the floor, her defiance given over to a melodramatic exhibition of self-pity.

Barbara ignored the show. "Here, we'll make a chart and you check off each time you check Julio. You check at nine, eleven and three. And remember, for some reason Julio's presence here must be kept a secret. But you probably know a lot more about that than I do. Okay, let's get to work."

Two of the first aid students showed up to help; it was another busy day at the clinic. Gabriela slowly got over her snit. Barbara realized that there was a lot more going on in and around the village than she'd been aware of. Smiling, she thought, "And probably I'm the only one in the village who thinks Julio's presence in the cottage is a secret!"

Barbara welcomed the afternoon *siesta*; it was a much needed break. After checking Julio, who continued to improve, she glanced at her stack of mail before nodding off with a smile on her face. "Well, I still have that to look forward to."

When her alarm woke her, she had been dreaming of the easy life she had led in Lewiston, Pennsylvania. It had never felt like an easy road but hindsight painted a pretty rosy picture, especially when compared to the grueling schedule of her mountain-top clinic in Honduras.

Julio remained stable and his urinal indicated adequate kidney function. Drainage remained minimal on the dressing.

"Oh geez, tonight is first aid class again. Great. What a week it's been."

The afternoon and the class went well. Thursday was another blistering sunny day. About eleven a.m., the courtyard was again in a uproar as Dr. Kane arrived with his bodyguard Caesar, in his noisy SUV. Barbara hurried to look at the schedule. "Did I forget to schedule patients for Dr. Kane?"

He was not scheduled till the following week. "Well, at least I'm not losing my mind."

Gabriela was also caught off guard. Dr. Kane walked into the clinic as if he owned it. He took off his Yankees hat and bowed, looking silly with his long gray pony tail dangling over his bulky shoulders. "Gabriela and Nurse Barbara, I've heard through the jungle grapevine that you've had your hands full this week. I was in the neighborhood and thought I'd stop by."

Barbara couldn't help but smile, remembering their contemptuous interaction on the day they met. He was actually trying to be nice today. "That's very kind of you, Dr. Kane. We've had an exceptionally busy week." She checked the patient log sheet, though. "Only three more patients to be seen before lunch."

She quickly asked Gabriela to finish up the morning patients. Then she turned to Dr. Kane and asked, "Would you like to join me for a glass of cold tea in the cottage? It's almost time to break for lunch and *siesta*. Gabriela can handle things here until I return."

He looked at her skeptically, somehow sensing there was more to the invitation than food and drink. "Yes, I think that sounds good."

She apologized for the state of her home, and after relocking the door, poured three tall glasses of her delicious cold tea, explaining that her small refrigerator would no longer make ice. "Please come into the living room and sit down. I'm really glad to see you. I have many questions for you."

"Three glasses of tea for two people?" he asked with a puzzled expression.

"Well, maybe before you sit down you should come to the bedroom with me; I'd like your medical opinion on something. Please come with me."

He followed her through the living room with sheets and pillow still on the sofa as if someone were using it as a bed. He stopped cold when he saw the sallow young man in her bed. "My God, Barbara, what do you have here?!"

"Julio, this is Dr. Kane. He has come to examine you and help you get well faster."

Julio did not look happy to have the doctor there. Barbara reassured Julio and he relaxed slightly.

She explained the crisis situation to Dr. Kane and how she had felt forced to reluctantly handle it. "I did get this bullet out." She showed him the small plastic bag with the weapon of death and destruction inside. "His vital signs remain weak; he did lose a lot of blood. His respirations are weak but somewhat stronger than two days ago. BP is slightly higher now. It had been as low as 50/30. Today it was 62/40. I've been pushing fluids. He's had no solids yet. Urine output is adequate, considering intake. Bowels have not moved in four days. He has not been out of bed yet. He is very cooperative with deep-breathing exercises. He has an older brother who appears to be extremely close and devoted to him. He wanted to take Julio with him the day after they arrived. I told him his brother was not strong enough to travel, so that is it in a nutshell. Older brother told me Julio's presence here must be kept a secret."

"Well, Julio, my boy, let's have a look at that wound," the doctor said. He checked Julio's lungs and then encouraged him to sit up on the side of the bed, dangling his legs for about five minutes. After that the doctor assisted Julio to take a few steps around the room. Julio's face was wet with perspiration but he was proud to have walked even such a short distance.

Barbara wiped his face and offered him the cold tea. "*Gracias*, Nurse Barbara, *gracias*."

"You rest now," she said, touching his cheek lightly as she left the room with Dr. Kane.

The doctor sat down on the side chair by the sofa, slumped over with his head in his hands. Barbara quickly removed her bedding from the sofa and set the tea on the magazine table.

"Well, Dr. Kane, do you think he's going to make it?" she asked hesitantly.

He slowly sat back in the chair and looked at her. "Yeah, I expect he'll make it. You did a damn good job getting that bullet out. The wound appears to be healing without complications. The stitches look great. Have you assisted with surgeries before?" He took a long drink of his tea.

"No, I haven't. Well, I was lucky, or perhaps I should say Julio was lucky; the bullet caused no major organ damage. So it was a simple search and rescue with much prayer. No, I've never worked in an operating room; as for stitches, I've done needlepoint for years. And once I was ready to close him up…stitches are stitches." She answered honestly and then took a drink of tea, which quenched her thirst.

"I have a question for you. Was Julio's brother with him, a big guy in an army fatigue type uniform?"

"Cergio, yes he was! Do you know him? Did you know Julio before today?"

"I'd heard Cergio had taken his little brother into the business. He and his two older brothers are famous in these mountains. The Molinos brothers are big drug traffickers, use remote mountain borders to transport their product through to Nicaragua and from there to fishing boats and up to the south Texas coast."

Barbara sighed. "There was another injury, a young man with stab wounds to his left shoulder and right thigh. Gabriela cleaned and dressed his wounds. Cergio took him with him the next day. He wanted to take Julio, too. But I told him Julio could die if moved, that he needed at least a week before leaving. I didn't think the other one should've left so soon either....

"I suspected something illegal about them but I didn't feel I had any choice but to do the best I could to help the injured. It is easier to provide round-the-clock nursing care here in the cottage. Gabriela has a key and checks on him several times a day. It's easier for me to have him here than running to the clinic throughout the night *and* trying to keep his presence a secret during the day. Though I seriously doubt it is a secret. Why even Gabriela admitted she knew them after Cergio left."

"What we have here is a complicated situation," Dr. Kane remarked.

"Do you have any words of wisdom to offer, Doctor?" Barbara asked.

"Well, first of all, stop calling me Doctor. We're both professionals and we are of a similar age group. So please, call me Mike. All my friends do."

Barbara chuckled, as she thought, "You have friends!?" While she answered, "Okay, Mike it is. Would you like a bite of lunch? I have to fix something for myself anyway."

"Sure, let's see if you can cook as well as you can take bullets out and stitch up holes." He stretched out on the chair, making himself right at home. "So how many days has Julio been here at the compound now?"

"This is his fourth day. Cergio will probably be back on Sunday or Monday. Why do you ask?" Barbara queried. "You're not going to send the authorities to ambush them, are you? I want to stay completely neutral here. I really do."

He didn't answer her with words; instead she heard the steady sound of a blocked nasal passageway, snoring.

She thought, "I guess I'm not the only tired one." She set their tuna sandwiches in the frig, adjusted the timer to wake her in an hour, and laid down on the sofa for a much needed *siesta*.

A startled Barbara stretched and jumped up when the timer rang, knowing if she rolled over, it'd be even harder to get up. She set the table for their simple lunch of tuna sandwiches, mango and tea. Dr. Mike Kane began to stretch and yawn. He looked around a few seconds as if trying to figure out where he was.

"Lunch is ready, Mike. Tuna sandwiches, hope you like them; we also have fresh mangos and tea. Sorry, but we have a limited menu around here."

"Sounds good to me. God, a man could get a bad back from napping on that old chair!"

"Glad you were able to get some rest. I have to get back to the clinic in a few minutes. Sorry, but we have no way of notifying your appointments to come in this week rather than next," Barbara informed him.

"Hey, like I said, I just stopped by, sort of a neighborly visit. Mind if I give you a hand seeing patients this afternoon? Maybe you could close early, Barbara. You look exhausted."

"Would you really do that? It'd be awfully kind of you. And it's an offer I can't refuse!" She finished her lunch. "I'll have to check on Julio before I go."

"Don't bother, I'll see to him when I finish eating. By the way, thanks for the lunch."

"Okay, here's my last house key. Last one out locks the back door. And I'll need that key back when you come to the clinic." Barbara smiled as she glanced at her stack of letters on her way out.

"Looks like you got mail. Lucky lady," Mike said as he followed her eyes to the counter.

"First time in three weeks. It all came on Monday, just shortly before Cergio arrived with our wounded patients. I haven't even had time to open my letters. See you later."

Mike helped himself to another glass of tea and saw it was getting low and soon noticed Barbara had already had teabags soaking in water for the next gallon. He hated to admit he was impressed with this lady. And she did seem to be a lady. He knew he shouldn't snoop but was curious about who wrote to her. Shuffling through her mail, he found five out of nine letters had return addresses from other Malones. Probably relatives. Two were posted in Honduras, probably Peace Corps friends. He thought, "Come on, old boy, get hold of yourself! Her mail is none of your business." In his haste, one fell to the floor, return address: Ms. Alvie Novak, Peace Corps Compound, Cabela, Honduras. "Oh my God, no, no...."

He felt his hand begin to shake as he put the letters back as they were and went into check Julio's dressings and vital signs. He gave the boy fresh water and offered him some yogurt he'd noticed in the refrigerator. Julio was showing continued improvement and did well with the yogurt. Mike gave him a bucket to use in case he became nauseous from the food but luckily Julio didn't need it.

Then Mike went to the clinic. Gabriela was astounded; she'd never seen Dr. Kane help with anything as a volunteer. He helped move the desk back from the portico to the reception area. Gabriela took her seat at the desk. Dr. Kane saw all the diarrhea patients in treatment room one. He always included teaching the necessity of boiling all water to be used for food preparation and for drinking. Barbara worked out of treatment room two and concentrated on the scabies patients.

There were so many infected children that day and most of the parents had brought their healthy children along. People were frightened and refused to leave children at home unattended, therefore the sounds of noisy barefoot children filled the air as they played under the sparse shade of the cluster of fruit trees in the center of the compound.

By five p.m. they'd seen all thirty-seven patients who'd been waiting. Barbara asked Pablo to close the gate and turn away any latecomers unless it was an emergency. She thanked Gabriela and the first aid students for all their extra help during the week and sent them home early. Gabriela winked at Barbara as she discreetly gave her the extra key to her cottage. Karena would arrive around six thirty to clean the clinic.

Dr. Kane accompanied Barbara back to the cottage. They found Julio sitting on the edge of the bed doing his deep-breathing exercises. She checked his dressing and was relieved to find no break-through bleeding. Dr. Kane spoke excellent Spanish. "Let's go for a walk, big boy. You need more exercise. Here, hang onto me. Yeah, that's right."

They walked around the tiny cottage, not wanting to venture out into the compound in case someone might discover the secret patient. "How did you do with the yoqurt? Maybe we can whip up something even better for your dinner tonight."

Ten minutes later Julio said in a weak voice, "*Señor*, Doctor, I feel very tired. *Por favor…siesta? Gracias*." Dr. Kane assisted Julio back to bed. Julio lay there exhausted, even as his face glowed with a look of hope and satisfaction.

Dr. Kane joined Barbara in the kitchen. "I think he's going to be all right. You'll have to let Cergio take him when he returns. I've no doubt you can make him see it's absolutely imperative that Julio take it easy for a few weeks." He smiled. "If there's one thing you can do, Nurse Barbara, it's communicate! People take notice when you talk."

"Well, thanks, I think." Barbara looked at him skeptically and continued. "You know this is the first time since I've been in Honduras that I truly wish I could pick up a phone and order a pizza! Would you like to join me for a potluck supper?"

He stood like a giant in her small kitchen, arms folded, shaggy gray ponytail and penetrating brown eyes staring at her. "I'll accept on two conditions; first I can help prepare the food and secondly if you'll tell me why you are here."

She copied his stance and returned the stare, her tired blue eyes piercing his concentration. "Good. The vegetables were donated by a few of the afternoon patients. Some are so proud, they won't accept free medical care. Anyway there's boiled water to wash the veggies in the large pot on the stove. I have a can of beef stew. Would you like that with the salad?"

"Sounds good to me," he answered. "Maybe we can give Julio some bread to dunk into his stew broth."

After dinner, they were pleased to see Julio had tolerated the food well. Mike Kane encouraged Barbara to tell him about herself.

"Okay, I am a widow with four adult children, and I'm from a small town in Pennsylvania. I'm an RN and wanted a change in scenery for awhile. What else could you possibly want to know?" Barbara was so tired, tears almost escaped. After a brief hesitation, she asked, "So, what's your story? Why are you here?"

"It's a long story; I'll save it for another time. Thanks for dinner. I want you to get some sleep. I'll check on Julio and let myself out. You sleep, Barbara. I'll use the extra key to lock up when I leave." He fluffed her pillow and covered her with a sheet. His hand hesitated just a few seconds too long on her cheek as he said, "Good night, my dear."

"Thanks, Dr. Kane, but who said you could have the extra key?"

He grinned. "Don't worry. I'll bring it back in the morning and remember, my name is Mike!"

Barbara awakened at six a.m., feeling rested and ready to take on the world. She quickly checked on Julio, who reported a restful night. He now only requested Tylenol twice a day. He sat up by the side of the bed. Barbara checked both dressings, no fresh drainage. She decided to wait till Dr. Kane came and have him check and maybe even change the dressing today. For breakfast she fixed scrambled eggs for Julio and herself. She took Julio a bedpan of warm water, towel and washcloth to wash up. It made her feel good to see the young man getting stronger.

Barbara felt she was getting back into her stride, arriving at the clinic fifteen minutes early. Gabriela was next, smiling like a cat who'd just swallowed a canary.

"Morning, Gabriela. You look like you've had good night's sleep."

"Yes, I feel good. It is Friday. I feel ready for two days with no work. This has been hard week. How is Julio? Did Dr. Kane like our care of patient?" Gabriela asked.

Barbara answered with a smile, "Julio is doing quite well. He sits up in bed by himself, he walks with help. His vital signs are stable. He now takes Tylenol only two times a day. The wounds are healing and he is eating a soft diet without problems. Dr. Kane said we did a good job taking care of him."

"That is good because I'm sure Cergio will come soon for brother and he be happy to see Julio get well," Gabriela said as she walked away.

There were already patients lining up to sign in for the clinic when Gabriela went back to the reception desk. Soon Dr. Kane walked in, booming. "*Buenos días!* I'm here to work."

Barbara came out of the supply room, amused. "Well, this is a surprise! Are you sure you have time to stay in Rebita this long? What about the other clinics you provide services for?"

"Now, Nurse Barbara, don't you worry, I took care of my responsibilities and now I'm going to help you with yours," Mike Kane replied with a wink.

Barbara thought, "He winked at me! My God! Winked. How weird. But it will be helpful to have him around today." She said, "Well, if you're willing, I won't turn down your offer. You can work out of treatment room one and I'll work out of two."

The day flew by and everyone was able to go home on time. The patients were happy to have seen the big doctor. Barbara was baffled as to why he was there in the first place and with no apparent plans for leaving soon....

"Barbara, I'd like to cook dinner for you tonight if I might borrow your kitchen. What do you think?" Dr. Mike Kane asked.

She smiled, feeling a bit confused and flattered by the unexpected attention. "I'd have to be a fool to turn down an offer like that! Sure, you can use the kitchen."

"Well, then let's check on our patient." They were pleased to find Julio trying to hobble his way around the edge of the bed.

Dr. Kane went to his SUV and brought Julio a primitive cane that Caesar, his assistant (i.e. bodyguard), had made the night before. He taught Julio how to use it properly and before long he was hobbling around the small cottage.

"Don't overdo it now," the doctor cautioned. Mike set a place for him at the table and told Julio it was time to start back to a more normal routine.

Mike told Barbara to relax in the living room. He suggested, "Why don't you start to read your letters while I cook dinner?"

Barbara gave him a perplexed look and went into the bathroom to freshen up. It had been another scorcher. She noticed her khakis were hanging on her at least two sizes too large. Good thing she had a belt. The way she perspired, she felt like her weight was sweating off drop by drop.

She was soon settled in the comfy side chair, anxious to hear the news from home. Tomorrow she would talk to the police about using the village phone to call home. It had not worked out for two weeks now and she didn't like that at all. She'd promised her parents and Mother Malone to call home every week, and decided, "I'll just explain that sometimes it's impossible the way the phone service works down here. I just don't want them to worry."

Before finishing the second letter, she had dozed off. The sounds of the doctor and Julio talking in the kitchen as well the sounds and smell of fried chicken were pleasant to wake up to after months of solitude. It was also good not to feel as tired as she usually did on a Friday evening. And indeed, it had been a particularly exhausting week.

After dinner Julio skillfully maneuvered around the cottage with his cane and said, "Look how good I walk now, Nurse Barbara."

"I'm impressed, Julio. That's really good! You learn very quickly." Barbara praised the proud young man.

"Your recovery has been going so well, you shouldn't overdo it. You'd better go to bed now, Julio," Dr. Kane cautioned. "Would you like something to read? Caesar, my assistant, has some Spanish magazines that I'm sure he'd share with you."

"Maybe *mañana*, I tired tonight. Big day! I walk again. *Gracias*, good Doctor and Nurse."

"I'll be in to check your dressings in a few minutes, Julio," Dr. Kane told him.

"How are you feeling now, Barbara?" Mike asked.

"I'm really glad it's Friday. I feel like I need the weekend. This was my most stressful week so far. I tried to do the right thing and in my heart I feel I did. But in my mind, I'm not so sure," Barbara confessed. "Have you ever been in situations where you had doubts about your decisions and actions?"

Mike looked at her and was amazed anyone could reach their fifties or maybe forties, with four adult children, and remain so idealistic. Her self-cut, short, sun-streaked light brown hair with traces of gray suited her well. "To answer your question, more times than I care to remember. Ruminating about it is a waste of energy. Each of us must make our decisions based on the choices and information we have at the time. When we learn we've made a wrong choice, we simply have to learn from that choice, move on and be careful not to make the same mistake twice."

"You sound like my father. He used to tell my brother and me that every time we'd make a 'stupid choice' as he called it! He's such a big teddy bear, though, I really miss him. He's always been my rock. I sure hope I can get through to talk to him and my mother tomorrow. International lines have been jammed when I tried to call for the last three weeks." Barbara wasn't aware of the faraway look in her eyes as she talked about home.

"You sound like you're close with your parents. I don't see that kind of connection very often anymore. You're lucky you still have them. What did they think about you coming down here with the Peace Corps?"

"They weren't very excited at first but came around to accept and support my decision. That's the kind of folks I have. What about you? Why are you in the mountains of Honduras?"

Mike hesitated and then looked at her with a grin. "I wanted to practice real medicine as far from bureaucratic paperwork and the greed of established civilization as I could get. I got tired of all the superficial materialism."

"So that might explain your choice of hair style. Although I'm sure it's not as cool or comfortable as a shorter hair cut would be. But how does that monster SUV fit in with your aversion to materialism? It seems like a clear contradiction to me," Barbara said honestly.

"Geez, you go right to the meat. My hair is my business."

"I never said it wasn't, sir!"

"And a doctor's gotta have dependable transportation in these mountains that barely have roads. Hell, I wouldn'ta' been able to get through to you this week if I didn't have that beauty out there."

"You know, I've been very curious about why you came and why you're still here. It just doesn't make sense to me."

"What if I told you I had a crush on you, Barbara?"

She blushed but laughed nonetheless. "Oh, yeah, right. I remember the first time I met you when you were so totally charming. Yes, I just knocked you off your feet."

"Well, I have to admit I remember that day too. You're the first woman I ever met who told me I looked like I already had one foot in the grave. Thank you very much." Mike laughed and shook his head. "What do you say we go out on the porch to get some fresh night air?"

"Okay." She stood up and walked outside with him. "But I offer no apology for that day, you had it coming. Where do you get off treating Peace Corps workers like servants or dirt under your feet?" Then she continued, "That's why I'm confused about what's really going on this week. It doesn't fit your normal pattern of behavior. And no, I don't buy the crush story for a minute. I'm about forty years older and wiser than that."

Mike said in a very hushed tone, "Let's sit on the portico by the clinic, if you don't mind."

Barbara locked the door and walked beside him, her curiosity mounting with each step.

Chapter Fifteen

Mike almost whispered, "Let's talk very quietly, sometimes the walls have ears when we least expect it. You're right, there's more to my being here than just neighborly concern. As you know, Julio is part of the Hermandos Molinos gang. Hell, he's the baby brother, Mama's pride and joy. While they are ruthless in their business, they have extremely strong family bonds of loyalty and revenge."

Barbara was puzzled. "So, what have I to fear? He's getting well."

"True and lucky for you that he is!" Mike stared at the moonlit sky. Then he turned back to Barbara. "Look at you, you must have lost at least thirty pounds in the four or five months you've been here. Your clothes hang on you. You're working like a slave. You've put yourself in harm's way...of course, you did the only thing you could've under the circumstances. But you've a family and a life back in the USA. Why don't you just resign and go home? Things are much more complicated than you realize here in these tropical mountains."

"Mike, I think your intentions are honorable; I do appreciate your concern, but you obviously don't know me. Then of course, how could you? We've only met through our work a few times. I am a very stubborn and proud woman. All my grandparents were Swedish immigrants. When I make up my mind to do something, I rarely turn back. I don't mind losing some weight. I'll ask my mother to send me a few new clothes; I feel perfectly fine. Tired sometimes, but that's expected given the work load and the heat. Besides, I was starting a middle-aged spread and losing a little weight has been good for me."

"Well, you're getting too thin, no more weight loss. Please start eating more. I have concerns about Cergio's return to get Julio as well as his continued recovery while they are on the run. They had some trouble down in Cabela late Sunday night. Five people were killed, ten wounded, not counting the two gang members treated here in Rebita. Now the government soldiers will come to hunt them down. I don't want you or any of your clinic staff to be accused of collaboration with the enemy. I don't want either side to turn on Rebita or any of its people."

Barbara reached over, lightly touched his hand and said, "I do appreciate your concern. If the government soldiers come, I'll just explain what happened. When they realize that we've only upheld recognized International Medical Standards of Care, they'll understand. Trust me; I'm tougher than I look."

He stared at the sky and gently squeezed her hand as he whispered, "Do you really think they'll accept you moving Molinos into your home and giving him your own bed as unbiased standard of care? I hope you know what you're doing, Barbara. I surely hope so."

"Cergio made me feel it was imperative that I do everything I possibly could to save his brother *and* it had to be kept a secret." Barbara began to feel uneasy about her decision again. "Perhaps we should head back to the cottage and check on Julio."

"Always the nurse, aren't you?" Mike smiled at her and shook his head.

"Maybe so, aren't you always the doctor?" she countered.

"Before we go back inside, I think there's something else you have to know, Barbara. Last Sunday night Cabela was having some kind of local festival. Lots of people were out, several maraji bands, dancing and drinking. People were out later than usual…when the trouble began with the Molinos gang and their local contact, who had set them up with the government agents. Nothing went as it was planned. Eight children from three families were seriously injured by bullets or shrapnel as well as a local policeman and a government agent. The local contact, his wife, two government agents and a Peace Corps worker were killed…."

A stunned Barbara turned to him. "Who was the Peace Corps worker…who?"

"A young teacher, her name was Alvira Novak."

"NO, NO…NOT ALVIE!" Barbara screamed. Hot tears poured from deep inside as her breathing became more and more shallow. "I can't stand it if Alvie is gone."

She collapsed into an inconsolable sobbing heap.

Miguel came running, rifle in ready position. "*Señora* Barbara, are you okay? What happen?"

Mike explained, "It's okay, Miguel. Nurse Barbara just received bad news. Thanks for checking. And please let me know if there's any unusual activity around the compound tonight."

Mike kneeled down beside her as she continued to sob. "I'm so sorry, Barbara, I didn't know you were friends. Now I'm really glad I'm here with you." He put his arm around her trembling shoulders and tried to comfort her.

But there was no comfort for Barbara. Relief from the disconsolate weeping and the pain deep in her heart was beyond attainment that night. Mike decided it would be best for her to sleep in the clinic and helped her inside. He moved a treatment table mattress pad to the floor and quickly found a pillow and bedding for her. He found emergency valium in the supply room and insisted she swallow a five-milligram tablet. He sat next to her on the floor, holding her hand and gently massaging her forehead as she slowly drifted off to a restless sleep.

He thought, "My God, I never expected her to have such a strong reaction, the poor girl. I sure can't figure this woman out. Every time I think I'm beginning to understand her...I seem to get another curve ball and end up at square one again."

He pondered, "Only God knows how she'll deal with Julio and Cergio, now that she knows they're responsible for her friend's death."

Two hours later, he stood up stiffly and decided he'd better check on Julio. He stopped by his SUV, inconspicuously parked behind the clinic. Dr. Kane nudged the slumbering Caesar to be on high alert for at least the next forty-eight hours. Caesar knew exactly what his boss meant. They'd been through this before.

Julio was resting comfortably in Barbara's bed. From the beginning Mike had had difficulty feeling professional empathy for the ailing *bandito*. He had marveled at Barbara's compassion. Mike decided to sleep the rest of the night on the cottage sofa; sleep came easy despite his apprehension about the coming day.

The Garcia family "bed and breakfast" never asked questions as long as he paid for the rooms he and Caesar used when in Rebita. He had paid in advance for ten days when he arrived...still, small towns were alike in one respect throughout the world. Gossip. Barbara's reputation was shot and she didn't deserve it. Well, he'd worry about that later. He couldn't help thinking, "Damn those Molinos!"

Mike hurried to the clinic with a cup of hot tea for Barbara. "How are you feeling this morning?"

She sat on the mattress, knees to her chest and back against the wall. The vacant stare on her red puffy face alarmed Mike. He sat in front of her and said, "Good morning, Barbara. I've brought you a cup of tea. Did you get any sleep? I know how hard this must be for you."

Slowly she brought him into focus. "Morning, Dr. Mike Kane, I doubt if it's a good one, though. Yes, I did manage to sleep a little last night, thanks to you. I'm glad you brought me here. I couldn't have gone back to the cottage to sleep, not last night. It's kind of you to understand. Thanks for the tea." With a shaky hand, she sipped her tea. Fresh tears leaked from her sad eyes.

"Barbara, your friend Alvie must have been a very special person. The people of Cabela were extremely angry and sad about losing their teacher. The Molinos lost the support of the town, which has long been an unofficial place of sanction for them. Cergio portrayed himself as an Honduran Robin Hood and randomly gave gifts to help village projects, donated jalopy police cars, money for the churches and schools and to many individual families. I always saw it as bribery, not that Robin Hood bullshit.

"But then they saw Robin Hood in action, with the air full of bullets and so many people hurt and killed. Even their beloved teacher killed…and you know; Alvie may well have survived if she had taken cover but she saw a group of terrified small children on the street. They'd been separated from their parents in all the confusion. She ran back to help bring them to safety. Eight of those children were wounded and would have surely died if it hadn't been for Alvie taking the bulk of the bullets in the hail of gunfire. In the short time she was in Honduras, she'd already touched so many lives."

Barbara said softly, "That's how Alvie was. She had a gift for life, she sparkled. Anyone lucky enough to know her was richer for it. I still can't believe she's gone. Mike, how are they managing so many injured in a small village clinic?"

"They closed the school in Cabela as well as the clinic. Both are now being used as field hospitals. The Peace Corps temporarily closed Valencia School and clinic and assigned those volunteers to help the nurse and her assistants in Cabela for a few weeks until things are more back to normal. I arrived Monday morning, for my regularly scheduled day. But it was anything but normal…I spent the whole day in makeshift surgery, removing bullets and stitching up holes, holes that should never have been there. As soon as Cergio takes Julio off your hands, I have to go back down the mountain to Cabela and check on the patients."

"Could I go with you? I'd share in the nursing care. And some of the others would be able to get a little needed rest."

Mike looked at her skeptically. "Are you sure you're up to that, Barbara?"

"There's a bit of a selfish angle to it. You see, Alvie was my roommate in training. She was younger than my children, yet she became one of my dearest friends. There was one other person who was part of our circle of friends, Ethel, the nurse at Valencia. I think she and I need to spend a little time together. I could use a break from Rebita for a few days. And busy hands can help keep a sad heart from breaking."

"Of course, I'll give you a ride when we go. I'm glad you're able to talk about it today. You had me worried last night."

"Sorry, Mike. I was just so shocked. I couldn't believe it. Alvie was so bright and full of life. She had a great sense of humor and was completely committed to teaching. I'm okay now, I really am. But it's still hard to believe."

"May I fix you some breakfast? I need to go check on Julio," Mike stated.

"No thanks, I'm really not hungry this morning," Barbara answered.

Mike decided he'd tempt her with a breakfast anyway. The way she was dropping weight, she'd soon be a poster ad for anorexics, although he didn't think that was her problem.

Julio was in the kitchen fixing a cup of tea. "*Buenos días*, Doctor, where is Nurse Barbara? I find nobody in house when I wake up. But I feel good today."

Mike said, "I'm glad you feel better today, maybe your brother will come for you soon. You could probably go anytime now. Let me change your dressing before I fix us some breakfast." As he changed the dressing, he said, "Looking real good, Julio, I've never seen anyone heal faster, but you're not all better yet. So don't be too active too soon."

Mike thought, "I wonder if the ten injured patients in Cabela are healing as well. I certainly hope so."

"*Gracias*, Doctor. Where is Nurse Barbara?" Julio asked again.

"Nurse Barbara became very ill last night and is resting in the clinic; she didn't want to expose you to any unnecessary germs. She said to wish you good luck and good health when you leave. Would you like eggs and cheese for breakfast today?" Mike asked.

"Oh yes, thank you, Dr. Kane, eggs good. I sorry Nurse Barbara is sick. She save my life. She is good person," Julio said as he sat down at the kitchen table.

After eating breakfast, Mike cleaned off the table and then fixed a plate of fresh eggs, cheese and toast for Barbara and a fresh cup of tea. He hoped she'd eat some of it.

Julio was restless and tired of staying inside the small cottage for six days. Mike reminded him of his brother's order to keep his presence a secret in the village and that Nurse Barbara would be in trouble with his brother if Julio was seen. Julio tried to settle down with little success. "I have to take this food to Nurse Barbara, I'll be right back. You stay here, okay?"

Julio nodded, though he looked like a caged rabbit about to jump.

Mike took the breakfast to Barbara and said, "Please try to eat. Do it for your family if not yourself. I'll be right back."

Then he hurried around back and found Caesar reading under a shade tree.

"Hey, could I have a few of your magazines to loan to Julio? He's feeling better and getting restless while waiting for his brother. How is everything going out here?"

Caesar shrugged and nodded to a stack of magazines in a box under the tree. "Okay, Doc. Help yourself."

Mike found Julio still pacing in the small cottage. "I'm sorry you're stuck here like this, I hope these will help you pass the time."

Julio was pleased with the magazines, and finally started to relax. "Ah, Doctor, these good. *Gracias*."

"Glad you like them, Julio. I'm going to the clinic to check on Nurse Barbara. I'll be back soon."

Engrossed in a four-wheeler magazine, Julio didn't even look up as he said, "*Adiós*, Doctor. *Por favor*, tell Nurse Barbara, get well!"

Mike picked up the stack of letters as he walked out and wondered, "Finally today she may have time to read these. I hope so." When he looked at the unopened letter from Alvie, he felt sad. Her handwriting had been almost elegant.

Mike was startled to find the clinic empty. "Barbara, where are you? Barbara!"

"Hey, don't panic, Mike! I'm back here in treatment room two."

"I brought your mail; thought you might have time to read it today. How're you doing?"

"Better than last night. Where did you learn to cook eggs? Breakfast was delicious. You could open a breakfast bar back in the States."

"Thanks, but I doubt I'll become a short-order cook. I was hoping I could tempt you to eat, you've been skipping too many meals, Barbara."

"How is Julio this morning?"

"He's feeling much better, restless and ready to move on. He was sorry to hear you were ill. He credits you with saving his life, and rightfully so. I borrowed some magazines from Caesar and he's contented with those for now. I hope Cergio comes for him today. Now that he's feeling better, it'll be much harder to keep him occupied and out of sight."

"Do you remember what you told me when you first saw Julio in the cottage? 'This is a complicated situation.' You certainly were right about that."

Mike asked, "Do you have a deck of playing cards in the cottage? Maybe I can get him interested in a card game. I'm sure the magazines won't hold him long."

"Yes, still unopened. You'll find them in the back of the dish towel drawer in the kitchen. Good luck. Even if he doesn't know how, he's a bright young man. He'll pick it up quickly."

"He'll know, Barbara. I swear; some of them must learn to play cards even before they can walk!"

She gave him a skeptical look and said, "In that case, you better not play for money."

"You sure you're okay here? Do you need anything else?" Mike couldn't help wanting to protect her; there was just something about her…and he wasn't sure what it was. Barbara had a strong elusive independent trait yet still some sort of vulnerability that she'd never admit existed. But it did.

"Well, if you'd take the breakfast tray back and maybe bring me a bottle of drinking water, I don't care if it's cold. I'd be very grateful. And Mike…thanks."

Barbara sat at the reception desk and began to read her letters. She opened the children's first. She was astonished to learn of Jessica's changes…moving back to Lewiston, a new job at Lewiston Hospital, temporarily living with Grandmother Malone ("until I find an apartment and *No Thanks* I don't want to live in the family home, way too big for me. I could live with Michael, but I told him I liked dating him too much to make him my roommate"), and a boyfriend! Jessica?! She did sound excited and upbeat in her letter.

Janie's letter was full of news about her co-starring role in a TV Movie of the Week. Barbara thought, "I always knew she had a special spark and it's about time those show business people opened their eyes to see the obvious." Janie sounded happy with her soap role and also as if her feet were solidly on the ground. Clean and determined with new friends from work. Barbara smiled softly and said, "Thank you, God!" as she folded Janie's letter.

Billy and Liz were planning their summer honeymoon trip. They wanted to spend a week with Barbara in Rebita. Prior to the events of the past week, this would've been a welcomed event. Now she was uncertain, she'd never want to put them in harm's way. "I could take a week off and meet them in Tegucigalpa or at a beach resort. Yes, I'd feel more comfortable with that."

Bobby was still unhappy with his job. But he barely mentioned it. He'd always had lots of girlfriends over the years whom he'd barely mentioned. "But here's a letter to me, his mother; that could've been sent to her. It's all about how great she is. Ashley, a very pretty name. Well, good grief, if she's half as good as he thinks she is, then maybe he'd better make sure she doesn't get away!" Bobby. She just shook her head and smiled, thinking about him…and then Billy, Janie and Jessica. "Four unique individuals and I love each one of them so much. My life would've been so empty without my children." She sighed.

Mother Malone's letter was predictably happy. She'd always had a particularly close relationship with Jessica. They seemed to function on the same wave length. She was thrilled about her move back to Lewiston and, "I hope she won't be in a hurry to find an apartment."

Mom and Dad's letter was filled with news about people she knew in Lewiston. Who died, retired, married, divorced, graduated, had a baby, was sick or hurt, and even who moved where. Barbara smiled. "When I go home, at least I won't be behind on what's been happening while I was away."

Of course, they expressed surprise about Jessica moving back home and were pleased as punch with her decision. They were proud of Janie's continued success in television work. They'd talked with both "the boys" and reported they both sounded "good." Barbara sighed again. "What does 'sounded good' really mean?"

She was glad to read that Eric and his family were well. Barbara felt a pang of guilt when she remembered her niece, Erica. The twelve-year-old had been so intensely interested in the Peace Corps, Aunt Barbara's job and Honduras. "I promised I'd write and tell her all about it, and here it is seven months later, I must remember to write to her. Maybe Mother has sent copies of my letters to Eric, too. I hope so, must ask about that when I talk to them. I don't know how I could've ever managed here without their help back home."

Alice told news of her family and their mutual friends. She wrote, "I let you go because I couldn't stop you, you're soo stubborn. But every day I miss you and pray that you'll come safely back home."

Barbara smiled. "Ever faithful Alice! Impossible to imagine life without her friendship, we've always been there for each other. Funny but I can't remember a time in my life when I didn't know Alice. We started in the neighborhood sandbox...and we've been together ever since."

Next she opened Anita's letter. She could almost hear the Brooklyn accent as she read news about her acceptance into a Nurse Practitioner/ Master's Degree Program at the University of Pittsburgh. Anita wrote, "Based on my experience in Honduras and scores on the qualifying entrance exams, I'll start classes in August for a two-year program. I've been granted generous scholarships and with the Peace Corps tuition reimbursements, combined with my part-time work in the ICU, I'll survive just fine. During school breaks I'll pick up extra hours. I bought myself a good dependable used car with my banked Peace Corps pay.

"What I especially like about this deal is I'll be a licensed medical professional who can diagnose and treat patients independently as part of a treatment team. I'll graduate without a school debt hanging over my head. Hooray! Who says dreams don't come true?

"I spent the obligatory three days visiting my folks. It wasn't bad. The little brothers are getting a bit older and more interesting; I still seem to have about as much in common with my parents as I would your average Martian!

"Please tell Gabriela, Karena, Armondo, Pablo, Miguel and all the others I send my love. How're you holdin up with good old Dr. Kane? I'll never forget the first day you met him when you sat him on his ass with that 'one foot in the grave' crack. God, he had it comin' if anyone ever did! But despite his testy nature, he's one of the best doctors I've ever worked with. Hey, don't you work too hard."

She smiled as she folded the letter and put it back into the envelope. Then she picked up Ethel's letter. It was in her typical upbeat style; that's what Barbara first liked about her. After getting to know her better, she realized it wasn't just a style. It was simply Ethel's way. She described with humorous detail what life was like in the village of Valencia. Sharon, the young Peace Corps teacher living and working in the compound, and Ethel had quickly developed a strong bond and warm working relationship. Ethel wrote, "I feel like the Pied Piper, everywhere I go, these youngsters keep adopting me as their 'other grandmother.' I feel fortunate to have the health and stamina to be here and if I pick up a few more dozen grandchildren, so be it. My life is enriched by my friendships with such remarkable and dedicated young folks. It gives me faith that despite all the horrors in the world today, there is hope for a better world someday. Okay, now, when are we three PCVs going to have a vacation together? I've enclosed three dates, please choose which is best for you and get back to me ASAP. I sent the same dates to Alvie and I'm sure she'll get right on it because she's always ready for a good time. And when we three get together, we do have fun! It doesn't matter a bit that we're from three different generations. Oh, I'm so ready for a break with my training buddies! We're lucky to have been assigned in the same general area; do you think it was perhaps fate?"

Ethel affectionately described her four local nursing assistants, and the warm friendly people of Valencia. She also reported her family was well and thriving back in the USA.

There was only Alvie's letter left. Barbara slowly picked it up and opened it. Alvie started out as she had in all her other letters. "Hey, girl, how's it goin' up there on top o' the mountain? Down here in the valley life is sweet." She described all the preparation the villagers had put into making ready for the big festival week. She wrote of a few favorite students and how seriously they all take their educations, yet how their life expectations were so different for using their educations than their counterparts in the USA.

Alvie wrote, "P.S. I just received an Ethel letter. She sounds like she loves her work. She has a great idea about us three PCVs getting together, away from our home bases for a few days. I'm definitely in! The best time for me would be the second week of June. How about a small resort by the ocean? If that time is bad for you, I can be flexible."

Unaware of her own tears, the letter dropped from her shaking hands as Barbara fell forward, sobbing with her face in her hands as her stifled her cries. "Oh God, why? Why?…Alvie!" went unanswered.

When Mike came back two hours later, Barbara had regained her composure, though her face and eyes remained puffy and red. She had neatly refolded all the letters and was almost finished writing a relatively short letter to her parents to share with the family. She tried to keep it upbeat, but had never been able to hide true feelings from them. This time she hoped she could. She didn't want to cause them concern.

"How're you doing? I see you've read your mail. Good news from home I hope."

"Yes, everyone seems to be doing fine. Anita, the nurse I replaced, wrote and said to tell you, 'hi'; she's going on to school to become a nurse practitioner. She'll be a good one."

"Probably will."

"She said you were the best doctor she ever worked with."

A trace of a smile crossed Mike's face. "She said that, huh? Well, I'll be."

Barbara couldn't help smiling. "She did write that followed by the words, 'despite his testy nature.' Why haven't you been testy this week? Heaven knows you sure enough were the first day I met you here at the clinic. But you've been so helpful and kind to me the last few days; hardly seems like you're the same person."

"I have? Well I didn't mean to be kind; I'll have to be more careful about that. Must be that tea you're always offering!" Mike teased.

"Well, I'll just have to keep plenty of it on hand whenever you're around."

"Was it hard for you to read Alvie's letter?"

Barbara nodded. "I could almost hear her voice saying the words. It was good to read but very sad at the same time. Does that make any sense to you?"

"Of course. Are you feeling any better now? Do you want to go to the police station and try to call your family this afternoon?"

"No, I've written a letter to my parents to share with the family. I'm afraid I'd upset them if I called to talk. They'd know in a few seconds that I'm upset about something. I'll wait and call next week. Surely I'll be more like my old self by then.

"How did your afternoon go with Julio?"

"He's a hell of a card player, very shrewd, great concentration."

"I'm not surprised. Thanks for keeping him occupied."

"What would you like for dinner tonight, Nurse?"

"What are my choices, Doctor?"

"After checking your meager pantry supplies, I think we have a choice between macaroni and cheese with canned bake beans or canned baked beans with macaroni and cheese. Which would you prefer?"

Barbara smiled. "It's a tough choice but I think I'll take the beans and macaroni and cheese."

Barbara avoided Julio again by sleeping the night at the clinic. Before sleeping she reflected, "Odd that I mourn Alvie more than I did the man I was married to for thirty-three years."

Mike played cards with Julio until almost midnight. Finally he complained, "Okay, Julio, it's time to sleep. I think you've beat me enough for one day, don't you?"

Mid Sunday morning, two hours after breakfast, they heard a commotion in the compound, the sound of jeeps and shouting. This time Pablo opened the gate and allowed the visitors in without question. Mike walked to greet

Cergio and his men; he invited Cergio into the cottage to see Julio. The two brothers embraced.

Cergio said, "Julio, you look good. Turn around and let me see you. Lose some kilos, yes? But now you healthy. Let me see wound."

Julio unbuttoned his "new" donated shirt gently and pulled the dressing back for examination.

Mike interceded, "Your brother is healing very quickly but is not all better yet. He needs to be careful and not be too active for at least two more weeks. Here, let me apply a sterile dressing before you leave. Watch how I do it. Then you will be able to do it every day. Always clean hands before and after each exposure to wound area. We will give you extra supplies for daily dressing changes."

Cergio looked around. "Where is Nurse Barbara? She save my brother's life. I want thank her. I have gift for her."

Julio said, "Nurse is sick today at the clinic, she not want give me germs. So, she stay away from me today."

Mike concurred with Julio's report. "You can leave the gift here at the cottage and she'll see it when she's feeling a bit better. That's generous of you to give Nurse Barbara a gift. She only did what she felt was the right thing to do."

Cergio signaled to his men to unload the package. It was quite large. Cergio beamed with pride as his men carefully unloaded and carried the box to the center of the small living room.

Mike prepared the group cheese and tuna sandwiches, tall glasses of cold tea and cut mango for lunch. Cergio announced, "We'll be leaving after eat food. I no want us be sitting target for government soldiers. They after us all the time."

When they were gone, Mike walked to the clinic and helped Barbara carry her things back to the cottage. "I have a sandwich and a cup of fresh mango waiting for you."

"Thanks for everything, Mike. I don't know how I would've made it through the past few days without you. I suggest you show this side of your personality more often and you just might lose that testy reputation you've earned.

"It is a relief to get my bedroom back and be able to put my little house in order again. Do you think Julio was truly well enough to leave?"

"Definitely. As long as he takes it a little easy for the next couple weeks. I showed Cergio how to change the dressing and explained the necessity of washing before and after wound care. Gave him extra dressing supplies. If not, it could cause tears in the stitches and wound hemorrhaging. He loves his little brother and will watch out for him. I think Julio will be all right."

"They both said to tell you good-bye. Cergio had his men carry in a large box; it's in the middle of your living room. 'A thank you gift for Nurse who save my Julio.' They can't say enough good things about you."

"Did you set them straight? And tell them I was just lucky. I wonder if other 'innocents' will be killed when Cergio's gang has its next disagreement…I know all life is precious and I had a professional obligation to help them, but what about Alvie…and the others?"

Mike shook his head and said with grave severity, "When we pledge ourselves to the medical profession, it is our responsibility to help those who suffer, not to judge their lifestyles or politics."

Barbara bit her lip as she stared out the small kitchen window, seeing nothing at all as tears welled up in her eyes.

Mike walked over and stood beside her companionably. He put his arm on her shoulder and said, "I know it's hard to treat everyone equally regardless of which side of the fence they hang their political hat. Sometimes it's nearly impossible. But we have to keep trying."

Barbara patted his hand and walked to the living room. "I know you are right, of course. Thank you for being here this past week. I really appreciate all the help you've been to me at the clinic, at home and coping with Alvie."

"You are most welcome, my friend, I plan to move out at eight a.m. sharp. Do you still want to go along?"

"Yes. I'll be ready. I'll have to go to Gabriela's and tell her I'll be gone for about a week. I think she'll be able manage routine complaints here at the clinic during my absence. She'll understand."

"Do you want some help opening your gift?"

"No, I'll open it when I get back, I need nothing and I'd have preferred a simple thanks instead of this grandiose…." She motioned toward the huge box and frowned.

The next morning Gabriela and Pablo waved *adiós* as the SUV left the compound. They arrived in Cabela a few hours later without incident. Barbara felt refreshed and ready to work. Despite the bumpy ride, she'd managed to sleep during the trip down the mountain.

Dr. Kane made his usual blustery arrival at the Peace Corps compound. Carolyn, the local Peace Corps nurse, hurried out to the SUV. "Dr. Kane, two patients need a doctor ASAP. Treatment Room one." He ran to the clinic with the nurse.

Barbara told Caesar, "I'll get my bag later. I'm going to see what I can do to help."

Caesar nodded. "No problem, Nurse Barbara. See you later."

Barbara walked into the small makeshift hospital, former clinic. There were four beds in the reception area; the patients appeared to be recovering but still in a great deal of discomfort. A nurse aid approached her. "May I help you?"

"I've come to help you. I'm a nurse. Is Nurse Ethel here?" Barbara answered.

"*Sí*, Nurse Ethel in school hospital over there." She pointed a short distance across the courtyard from the clinic.

"*Gracias*." Barbara rushed to the school.

She stood at the door of the one-room school house converted to a six-bed hospital ward. It was a frenzy of activity. There were family members at the bed sides of the patients, four nurse aids and Ethel trying her best to provide care and allay fears.

When Ethel glanced toward the door and saw Barbara, she shoved her way through the crowded room and hugged her as they both wept for Alvie. "You know, it should've been me. I'm old. I've had a good life. She was so young, just getting started with her life's work. It's so unfair."

Barbara responded, "No, Ethel, it shouldn't have been you or Alvie or anyone. Oh God, I'm going to miss that girl."

They stood there sobbing and hanging onto each other as if their lives depended on it. At that moment, maybe they did. A nurse aid brought them a box of tissues, and a question for Nurse Ethel. Ethel composed herself and said, "*Un momento*," to the nurse aid.

And to Barbara, "Glad you're here; we could sure use some extra help. Wanna give me a hand with Maria in bed three? Ten years old, gunshot wound, bullet lodged in lower back. We've been trying to keep her as comfortable as possible. Soon as Doc is done at the clinic, Carolyn'll send him over here. Surgery is risky but she can't live like this, poor little thing." Ethel shook her head and turned away, not wanting Barbara to see the tears in her eyes. Too late, Barbara saw and knew the anguish Ethel felt.

She patted her friend's hand and Ethel gently squeezed back, nodding her head ever so slightly. "Thanks for coming, Barbie."

The situation in Cabela was even worse than Barbara had anticipated. Carolyn appeared near exhaustion. Finally, five days later, Ethel banned her from the clinic for twenty-four hours, gave her a five-milligram tablet of diazepam and sent her to quarters to sleep.

Barbara ended up staying for three weeks, working nonstop except for seven hours off each day for sleep. Dr. Kane was there most of that time except for two days each week when he and Caesar would drive to other villages to provide medical care and then hurry back to Cabela. Little Maria and another patient died in spite of their efforts. It was a gut-wrenching, heart-breaking experience for Barbara whose only real work experience had been teaching Red Cross courses and volunteer work prior to joining the Peace Corps.

Chapter Sixteen

BOBBY

"Billy, promise you'll call me as soon as you hear anything about or from Mom. I don't care what time it is. Good talking to you."

No one had heard from Barbara in over a month. This was not like their mother. They learned through internet alternative news that there was unrest and deadly altercations between government soldiers and rebels or *banditos*…in a village very close to Rebita. There had even been a Peace Corps worker killed. None of this had been even hinted at by the mainstream media. Calls to the Peace Corps seemed to be stonewalled. The brothers had left home and work phone numbers and their mother's name, location and Peace Corps identification number with the PC office. The workers they talked to had promised to relay any pertinent information about their mother as soon as it was received by their office. Seven long days later and still…nothing. Morfar always used to say, "No news is good news." But now even he was having a hard time covering up his concern.

"Grandmother Malone, what a nice surprise," Bobby said when he answered the phone. "How are you? Is my sister behaving herself? I still can hardly believe Jessica, of all people decided to move back to Lewiston! She's living proof that miracles still happen."

"To answer your first question, I'm worried about your mother. We've not heard from her for over a month. That's not like Barbara. I realize letters can get lost in the mail, especially international mail. That's why I'm only worried and not in total panic."

"I'm sure one of us will get a letter any day now. Mom will write and send out mail first chance she gets, I know she will," Bobby said with more conviction than he felt. Sometimes his persuasive legal training came in very handy.

"As for your second question, Jessica is an angel. She makes me feel young and almost like the daughter I never had. She seems happier than I've ever seen her. It's a delight to have her home with me, even if it's for a short time."

"Is Jess still looking for an apartment? I thought she'd probably move in with Michael."

"Well, she says she doesn't want to ruin their relationship by too much familiarity. You know, Jessica has always had a mind of her own. I told her to take her time. She's most welcome to stay here as long as she likes."

"I can't imagine where Jessica ever got such a stubborn independent streak! Grandmother, have I ever told you how much I love you? You've always made our lives more interesting, by just being you. You're truly one of a kind."

"Bobby, you have such a way with words, you must have a zillion girlfriends."

"Actually, I've met someone, a very special girl. I know you'll like her. I want to bring her home to meet you and the Olson grands as soon as possible."

"That's wonderful, Bobby. When're you coming? How about Memorial Day Weekend? We could invite everyone...."

"Sounds like a great idea. I'll check with Ashley and see if she already has plans. Remember we're just dating. This is not an engagement party."

He could almost see the ironic smile on his headstrong grandmother's face through the phone line.

"Of course, whatever you say, Bobby...I'll get back to you after checking with the others about Memorial Day."

Promises were made to let each other know *immediately* when any word arrived from Barbara.

He called Ashley and felt himself begin to melt at the sound of her voice. "Hi, Ash, are you busy?"

"I'm never too busy to talk to you, Bob. How are you? Any word from your mom yet?"

"No word yet. The whole family's just trying to bolster each other up. How was your day? I'm doin' better now though, just hearing your voice, Ash."

"Well, okay as far as work goes. Tomorrow will be my last day at McDowell's. His secretary will return from family leave and I'll bring her up to speed. She stopped by today, seems like a very pleasant person. I'm ready for a change. The office atmosphere at McDowell's is so stifling. I don't know how you stand it. But I'm glad I had the work assignment since I met you there."

Bob stammered, “Sorry to hear you’ll be leaving. Of course, I knew you were a temp, but I’ll still miss seeing you at work. How about a farewell lunch tomorrow?”

“Sounds great, no one I’d rather have lunch with. Meeting you has been the best thing that’s ever happened to me,” Ashley said softly.

“I just finished talking to Grandmother Malone. She’d like to meet you and has invited us for Memorial Day Weekend. How do you feel about meeting some of the clan? They’re all dying to meet you.”

“Let me think about it, Bob. I’m not sure if I’m ready for that yet.”

“What is it you’re not sure about…a future with me or meeting my family?” Bob asked tentatively.

“Oh, dear, dear Bobby…I hope and pray we have a future together, but I think it’s far too early in our friendship to speculate on longevity. Meeting your family should come after we’ve decided we aren’t just dating casually. You know what I mean, Bob?” Ashley asked.

“I think so. All I know is I’ll dread going to work with you not there. Seeing you has been the one highlight of my work day.” He continued with a deep frown and a very discouraged tone. “And I can tell you that I’ve never felt you were just a casual date. You’re the first woman I’ve ever met that I’ve known from day one that I’d even consider spending the rest of my life with. I love you, Ashley.”

“Bob, I’m so flattered and I wish I could safely say the same but I’m just not sure yet.”

A very disappointed Bob replied, “Of course, I understand.” But inside he felt like he’d been kicked in the stomach. “So, what’s next, Ash?”

“I think I’ll take a week or so off and relax. I’ll go visit my grandmother in Cleveland for a few days. She’s not well but won’t talk to me about her health. We’re very close and it’s time for another visit.”

“When do you plan to leave for Cleveland? May I drive you to the airport?”

“Dear, dear Bob, you’re all I think about and I’d like to be more certain it’s not just infatuation before I meet your family. I appreciate your offer for a ride to the airport but I always drive to Cleveland. I listen to audio books…besides it saves me all the hassle of air travel and is less expensive. I’ll call Grandma before work tomorrow so I should know my travel plans when I see you for lunch, okay?”

“Sounds like a good plan, sleep well, Ash. I’ll meet you in the lobby about noon tomorrow.”

Bobby called his grandmother immediately. "I'm still available for Memorial Day but Ashley has already made other plans. You'll have to wait for another time to meet her. Sorry."

Grandmother Malone could hear the disappointment in his voice. "There's plenty of time for that, Bobby. We don't have to do it on a holiday and maybe she'd prefer meeting us in smaller groups rather than all at once. You'll both know when the time's right."

Bobby hesitated and then said, "Thanks for understanding, Grandmother. I'll talk to you soon. Please tell Jess I said 'hi.'"

"And thank you for calling back so promptly. I love you, Bobby Malone."

The farewell lunch was fun and lighthearted. Still Bobby felt apprehensive. The thoughts of working at McDowell's without Ashley in the building left him feeling empty and cold. Even on days he didn't see her, just knowing she was there was enough stimulation and motivation to tackle and complete the never ending paperwork. Now he was on his own. That's what he had always said he wanted. Tonight he realized he had changed his mind. He wanted to be part of a two-person team and he wanted Ashley to be his partner on that team.

BILLY

Liz hugged Billy and asked, "Has Bobby heard from your mother?"

Billy rested his head on top of her soft fragrant dark hair and said with a choked voice, "No, not yet." He felt hot tears burn his eyes. "Why did she have to go off to the mountain jungles anyway?"

Liz gently stroked his face and reassured him even though she too was very concerned about Barbara's safety.

"I'm sure we'll hear from your mother this week, Billy. I'll bet she'll even tell us when she wants us to come for our vacation. Remember, no news is good news. I know I'm just too ready for a break from teaching. I'm glad there's only three weeks until summer holiday."

Billy gently kissed Liz. "I don't know what I'd ever do without you. Somehow you help me stay balanced and focused; I'm more than ready for summer vacation too. Teaching summer school will not even be an option this year. I need a break."

"Have you ever thought of planting a garden, Billy? I love fresh tomatoes and cucumbers. Maybe it would do us good to dig in the ground and would surely make us proud to watch it grow. What do you think?"

"You never stop surprising me, Liz. A garden! That's not a bad idea. I'm sure the landlord wouldn't mind. Have you ever planted a garden before? Do you want flowers, too?"

"Well, no, not exactly. One summer I stayed with my grandmother and helped her as much as a seven-year-old could. I'll never forget how wonderful the fresh, out-of-the-garden warm tomatoes tasted and how fascinating it was to watch them grow. And yes, I think a few pretty bright red flowers bordering our vegetables would be great. Thanks, Billy, that's one of the many things I love about you. You really listen to me when I say something. You don't always like my ideas, but at least you consider them and explain why you agree or disagree. I'm so excited; we'll have our very first garden."

"Of course I listen to your suggestions. You keep our lives interesting. But we'll have to learn how to garden together since my gardening experience is almost a perfect match to yours. I helped Morfar with their garden when I was five, six and seven years old. I remember the challenge of weeding and I believe I promised myself, 'Never again.' Yet here we are…planning our first garden." He mockingly shook his head in disbelief.

"It'll be fun Billy, just wait and see." Liz squeezed his hand and smiled.

"Okay, okay." Billy laughed and kissed her lightly on the cheek. "Now if you'll excuse me, I've got to correct these papers for tomorrow. It shouldn't take more than a half hour or so."

The next morning during a break, Billy pulled out a cell phone and soon he was talking to Morfar. "Any word on Mom yet?"

"No, son, I'm afraid not. How're you today? Are you able to sleep all right? Your mormor is rightly gettin' herself half sick with worry about your mother, not sleepin' good at all."

"Sorry about Mormor's sleep problems. What do you think we should do next if we don't get some word on Mom soon?"

"I figure with international mail not as dependable as it could be, we oughta wait and pray another two weeks and then really start shakin' the bushes. Nobody is gonna mess with my girl."

"Okay, that sounds like a fair deadline before taking action. Morfar, I wanted to ask you some gardening questions, Liz and I are planting a garden this summer. You remember what a miserable gardener I was as a kid? Well, she's had even less experience than me. She thinks it will be good for me and help me stop worrying so much...I don't have positive gardening memories. I recollect dirt, sweat and tedious weeding and watering. Do you think I might be a bit better as an adult or are some of us just not the type?"

Morfar laughed. "If I ever heard of a reluctant gardener, it's you, Billy. Give it a try. I remember you didn't like girls or school when you were my helper and you've sure changed your mind about both so maybe havin' a garden won't be as terrible as you're thinkin' it'll be."

After writing down a few detailed gardening tips, Billy thanked his grandfather, talked with Mormor a few minutes and said, "Good-bye." He always felt better after talking to them. They were pure salt of the earth.

He was smiling when he met Liz in the parking lot after school. She gave him a questioning look. Billy's smiles had been few and far between. "Is there news about your mother?"

Billy always liked her perplexed expression, a slightly crooked half smile and her right eyebrow arched suspiciously. She was beautiful. Despite his worries, he felt lucky to have her in his life. Billy spontaneously hugged his wife and said, "No news on Mom, yet....Liz, have I told you lately how much I love you?"

She smiled and blushed just a little as she whispered, "Well, actually it's been awhile. You know, I love you, too...you big old romantic, Billy Malone."

They embraced under the trees in the school yard near the staff parking lot on a very warm day with only two weeks of classes left before their summer breaks.

JESSICA

"Hi, Grandmother. Mmm, what's cooking? It smells wonderful and I'm starved, work was a zoo today." Jess gave her grandmother a quick hug, took a step back and asked, "Are you feeling all right? You don't look so well."

"Yes dear, I'm fine, just a bit tired. What time would you like dinner?"

"How does an hour sound? That'll give me a chance to unwind and check my mail, if that's okay with you."

"Certainly, Jessica, but the bad news is, you didn't get a letter today, no one has heard anything from your mother yet. I talked to Bobby today and he'd just talked to Billy."

Jessica swallowed hard, trying to keep her tears welled up. "Maybe I should call Janie this evening. What about Mormor and Morfar?"

"Good idea to talk to Janie, though I'm sure she'd have called us if she received a letter. Perhaps you could visit Mormor and Morfar. He keeps saying, 'no news is good news.' I know he's trying to bolster us but at the same time, I think he's trying hard to convince himself."

"I'm sure you're right, Grandmother. I'll have plenty of time since Michael has a school program tonight. I've got some work cut out for me with that young man! He just doesn't have enough respect for my time. He calls spontaneously and expects me to be happy just for the chance to be with him at the drop of a hat…for a couple hours.

"Don't worry, though, Michael and me are okay. He shows more respect for me than any other boyfriend I've had. Of course that in itself is not exactly an achievement. He simply has to learn that I have a life too. And living alone for so long, well, I need some space. You know what I mean?"

"Of course, I do, Jessica. I still keep hoping you'll stay on with me a bit longer. As far as I'm concerned, you can stay with me as long as you want to. I love having you here and I promise to give you as much space as you want."

"Thanks. You know, Grandmother. I might just take you up on the offer of staying here indefinitely. If I save the amount of my rent each month, and if things continue to go well with Michael and I…well, who knows what tomorrow might bring. Besides, it's kind of nice to be spoiled and pampered by you. It makes me feel a little embarrassed but very special too."

"Jess, you are special! You've made me so happy. Having you here has given me a new lease on life. I'm so glad you've moved back to Lewiston. Now, I'm going to read in the sunroom while you relax before dinner." She gave her granddaughter a hug and kissed her forehead softly before leaving the room.

JANIE

Janie answered the phone. "Jess, hi! How're you doing? Haven't talked with you in ages."

"I'm good, how about yourself?"

"Well, my life has definitely been on the upturn since I got the part in the soap. I'm suddenly getting parts and between the soap and the movie shoots, I'm exhausted when I finally get to bed. But that's good, 'cause then I don't feel like taking anything to help me sleep…you know what I mean."

"What movies are you in? I haven't seen you in anything but the soap and little sister, you are *hot* in that part."

"Well, one movie is in the can and won't be on television till next winter sometime. I don't know what they've finally decided to call it. I just signed on for my third movie. We'll start filming next fall. Now I'm working on one for the cinemas, I play the younger sister of Kamila Zoot. It's a great story and she's wonderful to work with. Each director has his own set of ideas and the different actors have their own unique styles. I'm learning so much. Most of them have been very impressive and professional."

Janie continued, "So how are things really going for you in Lewiston? Do you like your job at the Lewiston Hospital? How is it to live with Grandmother Malone?"

Jessica replied, "I know this is going to sound very out of character for me. But I love the work, great group of co-workers and the patients have been challenging, which provides enough stimulation for me to stay interested. Living with her gives me a real peace of mind. Sure beats the isolated independence I had when I lived downstate. Grandmother made me an offer I couldn't refuse. Now I've agreed to live with her indefinitely. She says I've given her a new lease on life. We have so much fun. What a character! I could easily forget she was *old* if she wasn't my grandmother."

"Glad to hear it. You do sound more contented than I've ever known you to be. Do you often see the other grands? How are they?"

"I see Morfar and Mormor three or four times a week. They're always busy puttering around on their projects. Right now it's spring garden preparation, spring cleaning, and various church activities."

"Hey, have you heard from Mom lately?" Janie asked.

"No one has for over a month, I was hoping maybe you had. Morfar says 'no news is good news' but I think he's trying to bolster himself as much as to allay our concerns. They've become chronic worriers about Mom. It is so unlike her not to write or call someone for that matter."

"I didn't know enough to be worried; I thought one of you must have received a letter and not sent out copies to the rest of us yet. This is not like Mom. Please as soon as anyone hears anything, call me. Immediately," Janie stated with a new sense of boldness.

"I promise we'll call. And don't worry, I'm sure Mom's okay. It's only been a month."

"Isn't there a number we can call for information at the Peace Corps? Surely we don't have to just *wait*!" Janie's voice was becoming tense.

"Bobby has already tried that and they reassured him and told him to wait, that they've received no bad news about our mother," Jess answered. "On a different subject, are you seeing anyone now?"

"No, I really haven't had time for a social life and half the men I've met have been gay, great friends but just not interested in anything I could offer romantically. Half of the rest are married and most of the women I know wouldn't want the leftovers anyway."

"Hang in there, kid, who'd have ever thought I'd have another go round with romance and here I am, sometimes even fantasizing about what our children will look like! No! I'm not trying to tell you anything, no babies in the oven. It's just that you only need to meet one special person, take it slow, and well, you just never know. If it can happen to someone like me, it surely will for a doll like you," Jessica reassured her little sister.

There were many things the sisters never shared with each other about their personal lives and would never venture to intrude on one another's privacy. They were proud and confident in their mutual respect.

Again promises were made to call immediately when someone received word from Mom. While each sister knew the other would disregard it, they encouraged each other to stop working so hard.

Janie prepared for bed and lay in the darkness silently praying for her mother's safety. A few lonesome tears trickled down her cheeks as she drifted into a restless sleep.

Chapter Seventeen

BARBARA

After one week back in Rebita with the ordeal of the last month behind her, Barbara finally sat down to write a long letter to her family. She wrote apologies and explanations for her delayed correspondence, polite questions about each of their lives and still had written only two pages. Usually her letters were at least six pages of entertaining descriptive communications. But she couldn't think of anything else to say. Barbara felt a strange unfamiliar emotional distance from her family. The horrors she had witnessed in helping care for the victims in Cabela were not something she could share with anyone who wasn't there. She felt as though she was under a great cloud of sadness that followed her everywhere she went.

Gabriela and the first aid students had done an excellent job keeping the clinic up and going. Supplies had become dangerously low until a large supply order had been delivered just yesterday. Barbara had spent the previous afternoon at the clinic unpacking the order, doing inventory and preparing the next supply order. This was a necessary safeguard measure to prevent running out of needed stock.

The huge box in her small living room was proving to be an unneeded irritant. Barbara reluctantly opened it to find a wide-screen television. "Good grief! And what am I supposed to do with this? We have no antennas or satellite dishes, let alone electricity." She decided to talk to the village priest and see if he had any suggestions. "I know for sure I don't want it and absolutely have no room for this thing. But I certainly don't want to offend Cergio by publicly rejecting his gift."

Padre Daniel looked pensive, and asked, "Please, would you give me a few days to think about the television problem? How big you say it is? Not to worry, Nurse Barbara, I will talk to you in a few days."

Barbara had accepted an invitation from Gabriela's family to join them for dinner Saturday evening. She decided to close the envelope and have it ready to be posted at the earliest possible opportunity. She looked at the clock, three hours before dinner; she decided to take a *siesta* in an effort to chase the clouds of gloom away.

Later as Barbara walked to Gabriela's home, she couldn't help noticing the quiet natural beauty of the mountain village. Rebita looked peaceful, contented and alive, completely the opposite of how Barbara felt as the cloud of sadness shadowed over her. She prayed for release from this overwhelming despair, but the ghosts of the last month were never far from her mind.

She stopped in the market to buy fresh flowers for Gabriela's mother. The villagers were warm and friendly, always so kind to her. Barbara's facade of smiles and compassion was beginning to crumble. Determined to get through the evening, she silently repeated her mantra, "I can and I will. I can and I will. I can and I will!"

Gabriela sat on the veranda of the small home she shared with her parents and various family members. She lovingly held a beautiful baby girl on her lap as she softly sang a vivacious Honduran melody. She looked up as Barbara walked toward the house. "Nurse Barbara! Welcome to our home. It is good you to come here. You our family. We your family."

Gabriela embraced her warmly. "This is baby Lilia, baby of my brother, Phillipe. They live in house of my mother and father. Is she not pretty baby? Phillipe not home today." Lilia was dressed in bright red and yellow ruffles with matching bows in her black curly hair. A prettier baby would've been hard to find. Gabriela was definitely attached and proud of her niece.

"*Hola*, Lilia, you are such a sweet little girl and I like your pretty dress. Aunt Gabriela is a good nurse. You be proud of her, okay?"

Baby Lilia's bright brown eyes twinkled as she giggled and seemed to nod her head in agreement. Barbara touched the baby's hand and said affectionately, "You're not only beautiful but smart, just like your Aunt Gabriela."

Just then Gabriela's mother and father, Lilia and Oscar, came out of the house to welcome Barbara; they were short, stocky, solid mountain people. Their leathered brown skin epitomized their life of struggling to make a home for themselves and their family. Spanish was the official language for the rest of the evening. They were warm, kind and considerate hosts who *almost* helped Barbara escape her cloud of depression. The food was delicious spicy tortillas, chicken and rice and wonderful cakes for dessert, all served and eaten at a delicious slow pace with plenty of wine to wash it down.

Lilia said, "We are very proud of our Nurse Gabriela, she help us live like this. We have beautiful home and everyone respects us in Rebita. She is good girl."

Gabriela blushed. "Mama, please!"

Barbara laughed and said, "Lilia, my daughters react the same way when I say good things about them but there's nothing like a mother to set things straight. So, where are your other children now? How many grandchildren do you have?"

Lilia and Oscar looked at each other and smiled. "We have eight children and twelve grandchildren. Gabriela, Phillipe, his wife and baby Lilia live with us. Also Geraldo, his wife and three children, they live with us. One daughter, Adrina, marry to man from Cabela and live there. They have four children. The others live here in Rebita. Family is good, very important."

"Absolutely. I have two sons and two daughters in the US. They're all grown up. No grandchildren yet. My parents are there too. I miss them all very much."

Lilia and Oscar gave a brief look of surprise; few people Barbara's age in Honduras still had their parents and if they did, wouldn't leave them to go to a strange country.... Oscar asked her, "Why you in Honduras when you have family and so much work to do in US? We know some things here in the mountains, many sick people in US. Not enough nurses. I not understand." Lilia nodded her head in agreement, a puzzled expression on her face.

Gabriela was quietly attentive. Barbara answered carefully, wondering if she had already told them too much. "My husband died of heart attack last summer. I just wanted to give something back to help others and to get away for awhile. I don't know if that makes any sense to you or not. It made so much sense to me back then. But this last month, nothing is making much sense anymore."

Lilia saw the tears in Barbara's eyes and gently put her arm around the foreign nurse's bony shoulder. "We happy you came to our village, you work too hard. You must eat better, look how skinny you are. You help by teaching villagers to be nurses. This is good. We so proud of our Gabriela."

Barbara patted Lilia's hand and thanked her for the kind words.

The conversation continued on a lighter note. Barbara met Gabriela's brother Geraldo, his three children and lovely wife. They all seemed to get along well. Still Barbara couldn't imagine so many people living in such close quarters; the house didn't seem *that* large. Geraldo was young, handsome and charming. His wife had raven black hair. She was very shy and quite beautiful. Their children were simply beguiling. The couple were still young and time had not taken its toll on their appearances yet. Inevitably it would.

Oscar walked back into the family fold with a bottle of tequila. "Last call for bedtime drink of Hondura's best." Gabriela followed behind her father with a tray of glasses for adults and a bottle of water and cups for the children. Barbara was served first, after everyone had their drinks, Oscar toasted, "Nurses are helpers of the blessed Virgin Mother."

All glasses were turned bottoms up. Barbara had never been much of a drinker and embarrassed herself when she choked and coughed for air after a hefty swallow of the bitter drink. The Chavez family roared with laughter as she stammered to regain her composure.

Barbara put her arm through Lilia's as she was leaving. "Thank you for a wonderful evening. The food was delicious and it was so nice to meet your family. You're a rich woman to have them all so close by."

Lilia responded by patting Barbara's hand. "And even more rich to have you my friend, Nurse Barbara."

Barbara walked back to the compound by the light of the moon. It was a lovely warm night in Rebita. She thought, "It was a good evening, I feel a little better because I went. The Chavez family was really very kind to me. And I think Lilia and I might even become friends."

Sleep came quickly with the combination of alcohol and exhaustion due to the sporadic sleep patterns and extreme stress of the last month.

The next day she took advantage of the opportunity to relax with her tea and stale muffins. Smirking wickedly she thought, "At least they're not moldy." Late in the morning, Barbara walked to the open market to buy some badly needed supplies for her barren kitchen.

Before starting back to the compound, she chatted with several acquaintances and patients. As she turned the corner she noticed the *comisaría de policías* and decided to ask to use their phone to call home. They were very pleased to help her. Barbara was suddenly almost a hero in the small village. Everyone seemed to know "the secret."

She called her parents, her mother answering on the second ring. "Hello, Mother, oh God, it's good to hear your voice!"

At first her mother was quiet and then she cried and babbled on.

"Mother, I'm so sorry I didn't call you sooner, I have a letter ready for the post. Please don't cry. I'm okay. I've been working very long hours and things got a little crazy. Ah, Mom, please stop crying. I'm fine, I really am. I love you, Mom."

"I love you too, Barbie. Please, be careful, dear."

Then her father took over the phone. "Barbara Ann? Why in God's name haven't you called or written? We haven't heard a word from you in nearly six weeks. We've been worried sick. How are you anyway?"

"I'm fine, Dad. Really I am. I'm sorry I wasn't able to call or write for awhile. You should receive a letter soon. I'm calling from the police station. It's the only phone in the village and doesn't always work. How are you doing?" Barbara blinked hard to block her tears as she listened to the tormented voices of her parents.

"Well, at least you're still alive." He sighed, loud enough to be heard in the Honduran mountain village from Pennsylvania.

"Of course, I'm alive, Dad, I'm fine. I'm so sorry to have caused you all so much worry. I promise not to let that happen again. How are the children? Mother Malone? Alice? Eric? Please tell them all I think about them and miss everyone so much. And thank them for all the letters and to please, please, please keep writing."

"First of all, everyone is okay; just crazy with worry about you. Now that we know you're still kickin', everybody'll be a whole lot better. Jessica just walked in; she wants to talk to you herself. You be careful down there. I love you, little girl!"

"Dad, you know I love you. And I'm not a little girl; I'm fifty-three years old! Please give Mother a hug from me. I hope to see you both soon. I miss you so much."

"Barbara Ann, might as well face it, you will *always* be our little girl. Now talk to Jessica."

"Mom! My God, we've been nearly sick with worry. How are you?"

Barbara smiled as she listened to her daughter's voice and thought, "This child will always be blunt, depending on the direction of the verbal bullets, either a personality plus or negative." Then she answered, "I'm fine, Jessica. It is so good to hear your voice again. I'm truly sorry to have caused you all such worry. I have a letter ready for the post. I tried to explain the situation here. It got sorta crazy for a few weeks."

"Thank God you're okay. It's great to hear your voice again, Mom. I really do miss you. Did you know I'm living with Grandmother Malone now? And I'm happier than at any time in my adult life. It's so much better than the isolated loneliness of independence I had in a city of strangers."

"You and Grandmother Malone always were like two peas in a pod. I'm glad to hear you're content. I hope the new job and the boyfriend are also positives in your life. Dear Jessica, you deserve to be happy. Oh darn, the policeman just signaled that he needs the phone and my time is up. Please give my love to Janie, Bobby, Billy and Grandmother Malone. I love you, Jess. Good-bye for now."

Barbara smiled. "*Gracias*, Arturo, *gracias*." She told him again to bring her the phone bill when it arrives. "I want to pay my own phone bill."

Arturo was a gentleman and an officer. "*Sí, señora, sí.*" All the while smiling from ear to ear. Two missing front teeth couldn't deter his chivalry as he bowed to Barbara with his tattered hat held across his waist.

She often wondered if he understood anything she said to him in English or Spanish, when it suddenly dawned on her that he might be almost deaf. She decided to check his hearing next time he came by the clinic.

Barbara walked from the market carrying her bags but the load felt distinctly lighter. She could even feel a little sunshine break through her cloud. She thought, "Talking with Mom, Dad and Jessica was the best thing that could have happened to me today, especially with a good night's sleep. Yes, life will go on and so will I."

Barbara decided to start a journal, to record her observations, feelings and daily life experiences and spent the rest of the weekend cooking, reading and writing letters.

After church on Sunday, Lilia made a point to talk with Barbara. "Please come to my cottage for a glass of iced tea some evening, Lilia. I'd love the company and it'd be fun to share life experiences. I'm home every night."

"*Sí*, I'd like very much come your house. You good *gringo*, Nurse Barbara."

So, the friendship began…two middle-aged women from two different cultures.

Barbara hung around to talk with *Padre* Daniel about the gift television set in her living room.

"I think perhaps I may have a solution to your problem without causing the gift bearer insult. Please let me think about it for a few more days. I will stop by the clinic in a few days and we'll talk about it then."

"Thank you, *Padre*."

By Monday morning Barbara was feeling more like her old self again. The clinic was busy at a steady pace but not overwhelming, and the weather remained very hot but somewhat less than the previous weeks had been. Gabriela was her usual competent good-natured self. First aid classes would start again Wednesday evening. Barbara decided to make certificates of appreciation with cash attached for each of the students at an informal ceremony during the class. The last month had required so much extra effort from each of them. She also made one for Gabriela and attached a bonus for duty served above and beyond expectations. Barbara hoped her Spanish was adequate for the task at hand and didn't want to ask for help as the certificates were intended to be a surprise. Barbara was especially thankful she had brought some extra cash with her and secretly changed to Honduran pesos while in training in Tegucigalpa. She stubbornly resolved, "Recognition and rewards are important for everyone."

Wednesday evening after the class, Barbara announced, "Gabriela and everyone, please stay for a few minutes. Have some iced tea and biscuits. I have something I'd like to share with you. Because you've all been such wonderful nurse helpers, we could never have done the work we've done without each one of you the past few weeks." Barbara smiled when she noticed the hesitation of some of the students to taste the tea. "It's okay, really. Just taste it, and it's not *loco* water. It only tastes good and quenches your thirst. Anyway I have a surprise for each of you. And you must understand this is special. Just because of our troubled times this last month."

The students were thrilled. This was the most money most of them had ever seen in their entire lives, and the first official certificate they'd ever received. The students hugged Barbara and thanked her again and again. A few even said they liked the iced tea. She smiled and thought, "The others probably weren't brave enough to even taste it."

Interestingly, as Barbara got to know the villagers one person at a time, they became like her extended family. They had such a strong sense of community. In many ways they were like one very large functional clan.

Thursday and Friday went by uneventfully. Lilia stopped by on Friday evening. Gabriela had grown increasingly curious about what they could possibly have in common. She frowned. "Nurse Barbara and my *madre*? Will they talk about…*me*?" She decided to follow her mother and listen to their conversation through the window. Gabriela felt only the tiniest glimmer of guilt.

She begged Miguel, "Please no tell anybody I here, I play trick on my *madre*. Please keep my secret. Okay?"

Miguel smiled, nodded and waved her through. He sighed and thought, "What a waste, a beautiful woman like Gabriela and not even married."

Gabriela perched herself snugly under the open living room window on the small front porch. She listened intently and was shocked to hear them laugh as if they were young. She thought, "Do they not know they old? They laugh like young people!" She realized she'd never known this side of her mother before....

Barbara and Lilia, unaware of their eavesdropper, shared a glass of Honduran white wine with a small plate of crackers and cheese. Despite their cultural and language barriers they found much in common to talk and laugh about. Perhaps because both had been so isolated from girl talk outside their circles of duty, that it was just a relief. Spanish was their common language since Lilia was not bilingual. Whatever it was, something clicked between them.

They laughed at their distinctive differences. Lilia's dark brown eyes, dark skin and long braided black hair. Barbara's light skin, blue eyes and short gray streaked sandy hair. Lilia's stocky stature compared to Barbara's gangly height towering at least twelve inches above her Honduran friend. Two things they shared in equal measure were innate intelligence and healthy senses of humor.

Lilia told Barbara about her wedding day jitters when she married Oscar at age fifteen. "Big celebration and my father, proud man. Oscar was like scared little boy who smelled like de brewery. Oscar was seventeen. We married thirty-one years and it seems like only yesterday. He so proud when we have each baby! He good man for me."

Lilia's face glowed as she continued. "You been to Honduran wedding yet? Something to see! So pretty and big happy time for all de families."

Barbara stated, "I do hope to attend a wedding while I'm here. I married my husband when I was nineteen. He was twenty-one. It was a big fancy affair and I truly can say, I hardly remember it anymore. It was not a good marriage, but I did have a good life as a mother."

"Oh yes, being mother very important, a job that never ends. But I do like my peaceful times, when Oscar at his work and Gabriela, Geraldo and family are out...I make a cup of tea and sit down to pray the rosary. It's inspiring and refreshing."

"Lilia, have you ever seen a movie?"

"No, not here in Rebita. But my cousin's friend travel all the way to Valencia one day and saw a movie. Big people move and talk on big flat white surface. Like a moving picture that talks. She say it very exciting."

"That's right and the movies tell stories. I have a gift from Cergio when Gabriela and I took care of his brother. It is a large television, in that box. *Padre* said maybe we can use it for the whole village and have an outdoor movie night in the square about once a month. I've ordered a VCR and a few videos. He will store the television and video player in the storage room of the church. What do you think? Will people come? Will they like it?"

"Here in Rebita?! This is such big news and so exciting. Will we have enough electricity? You are so kind to our people."

"I'm happy you like the idea, Lilia. I didn't know what to do with the gift; I didn't want to offend Cergio. As you see, I don't have enough room for it here or at the clinic. But when *Padre* made this suggestion, I have to admit, I thought it was the perfect plan. This way the whole village will have a chance to enjoy the gift. *Padre* said the Lord will provide electricity for our movie nights."

"Tell me, Barbara, is de movie night a secret or can I tell my family and neighbors?" Lilia was smiling like the cat that just ate the canary!

Barbara laughed. "It is no secret, you can tell anyone you want to. Would you like another glass of wine?"

"Oh yes, *gracias*."

Barbara sat back on her chair sharing a comfortable silence with her new friend as they sipped their wine. Finally she turned to Lilia. "So, did you ever have a chance to go to school? Did you ever learn to read or write?"

"No, I not go to school. My *madre* taught me how to take care of de home and cook. I wish I could read, but in those days, taking care of de home and family was most important education for *muchachas*." Then she smiled and lifted her glass. "A toast, I keep good house for my family!"

"To Lilia who keeps a beautiful home for her family!" And they both laughed like school girls.

"Maybe nine years ago, the *Padre* developed a part-time school for villages. He teaches three mornings and gives assignments. His assistant teaches two afternoons. All eight my children read, write and add numbers. They all speak some English. And my beautiful Gabriela is nurse with you for the Peace Corps of United States. I so proud of her. I proud all my children."

"As you should be; you are a good mother."

"Please tell me about your children, are you friends with them?"

"It's a little hard to answer your question. First I am their mother. To me that means I'm their friend, too. However, I doubt they've always viewed me as their friend. I think they do more now that they're older and have adjusted more to their father's death. I have two daughters, Jessica and Janie, and two sons, Billy and Bobby. What more can I say? I love them and I still left them. But I do miss them. They all live out on their own. Billy married a very nice girl just before I left, they're both teachers. No grandchildren yet."

Lilia yawned and said, "I feel so tired now, thank you for happy evening. I go my house now." She smiled at Barbara, and gave her an affectionate hug. "It good to laugh with my *amigo*, Nurse Barbara!"

Barbara returned the hug and agreed. "Indeed, it is good to laugh with a friend. *Buenas noches* and do come back again soon."

Gabriela scrambled behind the cottage as the front door began to open. She still felt unsettled and a bit confused about her mother and her boss becoming friends. "But why not? They both nice ladies." As she sneaked out of the compound, she asked herself, "Why do I feel so insecure and suspicious all the time?" Rather than ponder her questions, she took shortcuts and managed to arrive home before her mother. She thought, "Perhaps it is better to let sleeping dogs lie. At least I know my mother thinks of me with pride and as a friend. That could change if she knew I was sneaking around spying on her!"

Gabriela smiled as she lay quietly in bed. Moments before sleep came, she thought, "Imagine, movies in Rebita!"

Word spread through the town quickly that a free open-air movie would be featured each month in the town square. Most of the native mountain village people had never seen television or a movie. It was hard for them to imagine but they were all anxious for the first one.

Barbara continued to write letters home and in her journal. She still felt an empty sadness regarding Alvie. Rain fell almost every night while the village slept; each morning started with a heavy moist mist soon replaced by the hot tropical sun. The first aid class was excelling and their competence had actually made the clinic just a bit easier to handle since they were often able to help neighbors and family avoid direct clinic involvement.

Supplies and letters began to arrive on a regular basis and life in Rebita picked up a normal cadence. The video player arrived with the six videos Barbara had requested. The first movie night was set for a Tuesday evening. It was the main topic of conversation for days before the planned event. Cergio became an even bigger hero with many of the villagers because he had given them a movie machine.

Tuesday morning about ten a.m., an SUV's roar alerted Barbara and Gabriela that Dr. Kane had entered the compound. A few minutes later he walked into the clinic, looking much older than Barbara had remembered. He nodded and tipped his hat to both women accordingly as they said, "Good morning, Doctor Kane."

"So, how have things been since I was last here?" he asked as he was checking over his list of patients to be seen that day.

Gabriela answered, "We have a peaceful month. Tonight we have our first movie in Rebita. Everyone excited! I work now."

"So how is our Nurse Barbara? You look a little better than the last time I saw you."

"Again I must thank you for all the help when I cared for Cergio's brother. And dealing with Alvie's murder. That was a rough time for me and I truly appreciate all you did for me." She reached over and put her hand over his and gently squeezed. "Thanks, Mike. I think I'm way better now than I was then. May I invite you to dinner tonight and then a movie?"

"That's an offer I can hardly turn down, but a movie? Same one Gabriela was talking about?"

Barbara nodded. "Remember the large box Cergio gave me to show his appreciation for saving his brother? It was a large-screen television. I had no room or personal use for it. And we have limited electricity from our generator…I didn't want to offend Cergio by refusing his gift. So, I talked with the village priest. He suggested using it in the town square once a month for free movies for all the villagers. Most of them have never seen a television or movie. He will store the television at the church and use a borrowed generator for electricity."

"Well, I hope the copyright folks don't get after you!" Mike said with a diabolic smile. "Actually it sounds like a great idea. I'd be honored to dine with you, Nurse Barbara, and to accompany you to the movie."

Barbara smiled. "Good. Be at the cottage about five thirty p.m. Potluck as usual."

It was a routine afternoon. Barbara thought, "Thank God for predictable patients, and to think at one time I thought routine nursing would be boring! Foolish me!"

Chapter Eighteen

She prepared a simple casserole dinner but also included pudding for dessert. It wasn't a bad meal combined with bread, salad and wine.

Mike arrived ten minutes early. "I know it's not proper to come early for a dinner but I'm here and it's too bloody hot to wait outside when I can be in your cozy little cottage out of the heat. These are for you." He handed her a small bouquet of fresh bright colored wildflowers.

Barbara stood at the open door smiling at him. He was truly an original. "Welcome and thank you, they're beautiful." She went to the kitchen to find a vase for the flowers. "Would you like a glass of iced tea?"

"Sounds good. Your place looks a lot better when not converted into a private hospital." Mike made himself comfortable in the overstuffed side chair.

"Thank you. Here's your tea." She sat down on the sofa across from him with her own glass of tea. "So, please tell me, how's Ethel and the crew down in Cabela? When did you last see them?"

"Ethel is a survivor; she seems to take everything in her stride. Really, quite a remarkable woman. Excellent nurse. But then I have to hand it to the Peace Corps, they always have the best nurses. From what I hear about the shortage of nurse in the states, the Peace Corps recruiting techniques must be the envy of more than a few hospital CEOs and they're finally beginning to offer nurses a fair wage. Still the Peace Corps always manages to find a few good nurses and get them for little more than volunteer wages. Amazing.

"They're slowly getting back to their regular routine in Cabela. School is in session again. The hospitalized patients have been mostly sent home with close follow up. We still have two of the more seriously wounded ones in the clinic round the clock. They're improving each day."

"Which ones are they?" Barbara asked.

"Little Rosita and Paulo, a forty-year-old worker who was just at the wrong place at the wrong time."

"I remember them. She's such a sweet little thing. I'm happy to hear they're getting well. So, what else is new?"

"Well, a good looking skinny nurse invited me to dinner and a movie. That hasn't happened to me in years. I find it quite a curious occurrence."

Barbara laughed at his comments and teased, "Let's just say that a lonely widow is in hot pursuit so you better be careful, Doc!"

Mike blushed. "Well, I, I…ah hardly know what to say. Except that I'm flattered." He stared awkwardly into his glass of iced tea.

Barbara went to check on dinner. "Hey, Mike, don't you recognize a joke when you hear it?!"

They enjoyed the dinner and by his second glass of wine, he was becoming more relaxed. Barbara had talked more openly about her past than she'd planned; he was just so easy to talk to. "So, Dr. Kane, it's your turn. Tell me your story."

"There's really not much to tell, I'm just an old medicine man trying to help the Honduran mountain folks the best I can." He continued to stare into his wine glass, clearly uncomfortable.

"Have you been or are you married? Do you have children? Where are you from in the States?" Barbara was determined to make him talk. She filled his empty wine glass and offered him after dinner tea.

His guards were down by the time he finished his third glass of wine. "I'm widowed. It was a very nasty end to a long good-bye. We married during my second year of med school. Sue worked as a secretary to help support us but also to give her something to do during my long hours of class and training. Mostly my folks paid the bills. Mom and Dad were both physicians. By the time I finished my residency in family medicine, we had little Mike and Betsy. My future was set. The children were smart, healthy and beautiful.

"I started to work in my parents' office immediately. Good money, security and familiar surroundings. However, Sue became more and more discontent. She felt her position as a doctor's wife deserved more respect and distinction than she was receiving in our small town. I couldn't make enough money to please her; each month we slid deeper and deeper into debt. By the time Little Mike and Betsy started school, we'd started a pattern of arguing about money every time we were together. My parents even tried to talk to her. That was a disaster!"

"Then she started to drink very heavily and to be out late at night with what she called 'a group of new friends.' It wasn't long before I saw signs of drug use. So what did I do? I worked longer and longer hours. I avoided being home with her as much as possible. We argued less. The years went by and little Mike was suddenly taller than me. It seemed like overnight I had two angry sulking teenagers, demanding their own credit cards and wheels. Betsy had spiked pink hair. By then Sue spent most mornings recovering from the night before. She wasn't raising our children and neither was I." Mike's dark eyes filled with tears. Barbara sat patiently waiting...she put her hand on his to reassure him.

He wiped his eyes with the back of his huge right hand and continued. "I've never talked about this with anyone before...I respect you, Barbara, and trust you will not spread it through the Peace Corps volunteer community." She felt his intense dark eyes bore straight into her very soul.

She nodded. "Of course you can trust me, Mike."

"A week before young Mike was to graduate from high school, I took an evening off to talk to him about his future. His grades had been consistently deplorable. He saw me walk into the kitchen and sneered, 'What the hell are you doing here?' The smell of alcohol hung heavy in the air. I tensed up and shouted, 'This is my home. I pay the bills around here. I'm your father, remember me?' He walked over and put his face within an inch of mine, and said with pure hatred dripping from his voice, 'No, I don't know you. Maybe there's something vaguely familiar about your face. Ah yeah, maybe I've seen your picture somewhere before.' I grabbed him by the shoulders and tried to shake some sense into him. Betsy had been sitting at the counter pretending to ignore us. She became frightened and screamed. Sue ran into the kitchen and saw us. 'You son of a bitch! You leave my son alone!' and started pounding on me like I was a punching bag. Mike pulled free and glared at me. 'God, you're some kinda piece of work. You fuckin' idiot. I'm outa here.' Betsy shouted, 'Wait for me!' She grabbed her purse and was gone but not before giving each of us a look of total disgust.

Sue lit a cigarette and looked at me with a coldness that chills me even now. Then she whispered hoarsely, 'Well, Doctor, how you gonna fix this mess? It may take more than one evening at home.' I don't remember much more until the doorbell rang about midnight. Sue had passed out on the sofa before ten. A state policeman regretfully informed me about the accident.... They were both pronounced dead at the scene. Just like that, I lost my children. But in their minds they didn't even have a father. They were right;

of course, I hid from my domestic problems by working, working, working. Sue was inconsolable. Six weeks later she took a fatal overdose. I had let them all down. Both my parents had died long before my home went into total chaos. I was thankful they weren't around to see the end. I functioned on automatic for a year but grew sick and tired of the curious and sympathetic stares.... So, finally I decided to check out the need for medical doctors in Honduras. I'd been here as a young college graduate and worked in health services before I started medical school. I sold everything, cashed in my pension and moved lock, stock and barrel. Anyway, that's my story. Nothing I'm proud of." He wiped his eyes again, excused himself and went outside for air.

As Barbara finished cleaning her tiny kitchen, she thought, "My God. What can I say to this man? Lord, don't ever let me feel sorry for myself again!" She wiped tears from her cheeks as she washed the dishes. "I'm so lucky that my children are alive and well, not perfect, but who cares? Their imperfections only make them more interesting. Poor Mike, what a terrible guilt he carries."

Later she joined him on the front porch with two small glasses of iced tea. "Want some company?" She gave him his drink and sat down beside him on the step without waiting for an answer.

"You're really something; you come barging out here, always with your iced tea. Did it ever occur to you that I might prefer to be alone with my misery...what do you want from me anyway?"

"I just want to be your friend. You were good to me. I didn't even know I needed a friend and there you were. Besides, this is my front porch!" She ever so lightly touched his forearm with her hand to reassure him she wasn't put off by his testy nature. "Know what I think? I think you use your size and your gruff demeanor as a barrier to keep anyone from getting close to you. You used your work when you were younger. Now it's work combined with your grumpy reputation that prevents you from having to deal with people on an interpersonal level."

"Listen to me, Barbara. I've managed just fine for eight years here in the mountains without friends. I'm not changing my status quo. Not for you. Not for anyone. You're a nice person. You should go back to your Pennsylvania and your family. You have choices. I don't."

"You just don't get it, do you? I am going back to Pennsylvania *when* my tour of duty is up. I made a commitment and I intend to keep it. Life is far too short to live as an island and I believe you know that very well. Are you saying you're going to carry this terrible guilt you feel for your family as long as you live? Do you enjoy the martyr complex? It sounds like you weren't a good father. But accidents happen. Sue made her choices. And you still have choices. Everyone does. Sometimes life is unfair. Just think about it, okay?" She stood up to go inside.

Mike slowly stood and faced Barbara. Unable to be gruff with her, he finally said, "Thank you for a delicious dinner. It was a refreshing break from my usual fare. And thanks for listening to my story." His eyes filled with tears and he bit his lip. He looked at her and with a choked voice said, "Thanks, friend." He gently stroked her cheek with his hand as he turned to leave.

Barbara put her hand over his and lightly squeezed. "Good night, friend. I'll see you in the clinic tomorrow."

She picked up their glasses and went back into her little cottage. As she prepared for bed, she couldn't help thinking about poor Mike's burden. "I hope I wasn't too hard on him." However, sleep came easily to the exhausted nurse.

Chapter Nineteen

The next morning, Gabriela arrived breathless at the clinic. "Nurse Barbara, you miss the movie! Where were you? What happen? You help Rebita get first movie and then you not go!"

"First, tell me, did you like the movie? Did most people like the movie? Please tell me all about it. Could everyone see and hear okay?" Barbara was astounded that she'd forgotten all about the movie.

"Everyone like movie. Some people cry when finish. *Padre* make high table and set movie machine on. Everybody could see and movie machine so loud, everybody hear. But why you not there?" Gabriela answered and again questioned Barbara.

"Gabriela, something came up and I just forgot about it. I'm sorry. Next time I'll be there, I promise. I'm really glad you liked the movie. What was your favorite part?"

"So what it matter my favorite part? You not see movie, you not there last night!"

Gabriela's temper flared again.

"I've seen the movie before, when I lived in the United States, I remember it well, the part where the boy found his friend who'd been lost was always one of my favorites. Well, let's get to work." Barbara didn't feel like fawning over Gabriela until she felt important. She thought, "I'm just not up to it today."

Gabriela pouted for a half hour or so and then got into the swing of things with her normal enthusiasm. About eight thirty she walked by Barbara and whispered, "I liked the same part you did."

Dr. Kane arrived around nine a.m. "Good morning, Doctor." Barbara greeted him officially.

He took her cue. "Good morning, Nurse Barbara and Gabriela. Beautiful day it is in Honduras today."

Gabriela looked at him with a puzzled expression. "You okay, Dr. Kane? You never come work with smiling face. Must be sick!" She walked away, shaking her head in disbelief.

Barbara whispered as she walked by Mike, "Hey, don't overdo it! But it is great to see you smiling. You look ten years younger."

He answered, "Thanks, I think. Sorry we missed the movie last night."

The clinic was busier than usual and the day flew by. All the patients were talking about the movie, for most of them it was their first. They were all eagerly awaiting the one scheduled for next month.

Mike decided to stay in Rebita an extra night and get an early start in the morning. He invited Barbara to dinner in the village. "Don't worry, I'll order safe food for you. I promise it won't make you sick. What's the matter; can't trust a friend?"

"I'd like that very much. I do get tired of my own cooking and yes, I do trust my friends."

He had a glass of her famous iced tea while she showered and changed for their dinner out.

Barbara hadn't prepared for an evening out with a male friend since she was nineteen. She looked in the mirror and evaluated herself. "Pale by Honduran standards but deeply tanned according to my Swedish ancestry. No make up, self-cut short streaked sandy hair, dark circles under my eyes…oh well; what you see is what you get." Of course the streaked hair was the natural graying process that insidiously affects almost everyone after the age of fifty. She looked at herself in the mirror one last time and thought, "At least I'm clean and lean."

Mike looked at her approvingly when she joined him in the living room. He appeared nervous. "This isn't a date, you know. We're just a couple isolated friends catching a dinner together, that's all."

Barbara smiled. "I never thought it was anything else. Would you like some more tea? I'm going to have a small drink before we go. I'm always thirsty in this heat."

"No thanks. I'm good," Dr. Kane replied. He looked terribly uncomfortable and nervous sitting on the sofa, staring at the floor.

"Is something wrong? It's okay if you want to cancel the dinner invitation, I've plenty of food right here to fix a quick bite for one or two…."

"Would you mind if I did cancel? I tried to act friendly and normal to make you happy today. But it took a hell of a lot out of me. I know you were right telling me all that last night. However, I don't know if I can change. Old habits die hard. Today, being nice made me feel like a big phony. No one down here expects me to be nice. I have my reputation to protect." Mike spoke in a steady controlled voice.

"Well, I for one try to treat others as I want them to treat me, and Mike, I've seen your kind side. I think that's the real you. And this persona of a grumpy calloused jungle doctor is the phony. When you took care of Julio and the injured in Cabela, I understood why you were a doctor. Your parents must have been very proud of your medical skills as I'm sure your wife and children were, in their own ways."

"Listen, Barbara, I'm sure you mean well. But you don't know me. And stop with this goody goody act. No one believes in that damn golden rule shit anymore. Grow up! I'm leaving and don't say one more word to me, you think you know me and you're wrong. Dead wrong." He left abruptly, not wanting her to see the tears in his eyes. But she saw them.

Barbara watched him leave without saying a word. She prayed, "Dear God in Heaven, please watch over that stubborn Dr. Mike Kane. He's battling the demons of his past and right now he's not winning the fight. Please guide him and show him the way. I truly feel he's finally ready to face his memories and accept the good and the bad. Please, God help him, Mike doesn't even know he needs you. Yet, he needs you now more than he ever has. Thank you, Lord. Amen."

Life went on in the Peace Corps compound. Barbara assisted the local midwife in a few deliveries, broken bones were set, plus the normal mix of diarrhea, respiratory infections and scabies kept Gabriela and Barbara busy.

Barbara wrote long letters to each family member. She reassured each of them that the Peace Corps would let them know promptly if she had any serious problems. "They are very conscientious and take good care of our needs while we are here. Please rest assured that I'll be fine, I'm well and I feel like I'm doing something very important here."

Barbara's first journal was almost full; she kept all the letters from family, individually filed in chronological order. Sometimes when she was thinking about one in particular, she'd read that file and pray fervently for blessing and guidance for that one. This made her feel close to her family and to God. She felt her faith grow by leaps and bounds on the Honduran mountain.

A letter from Ethel had arrived two weeks ago inviting Barbara to a weekend party at the Peace Corps compound in El Progresso. It was scheduled for this weekend. Barbara had used the police telephone to call for a car to pick her up Thursday morning. She calculated she should arrive in Valencia by Friday night. She estimated she'd be back in Rebita by Tuesday or Wednesday. "A lot of traveling for a weekend, but it'll be worth it." Gabriela reassured her that she and a few of the first aid graduates could handle the clinic for a few days. So Barbara locked up her cottage and was off for a change-of-pace weekend.

Dr. Mike Kane arrived at the clinic on Tuesday. It was his third visit to Rebita since the painful night he told Barbara about his family. He felt a sense of loss when Gabriela said, "Nurse Barbara not here. She away for long weekend."

Barbara had been courteous, kind and professional during his last two visits to Rebita. She had not offered him any hospitality and he hadn't had the nerve to invite her to dinner again. He thought, "It's best this way. But *why* do I miss her when she's not here? That's never happened with any other volunteers. And I wish she'd get out of my mind. Maybe because she's the first to see me and accept me as a person, probably that's it. Yeah. And I screwed up royally. But it's better this way, I have a feeling she's already been hurt enough somewhere along the way. She doesn't need any more crap. I messed up Sue's life enough, no sense screwing up another life. Especially someone as special as Barbara. Good God! Did I say she was special? I better do my work and get the hell out of here!"

Barbara's rental SUV rolled into the compound at three p.m. Her driver and guide planned to stay the night with friends in the village. She paid them each a hearty tip as well as the fare, waving and smiling. "*Adiós amigos y gracias!*"

She unlocked the door, flopped her bag in a corner, opened the windows and turned on the ceiling fans; the cottage felt stuffy and stale from being closed up for a few days. Barbara splashed cold water on her face and brushed her hair. "That feels better!" She decided to walk to the village market to buy a few staples and on her way back, stop by the clinic.

Saturday morning, Barbara had bought a phone card in Valencia and called all the children, Eric, Alice, Mother Malone and, of course, Mom and Dad. It had been such a warm feeling just to hear their voices and reassure them that she was well and learning so much. "Yes, it's a very positive experience, hard work, long hours and appreciative sweet people. The time is going so fast!" She shared the story of the gift television and giving it to the village priest for once-a-month movie nights in the village square. Everyone was amazed that there were still people in the world who'd never seen a movie or television. She felt very lucky to have caught everyone at home. Her parents expressed concerns about Barbara's weight loss since they had shopped for a few new clothes for her in smaller sizes. She told them that most Peace Corps volunteers lose at least ten pounds due to a combination of heat, work pace, and dietary changes.

The mountain air was hot but not nearly as stifling as El Progresso. It had been a good weekend with Ethel and the other volunteers. It was nice to have a break from work, but an air of melancholy hung over the compound. Alvie had touched all their lives and she was gone. She had been the spark that ignited their laughter in other times. And it had been damn hard to laugh without her. If she'd have ever wanted a grand wake...well, that's just what they gave her. Since everyone was thinking about her all the time anyway, they unanimously dedicated the weekend to Alvie, God rest her soul.

Sharon and Ethel were their hosts in Valencia. Carolyn and Patrick were there from Cabela. Four other volunteers joined them from other villages in the valley. Those four had never had the pleasure of knowing Alvie. By the time the weekend was over, they felt like they did. They all agreed it was a good first step in truly accepting her passing. And therefore going on with their own lives. A few times Dr. Kane's name was mentioned with a bit of curiosity...Barbara never said a word. Her thoughts were interrupted; she turned around and smiled to see Lilia waving and running to catch up with her.

"Barbara, welcome back to Rebita! I miss you!"

She gave Lilia a hug. "I missed you too. How are you? How's the family?"

Lilia reported all was well, chatting away as they walked to market. They bought fruits and vegetables together and sat in a shaded café drinking cold sodas before going their separate ways. Lilia spoke enthusiastically about the movies she'd seen in the square. "I love movies. Movies show good stories, I cry, I laugh and sometimes I try help the people when I see danger. But never they listen."

"I'm glad you like the movies so much. Is it movie night next week again? I like movies too. Well, I better go back to the compound. I'm happy we met today, I'll see you later."

"*Adiós, amiga* Barbara."

Barbara walked back to the compound feeling contented and quite at home in the remote mountain village. She put her groceries away and walked to the clinic to check in with Gabriela.

Her mail had arrived Monday at the clinic. There was a small parcel from her mother, four letters, and two magazines. Barbara exchanged greetings with the dozen or so waiting patients.

Gabriela walked out of the small treatment room and saw Barbara. Being Gabriela, she couldn't just say *hola*. She shrieked and ran to her as if she hadn't seen Barbara for years. "I miss you, Nurse Barbara. Did you have good visit with friends? Yes? Clinic is good, no big emergencies." In hushed tones she said, "Dr. Kane is here today. I think he miss you, too." She winked at Barbara, smiled and walked back to the treatment room with the fresh gauze, tape and ointment she'd come out for in the first place.

Barbara took a deep breath and thought, "That girl can be downright annoying at times. But she's near irreplaceable here at the clinic. Besides, she's likable and fills this place with her amazing energy."

As Barbara gathered her mail to return to her cottage, Dr. Kane accompanied an older male from the back treatment room; his leg was in a fresh cast. The old man walked with the help of a young man (perhaps his son?) and a homemade cane. Dr. Kane spoke with them in rapid fluent Spanish and told them to come by the clinic each week to have the nurse check the leg and the cast. He reminded them to keep the leg elevated as much as possible. They thanked the doctor repeatedly; their gratitude was overflowing.

Dr. Kane smiled. "Welcome back, Nurse Barbara. We've missed you. I trust you had a pleasant time with your friends."

"Thank you, Dr. Kane. It's good to be back but it was also good to get away for a few days. I hope you've been well."

"I've no complaints…well, I best get back to work, can't keep the patients waiting longer than necessary."

"Indeed. See you later, Doctor Kane."

Back in her cottage, Barbara was anxious to open the package from her mother. She was pleased to find two pair of walking shorts, two pair of khaki slacks, three wash-and-wear blouses and two t-shirts. All in the smaller sizes she'd ask for. Barbara hastily tried on the shorts and slacks. Both were still a bit too big, but great improvements over the ones she'd been wearing. She said, "Oh, Mom, you are such a dear!" and decided her first letter that afternoon would be to her parents.

She opened the letter from Billy and Liz first, realizing she'd neglected to confirm anything with them for a visit this summer...they reported enjoying their first two weeks of summer vacation and wondering if she thought it wise of them to come to visit Rebita this summer. They had an alternate plan to go to Freeport, Bahamas, for ten days instead. Barbara thought, "I talked to them Saturday morning and they didn't mention coming here so they must've decided against Honduras for this summer. I'm glad. I still feel just a bit uneasy about this whole Cergio thing. I hope it's all behind us. Maybe they'll come during Christmas break or next summer. It's hard to believe I've already been here almost six months...yes, I think the Bahamas is a much better place for them to vacation this summer. They sounded happy on the phone and here in the letter, they're talking about their garden. Billy...a garden?!"

A letter from Janie was always extra special because she wrote less frequently than the others. She sounded good on the phone and her letter was also very positive. She reported working very hard, her character on the soap had a strong following, already opportunities for three movies have resulted from her TV work. Barbara smiled as she thought, "One was a top drawer theater movie with major stars, and to think she almost gave up her dream...Bill would've been so proud of her. Her circle of friends in New York City had been dubious at best, but now she seemed to socialize only with her work mates and her agent, Gloria. She sounds like a decent person who's genuinely trying to help Janie. Much better than that Arnie and his crowd. Well, I always knew she'd make it. She had that extra sparkle, really set her apart from the crowd. Janie even asked about visiting me in Honduras, maybe next summer. We'll see."

Mother Malone's was newsy and optimistic as usual but near the end she became almost sentimental. She adores having Jessica live with her. Barbara smiled as she read on, it was easy to hear the voice behind the words. "...and this Michael fellow, he does seem to be a nice enough young man, I just wonder if he's right for Jessica. The poor dear, I'm afraid she may just be afraid of becoming an old maid. They certainly don't seem to be in any hurry to move to the next level of commitment but that's fine with me. Maybe it's because they're older and have both been victims of failed love in the past; even though neither one has ever been married. I wonder if some of us who married so young may have had quite a different life had we waited till we were older to choose a life mate. But it seems men used to and probably still do...well, you know, prefer the young fresh sweet naive things we used to be. Well, as much as I miss your father-in- law, and I do, I'm relieved that I no longer have to play those games. Enough of that! Back to Jessica. She's a wonderful cook. Michael joins us for dinner several times a week. They get along so well, companionable as well as affectionate. Actually very sweet together.

"You're the only person in the world I'd say this to because we have a mutual understanding, I'd dare say even friendship. My grandchildren are the absolute joy of my life, especially Jessica. Whatever I went through to get to this point in my life was worth it because of them. I will always cherish you, dear, for including me in their lives and yours, the way things were with Bill…I appreciate that you didn't hold grudges against me. It is very hard for a mother to see her beloved child live a wayward life as an adult. Oh, how I do go on sometimes! I love you and miss you. Please be careful and take good care of yourself."

Barbara slowly folded Mother Malone's letter, unaware of the tears trickling down her cheeks. She sat in the cozy little living room suddenly flooded with unpleasant memories.

The last letter was from Alice. She wrote of her family, mutual friends and Lewiston. "Good news, I still go for brisk walks every morning. Bad news, I haven't found a dependable walking partner like you. Mostly I walk alone with my headset on. It's my 'reading time' as I listen to audio books and it's really a good use of my time. You wouldn't believe how busy I am between church work and helping with the grandchildren. And I really love it, sometimes I wonder, am I becoming *my* mother?!

"I dreamed about you for three nights in a row last week, the same strange dream every night. Didn't make any sense…but ever since I've had this premonition that we've lost you, Barbara. And not just for two years. I no longer feel such concern about danger for you; I know you'll come back to Lewiston. But I think you've moved on emotionally and will never feel at home here again. Good grief, does this make any sense to you? I must close. My grandbaby's crying. Guess nap time is over. WRITE ASAP! Love you and miss you, old pal o' mine….Alice."

Barbara's eyes were teary again but this time she had a wry smile on her face. She thought aloud, "Ahh, Alice, you know me too well and that's why we've been friends forever. I don't really know what your dream meant, but I feel more distance between Pennsylvania and Honduras than miles only. But I can't tell you what it's all about until I figure it out myself."

Her thoughts were interrupted by a persistent tapping on her front door. She was surprised to see Mike Kane, gray ponytail and all; she opened the door. "Well, hi. I must say this is a surprise! Won't you come in, it's a little more comfortable in here and I just happen to have a fresh pitcher of iced tea."

"Thanks. A glass of your iced tea is just what the doctor ordered. When you said, 'See you later,' this afternoon, I decided to take that as an invitation."

"Glad you did. Please, sit down. I'll get your tea."

"So you had a good weekend in Valencia?"

"Yes, it was great to spend time with Ethel and the others. We actually had an old-fashioned wake for Alvie. It was good for all of us. To know Alvie was to love her. Everyone feels such a loss."

"I'm glad you were able to go. You look nice. Is that a new outfit? Did you shop when you were down the mountain?"

"Actually, I asked my mother to do some shopping for me, my clothes wear out much faster down here and I needed smaller sizes. Mom did a great job in her selections. I just opened it this afternoon."

"Barbara, I want to apologize for my behavior a few weeks ago when I invited you out to dinner and then I walked out. I've been alone for a long time. My bodyguard is the closest thing to a friend I have. And you scare me, Barbara. It's not your fault. It's me."

She looked at him with teary eyes; her letters had put her in a very emotional state of mind. "Apology accepted. I never intended to frighten you. All I did was offer you friendship; sorry that was so scary."

"Barbara, you are not the problem, I am. I'd be proud to call you a friend...if you can put up with all my idiosyncrasies."

"That's very noble of you. I'd be proud to call you a friend too." But she did not invite him to share dinner with her.

Dr. Mike Kane hesitantly stood up, like he was waiting for something that didn't happen and finally said, "Barbara, I want you to know, I've missed you. I've thought about you more than I like to admit since that night I walked away. I'm serious when I say I'm sorry and I really want to be your friend."

"I've thought about you too, and I appreciate your apology. I'd just like to have some time to think about this friendship. Do you understand?"

"Of course I understand." But he didn't. "Well, I'll see you next month."

"Good-bye, Dr. Kane, and thanks for stopping by." Barbara slowly closed the door, leaning against it, and slid to the floor. Sitting there with her knees pulled in front of her, tears steaming down her cheeks, she prayed, "Dear God, *where* do I belong? Please help me find contentment for my heart and mind."

Chapter Twenty

BILLY

"Good morning, Mrs. Malone. 'Tis grand to wake up beside you in the Bahamas."

"Good morning to you, Mr. Malone. I must say; 'tis wonderful to wake up with you in paradise as well." Liz cuddled up to Billy.

He laughed tenderly and gently stroked her hair. "What *else* would you like to do today, Liz? It's another gorgeous day."

"What's your hurry, Billy? We've got all day." And she beguilingly snuggled against him. "I don't know...have you ever scuba dived, Billy? Would you like to take lessons? I think it might be fun."

An hour later, after their honeymoon diversion, with the rosy glow of fulfilled love and happiness, they resumed the scuba diving discussion.

"I had lessons at the YMCA when I was a kid. But I'd be up for a refresher course. I've heard the coral reefs are fantastic. Great idea. Are you staying in bed till noon, Mrs. Malone?"

Liz swung her legs over the bed. "No way, I'm coming! I'll hate myself if I waste a beautiful day just being lazy. We've places to go, people to see, scuba lessons to take. But first let's get some breakfast, I'm starved."

Billy gave his beautiful wife a morning kiss. "You know I'm kinda glad Mom didn't encourage us to go to Honduras. I think this honeymoon trip has been just about perfect."

"What do you mean 'about perfect'? I think it's been totally perfect! We've got each other and we've been in paradise for five days already. What more could we possibly want?"

"How about another seven days in paradise?" Billy teased.

"You're kidding, aren't you?" Liz gave him a puzzled look.

"While you were sleeping, I've been busy...I talked to the day manager and received a special discount for staying an additional seven days. Called the airline and used the hotel discount to pay the penalty for changing our tickets. Also called the neighbor to keep our garden watered for an extra week. I want to call Morfar and Mormor to let them know we're staying longer than originally planned, in case of an emergency. What do you think?"

"Billy Malone, you're not kidding, are you?" Her smile lit up the room. She wrapped her arms around him and nearly smothered him with kisses. "Thank you, Billy. Thank you so much. I love it here, I love you and I love being your wife."

After another day of water sports and beach combing, they freshened up for a late dinner at the hotel restaurant. Their table had a spectacular view of the moonlight dancing on the rhythmic waves of the Atlantic. A smoldering duo sang an enchanting mix of reggae and blues accompanied by a pianist. Already deeply tanned, Liz and Billy felt all was well in their world. Neither one had ever felt as happy and content as they did that night.

Liz toasted her husband. "I wish this moment could last forever. My life is perfect in this place with you tonight."

Billy took her hands and they glided onto the dance floor. They held each other tenderly as they danced to "Bridge Over Troubled Waters." Billy whispered, "I'll never forget this night, the way you look in your little black dress. Ah...Liz, I love you, totally."

She laid her head on his shoulder and whispered, "As I do you, Billy."

Their days and nights in Freeport blended together in a blissful blur. Reality hit them when they realized they'd have to fly home the next day. They went for a walk on the beach; the pulsating sounds of the surf provided their background music. "Billy, this has been the happiest two weeks of my life. I'm so glad we came."

He gently embraced her. "Me too. I think we should come back every year, just you and me."

They stood watching the waves come and go. It was a dark overcast night and the wind was picking up. Her hair blew in Billy's face. "Ahh, don't I love the smell of your shampoo and the sea mixed together like this? Do we *really* have to go back, Liz?"

"Not till tomorrow! I'll race you back to the hotel!"

And they were off to enjoy every minute of their time left in paradise. They picked up two Bahama Mama drinks at the poolside bar and headed for the elevator.

Chapter Twenty-one

BOBBY

"Your mother called today and said to tell you hello, she says she's okay and has sent a letter explaining her lapse in communication. Very apologetic, she was."

Bobby sighed. "Thanks, Morfar, what a relief to know she's alive and well."

"But I think something's happened, she sounded like she was under a lot of strain. Not up to talking about what was on her mind. Said she's started to write again and a letter is on the way.... So how're you doing, Bobby? I heard you had a lady friend to bring home, any truth to that rumor?"

"Well, yes and no. I have a special friend, Ashley. But she's not ready to meet my family yet until she sees where we are headed as a couple. She's wonderful and beautiful. She's in Cleveland visiting her revered grandmother for a couple weeks. I can hardly wait till she returns. God, I miss her!"

"Bobby, sounds like you got it bad, real bad. This Ashley girl must really be something to have my 'love 'em and leave 'em' grandson broodin' his heart out while she's off visitin' her grandmother. I like a girl who makes time for her grandparents. Yep, I'd say that's a real good sign."

Bobby couldn't help smiling at Morfar's comments. "I'll let you know when I'm coming, maybe even this weekend for a Memorial Day picnic. I'm not sure yet. I'm glad I was here for your call, was just on my way out for a few hours to catch up at the office."

"I gotta admit I'm impressed with your work ethic. Do you like your lawyerin' work any better than before? Shame to study all those years and then hate what you're doin'; course there are other areas of law you could pursue. Did you ever think of changin' to a field you might like better?" Morfar asked.

"All the time, I'm thinking about a career change. Yes, I still detest my work, my work atmosphere, the whole thing and I don't respect my manager, *but* I met Ashley there. She was working for the CEO while his regular secretary was off for maternity leave. She has an MBA and prefers to work as a secretary for a temp agency, says it's less stressful. Also, does part-time modeling. Overall, a very remarkable girl. She's part Irish, German and Swedish with the voice of an angel."

"I sure hope you figure out what it is you want. Heck of a lot easier to make a livin' when you get paid for doin' somethin' you like. Well, I suppose I best give this telephone a rest, we've been burnin' the wires for a good ten minutes now."

"Give me a couple more minutes, Morfar. Mom told me I had to pay my dues and I should stick it out for two years, with no less than one year. I've been there almost a year. What do you think?" Bobby asked. He'd always had the utmost respect for his grandfather's opinion.

Morfar sighed. "I think that's something you have to decide for yourself, Bobby. It ain't easy figurin' out what you wanna do with your life. If it makes you feel any better, I think you're on the right track."

"Thanks, Morfar. How's Mormor? Haven't talked to her in ages."

"She'll be mad at me for callin' you while she was out. She went for a'celebration walk' with our neighbor, Gladys. After the phone call from your mother, Mormor felt better than she has in weeks."

"Please tell her I miss her and I'll call later to talk to her. Thanks for being there for me, Morfar. Stay well and I'll see you soon."

"You take care of yourself, Bobby-Boy; we're very proud of you. Good-bye."

When Bobby returned from the office late that afternoon, he was pleased to hear Ashley's sweet voice on the answering machine. She finally gave him her grandmother's phone number.

He grabbed a bottle of water and called her. The melodic voice of a young child answered on the third ring. "Hello, Collins residence. May I help you?"

"Hello. May I please speak to Ashley?"

The child answered, "Of course, she'll be right here." Then he turned and called out, "*Mommy*, it's a man and it's for you." Bobby's world stopped spinning for a moment; a moment that felt like an eternity.

Ashley was on the line almost immediately. "Hello."

Bobby was unable to make himself speak.

"Hello, who is this?"

Still no answer from Bobby.

Then he heard her say to someone in the room, her grandmother? "Maybe we should get this number changed...."

"NO, no, don't hang up, Ashley! It's me, Bob."

"Bob! It's so good to hear your voice again. I've been thinking about you a lot actually. I've even talked to my grandmother about you. But why didn't you answer when I came to the phone...." Her voice trailed off....it suddenly dawned on her. "Mommy."

"I guess I was left speechless, which rarely happens to a lawyer as you know. The child sounds wonderful, how old is it and what is the name? Do you have any more surprises?" He knew his voice was a little flat, but he was doing the best he could given the situation. Bobby was still trying to absorb if and how that one little word might've changed his feelings or his mind about Ashley.

"I didn't want to get involved with anyone at all, then you came along and it was so easy and so comfortable. Then I didn't know how to tell you about Danny. He's five, his birthday was last Wednesday. We had a small party for him, took ten little boys and a few parents to Chuckie Cheese's Pizza. They had a great time. He's such a dear. He's handsome, smart, well mannered and I love him so much."

"I, ah...don't know what I'm supposed to say now. Where's Danny's father?"

"I really don't know. He dumped me before I even knew I was pregnant. I doubt if he'd even remember me. I met him on spring break in Florida. I was twenty. We were all out clubbing...I know that sounds irresponsible. It was." Ashley spoke softly and with a reluctance that only raw courage could overcome.

"But I don't understand why you work and live in a city several hours away from your child...." Bobby was truly puzzled by the entire situation.

"Well, one thing just kind of led to another...I never expected my life to be like this. I know it looks strange from the outside, but it's okay. Guess it's safe to say I'm in a transition phase right now. I don't know how everything will turn out."

"Ashley, no one ever knows how their life will evolve. Fourteen months ago I'd never have believed anyone who'd have told me my mother would be living in a tropical mountain village that doesn't even have plumbing, electricity or proper phone service, much less calling the natives her friends! That's what makes it all so interesting. We just never know."

"Have you heard from your mother yet?"

"Just today, she called my grandparents and my grandfather called me. Something's happened, but she's okay. She told him a letter is on the way but what about you, Ashley? A child is an adjustment for me. However, Danny certainly doesn't change the way I feel about his mother."

"Do you really mean that, Bob?"

"Of course I do. Ash, I've missed you more than you'll ever know; when are you coming back? Will you bring Danny with you? I want to meet him."

"I'm not coming back. I must stay here and look after Grandma. She's not doing so well. She's always been active and healthy. But now she's developed health problems. She should've called and told me when it started, but she's stubborn and proud. My mother lives here too. She works terribly long hours and is totally absorbed in her work as a researcher at Case Western. She didn't even notice Grandma's precarious state of health. Danny has been trying to take care of her, bless his heart.

"I'm an only child, an only grandchild, no cousins and both parents were 'only children' too. So she has no one else. She lives in this extraordinary old mansion on Lake Erie. Her father built it as a wedding gift for her mother just after WWI.

"Now to explain how Danny came to live with his great-grandmother. My father was furious when he realized I'd soon be a statistic for unwed motherhood. I was six months pregnant; he knew where I could still get an abortion. He insisted Danny would ruin the family bloodline. He ordered me to have an abortion. I refused. Mom backed me and so did Grandma. My paternal grandparents died before I was born.

"My parents' marriage had been on the rocks since I could remember. Mom moved in with Grandma and me. She said she finally had a good reason to leave him. We all prepared for and helped take care of the baby after he was born. Dad continued to pay for my education and give me a monthly stipend. But it wasn't a sacrificial gift. He's well off after so many years as a surgeon.

"Since I had so much help with the baby, I increased my study time and credit load. I graduated two semesters early. Immediately after that I began the Master's of Business Administration program at Case Western. Again I went full speed ahead and completed it in eighteen months. I worked fourteen hour days for six months and one day I just quit. No job satisfaction. I didn't want to repeat my parents' life. So I decided to change careers. Danny was getting cuter each day and I was tired of being tired and missing so much of his life. I joined a temp agency and eventually was transferred to your town for the assignment at your firm, due to my 'exceptional' background and skills.

"The most painful thing about all this is my father's total rejection of Danny. He refuses to acknowledge his existence and talks to me about almost everything *except* my son. He refuses to meet him. One day Danny and I were at the museum, and we accidentally bumped into my father. He had a date with him and started to introduce me. As soon as he saw my child, he turned his head and walked away like he didn't even know me. I hope and pray he'll someday meet Danny and accept him for the fine little boy he is. But I don't have my hopes up about it ever happening." Her soft angelic voice sounded very sad.

"Your father sounds like a very obstinate man, but surely he'll come around eventually. If you're not coming back for awhile, may I come see you in Cleveland, meet Danny, your grandmother and parents?"

"I must say you're persistent. Okay. Grandma said she wanted to meet you; it was her idea to leave a message and then have Danny answer the phone. She said it would be a good test of your mettle and intentions!" Ashley's face glowed with a radiance that only love could create. Her grandmother watched from across the room approvingly.

"Well, how about next weekend? It's Memorial Day and I could stay four days…God, I miss you, Ashley."

She spoke softly. "I've missed you, too. Grandma's been teasing me; she says every topic of conversation goes back to 'Bob.' You can stay here, we have empty guest rooms. I can hardly wait to see you again."

When they finished talking, he called Morfar and Mormor to tell them of his change of plans. "I was shocked when this child said 'Mommy,' and then Ashley came to the phone. I lost my voice for a minute or so. It felt like a long time before I was conscious of my reaction. But he sounds like such a nice little boy, has excellent manners. Can you believe her father refuses to acknowledge the child's existence because Ashley is an unwed mother? He has only one child and one grandchild. I found his extreme obstinate nature very strange. Her mother sounds like a workaholic. The grandmother is the one Ashley is really close to. Anyway, I hope you can forgive me for not coming to Lewiston. She made me an offer I just couldn't refuse."

Mormor smiled and thought, "The idea of seeing Ashley in two days has Bobby in such a dither. I hope he won't be disappointed with his reception in Cleveland, and hits it off well with little Danny. It would be nice to have a young child around again!"

Morfar and Mormor decided to have their afternoon tea on the front porch; it was an unusually warm spring day. Morfar took a sip of his tea as he slowly rocked back and forth in his rocking chair. "I always said, when Bobby falls in love, he'll fall fast and hard. And I think it's fair to say the boy's taken the fall."

Mormor's chair rocked at a rapid steady clip as her mind churned, creating new to-do lists. "I wish Barbara was here but I guess our lives will have to go on…she'll meet them eventually. I can hardly wait to meet Ashley and the little boy myself. I'd say it's about time he think about settling down and raising a family. I'll have to finish up his quilt, sounds like we'll be needin' another weddin' gift before long."

"Hold on there, woman! You're gettin' way 'head of yourself agin'. They may not even be seein' each other after Bobby meets the boy. Give 'em a little time." Morfar reached over for his wife's hand, shook his head and smiled. "It's darn nice sittin' here on the porch with you; the years have been mostly good to us. Wouldn't you say?"

She gently squeezed his hand as they sat in their rocking chairs. "'Tis true, life has been kind to us." She nodded off into a short nap with a sweet smile on her no longer young but still beautiful face.

Morfar lifted her hand and softly kissed it. He thought, "I was surely blessed to have this good woman as my life partner."

Traffic was heavy as Bobby drove to Cleveland for the Memorial Day Weekend. Ashley had given him flawless directions. Soon he was driving up a tree-lined driveway to an impressive mansion from another time. He left his bags in the car and walked up the veranda steps to ring the doorbell. A middle-aged uniformed housekeeper greeted him pleasantly. "Mr. Bob Malone, I presume."

"Yes, ma'am. Nice to meet you, I'm here to see Ashley Collins."

"Of course, we've been expecting you. I'm Wanda, been with Mrs. Miles near forty years now. Great family, what there is of them. Almost feel like Ashley's one of my own."

As they were about to enter the formal sitting room, Ashley and Danny burst in through the front door. She was even more beautiful than he'd remembered…the boy stopped and looked at him evenly. Ashley said, "Danny, I want you to meet Bob Malone. He's a special friend of Mommy's. I met him when I was away working in Pennsylvania. He's come the whole way to Cleveland just to meet you."

Bob couldn't help smiling at the small serious boy. He walked over to him and bent down to be eye level and said, "I've heard really good things about you, Danny. It's nice to meet you." Bob extended his hand to shake hands with the boy.

Danny stood with his hands clasped behind his back, resolutely staring at the strange man in his home. "Why did you want to meet me?"

"I wanted to meet you because your mommy is a special friend of mine. You really look a lot like her you know."

"Yes, I know that. Do you always try to meet little boys when you are friends with their mommies?"

"Well, to tell you the truth, your mommy is the first friend I've had who had a little boy. So, Danny, that makes you the first little boy I've met, maybe since I was a little boy."

Danny didn't move a muscle; then he said very softly, "Really?"

Bob continued to ignore Wanda and Ashley as he concentrated on the boy. "Really. May I ask you a question?"

Danny nodded.

"Do you question all your mommies friends like this when they come to visit?"

"Mommy doesn't have other friends, just me."

"Could I be your friend? What'a you say, Danny?"

He bit his lip and studied Bob closely, then looked at Ashley. She smiled at him and nodded her head; he slowly pulled his right hand from behind his back and extended it to Bob. "Okay, guess we can *try* to be friends."

As he stood back up he heard the shuffle of a walker on the shiny hardwood floors and he turned to meet the steely gray gaze of the family matriarch. "And you must be the famous Bob Malone. Turn around, young man. Yes, yes, he's got a good build to him, Ashley." With a sly smile, she winked at Ashley and nodded approvingly.

"*Grandma! Please!* Good grief, Bob, you'll feel like you're in the Inquisition if this keeps up. Wanda, please get us all nice drinks of ice water. Grandma, Danny, and Bob, let's all go sit down and relax a bit before dinner."

Grandma shuffled in with her walker followed by her great grandson. Ashley and Bob touched hands. He grinned and whispered, "Thanks for saving me!"

Her sparkling eyes smiled back at him. "I'm so happy you're here."

Grandma took control immediately after situating herself in her favorite chair. Danny proudly sat beside her, obviously very territorial with his women. He might share his mommy with a friend, but there was no chance he'd share any part of his great-grandmother with anyone. "So, Ashley tells me you're a great lawyer and that you hate bein' a lawyer. So what do ya wanna do with yourself if you wanna quit bein' a lawyer?"

Ashley rolled her eyes but held her tongue.

Bobby answered, "I'm really not quite sure, ma'am. I've got a few options. I've been gaining work experience and biding my time."

"I don't usually come on this strong but I need some answers. I'm a sick old woman and Ashley is my only grandchild. The apple of my eye. Sure she has parents but they're nearly hopeless human beings, so selfish and into their own interests. I just want to know your intentions with Ashley. She's been hurt once and it will be over my dead body before anyone else will get away with hurting that girl again. Do you understand?"

"Yes, I understand. Sometimes bad times help us appreciate the good times that much more. Mrs. Miles, I will try hard to protect Ashley from harm. I love your granddaughter with such intensity…I never would've believed this kind of love possible before I met Ashley Collins. She's a wonderful girl. And I think Danny and I will be great friends."

"You just might be good enough for my Ashley; we'll see before the weekend's out." Grandma's cool gaze bored through him like a drill.

Wanda came in with four tall glasses of ice water. "Thanks, Wanda, that's just what we need to cool down in here," Ashley told her as she took a deep breath as if preparing for a major confrontation.

Danny was on high alert. "I thought you were friends with my mommy, now you say you love her. Which is it, Mr. Bob?"

Bob looked at the worried boy and smiled. "I am your friend and your mommy's friend. Aren't friends supposed to love each other?"

"I guess so." The earnest little boy looked confused.

Wanda said, "Hey, Danny, could you help me make some special pudding for dinner? I could really use a helper."

He reluctantly stood to follow the housekeeper; Ashley mouthed a big "thank you" to Wanda as he walked away. Wanda winked at them and said, "Good luck to you folks." She smiled as she walked away and thought, "You'se gonna need all the luck you can get!"

"So, just what are we talking about here, young man?" Grandma demanded an answer.

"Well, huh…." He looked at Ashley for help. She just sat there looking gorgeous, watching him squirm with a faint smile and that twinkle in her eyes.

"I want to live my life with Ashley as my wife. I want to cherish our love and raise our children and little Danny. I am a lawyer. I will provide an adequate income, although not to the grand style of your home. I have a small trust fund. I want to marry your granddaughter, Mrs. Miles."

Bobby turned to Ashley and asked, "I love you, Ashley, will you be my wife?"

Grandma turned to her. "Well, what's it gonna be, Ashley? Don't be shy. Do you love this young man enough to marry him?

"I love him more than the whole world, Grandma." Then she turned to Bob. "But I'd like a courtship to give Danny a chance to adjust to the idea. Is that okay with you, Bob?"

Grandma interjected, "Maybe yes and maybe no, how long are you planning to give Danny to adjust?"

"I don't know, as much time as it takes. Why the rush?"

"I have my reasons, young lady! Now why don't you two go for a walk or something while I take a short rest. All this excitement has worn me out."

"Your grandma's a character! Somehow reminds me of my mormor and Grandmother Malone rolled into one."

When they were safely on the veranda they stopped and embraced. "I missed you so much, Bob Malone." And she kissed him.

Bobby's knees felt weak. "Oh God, Ashley, I've missed you too. I've told my family about you. They're dying to meet the woman who stopped me cold. Will you really be my wife, Ashley? I love you. And I can't imagine living without you."

"I guess you could tell that I've talked to Grandma about you." She looked embarrassed to admit it.

He answered, "I'm flattered and would've been hurt if you hadn't!"

Later he played catch with Danny and was impressed with the boy's coordination. After dinner he and Ashley played table games with him. By bedtime Danny kissed him on the cheek and whispered, "Would you like to see my secret cabin tomorrow?"

Bobby answered, "That'd be great, but how can it be a secret if you show me?"

Danny smiled and motioned for Bob to come closer. "Cause I know I can trust you." Bob felt the warmth of the two small arms as they circled his neck in an embrace, then he whispered, "You *really* wanna be my daddy, don't you?"

Bob was tongue-tied and felt the heat in his neck and face as he blushed. He thought, "How can this little kid do this to me? I'm supposed to be a fast-thinking, smooth-talking lawyer!"

He hugged the boy, and said, "Well, I'll have to talk to your mommy about that!"

Ashley took her time with Danny's bedtime rituals. Bob became engrossed with the Economist magazine and didn't notice the attractive, tall, middle-aged woman who walked in and sat down on the dark burgundy sofa across the room from him. She sat quietly watching him as she sipped her wine. Suddenly, she cleared her throat to get his attention.

A startled Bobby looked up from his reading. "Oh, hello. You must be Mrs. Collins. I'm Bob Malone, a friend of Ashley's."

She walked over and shook his hand firmly. "Good to meet you, young man. I'm not Mrs. Collins anymore; I took my maiden name back after the divorce, Joyce Miles. Please, just call me Joyce."

"Nice to meet you, Joyce. Your daughter is a very special person."

"We like her. I've heard about you. Seems Miss Ashley is quite taken with you. So you're an attorney, huh?"

"Yes, ma'am. And you're a research scientist? Are you currently working on an interesting project?"

"Top secret government stuff. Nothing that would be of interest to you. Have you met Mother, Wanda and Master Danny, yet?"

"Yes I have; great family. Danny is like a breath of fresh air, so full of life. I've never been around kids much. I like your grandson."

"I hardly think of myself as a grandmother, although, technically I suppose I am. My mother is Grandmother Superior; I'm just Joyce…without the joy. I was a piss-poor mother to Ashley; don't get me wrong, I like her. She's a great kid. But she's not at all like me or her father, thank God!"

For the second time within the hour, Bob found himself without words. He thought, "This woman is soo unlike my mother. If Joyce raised her, then how did Ashley turn out to be such a sweet person?" He said, "Ashley is certainly a daughter to be proud of."

"I know. Thank Grandma for that. So, Bob, tell me about your family. Any brothers or sisters? Are your parents still married to each other? Is anybody's parents still married to each other?!"

"My parents were still married when my father died of a heart attack last summer. Since then my mother joined the Peace Corps and is nursing in a remote village in the mountains of Honduras."

"My God! Your mother in the Peace Corps? Please go on." Her demeanor quickly changed from bored to attentive and interested.

"I have an older brother, Billy, he's a teacher and married a very nice girl last fall. She's also a teacher. My older sister, Jessica, just relocated back to our hometown, Lewiston. She now lives with Grandmother Malone. They're both very happy with the arrangement. Jess is a physical therapist and works at the hospital. My little sister, Janie, is an actress in New York City. She has a part in one of the daytime soaps and is working on some movie roles now. My maternal grandparents are well and active. My dad was an only child. My mom has a brother in California and I have three much younger cousins there. I also have two cousins in North Carolina, the children of my mother's deceased sister. We don't see each other very often anymore, but we stay in touch and cherish the times we do have with each other."

"Hell, you sound like a solid family man if ever there was one! Compared to us your family is like a whole clan. Interesting diversification, each one of you must be strong in your own right. I like that. And your mother down in the tropical mountain jungles. Cool." She took another long sip of her wine.

Ashley walked in with a smile. "Oh, hi, Mom, I see you've met Bob. Nice guy, isn't he? Finally got Danny to sleep, I tried to read him stories but all he wanted to do was talk about Bob! He's so excited." She walked over and kissed Bob lightly on the lips. "I hope Mom hasn't scared you off. She tries hard to be tough, but she's really an old softy, aren't you, Mom?"

"Young lady, that's enough out of you." But she smiled knowingly at the young couple as if reading their minds.

Grandmother came shuffling into the room. "Are you two girls at it again? I declare, I can't turn my back for a second. Is my little guy in bed already? He's had a big day." She settled into a chair and propped her feet up on a large hassock.

Bobby cleared his throat. "I've asked Ashley to be my wife. She said yes. I'd like to have your blessings on our marriage. I'd like to have a chance to be the daddy little Danny deserves and wants."

"Well, it seems we've only met and you're itchin' to crawl in bed with my little girl. Don't know if she's thought this through or not…but I say what the hell is the hurry?" With that Joyce poured herself another drink of wine.

"Mother, please stop carrying on like this."

"Joyce, I think that's quite enough. I expect you to use your best manners with Bob. He's done nothing to you. He is not like Charles and he is not your enemy." Grandma's voice was very firm. After that Joyce sat on the sofa very quietly. Then Grandma asked Ashley, "Are you sure, dear?"

Ashley answered, "I've never felt so certain about anything in my life. Danny likes him too. And of course, Bob likes Danny because they're both simply irresistible."

"I must ask you two girls to leave Bob and me alone for a few minutes." Joyce rolled her eyes and sighed. "Well excuse us..." and mother and daughter made a dramatic exit.

Grandma motioned for Bob to pull a chair up beside her. "Young man, did you plan to ask my granddaughter to marry you when you drove out here today?"

"Well, I was hoping to, but I didn't really know what kind of a reception I'd get. I mean I only learned about Danny two days ago. I knew I loved Ashley and thinking of a future without her in it...was well, just plain depressing," Bobby answered honestly.

"So, now that you've spent a little time with Danny, you still want Ashley even though she's a package deal?" The eighty-five-year-old grandmother watched his every reaction; her sharp brown eyes seemed to read his mind.

Without even a brief hesitation he responded, "Absolutely. I'd be proud to be the boy's father, ma'am."

"You may wonder why I'm so pushy about Ashley's future. My time is very limited. Doc says I may have a month or two. Probably less. I know Joyce can take care of herself. And perhaps Ashley could take care of herself, but with Danny, I think she could use some help. When she came home and told me about you, she was ready to run and hide behind the boy. I insisted she call you and let the chips fall as they may. I didn't know what to expect, but I like you."

"Does Ashley know?"

"Of course not. She has enough on her mind. Now with a weddin' to plan. Do you think your family would come to Cleveland for their brother's weddin'?"

"I'm sure they will, once they get over the shock of their bachelor brother getting married! Shouldn't I talk to Ashley's father?"

"He's agreed to come to breakfast tomorrow morning. Charles Collins, M.D. He's a cold fish and a real snob, but he's her father. I want to see my granddaughter happily married before I die, and I don't have much time left. That's the rush."

Bobby's mind was spinning when he went to bed that night. He finally managed to sleep a couple hours before daylight. He showered in preparation for the day, taking extra care to impress her surgeon father.

Ashley was up early, too. They met accidentally in the expansive upstairs hallway. "Good morning, Bob. How'd you sleep?"

"Good morning to you, Ashley, my sweet. I slept well enough. Lots to think about, you know. How about you?"

"I slept okay. Dad's coming for breakfast this morning. Mom should have left a half hour ago for work, I hope she did. When he comes, there's always a lot of commotion. I hope he's nice to you. If not, please don't take it personally."

She kissed him lightly on the cheek and they walked to the breakfast room hand in hand as if to give each other courage.

Grandma was seated at the head of the table. A distinguished, tall, middle-aged graying male sat to her left. When they walked in, he stood and extended his arms to embrace his only child. "Ashley, darling! Wonderful to see you."

"Good to see you too, Dad. I'd like to introduce you to my special friend, Bob Malone."

"Well, special friend, huh?" Dr. Collins raised his eyebrows questioningly as he shook hands with Bob. "Nice to meet you, young man. So how long have you and Ashley been friends?"

"We've known each other about three months, sir," Bob answered. He refused to allow this pompous man make him squirm.

Ashley interrupted, "Grandma, Wanda is giving Danny his breakfast in the kitchen this morning." She glanced at her father and true to character, he ignored her reference to his grandson. Ashley felt the tension build as it always did when she was with her father.

"That's fine, dear," Grandma answered softly and smiled at her granddaughter with enough warmth to melt an iceberg.

"So, young man, what do you do to make a living?"

"I'm a lawyer, sir. And I want to marry your daughter. I love her with all my heart and want to spend my life with her. I want to be a father to Danny. He's a great little guy. It's a shame you've refused to get to know him while you've had the chance." Bob's directness surprised Ashley and her Grandma. They unconsciously held their breaths for several seconds.

"Shame! How dare you! What do you know about shame? The shame is *she* conceived and carried a baby out of wedlock. I will never accept that bastard child as *my* grandchild. And *you* have the nerve to tell me you want to marry *my* daughter. My guess is you've already asked her." He turned to Ashley who sat in her chair with silent tears rolling down her cheeks. "And you, young lady, what did you say? Do you want to marry this man?"

"Yes I do, Dad. I accepted his proposal. We're getting married in three weeks. I'd like you to be at the wedding. It's going to be here at Grandma's. *And don't you ever* call my son a bastard again. I swear if you do, I'll never speak to you. I just won't tolerate that. The wedding will be small, just family and a few close friends. And you won't have to pay for a thing."

"Charles, would you like some more coffee? Perhaps if we eat our breakfast and get a little nourishment, we'll be able to discuss things a little more civilly." Grandma's suggestion was a gratefully accepted truce.

Dr. Collins ate as if nothing had happened at all. Ashley's appetite was nil as was Bob's. Grandma ate a slice of toast because that was about all her digestive system could tolerate. And she managed to keep a superficial conversation going....

"So, tell me about your family, young man? What kind of people do you come from?" Dr. Colllins stared at Bob, waiting for an answer.

Bob told him the same report he'd given Ashley's mother the day before. "Your mother in the Peace Corps, my God! Do you have any other nuts in your family?"

Before Bob could respond to Dr. Collins' rude comment, Grandma pulled out her daily planner. "Let's set the date. Charles, make sure you mark your calendar; I'll *never* forgive you if you miss Ashley's wedding."

Bob noticed Dr. Collins' respect for his former mother-in-law. He wondered, "Is she the only person he respects?" He found their relationship very curious and interesting and decided Ashley's father was the most arrogant dislikable man he'd ever had the misfortune of meeting.

Grandma assured Ashley's father that the women of the family would take care of all the details. He stood to leave, shook hands with Bob and announced he wanted all wedding expenses charged to him. "After all I have only one little girl and I insist on doing right by her. I just don't understand what the hurry is. Well, thanks for breakfast; I must get to the hospital."

Ashley hugged her Grandma. "How can you be so nice to him when he's so self-righteous and condescending. If he wasn't my father, I swear I'd never speak to him again."

"Ah, my dear, that's just it. Like it or not, he is your father. And he's a fine surgeon. Your mother loved him enough to marry him twenty-seven years ago. Don't forget that." Grandma excused herself to take a morning rest.

Ashley and Bob took Danny to the park for a picnic lunch. The next two days passed quickly and the wedding date was set. Bob left for Pennsylvania a changed and very happy, though somewhat frightened, young man on Tuesday evening. He had some important phone calls to make. He knew he'd shock his family and thought, "Hell, the speed of this wedding was enough to shock me and I was there. I *saw* it coming."

Chapter Twenty-two

JANIE

"Thank God for weekends," Janie mumbled as she forced herself out of bed and opened the shades to a beautiful sunny day. Her work weeks left her exhausted.

The phone rang. It was Gloria. She chided, "Doll, looks to me like you're tryin' to catch up on ten years' worth of actin' in six months. Better slow down or you'll burn yourself out. Don't overdo it, sweetie. Your big break was a long time comin'."

Janie responded, "Gloria, you tried so hard to convince me to go to the photo op public relations party last night. I just couldn't do it. I'm sorry. I'll try to be more acquiescent to your suggestions. God knows you've always been there for me. And I wouldn't have my contracts and work if it wasn't for you.

"*Maybe* you're right, *maybe* I am burning myself out…*maybe* I need to prioritize my life, *but* the truth of the matter is, I'm scared. Work gives me excuses to avoid people and avoid the pain that has been part of every relationship I've ever had. Arnie was the absolute pits. My track record proves I'm a poor judge of character, so I prefer to work."

"I don't know anyone who hasn't been burned at least once by trustin' others. Doesn't matter, you have to slow down and learn from your mistakes. Everybody does. Work is good. Socializin' and smoozin' is part of the game, too. I'll forgive you this time, but you damn well better not stand me up again…at least not without a damn good excuse!" Gloria barked and hung up.

Janie knew she deserved it, but still she felt stupid and inadequate. She sighed. "Shit!"

The phone interrupted her pity party. "Hey, Bobby! Great to hear a friendly voice, haven't talked to you in ages. How're you doing? What's new?"

"Are you sitting down?" he asked. "I've got some news for you."

Janie sat down with a sense of doom. "Has something happened to Mom?"

"No, nothing like that, Mom's fine as far as I know. I've got news about me. I've met someone and we're getting married in three weeks. I want you to be at our wedding. It'll be in Cleveland."

"*What* did you say? My God. Bobby, are you sure about this? Normal people don't just get married in *three weeks*! Have you had a recent head injury? Are you okay?! I can't believe this! I think you should see a shrink! Who is she? How long have you known her? Three fucking weeks! Ah, God, Bobby...this seems pretty damn unstable to me. And I'm supposed to be the family expert on instability, remember?"

He listened and finally sighed. "Are you done ranting yet, Janie? No, I've had no head injuries. Her name is Ashley. You'll like her; she's nothing short of wonderful. I've known her for three months. We met at work. She has no siblings but she does have a five-year-old son. His name is Danny, you'll love him too. He's a great little boy. And no, she's never been married."

"But why the rush? Three weeks!" Janie still felt completely blind sided.

"Well, it's kind of a long story. So, I'll skip ahead to the end. Ashley has workaholic parents. Both very successful. So her maternal grandmother raised her in the family mansion on Lake Erie. She and her grandmother are very close. Ashley doesn't know, but her grandmother has terminal cancer *and* has chosen not to take any treatment. Her doctor told her last week that she'll be lucky if she has two months left. She wants to see Ashley safely married before she dies. And no, I don't feel I'm being manipulated. I love Ashley and I wanted to marry her anyway. Little Danny is a great kid, too. I think I'm ready to be a father and a husband. I'm excited."

"I don't know what to say, Bobby. I'm just sorta in shock here. Whew!"

"I know it all seems kind of sudden. But trust me, I feel good about the whole thing. We're not having a big wedding, but I'm sure it will have more than enough pomp. We don't even know where we'll live. Ashley and Danny will stay in Cleveland as long as her grandma is there. I'll take as much time off as I can and every weekend. Probably a short wedding trip for now. Guess you can tell, we still have plenty of loose ends."

"You're really serious, Bobby. I can't wait to meet Ashley; she must really be something to turn you around like this! And a little kid in our family! Now that'll be a change for the better. Of course I'll be at your wedding. What can I do to help? I'll mark my calendar right now."

"Thanks, Janie. I knew I could count on you. I'll tell Ashley you've offered assistance. You may be hearing from us real soon. Trust me, you'll love her and Danny…they're irresistible."

"And thanks for calling. Sorry if I wasn't immediately supportive. You blind sided me! It's been great talking to you. I miss you, big brother!"

Janie circled the wedding weekend on the calendar and sat down with a cup of tea by her open window, watching the neighborhood come alive on a Saturday morning. She smiled as she thought, "Bobby, Bobby. You're quite the guy! Ashley is a lucky girl and it sounds like you're lucky, too. I wish I could find someone like you. I don't think I want an actor/showbiz kind of boyfriend again. Next time we talk, I'll just nonchalantly ask you if you've got any nice single friends. Now *that's* a plan."

Janie no longer felt guilty or inadequate about missing the publicity event the night before. However, she promised herself to make those affairs a priority in the future. "Enough time wasted on self-pity this morning. Gloria was right. But so was I. I'm going to have to limit my commitments. I'll have to decide, what do I want? Soaps, movies or the stage? I might be able to combine the three. But now I know I can't do them all at the same time."

Janie did a few chores and ate lunch at a small neighborhood sidewalk café. She relaxed in the sunshine and started to read the newest Grisham novel.

Two hours later as she was putting her groceries away, the phone rang.

"Hello, I'm calling for Janie Malone. This is Bobby's fiancé, Ashley Collins. I've heard so much about you and I've watched your show a few times. You're really very good. Forgive me please for this intrusion."

"Oh please, you're not intruding. I'm glad you called. I'd rather we were meeting face to face, but this will do for now. Is Bobby okay?"

"Yes, of course, Bob's wonderful. He told me he talked to you this morning and you were kind enough to offer assistance with our wedding. Well, I was wondering if you'd consider being a bridesmaid? I know we don't have a history together other than Bob, but we do have a future. I don't have any family and I've lost touch with all my old friends since I had Danny. My grandma has been my best friend. But she refuses to be anything but a wedding guest. She gets tired very easily these days."

"Ashley, I'm flattered. I'd love to be a bridesmaid. Wow! You don't beat around the bush. I like that."

They chatted on like girlfriends, discussing bridesmaid dresses. Ashley had picked out a favorite in a J.C. Penney catalogue…which would simplify shopping, individual fittings and traveling.

When they finally finished talking, Janie smiled as she finished putting away her morning shopping and thought, "Both of my brothers have had good sense in choosing wives. Smart boys they are, indeed. After talking to Ashley, I can see how Bobby decided to get married so quickly. She's sweet, intelligent and direct. What a combination! And I'm certain she must be extremely pretty to have turned Bobby around like she did."

Janie decided to call Jessica and Billy. By the time she had reached them, both had already talked to Bobby *and* Ashley. And they'd had time to adjust to the news. Both Jessica and Liz had agreed to be bridesmaids. Billy would be best man.

Jessica said, "Can you believe it, we're all going to suddenly have a nephew? God, I hope he'll like us."

"And why wouldn't he like us?" Janie asked.

"Well, I've never been around kids much; I don't know…what do you do with them? What do you say to a kid?" Jessica sounded truly bewildered.

Janie laughed and said, "You're asking the wrong person. I don't know. Maybe he's a little worried too, about gaining a whole new family. Let's follow Bobby's lead and maybe we should brush up on some child development. He's a five-year-old. I'll keep you posted if there's anything special I come across. I think I'll run over to the library this afternoon."

Jessica was quiet for a few seconds, then she said, "You know he may resent us 'cause he's had his mom to himself for five years and now he'll suddenly have to share her with all of us. I sure hope I don't screw up my first chance to be an aunt!"

"Jessica, you'll be a wonderful aunt. The best! Just relax. Hey, how're you doing living with Grandmother Malone *and* how's the friendship with Michael going?"

"Great to both questions. I can't remember ever being happier. I thought maybe Michael and I would be the next wedding in the family, but we kind of hate to take a chance on marriage ruining a wonderful friendship. We'll see. Grandmother seems to love having me here. We each do our own things, but we spend a lot of time just hanging out. I've come to know her as more than just a grandmother. She's told me so many stories about her life as a young girl. Sorry! I'm starting to ramble."

Janie smiled as she spoke. "I'm really happy for you. Please tell Grandmother Malone I said 'hi' and I'm jealous. I want to hear her girlhood stories too."

"Janie, how're things going for you now in the city? Grandmother tapes your show for me every day. We watch it together before going to bed two or three times a week. You are great. Doesn't seem like you're even acting. Some of the performers overact so much that their drama is almost a bad comedy! We're saving them for Mom to watch when she comes home. We're all so proud of you."

"Thanks, Jessica. I really like my work and I'm still clean. Arnie had the balls to call me a couple weeks ago and tried to lure me back into his web of drugged euphoria. I asked him not to call anymore. He told me I was an uppity bitch and probably a whore too. I hung up. Friends like that, who needs them?! Not me."

"Glad to hear that, but I was pretty sure you were clean, just from watching you on the soap. Don't work too hard, sweetie. I think this wedding's going to be fun. Can you believe Bobby, Mr. Bachelor, swept away like this? Ashley must really be something!" Jessica grinned. "My God, look at the time. Hey, I really have to go. We'll talk soon."

Janie found two self-help books at the library dealing with child development and new step families. She ordered a Chinese dinner and curled up for an educational evening with her library books. By two a.m. she had finished the child development book, carefully flagging the pages she'd decided to photocopy for Jessica. Sunday morning she slept till ten a.m. and went out for a bagel breakfast and a long walk. It was a glorious sunny day in New York City and people were *almost* friendly.

When she returned to her apartment, she had messages to call Bobby, Billy, Mormor, and Gloria. "Good grief!"

Janie called Gloria first…to get it over with. "Are ya still mad at me, doll? I had to come on a little strong to show ya I mean business. Just got another invite to a big PR photo op at the Waldorf Astoria Ball Room, mark your calendar for Saturday evening in three weeks. We're talkin' class and connections here. Wasn't easy but I talked them in to givin' ya two tickets. Well, what'ya say, doll?"

Janie swallowed hard. "I can't do it that weekend. I've made other plans. Sorry, Gloria."

"So change your plans, this is a real opportunity. Ya gotta go. *This is business.*" Gloria was yelling again.

"Listen carefully, Gloria. I appreciate all you've done for me. But I don't like the tone you are using with me. My brother, Bobby, the lawyer, is getting married that day and I'm a bridesmaid in the wedding. It's in Cleveland. I'll be flying there as soon as I finish work on Friday. I can't come to the Waldorf PR that Saturday and that is my final answer. *This is family.*" Janie sighed as she finished asserting herself.

"Well, *excuse me.* I almost forgot you're just a little small-town family girl. You jes' go on and have a good time. I'll call you if anythin' else comes up, bye now." Angry sarcasm dripped heavily from Gloria's voice as she hung up.

Janie shook her head and took a deep breath as she thought, "Gloria, Gloria. I'm not your puppet. Guess I seemed like one for a long time and now that I'm thinking for myself...well it must be hard for you. Hang in there, it'll be okay."

She called Mormor and as always it was good to talk to her mother's mother. She was a sharp and sweet woman. No pretenses and no animosity towards anyone. Just true blue kindness and optimism that radiated from deep in her soul. Mormor was excited about the coming wedding and anxious to meet the bride and little Danny in person. "He'll be our first great grandchild!"

Bobby's message. "Hey, Janie, thanks for talking to Ashley and agreeing to be a bridesmaid. She was so nervous about calling you, my actress sister! You put her at ease and she really likes you. Thanks. I'll catch you later."

Billy's was brief and to the point. "Call me ASAP."

Billy picked up on the third ring. "Hi Billy, how'd you like the Bahamas? Hey, what's up? I got your message, sounded urgent. Is Mom okay?"

"Hi Janie, thanks for calling back so quickly. The Bahamas were nothing short of wonderful. We both loved every minute; we even stayed an extra week. It's a hard place to leave. As far as I know, everything is still okay with Mom. I called because Bobby called me this morning and I'm in shock! Then a couple hours ago, his fiancé called to talk to Liz and asked her to be a bridesmaid in the wedding. And can you believe, Liz said yes! Three weeks! And a kid to boot. I don't know what's happened to him. My God!"

"I think I know what happened. He fell head over heels in love," Janie answered softly.

"You don't think we should try to put the brakes to this whole affair? I don't know how you can be so calm about your brother potentially ruining his life." Billy's rapid loud speech didn't mask his anger at all.

"Well, I don't see us having any options. We either accept and support our brother or we risk pushing him away and losing him forever. I talked to her on the phone today and she seems like a really nice person. I'm going to be a bridesmaid, too."

"God! Do you know that you remind me of Mom when you talk like that?" Billy sounded slightly less agitated.

"Well, if I sound like Mom, I come by it honestly…after all, we are related, you know," Janie replied.

"And now Liz is mad at me and thinks I must be sorry I married her because of my 'overreaction' to Bobby's plans. Liz thinks this fiancé sounds like a genuinely nice person." Billy no longer sounded angry, only tired and sad.

"Well, maybe you could practice saying her name, '*Ashley*', so you don't end up calling her 'that woman and fiancé.' Give her a chance and give them a chance. She must be something to get Bobby turned completely around so quickly. Hey, guess what I read last night?" Janie cleverly diverted the subject.

"I don't have any idea, do tell me." Billy was curious now.

"Yesterday afternoon I went to the library and checked out a book on child development. I don't know any small children and I wanted to be prepared to meet Danny. He sounds delightful. I want to be a good aunt."

"Geez…I don't know what to say…" Billy hesitated.

"What did you say to Bobby when he called you? He asked you to be his best man, didn't he? So, what did you say?" Janie had never experienced the role of a responsible sibling before; everyone had always had to fix her messes, and there'd been plenty of them. But that was then and this was now. She preferred the responsible adult role and decided it was time to be a grown up. She thought, "Better late than never. Right?"

"I told him I'd do it. But I offered no congratulations or enthusiasm. I didn't show my anger and concern. I was brief and short with him." Billy's voice sounded regretful.

"One thing you've always been, Billy, is a terrible actor! Of course, he had to know you were upset. If he didn't notice, he'd better withdraw from the family!

"You never could fake anything and that's good. You're genuine. And because you are, I think you should go for a walk with Liz. After you've had a chance to think and talk it over with Liz, please call your brother and really talk to him. About his wedding and his new life." Janie smiled and thought, "I really like being the calm adult. And I think I'm pretty good at it, too."

She ordered a pizza and got comfy as she started the step family book. It was mostly common sense. If one always practiced the Golden Rule…but of course feelings interfere, family positions are threatened and boundaries are crossed when two families combine. At least in Bobby's situation there was only one child involved. The main thing for adults to remember is that it's not the child's fault. Children are innocent bystanders whose world fell apart. They want to feel safe and it's up to the adults in their lives to help them feel secure. "This book is very helpful; I'd have to photocopy the whole book if I was to send her the highlights. I'll have to tell Jessica to get a copy at the library or even buy one," Janie thought as she finished the book by eight p.m.

"Now I have to learn my lines for the next few days. Thank God, this is my last week of filming for the TV movie," she muttered as she ate another slice of the now cold pizza.

JESSICA

Jessica paused and then tapped lightly on her grandmother's bedroom door. It was ten p.m., if she was still awake. "I'm sorry, did I wake you?"

"Jessica? No, no, of course not. You know I always read till midnight. Is anything wrong, dear?"

"I don't know. I just felt like talking for a few minutes. I'm exhausted, but I don't feel sleepy, my mind is racing, and I can't seem to slow down enough to sleep. Do you ever feel like this, Grandmother?"

"More than I like to admit. I don't know why we must suffer so; I've wasted too many precious hours of my life. After your grandfather died, I had a terrible time trying to sleep. And I'd never felt so alone. I've always been thankful for your dear mother. She's consistently included me in your lives. Your family has been my life line. I know there were times I could've made our relationship much easier for her and I regret that I didn't...Barbara's a gem and I truly cherish her. I really do miss her."

"Me too. I wish she was back home with us or we could at least have a real conversation with her...I'm afraid I spent too many years distancing myself from my mother as much as possible. What was I trying to prove anyway?"

"It's called growing up, Jessica. And your mother realized and didn't take your 'distancing' personally. Now what's really on your mind?"

"Well, with Bobby getting married so fast. I told Michael about it and he just smiled. I want him to go to the wedding with us, of course." Jessica hesitated.

"Is he going? What did he say?"

"Yes, he said he'd come, but he's just so passive about commitment. I know I've always said I'd never get married. But now given the chance, *maybe* I would. He seems to be very content the way things are for us right now. And he's not ambitious. Michael has little interest in material things. I agreed with him at first, but I don't know if I'd really want to live a life of austerity. I know I don't feel comfortable in his Spartan apartment."

"Jessica, my love, relax. Everything happens in its own time. Just enjoy your brother's wedding. And enjoy your Michael."

"Thanks, Grandmother. I better let you get some sleep and try to get some myself. I have to get up for work by six. Good night and thanks." Jessica blew a kiss and started to close the door, then impulsively turned around and said, "Do you know how much I love and admire you, Grandmother?"

She looked at her granddaughter with a startled expression, which immediately turned into a warm smile, and with both arms extended, she said, "Jess, darling, come over here!"

Jessica sheepishly returned to her. The old woman hugged her with a firm gentleness and then held Jessica's face with her thin wrinkled hands covering her cheeks, looked into her eyes and said, "And don't you ever forget to stand tall, be proud and know you are loved. Now go to bed. I have a bridge luncheon at the club tomorrow and I need some sleep. Good night, love."

Surprisingly, the next morning they awakened early and felt refreshed. Grandmother had the daily crossword puzzle all but completed before seven a.m.

Jessica met Michael at their favorite romantic restaurant at seven for a nice dinner. They chatted about the normal mundane everyday concerns. Michael told her about his current problems in the classroom…students, parents, administration and curriculum. And topped it off with a few good jokes, delivered with perfect timing. Jessica realized she truly liked his companionship and would be devastated if they stopped seeing each other. She reached across the table and touched his hand. "Michael, I love you, I truly do."

He blushed and said, "I love you, too. I almost forgot I have a surprise for you." He then pulled a small grey leather box from his pocket. "This is for you, my beautiful Jessica. Will you marry me? I guess Bobby's wedding plan put me in the mood. Well, what do you say? Will you give me the privilege of being your husband?"

Jessica opened the box. A magnificent solitaire diamond glowed in the dimly lit restaurant. Michael sat watching her with his elbows on the table, his chin resting on his two hands. It seemed to him that only Jessica's eyes glowed more than the diamond ring. He thought, "I'm one heck of a lucky guy."

With tears of joy and her face in a blissful trance, Jessica shouted, "Yes, yes, yes!" Then in a lower tone, "I'd love to be your wife. I think we'll make a great team. But I have to ask you, what took you so long to finally ask me?"

"I felt we were young and there was no rush, but I knew I wanted to spend my life with you. I love being with you, Jessica. I guess Bobby prompted me a bit with his announcement. If you don't like the ring, it can be exchanged."

"I love it and I'd never consider changing it. After all, you picked it out. It shows what good taste you have in rings as well as women."

They laughed over two small glasses of wine to toast each other and their engagement. By the end of the evening they had made quick stops to show off the ring and announce their official engagement at Mormor and Morfar's, two of Michael's relatives and then back to Grandmother Malone's. Everyone was delighted and no one was surprised; except, perhaps Jessica had been caught a bit off guard.

Michael and Jessica agreed to set a date for the following summer.

Chapter Twenty-three

BARBARA

"Anybody home? Yoo-hoo, Barbara!" Lilia pounded on the cottage door at seven a.m. on Saturday morning.

Barbara suddenly sat up, rubbing her eyes, startled by the persistent knocking on her door. She recognized Lilia's voice, grabbed a robe and hurried to the door.

Lilia stood there grinning from ear to ear. "*Buenos días*, Barbara. I have good news for *amiga*." Lilia was so excited she could hardly contain herself.

"*Buenos días* to you!" Barbara yawned sleepily.

"Ahh, Nurse Barbara, you sleeping? *Lo siento*." She sighed and continued, "But already sunny for two hours, why you still sleep? I no *comprende*."

Barbara smiled at her friend. "Please come in, *buenos días*, Lilia. Want some tea? I need a cup."

Lilia followed her to the kitchen and sat down at the table. It was already getting hot. "Another scorcher," she thought as she turned the ceiling fan on low. It really did help. She poured two cups of tea and Lilia pulled a tray of fresh muffins from her bag. "I make these for my Oscar this morning. Special treat."

Barbara sat down across the table from her. "Mmm, delicious, *gracias*." And she ate two muffins as if she'd been a starving refugee. "Okay, so tell me the good news, Lilia."

"Oscar and me, big *fiesta* next week. Saturday night. All de children come home. Whole village come. Big fiesta. You must come, Nurse Barbara. You my good friend." Lilia glowed as she talked about her fiesta.

"Yes, of course, I'll come. Why a party now? Something special?" Barbara asked.

"*Sí, sí*! We marry for thirty years. Celebrate marriage, children, grandchildren and de family. We celebrate good life! We like *fiestas*."

"Congratulations, to thirty years of the good life." She toasted her cup of tea to Lilia who joined her in the toast.

With their cups held high, they laughed and said together, "To de good life!"

Barbara held up her cup. "One more toast, to my *amiga*, Lilia."

Lilia laughed and held her cup high. "To my *amiga*, Nurse Barbara. More tea, *por favor*?"

"What you do today?" Lilia asked.

"First I'll shower and dress. Do my laundry, then vegetable shopping, call my family from the police station, come back and write my letters. Not very exciting, but a nice change of pace. What about you?" Barbara answered.

"I cook for de family. Oscar and me have to plan de food for de *fiesta*, *mucho* work to be done."

"Is there anything I can do to help?"

"No, *gracias*. We do de work. You come *fiesta* next week," then she hesitated and smiled slyly as she said, "Dr. Kane coming stay de weekend and come to our *fiesta*. Great honor for de doctor come to our *fiesta*. He *es* good man." Lilia lifted her eyebrows in a knowing and teasing manner. "You and Dr. Kane dance good together. *Sí*?"

"Are you trying to be a matchmaker, Lilia?"

A puzzled expression clouded her face. "Matchmaker, *que es* matchmaker?" the Honduran asked.

Barbara tried to explain. "Dr. Kane good man. But not my man. I no want a man. *Comprende*?"

Lilia's smile did little to conceal her enjoyment of the moment. "*Sí, sí*. Doctor have nobody. Doctor like Nurse Barbara. I know. Gabriela tell me, 'Doctor likes Nurse Barbara,' everybody in de clinic see doctor look at you. *Sí*. We know. Next Saturday *everybody* dance at *fiesta*. I go now."

Barbara folded her arms and pretended to be peeved at her friend, but Lilia reached up with both her arms and gently squeezed Barbara's face. "Be happy, *amiga*. *Fiesta mucho* fun. *Adiós*."

"*Adiós* to you, you early bird! *Hasta luego*."

Barbara closed the door and looked at her clock, eight thirty a.m. She thought, "Well, I've eaten, had two cups of tea, and chatted with Lilia. It's definitely time to start the tasks of the day. What kind of rumors are floating around the village about Dr. Mike Kane and me? I definitely must talk to Gabriela on Monday. The fiesta does sound like fun, though." She sighed, shook her head and smiled.

Barbara was able to reach her parents on the first try. When she said, "Hello, Dad," he immediately shouted to her mother, "Mom, get on the other phone, it's our Barbara, the one that's livin' down in them tropical jungles."

"Dad, how're you doing? You sound just like always. I'm well, thanks for asking!" she teased.

Before he could respond, her mother picked up and fired a whole raft of health and wellness questions off at her and Barbara tried to satisfy her mother's concerns. Then her father solemnly said, "Big news, Bobby's getting married in three weeks in Cleveland to a very nice and beautiful girl he's been dating for three months. Her name is Ashley. Sounds like a solid decent family background. She has a very smart and handsome five-year-old son…she's never been married. Barbara, you're going to be a grandmother!"

"Oh my God, Bobby?! She must be very special to have swept Casanova off his feet like this. Is there any reason for the rush? I don't understand."

Her mother answered diplomatically, "It seems Ashley is an only child with no cousins, aunts or uncles. Her parents are divorced and mostly interested in their own careers. She and her grandmother are very close. The grandmother is quite ill and not expected to live more than another month or so. Ashley knows her grandmother is not well but not about her imminent death. The grandmother asked Bobby his intentions. This girl literally swept him off his feet; he wanted to marry her after their first date! The grandmother asked him to allow her the pleasure of seeing her granddaughter married before she died. So, that's why the wedding is in three weeks."

Her father added, "I always told your mother, when that boy falls in love it's goin' to be fast and hard. I was right again, you keep that in mind, little girl. Father knows best."

Barbara couldn't help smiling as she listened to her father gloat despite her initial shock about Bobby's wedding plans. "Well, it sounds exciting. I don't know if I'll be able to arrange to come home with such short notice. I certainly want to meet her and the child. And, of course, see Bobby get married." The words felt thick and foreign on her tongue…"see Bobby get married."

Barbara knew when she joined the Peace Corps she'd no longer be part of her children's everyday lives. "I think it's wonderful. Please tell them my thoughts are with them and congratulations. I'm really going to try to come home for the wedding. Please take lots of photos if I don't make it. Do you have any other news?"

"Well, yes dear, there is. Jessica and Michael were engaged this week. I guess Bobby's news inspired Michael to get off the fence of indecision. But they don't plan to marry before next summer." Barbara sighed as she listened to her mother's latest inside information about her children's lives.

"That's fantastic. Please tell them I'm happy for them and wish them well. I hate to ask if there's anything else I should know...."

Her father teased her. "Gettin' a little homesick down in them mountains, are you now? Here's your mother."

"No, Barbara, everything else is about the same old status quo. How about you? How are things with you, dear?" Her mother's voice was tense with concern. "Is there anything else you need? Please don't hesitate to let us know, we're always here for you. We miss you so much, Barbie. Bye." She heard her mother's voice begin to crack and knew that meant she was crying again.

"I guess that's all your mother's up for today. You wouldn't believe how that woman worries about you. Just remember, you'll always have a home to come back to. You don't have to hide away in the jungle."

"Dad, I'm *not hiding*. I'm sorry I'm causing you both so much anguish. But I really like my work and life here in the village. I'm going to try and get home a few days before the wedding. I'll bring lots of photos with me. Please don't say anything more about me coming home to Mom. I don't want to disappoint her if my efforts fail. I have to go. Please give my love to all. Bye, Dad."

Barbara walked in a daze through the open-air vegetable and fruit stands in the village plaza. She carefully chose fresh produce, fresh bread, a small chunk of cheese, eggs and a fresh chicken to prepare for her Sunday dinner. It would easily keep her in meat for the rest of the week. She said a silent prayer. "Dear Lord, please keep the generator working to provide electricity all week. It's been getting a real workout with this heat wave. And if it be your will, help me find a way to get home for Bobby's wedding."

Barbara was careful to speak pleasantly and as personably as possible to all the villagers that crossed her path, though her heart was not in it. Barbara felt another bout of guilt coming on; concern for her mother was causing her to question her decision to be here at all. Then she had some rational thoughts. "I'm just a little homesick after talking to my parents. My life in Lewiston was really quite empty and boring. The children were gone. My parents had each other. Mother Malone had her club friends. Alice had her family and I was alone. Since long before Bill died, I've been alone. Of course, I miss them, but I had become little more than a periphery observer in my children's lives. Here I feel needed, useful and fulfilled."

Barbara sat down in a shaded outdoor café and ordered a bottle of cold water. Lorena, a first aid graduate, walked over and sat down across from her. "*Hola*, Nurse Barbara. How are you today?"

Barbara encouraged the girl's dream to attend university to learn to be a real nurse. "I'll check to see if there's any kind of scholarship money available and how far you'd have to travel to attend a university. Please don't give up your goal; I know you'll make a wonderful nurse."

Suddenly the peaceful Saturday morning sounds of the plaza were interrupted by men shouting and loud motors. An alarmed Barbara asked, "What is happening?"

"The government soldiers are here. They come maybe once a year. We lucky, they hate road up the mountain, or maybe they come more often!" Lorena shrugged with reluctant acceptance.

A jeep and three noisy large trucks with canopies and benches pulled to the center of the plaza. Twenty soldiers climbed from the back of each truck.

Lorena leaned over to Barbara. "Stay quietly in the background and let the *Padre* handle the soldiers. He's done it many times before."

"Lorena, you speak excellent English. Have you ever traveled from the village? Where did you learn to speak so fluently?"

"Mostly from the Peace Corps workers who've been here over the years. I did it for money and security. Ut-oh, grab your bags. Here come the soldiers. Just be calm." Lorena was no more than fifteen and her calm enthusiasm for life was contagious.

"*Señora, señorita,* we are looking for Cergio Molinos and his *banditos*. Have you seen them?" He pulled out a photo of Cergio and flashed it at them.

Before they could answer, *Padre* Daniel walked with humble authority across Plaza de Rebita and called out, "Ah, *Capitán*! At last you visit Rebita. It has been too long. Please, please sit down, be comfortable," and he ordered cold drinks be served to all the soldiers, starting with the *capitán*. *Padre* Daniel was a master at innocent small talk and he used his skill without a hint of manipulation.

Barbara left money on the table for their drinks and she and Lorena slowly walked away from the plaza. "Nurse Barbara, I must go. You hurry back to compound and tell everybody you see; warn families to stay inside while soldiers here. *Adiós*."

Barbara noticed the plaza was quietly emptying and several of the open-air fruit stands had silently closed. Back at the compound, Pablo looked worried when she told him the soldiers were at the plaza. He said, "Nurse Barbara, go inside and stay there, *por favor*."

"What shall I say when they ask me about Cergio? Should I admit I helped them a few months ago?"

"*Sí*, they already think they know. Careful what you say," Pablo warned.

Barbara started toward the cottage then turned. "Pablo, how long do you think they'll stay in Rebita?"

He shrugged. "Only God know; maybe two days and maybe long time."

Barbara had just finished cleaning her vegetables and fruits and all her shopping was safely stored in the small refrigerator. She poured herself a glass of iced tea to drink with her lunch and set her letter writing box on the table for the afternoon.

Just as she started the first letter, there was a loud knock on the front door.

"*Hola, Capitán*, we meet again. Sorry, I could not wait for you at the plaza this morning. I had to bring my food home for the ice box. Would you like to come inside, it's a bit cooler in here."

"*Sí, señora*. I must ask you some questions about Cergio. How long were they here? Why did they come?" the *capitán* asked. He watched her responses carefully.

"Yes, Cergio came here the day after the bloody battle in Valencia a couple months ago. We operate a Peace Corps Medical Clinic here. I am Nurse Barbara Malone. We try to help people get well, regardless of their politics. He had two wounded 'soldiers.' One was a stab wound and one was a gunshot wound to the chest cavity. Cergio threatened my staff and me with a gun. I felt we had to help the injured *and* we did try to keep his presence confidential. Please do not blame any of the villagers. I was in charge and I made the decisions." Barbara maintained eye contact and managed to keep her voice professional and confident. Inside she was shaking. Lilia and Oscar had told her horror stories about the military. She wondered, "Where will this inquisition lead?"

"Thank you, Nurse Barbara, for your candid answers. May I ask you a few more questions, *por favor*? Forgive, my English not so good." He was a young, handsome, obviously well-educated Honduran who spoke almost flawless English...except when he wanted to appear humble.

"Of course, what else can I tell you? Excuse my manners, would you like a drink of iced tea, *Capitán*?" Barbara asked.

"*Gracias*, that would be very kind. Did they say where their base camp is? Have they been in contact with you or anyone else in the village since they left? And when did gunshot wounds patient leave?"

Barbara turned as she was pouring his iced tea, smiled and held up her hand for him to stop. "Please, *Capitán*! Too many questions, too fast. No more questions until I answer these. I'll have to start taking notes if you cluster anymore with the ones you've already thrown at me. Okay, let's see…absolutely no idea where their base camp is located. Although I'd guess it's not a permanent location and they move around. *But* remember, that's just a guess. I doubt if they've been in touch with anyone else in the village. I'm sure they've had no contact with any of our clinic personnel. It's been at least two months since the gunshot patient left. Cergio did bring me a gift of appreciation for caring for his soldiers, a large-screen television. You can see from the size of my cottage that it wouldn't work well here…."

"So, where is this big television? Your iced tea is very good, American iced tea, yes?" The *capitán* seemed a little too interested in the television to suit Barbara.

She wondered, "Am I digging my own grave?" But she answered, "I didn't know what to do with it. I didn't want to insult Cergio. So I talked to the village priest and he stores it in the church storage room. Once a month *Padre* Daniel hosts a movie night for the entire village in the plaza. I ordered a video player from Tegucigalpa and a few movies. Most of our villagers had never seen television or movies before. Now they love it and talk about the movies for days."

"One more question, Nurse Barbara; if Cergio or any of his men are hurt in the future and come to your Peace Corps Clinic, will you provide care for them again?" His eyes bored into her soul and his voice was tight and pinched.

"Yes, we would. Our mission is to provide care to anyone who needs it, including you or your soldiers. I hope we will not need to care for any more battle wounds. There was a young Peace Corps volunteer killed in Valencia that day. She was a very special friend of mine. It was very difficult for me to provide care to the ones responsible for her death." She answered him evenly, though tears filled her eyes, defying her attempts to squelch them.

"Thank you, Nurse Barbara. I hope I won't need to bother you again. I'm very sorry about the loss of your friend. I'm curious, how do you get electricity up here anyway…for the monthly movie and your ceiling fans?"

"The Peace Corps provides us with a generator for the clinic and our living quarters and once a month the priest borrows it for the movie night. He tells the village that God provides." Barbara smiled, shrugged and said, "What can I do?"

The *capitán* nodded and returned a smile. "Ahh, I see. Well, thank you again. It has been a pleasure talking with you. Honduras is fortunate to have the Peace Corps and nurses like you to help our people. And thanks for the tea. Good day to you, Nurse Barbara."

He was finally gone. She watched *el capitán* strut across the compound, not surprised that he stopped to question Pablo. Barbara muttered, "Thank goodness the rest of the staff is off on weekends." A half an hour later he and his entourage of soldiers left the compound. Barbara paced nervously in the cottage. She waited twenty minutes before taking Pablo a large glass of iced tea.

"How did it go with *el capitán*, Pablo?" she asked.

"*Gracias*, Nurse Barbara, good tea. Ahh, *sí*, *Capitán* ask *mucho* questions. I no trust that one. He sly one. Speaks with fork tongue. He say he like Nurse Barbara but no, no trust that one. *Capitán* say one thing and do another."

"What did he ask you, Pablo?"

"He ask, do I know Cergio? How many time Cergio come Rebita? How long they stay? Who their friends? Where they stay? I not know these things. I tell him only what I know is de truth. I tell him Nurse Barbara is angel and help *all* de sick and hurt. I tell him you no bad person. I tell him he should no more talk you. Nurse Barbara good person."

Barbara couldn't help laughing; the longer Pablo talked, the funnier it all sounded to her. "*Gracias*, Pablo. Do not worry about me, I'm a big girl. I can take care of myself. Besides, I have you and Miguel for when things get tough. *Hasta luego*."

Pablo watched her walk back to the cottage. He sighed and shook his head as he thought, "Nurse Barbara not so strong, I know. She is *mucho* sad *señora*. Every day I see her sad eyes. She is mystery nurse, *mucho* older than other nurses from Peace Corps and she work almost all the time. She work too much but I know she good person." Pablo smiled. "And Dr. Kane know this, *sí*, we men will take care of Nurse Barbara. *Sí*, Dr. Kane like this one *mucho, mucho*." He found himself daydreaming about Lilia and Oscar's *fiesta* next week. Pablo loved *fiestas*. Good food, drink, everyone dressed in their finest, dancing, music. "Ahh, *sí*, it be a fine time indeed."

Barbara forced herself to write her Saturday letters and put the interrogation out of her mind. Somehow she completed her task. She felt relieved after proofreading that she'd managed to write interesting newsy letters without mentioning the stressful situation at hand.

A foreboding calm settled over Rebita. Everyone in the village whispered the same question, "How long will *el capitán* and his soldiers stay?" And no one knew the answer.

Padre Daniel's Sunday Mass was filled to capacity. *El capitán* and many of his soldiers were there. The congregation was more subdued than usual. Barbara hoped the *capitán* wouldn't notice this cloud of self restraint since he hadn't been there during a normal exuberant Mass. Barbara's mind drifted and she couldn't help comparing Cergio and Julio to the *capitán*. Clearly the villagers trusted the *banditos* more than the government army. Still, she couldn't forget poor Alvie....

After church, Oscar and Lilia insisted on walking Barbara back to the compound. She agreed reluctantly, but only if they'd stay for lunch. As they walked, Lilia said, "Something bad hangs over Rebita."

When they turned the corner to the Peace Corps compound, Pablo was nowhere in sight. And the gate was wide open. Barbara started to run, breathlessly shouting, "Oh my God! Pablo! Pablo! Oscar, Lilia...something is very wrong here."

Barbara ran through the gate a few seconds before Lilia and Oscar, frantically calling Pablo's name. No answer from her loyal friend. Suddenly she noticed something shining in the dust. She bent down to see what it was, only to find Pablo's crucifix. Barbara clutched it to her heart and in a voice completely void of emotion, said, "He'd never lose this. He treasured it above all else."

Puffing and panting, Lilia and Oscar caught up with her. "What is it? Did you find something?"

Barbara extended her open hand where she held his crucifix; both Lilia and Oscar crossed themselves and muttered a prayer for Pablo. Barbara said nothing, just sat there with hot tears burning her cheeks in the midday heat.

After slowly assessing the scene, Oscar tentatively followed the marks in the dry dusty compound to the lush tropical growth to the right of the gate, closely followed by Lilia and Barbara. He saw the pool of blood only seconds before the women...Pablo's throat had been cut. His eyes were still open with an expression of terrified anger and fear frozen on his face forever.

Oscar immediately crossed himself and began to pray, "Hail Mary, Mother of God, have mercy on our brother's soul..." He reached over and closed Pablo's eyelids.

Barbara and Lilia held hands as they wept at the loss of their good friend and the unfairness of his murder. Oscar walked the women to the cottage. "I go for *policía*. You stay in cottage." He pointed his finger at both of them as he spoke. "Stay here, keep door locked."

They sat at the kitchen table in silence. A few minutes later, Barbara offered Lilia a glass of iced tea. The tea was lukewarm. Then she noticed how unusually warm the cottage was. She said, "I'm certain I left the ceiling fans on low this morning." She went to the control panel and sure enough, they were both set for low.

"Lilia, I have to check the generator, maybe Pablo never had a chance to refuel it this morning. I don't seem to have any electrical power in the cottage."

"I come to generator with you."

Barbara was shocked to find the generator was gone. "Oh my God! Lilia, come back inside with me. The generator's been stolen. Somebody killed Pablo so they could steal the generator." They went into the cottage and locked the doors. Both women were shocked and quiet. And hotter as the minutes passed to hours.

The practical Lilia said, "Barbara, I open windows for fresh air. Okay?" Lilia opened the windows and checked the refrigerator. She put the chicken in a pot of water to cook and put the dozen eggs in another pan to cook. She shook her head. "Too much food for one day, now you must shop every day. No worry. I shop for you when I shop for my family. I send food with Gabriela after *siesta*. This help you until you get new generator, *sí*?"

No answer. Just silence. Alvie's death had been a terrible shock and loss. But *this* time, her own guard had been murdered right in her own front yard, *while* she was in church. Because someone wanted the damn generator. Barbara's grief for Pablo and his family was real. But so was her anger toward the ruthless murderers and thieves. Whoever they were....

When Lilia heard Oscar and Policía Arturo on the front porch, she quickly opened the door for them. Barbara looked at them with a sense of hopelessness and despair.

Lilia served lukewarm tea, a vegetable tray with bread and still warm hard-boiled eggs.

"*Gracias*, Lilia. *Hola*, Arturo." She nodded to Oscar and spoke slower and louder to communicate with Rebita's *policía*.

Lilia noticed through the window that Pablo's brothers were already removing his body to prepare for tomorrow's burial. She thought, "I ask Barbara if we give chicken stew to Pablo's family for funeral dinner." Then she caught Oscar's attention and motioned for him to follow her behind the cottage.

"The killer steal the generator. Now Nurse Barbara no have electricity for the clinic. Who do this bad thing, Oscar?" They looked at each other evenly, they both knew but neither would dare say the name.

Arturo questioned Barbara in Spanish. "Have you noticed any unusual activities the last few days?"

Barbara looked at him. "No. Nothing. Except *el capitán* and his soldiers came yesterday. They questioned me *and* Pablo. We were the only ones here. He did seem unduly interested in the generator and the large screen at the church. Perhaps you could give *Padre* Daniel a message to leave the church and the storage room unlocked and unguarded tonight."

A surprised Arturo exclaimed, "You told him about *the television*? Oh my! Oh my! Perhaps Nurse Barbara could tell me *why* you tell *el capitán* about the television."

"Pablo told me before he arrived, 'be careful but tell *Capitán* everything. Because he probably already knows everything anyway.' *Capitán* is arrogant. Pablo felt nervous after he was questioned too. We didn't like him," she answered.

Oscar returned and in loud rapid fire Spanish told Arturo about the stolen generator. Arturo immediately went to look at the second crime scene. He slowly walked around the sight of the missing generator with his arms folded together. "Oh my, oh my, this is a problem. *Sí*, a great dilemma!" And he scratched his head.

Back in the house, he helped himself to another plate of food and gestured for Lilia to refill his tea. "*Gracias, gracias*." Then he turned his attention to her friend. "Nurse Barbara, can you think of anything else you should tell me? Anything at all?"

Barbara concentrated with all her might and could think of nothing. "I'm sorry, I can't think of anything else. If I remember anything I'll send for you. Thank you for coming, Arturo."

Oscar walked Arturo to the gate and closed it after he left. There was still a drying puddle of Pablo's blood in the brush. Oscar decided to clean the scene and dumped buckets of water until the blood was rinsed away. He didn't want Gabriela, the other workers or the patients to see Pablo's blood.

He walked back into the cottage. "How are you doing now, *señoras*?"

Lilia answered, "Some better, thanks, Oscar."

Barbara answered, "Me too."

"I'm going to look for Miguel. You need another guard now and I'll keep my eyes open for anything unusual. You go ahead and finish up the food preparations for Pablo's family. We can take it and pay respects to them when I return."

"Thanks, Oscar."

"My dear Lilia, what would I have done without you and Oscar today?"

Lilia sat down beside her. "It would be terrible if you come home alone today and find poor Pablo. Your house not so hot with the windows open, *sí*? You like if we take big chicken stew to Pablo's family tonight?"

"That's a wonderful idea. *Gracias* for taking care of everything today. I really appreciate you." She reached out and squeezed her friend's hand. "*Gracias*."

An hour later Miguel was at the door. "Very sad to lose our Pablo. He good man. Nurse Barbara, *por favor* I work day guard at clinic. Please hire for new guard at night. *Gracias*. Sorry for the trouble. Pablo good man."

Soon after Miguel went back to his guard post, Oscar arrived accompanied by two potential guards. They both spoke only Spanish. All questions were answered promptly and without difficulty. Juan was seventeen and Angelo was sixteen. In Rebita, they were considered adults. They were respectful to Oscar, Lilia and Barbara.

When Barbara indicated she had finished her interviews, Oscar walked them to the gate. They stayed to chat with Miguel while Oscar went back to the cottage. He walked into the cottage and Lilia asked, "What you think of those boys? You trust them?"

"*Sí*, they make good guards. Barbara, what you think maybe three guards instead of two? Then maybe guards have some days off for relax?"

"Good idea. Miguel wants to move to the day guard job, which is no problem. Please ask them if they can work with Miguel tonight for training. And tell Miguel I need to see him as soon possible."

Two minutes later, Miguel was in the cottage again. "Miguel, I need you to train the two new guards tonight. Tomorrow I need you to work day time and then you'll be off tomorrow night. We will have three guards now so that everyone will get a fair amount of time off. Please come in day after tomorrow and we'll work on setting up the schedule for all three. After that, you will be responsible for making the schedules for each of you."

"*Gracias*, Nurse Barbara. I do a good job. You see."

"I know you will, Miguel. Good luck. And don't worry. Our little compound will be okay."

"*Gracias*. *Buenas tardes*." Miguel ran back to the gate with his news. Three young Honduran men were happy for their good fortune though still grieving and angry about Pablo's murder.

Lilia announced, "Time we go Pablo's family." She had covered the large hot pan with dish towels and found a large sturdy cloth bag with handles to carry it through the village.

Barbara quickly combed her hair and splashed water on her face. Oscar joined them at the gate and they walked slowly through the somber village. Pablo's parents and young wife sat under a shade tree in the front yard. His two boys, ages three and five, played near their grandfather; two-year-old Maria clung to her mother. Lilia, Oscar and Barbara offered tearful condolences to all the family. They graciously thanked Lilia and Barbara for the chicken stew. Barbara was astounded by the quantity of aromatic foods stacked all around the small kitchen. It appeared that almost everyone in the village had brought food to Pablo's family.

Barbara closed the clinic the next day in honor of Pablo. Miguel was holding his own at the gate despite the almost triple shift. "No problem at the gate. Everything okay. I sleep good tonight."

Gabriela had visited Barbara for morning tea before walking to Pablo's funeral mass together. As they approached the plaza, the *capitán* approached them. "Sorry about the trouble at your Peace Corps home. If I can be of any assistance, please feel free to contact me." He bowed gallantly when he had finished his condolence speech.

Barbara thanked him for his concern, and realized even in the jungle, hypocrisy thrived.

That night the large-screen television mysteriously disappeared from the church, as well as the videos and VCR. The thieves had left the storage room door wide open so *Padre* Daniel had noticed immediately when he prepared to open the church for the morning activities.

The *padre* hurried across the plaza to the *policía*. "Arturo, Arturo! Somebody steal in the church!"

Arturo rushed to the front of the jail from his small living quarters in the back. "Ahh, sorry, *Padre*. This bad news. Very bad news. Sorry. I come now. We report crime." He grabbed his notebook and walked across the plaza with his fretful friend, *Padre* Daniel.

"The television, the VCR, the videos…they all gone. Who would do such thing to small village church? I not understand. I leave church and storage room unlocked like you said. No damage except for theft," the *padre* explained.

The crime scene investigation didn't take long. Arturo walked around the small storage room with his arms folded. "Very bad thing steal from church.

Very bad. Good that doors unlocked, nobody hurt and no damage church. Do you know anybody who mad at church? Any ideas about who steal from church?" Arturo rubbed his chin thoughtfully with his right hand as he concentrated on the second mysterious theft in as many days. He had been the *policía* for twelve years. Rebita was a quiet town. These were only his second and third theft investigations.

Padre Daniel shook his head. "I not know anyone angry with me or the church."

Later Arturo questioned *el capitán* and some of his soldiers. They all feigned innocence about the robberies and Pablo's murder. *Capitán* offered a theory. "Perhaps Cergio sneaked back into town and took his gifts back. Maybe Pablo tried to stop him. Just a thought."

Arturo nodded. "*Sí*, that *could* explain everything. I must check into it. *Gracias* for your help, *Capitán*."

"Arturo, here is my business card. Please call me if you have anymore questions. We'll be leaving Rebita before lunch today. *Gracias*."

"Very interesting," thought Arturo, as he stood with his arms folded, stroking his short beard, watching the soldiers prepare their trucks for departure. He thought, "I wish could inspect truck cargo. *El Capitán* acquired two very large suspicious objects while in Rebita. *He think I stupid*! He blame Cergio for stealing television! Cergio give us television, he not take away…but Arturo not *loco*. I not fight *Capitán* and government soldiers. I not start fight I can not win. Fight government soldiers make life hard in Rebita. My job is to keep people safe. *Lo siento*, Pablo." He wiped tears from his eyes with the right sleeve of his shirt.

Chapter Twenty-four

Dr. Kane arrived late Friday morning. The clinic had been busier than usual since it reopened Tuesday morning. Barbara had adapted to living like a real villager with no electricity. She missed her iced tea the most.

Lilia had notified everyone in the village by Tuesday morning. "No *fiesta* now, maybe in one or two months. Rebita must first mourn passing of Pablo."

She'd written a report to the Peace Corps on Pablo's murder and the stolen generator, requesting a replacement generator. She included a report on clinic services and activities as well as morale. Barbara also included a request for ten days' vacation to return to the USA for her son's wedding. She gave it to Arturo to take with him to Cabela when he made his weekly mail and supply trip down the mountain that morning.

Dr. Kane approached Barbara when things quieted down for their afternoon lunch *siesta* break. "Hello, my friend, how're you doing? I've heard you had some serious problems since my last visit. Would you like to talk? Friend to friend. I brought lunch for two. What do you say?"

She looked at him as if for the first time; her tired blue eyes penetrated his dark browns and wiped the perspiration from her brow with her thin tanned arm. "Sounds like an offer I can't refuse. Right now a friend, especially a friend with lunch, may be just what I need. Please come to the cottage; it's more private and out of the sun and probably a bit cooler than outside."

"I'll be there in five minutes." He hesitated and added, "And I'm looking forward to talking with you, Barbara."

She looked at him suspiciously. "Me too…I think," and then walked slowly on the clinic's shaded walkway to the cottage.

Barbara splashed water on her face and brushed her hair. She noticed the new slacks her mother sent were now almost as baggy as the ones they replaced. She smiled ruefully and thought, "They wouldn't need so many weight loss programs in the USA if more people would sign up to serve in the Peace Corps! Great for losing weight..." then she looked at her eyes, "and friends. Damn. Don't start crying again." She splashed more water on her face and took a deep breath. "I've got to pull myself together."

Dr. Kane knocked on the front door. "Lunch is here!"

Barbara quickly walked across the small living room and opened the door. The weather was exceptionally muggy. "Please come in. It sure is hot today." She smiled. "Would you like some lukewarm tea? It really is nice to see you again."

Mike grinned and said, "And it's good to see you. Where would you like to eat? Kitchen table okay?"

"Of course, what's for lunch? I'm starved."

"Would you believe a pepperoni pizza, already cooked and packed on dry ice? Made it myself last night. Thought it'd be a treat for my skinny friend in Rebita. I had no idea about all your trouble here...and Barbara, you've lost more weight. Not good, my dear. Not good at all. Yes, tea sounds great, as long as it's wet."

She set plates, silverware and poured two glasses of tea. "This pizza is fantastic. I didn't know I was so homesick for familiar food. And I don't know when I've had better pizza. If I ate like this all the time I wouldn't be this thin for long. It is sooo good. Thanks, Mike, this was really kind of you."

They finished two medium-sized pizzas for lunch. Mike teased her about eating more than him. He thought, "My God, she must be about starved here. I have to do *something*." Then he broke the comfortable silence. "My dear lady, may I have the pleasure of your company for this evening's dinner?"

Barbara was wary. She wondered, "Does he expect me to cook for him? I've nothing to cook and I'm out of practice." She asked, "Would you like a bit of fresh mango? I'd like a taste of fruit before my *siesta*."

"Sounds good to me, I love mango. But what about dinner, Barbara? We'd have more time to talk. Oh and I forgot to mention, I just happen to have a surprise dinner for two packed on ice. Forgive my presumptuous attitude about your availability status...what do you say?"

"I say you're incredibly persistent, and *yes* I'll accept your dinner invitation. You keep making offers I can't seem to resist today."

"Maybe you're just worn down by all that's happened and don't have much resistance left." He watched her closely for a reaction.

She only sighed, and quietly answered, "Maybe you're right."

"You were my guest for lunch, so you go rest and I'll clean up the kitchen. Do you mind if I use the sofa for a *siesta* when I'm through here?" he asked.

"Help yourself. I'll rest on the bed and set the alarm just in case we'd both sleep too long after that fantastic lunch. Thanks, Mike." She smiled at him as she left the room.

Her smile seemed like the most beautiful sincere smile he'd ever seen, anywhere. He felt a warmth and sense of caring that was entirely new to him. Dr. Mike Kane fell asleep on the sofa for his *siesta* with a contented expression on his face.

The alarm clock's brutal wailing abruptly awakened Barbara from her deep sleep. She pulled herself out of bed, splashed water on her face, neck and arms, put on a fresh shirt, and brushed her hair. She was briefly startled to see Mike sleeping on her sofa. Then she remembered lunch and sighed contentedly. She nudged his arm to wake him up. He, too, woke up with a start and then looked at her warmly. He covered her hand with his and softly said, "Good afternoon, my lady Barbara."

She grinned and shook her head, thinking, "It figures that my knight in shining armor would have a long gray pony tail!" She asked teasingly, "Did you crush sleeping pills into that pizza? We must've gone out like the lights. I've got to hurry, do you want tea or anything? Just help yourself. *Mi casa es su casa*. See you later." And she was off to the clinic. He found her work ethic curiously admirable.

He pushed himself to a sitting position and rubbed his head, thinking, "I could've slept till tomorrow. No wonder she asked me if I'd drugged the pizza! Guess we both must've been exhausted." He stumbled into the bathroom and splashed lukewarm water on his face, shoulders and arms, pulled a comb out of his pocket, pulled his hair lose, combed it and then pulled it tight into the hair band again. He tucked in his crumbled khaki shirt and on his way to the clinic stopped by the gate to visit with Angelo, the new guard, who'd been his patient on several occasions over the years.

Angelo was a young restless boy who was anxious to impress the doctor. He filled Mike in on the gruesome details of Pablo's murder, as well as the village rumors and speculation about who dunnit and why. Also, told Mike about the mysterious thefts of the village's television and the Peace Corps Compound's generator. "Sorry, sorry, Doctor, I almost forgot tell you we had government soldiers here when everything bad happen. They leave just few days ago. Now we have no more movie nights. Movies take us for big trips but we never leave Rebita. We like movies…and we have no more Pablo. Pablo was everybody friend. Now everybody miss Pablo, whole village sad."

"Pablo was a good man. It's a tragedy. Life is unfair sometimes. Well, it's been good talking to you again, Angelo. Congratulations on your new guard job. This is an important position. You're a smart young man. *Gracias* for telling me all the news. I've got to go see some sick people now." Mike Kane meandered toward the clinic.

Gabriela met him at the door, grabbed his arm and told him she had to talk to him. He thought, "This girl is nothing if she's not a drama queen!" But he said, "What's up, Gabriela?"

She had her hands on her hips and looked like she was going to explode in a rage. "What's up? Stupid question for you, our doctor, to ask! Open your eyes. I know you like Nurse Barbara. Everybody know. But not you. You don't see how she keep losing weight. How these bad things keep making her sadder and sadder."

"What do you suggest I do, Gabriela? I'm only here about two days a month."

"You the doctor, you think of something. We love Nurse Barbara. We want her be happy, well *and safe*. Now she learn her son get married next week, she want to go to wedding. She tell my mama. They girlfriends. Mama say, 'you must go to wedding' but Nurse Barbara shake her head, she cry and say, 'I don't know, I just not know.' Already more bad things happen to Nurse Barbara in Honduras than all other Rebita Peace Corps nurses together. You know that true, Doctor."

Mike Kane held his hands up and said, "Okay, okay, I give up. I'll think about it this afternoon and talk to her tonight over dinner. Oh…and thanks for sharing your concerns about Nurse Barbara with me, but you got the wrong idea about her and me."

Gabriela stopped him flat, raised her eyebrows and challenged him. "You think Gabriela wrong? I smarter than good doctor. I have eyes. I can see. You bring lunch for her today, and you bring dinner for her tonight. You care about this lady. Might as well admit it. You pick a good one. You show everybody you smarter than you look!"

"And what do you know about my lunch and dinner habits, *señorita?*"

She held her head high and walked away. "I *know* some things!"

Dr. Mike Kane inhaled deeply. He pondered, "That girl is downright exasperating, I've been offering free medical services to these mountain people for years and this is the respect I get?!" A few minutes later he walked into the clinic. There were only about twenty people waiting. A good sign for a steady though not hectic afternoon.

He looked at the list and started with the first name. The afternoon flew by. As Barbara locked up the clinic for the weekend, he asked, "May I use your kitchen facility again for tonight's dinner, Barbara?"

"Of course, when shall I expect you?" she asked.

"About an hour, I have a few errands to do and you can get a little rest."

"Sounds good to me, see you later." She watched him walk away.

The heat was nearly unbearable for Barbara; the small cottage was stifling, even with all the windows open. She thought, "Thank God for screens but electricity for fans is even better." Next she splashed water on her face and sat down on the overstuffed chair and promptly fell asleep. Mike's arrival, with a bag of fresh vegetables to prepare a salad for their dinner and the cooler with dinner on ice, was her wake up call. "You're spoiling me, Mike. I feel like a pampered princess!" Barbara tried to hide a smile; she was reluctantly savoring the moment.

"And now for the big surprise. Tonight's dinner is lasagna, Italian bread, fresh fruit and chocolate pudding. I made it last night and packed it on dry ice for the trip to Rebita. And of course, a fresh salad. All for you, my friend."

"It looks wonderful I haven't had lasagna since I joined the Peace Corps. Thanks, Mike, you're a great friend to have in the jungle. If you'll excuse me, I must go freshen up. A quick shower may make me feel alive again. This heat is hard to take."

"You go ahead; I'll set the table and heat up the lasagna." He hated to admit it, but he could not remember ever feeling this contented before.

The food was delicious. They shared a small bottle of Honduran wine and Mike's dinner was a smashing success. He insisted she relax as he cleaned up the kitchen. They toasted "friendship" with small glasses of after-dinner wine, on the front porch step, enjoying the slightly cooler evening breeze.

"Barbara, I told you my story. Why don't you tell me more about yours? I hear you have a son getting married next week. If you want to go home, I can help you get there."

She looked at him in shock. "How do you know about my son's wedding?"

"Gabriela, you know how she is. But she means well. She's worried about you. People have noticed how sad you look and how much weight you keep losing. I don't want to pry. I only want to be your friend. You've really told me nothing about yourself and I've told you my whole ugly story. Could you bring yourself to tell me *your* story? How did you end up in the mountain jungles of Honduras at this time in your life?"

She sighed and leaned against the porch post. "Thanks for dinner, it was simply delicious. You keep this up and I'll end up counting the days till your next visit. Mike, I don't know what you want me to tell you. I've not led an exciting life. I married young. It was not a good marriage, but I hung in for the long haul. I went back and finished my nursing studies about seventeen years ago. I've never worked except as a volunteer at the Wellness Clinic I established in our home town. My husband's family had money; it was beneath them for me to actually work. The best thing about our marriage was the four children.

"My oldest, Billy, is a dedicated high school teacher. He married his longtime girlfriend just before I left for training last year. She's a peach, also a dedicated teacher. They were honeymooning in the Bahamas just last month. They're very happy as far as I know.

"My second is Jessica, a physical therapist with a real firebrand spirit. She recently moved back to live with her paternal widowed grandmother in Lewiston. Seems to be a great match for both of them. She's working at the local hospital. Last week she became engaged to a boyfriend who's come into the picture since I've left. They seem to be very happy.

"My youngest son, Bobby, is a lawyer. Apparently he's had a whirlwind romance with a temp secretary who was working in his firm. This is what's so shocking. He's a smooth talker and has always been a Casanova-type...sort of like his father. Anyway he's fallen deep and hard; the wedding is next weekend. I understand she was raised by her grandmother who is terminally ill and wants to see her only granddaughter married before she dies. Bobby passed the muster. The family is wealthy. She has a five-year-old son and was never married. Bobby is quite taken with the child. My parents tell me she's a beautiful and wonderful girl.

"My baby, Janie, has been living in New York City for about ten years. She was a struggling actress for so long. A gorgeous and very talented girl. She's had her ups and downs. But just when she was about to give up, she got her first real break. She has a part on a daytime soap opera. The role was offered to her about the time I left for training. Now she's also had small roles in two movies and a co-staring role in a TV movie. This measure of success has been so good for her self-confidence. We're all very proud of her.

"My brother and his family live in California, my sister's family lives in North Carolina. She died several years ago...cancer. My parents are the cornerstone for the whole family. They're healthy, active and happy. I've enjoyed a warm relationship with my mother-in-law over the years. My husband died of a massive coronary on the golf course last summer. He was only fifty-five years old. He left everything to me and made a deathbed plea for forgiveness and love for me. Well that's about it. Hope it wasn't too long winded for you."

Mike watched her cheeks glisten in the moonlight from the silent tears. "Barbara, you are so fortunate to have family, and such a fine family." Mike shook his head. "Remarkable that they grew up exposed to money and they all still manage to have work ethics and values. I'm sure you've been a very strong influence in their lives. So, about this wedding? Are you packing tonight or in the morning? I can drive you to Valencia on Monday and you can take a bus from there to Tegucigalpa to fly home on Wednesday. You can't miss this wedding."

"I just didn't see how I could possibly go." Barbara stared into the darkness. "You'd really drive me to Valencia for the bus?"

"I said I would, didn't I? And I want you to do some serious thinking about whether you want to come back to Honduras. Personally, I'd like to see you return. But you'll have to make some changes, my friend, if you do."

She looked at him skeptically. "And what kind of changes do you recommend, Doctor?"

"First of all, you'll have to open the clinic fewer hours per week. Secondly, you'll have to figure out a stable nutritional balance for yourself. I'd say you're burning out here, Barbara. Overtired and malnourished. Look at yourself and think about it."

She carefully thought about his suggestions and finally looked at him. "I'm coming back. I signed up for two years and I'll honor my commitment. You can't get rid of me that easily!"

"I hope you do come back. But I don't want to see you come back and work yourself into an early grave."

"I promise I'll consider your advice. Well, I better go pack if we're leaving in the morning."

"Okay, see you then. You can spend Saturday afternoon and Sunday at my house. It's comfortable, you'll have a relaxing weekend. On Monday we'll get up before dawn and drive you to the bus depot." He stood up to leave.

Barbara walked a few steps in front of the cottage, then looked back at Mike. He baffled her, such a bundle of contradictions. She remembered her first impression of him and thought, "He's definitely a character and perhaps one of the *kindest* characters I've ever met."

He started to walk away, and she reached out and touched his arm gently. "Mike, I truly appreciate what you're doing for me." And she stretched up to lightly kiss him on the cheek. "Thanks. What time should I be ready in the morning? I'll have to talk to Gabriela about the clinic for the next couple weeks, but it won't be a problem. I did request time off from the Peace Corps office but had no idea how or even if a trip could be arranged so quickly. I felt it was nearly impossible. The request was sent with an incident report about our troubles here last week; I don't know how long it'll even take the envelope to get to the national Peace Corps office in Tegucigalpa."

He covered her hand with his and gallantly lifted it to kiss the back of her hand. "Good night, my friend. Be ready by seven thirty a.m. It's a long, bumpy ride, but I'll get you there. Don't worry, it'll all work out. Sleep well."

"The same to you, and thanks...Mike."

Barbara quickly packed a few essentials and set out a few pieces of fruit and bread to prepare lunches in the morning for the trip across the mountains. She set her alarm for six a.m. Exhaustion proved to be a dear friend to her weary soul, and sleep came easily.

By seven a.m. Barbara had showered, eaten a bite of breakfast and packed lunches into the cooler Mike had forgotten in her kitchen the night before. She'd walked to Gabriela's, had a cup of tea and some delicious fresh sweets with Gabriela, Lilia and Oscar.

Gabriela said, "No worry, I take care of clinic while you in USA. I taught by good Peace Corps nurses. I call first aid nurses if need help. You take good care and come back healthy and happy to us. *Adiós*, Nurse Barbara." Gabriela gave her a friendly hug.

Lilia hurried out with a small bundle of her fresh sweets and hugged Barbara. "*Adiós*, *gringo* nurse *amiga*, here good sweets for the travel. *Adiós*."

"*Gracias, amigos, gracias. Hasta luego.*" And Barbara hurried back to the cottage.

Chapter Twenty-five

At seven thirty a.m. Caesar and Mike roared into the compound. Barbara's things were quickly loaded and they started the long, rugged journey through the mountain jungles to Mike's home.

Three hours later, in a very dense area of the jungle, the familiar sounds of exotic birds and animals suddenly vanished. Caesar stopped with a lurch as Cergio, Julio and friends surrounded them with a dozen unfriendly guns. Rapid Spanish was exchanged between Cergio and Caesar. Then the doors were abruptly opened and Mike and Barbara were ordered out. As soon as Julio and Cergio recognized Nurse Barbara and Dr. Mike, all guns were put at ease.

"My friends, my friends! So sorry for inconvenience, please come sit down and tell me of life in Rebita. Such a pretty village." As he spoke, his comrades used their machetes to clear an area for them to sit and visit, small camp stools were provided from their backpacks.

Mike shook hands with Cergio and exchanged greetings.

Cergio shook Barbara's hand and bowed. "Nurse Barbara, my *madre* and all other family wish to thank you *mucho, mucho* for saving our Julio. *Gracias*."

She looked at Julio closely and asked, "How are you? Have you had any problems with your wound?"

He smiled, proudly pulled up his shirt to show her his surgical scars, and said, "I good as new. Nurse Barbara is good nurse. You save my life. Now Julio is friend of Nurse Barbara for always."

Barbara was impressed with the neat stitches that kept the scarring to a minimum and thought, "Needle point was certainly good preparation for surgical stitching!" But she said, "Thank you, Julio. I was only doing my job as a nurse to try to help you when you needed help. You were a good patient, you worked hard to get well."

She felt an overwhelming sense of frustration and confusion as nagging questions distracted her. "How can I sit here in the presence of Alvie's killers and accept their gratitude for saving Julio? How can I even care if he's recovered? What's wrong with me?"

Mike brought her back to the situation by putting his arm around her shoulder with a familiarity that startled Barbara. "Yes, *amigos*, Nurse Barbara is staying with me this weekend. We're special friends." He winked at Cergio and gave Barbara's shoulders an extra squeeze. "Now, won't you all join us for a small lunch? We weren't expecting guests but there's enough for everyone to have a little."

Barbara asked Caesar to get the cooler from the back and a light picnic lunch was shared with Cergio and company. Barbara thought, "Thank goodness for the extra sweets Lilia gave me this morning."

Mike told Cergio about the television theft and Pablo's murder in the village. Cergio's anger was clearly evident. "El *capitán* has gone too far this time! I will get new movie television for Rebita, this time it will be a secret from *Capitán*. We will help you find safer place to keep it. I will take care of evil *capitán* myself."

The picnic was interrupted by a midday tropical shower, already ninety-eight degrees and very humid. They quickly packed the empty cooler and bid farewell to their *bandito amigos*.

Barbara asked, "What if the government soldiers come by and find this cleared area? Won't they be suspicious?"

"Perhaps but the jungle regenerates so quickly that odds are if and when the *capitán* ever ventured this far from civilization, there'd be no evidence of our travel through here." Mike sounded confident. "Besides, what's to stop us from clearing an area for a picnic lunch and a chance to stretch our legs after a long morning of travel? Don't worry."

"Cergio sounded angry and determined to bring a new television for the village. That's really very kind of him," Barbara added. Then she asked, "*And* what was that special friend business and shoulder squeeze all about?"

"I hope I didn't hurt your shoulder or your feelings. Cergio was curious of our traveling together. I had to imply something he'd understand and believe. I don't think he'd have liked the idea of you leaving the jungle right now, even for a short visit home. You are their saving nurse."

"I see." Barbara nearly choked on the reality of his reasoning. "I guess I owe you. Thanks again, Mike."

Caesar drove on and on through the dense jungle; the sun seldom was more than an occasional flicker through the thick overgrowth of the tall trees.

Before Barbara dozed off, she remembered wondering how Caesar and Mike were so sure they knew where they were going. The road they were traveling looked more like an overgrown jungle trail; they could've been going in circles for all she knew. At four p.m. they stopped in front of a beautiful chalet.

Barbara opened her eyes and felt a bit confused until she recognized Mike and Caesar. Mike announced, "We're here."

She climbed out of the SUV and for a few seconds stood staring at the house, speechless. "How did you ever build such house in this jungle? It's magnificent!"

"Actually, I didn't build it. The government confiscated it from a drug ring years ago. It sat empty for two years, then I made the winning offer. It's not exactly located in the most sought-after neighborhood. No schools and the closest neighbor is five miles away. I paid ten thousand dollars and promised to provide medical care to the area for twenty years. They gave me the key on a silver platter."

Barbara had seen many beautiful homes, but this one was in a class of its own. Black-and-white marble floors with white stucco walls, it was built on a mountain bluff with a breathtaking view of the green jungle valley below. The first floor had extra high ceilings with elegant ceiling fans, which were very effective in keeping the rooms comfortable. The screened ceiling-to-floor windows were opened wide and a gentle breeze blew the long white sheers in a welcoming manner that seemed to say, "Come in and be safe within our walls." Barbara stood in the spacious foyer as if in a trance.

Mike had quietly carried their bags in and stood only slightly behind her, watching and waiting for Barbara's reaction to his home. Finally he cleared his voice and said, "Welcome to my home, I hope you will be comfortable."

She turned to him, her eyes shining and said softly, "This is the most beautiful house I've ever seen. I'm in shock…I never expected to see anything like this in the middle of the jungle! How do you keep it so clean? It's truly magnificent. I had a peaceful, safe and welcoming feeling just walking through the front door."

Mike smiled. "I rarely have visitors. It's just a little out of the way, you know. I have a middle-aged Honduran couple, Velia and Alejandro, who share my home; they live in the apartment in the back of the house. They're bright, energetic, native mountain people. They raised six children who all live in nearby villages with a couple dozen grandchildren. Velia does most of the cooking and all the cleaning. Alejandro takes care of the grounds and helps Velia with cleaning when needed."

Barbara turned to Mike. "I'm surprised…and impressed."

"Doctor, Doctor! *Bienvenido.*" Velia and Alejandro hustled to the foyer. A small child peaked from behind Velia's skirt, her beautiful sparkling brown eyes curious, but unsure at the sight of Barbara and Mike.

Mike greeted them like old friends and introduced Barbara. They were polite and guarded. Then he scooped up the little girl whose giggles filled the house with a natural joy. "And what do we call this little beauty?" Mike asked.

"Elena, child of our Maria. She visit us for the week, she very good helper," Alejandro answered.

"My friends are very rich in family," Mike said as he kissed the little girl's cheek and gave her to Velia. "Could we have dinner in about three hours? We need to rest and freshen up after our long journey. Barbara, allow me to show you to your room." He picked up her bag and led the way up the marble circular staircase. Six large teak doors opened onto the marble balcony with matching railings high above the foyer below.

Mike opened the third door and again she was left speechless at the quiet elegance of the room. The white sheers gently bounced by the open window. The room was spotlessly clean; the marble floors gleamed in the sunshine. Another elegant ceiling fan buzzed quietly, and the room temperature was perfect. The white fluffy poster bed looked comfortable and inviting, with its fluffy bright bedspread, matching pillows and the draped mosquito netting. "Mike, I don't know what to say."

"So, don't say anything, my friend. It's *siesta* time; I'll wake you in two hours if you're not awake. *Buenas tardes.*" He touched her face briefly and gently on his way out.

Barbara smiled as she closed the door and thought, "I joined the Peace Corps to help people and here I am in paradise and being treated as an honored guest at that. Life is full of surprises!"

She took a refreshing shower and was asleep within minutes after lying down in the lovely bed.

Mike knocked lightly on the door for her wake-up call. She quickly dressed in her only dress and sandals. Barbara splashed her face with cold water and brushed her hair till it shined and appeared somewhat styled, even though it was more than half gray now. She shrugged and closed the bedroom door behind her.

She found Mike by following the sound of his booming voice. He was in the living room talking with Alejandro about pending home maintenance projects. When she entered the room, both men rose to greet her as if she were an important guest.

Barbara apologized. "I'm sorry, I hope I'm not interrupting you. I just came to this room because I heard familiar voices."

Mike suggested, "No, not at all. Please join us. Would you like a drink?"

"Ice water would be great, thank you."

When he returned with their drinks, Alejandro soon excused himself to help Velia in the kitchen. Mike toasted, "To my dear friend, Nurse Barbara, may peace and health be your closest friends from this day forth."

She smiled and felt herself blush. "And to my dear friend, Mike Kane, whose kindness overwhelms me."

Velia served a delicious dinner. Mike had trained her well; it was bland by Honduran standards but perfect for a *gringo* with a weak stomach. After dinner Mike showed Barbara the majestic naturally landscaped grounds.

She said, "My compliments to Alejandro. He's a wonderful gardener."

"I'll tell him you think so, he'll be happy to hear that. He's very proud of his work."

Then he gave her a tour of the house. Every room was unique but true to the light airy quality of the first welcoming impression of the foyer. "You're very lucky to have Velia. She's an incredible housekeeper as well as a wonderful cook. This is truly the most beautiful home I've ever seen."

"Again I'll share your compliments with Velia. She is also very proud of her work and rightfully so, I might add. Actually the drug lords had very good decorators and we've just added a few touches to their general motif."

"Well, you certainly have a way of deflecting sincere compliments. It's so tranquil and beautiful here...that it's easy to forget it was built with drug money." Barbara bit her lip and her thoughts were with Janie in New York City and a young life almost lost to drugs.

"Barbara, my deflective comments are really just honesty. At first this place is almost enchanting, like something right out of a fairy tale. But I always remember the wealth that built this house came from destroyed families like mine. It helps keep it in perspective. I try to use it for some good. Caesar and his family live in the guest house beyond the garage. Velia and Alejandro use their apartment and the patio for family gatherings as often as they like. Their grandchildren and children are always welcome, sort of like my own extended family. They've certainly been more effective parents than I ever was. Of course, they all have total access to the pool."

"Mike, you manage to keep surprising me. I'm glad you have this house and I'm glad you share it so freely with your extended Honduran family. It'd be a shame if it was just another abandoned building. I certainly never expected to see such a lovely and sophisticated home in the mountain jungles."

"I know what you mean. I could hardly believe it when I first saw it. But trust me, the original glow dims and it becomes just a home. A home with a few ghosts roaming the halls."

"You don't believe in ghosts, do you, Mike?" Barbara was dumfounded by his remark.

"Not literally. But for me there are occasional eerie feelings derived from living here. Maybe it's because of the way I came to be alone in this world, I don't know."

Barbara spoke softly. "I'm sorry you have to keep reliving your personal tragedy, Mike. I hope some day you will be free of your nightmares. You deserve some peace of mind."

He looked at her intently for several seconds; it felt like an hour to both of them. Finally he said, "How do you always know what to say to make me feel like a whole person again?"

She smiled and answered, "Well, thank you. I never thought I was particularly gifted as a conversationalist. I'm glad I've helped you feel better. After all you are a whole person. I'd hate to think our friendship was…oh, completely one sided."

"One-sided? Barbara, what does a man have to do to prove his interest and concern for a friend?" Mike looked stunned with her reply.

Barbara was embarrassed when her eyes filled with tears. "Mike, you couldn't be more special than you have the last few days. I'll be forever grateful to you. I've been so tired. Are there any special plans for tomorrow?"

"It's special having you as a guest in my home." He gently wiped the tears from her eyes with his huge hands. "Velia has planned a barbecue for several of her children and their families tomorrow. They'll sing and dance and swim. They always have fun at their *fiestas*. There will be at least thirty people here. Caesar and his family are coming over, too. I really don't know what the occasion is. It will be a fun day. If you get too tired, please just excuse yourself and go to your bedroom and rest. These people really know how to enjoy themselves and they have admirable family love and loyalty. How about a small nightcap?"

"Thanks, Mike, I may need it tonight. I've so much on my mind, things to do when I get home and what I have to do to get home. And why I feel so good being here with you. Yes, a drink may be just what I need right now."

"Well, I think I can arrange to get you what you need then. I'll be right back."

After their drinks he closed and locked his windows and doors and turned off the downstairs lights. They walked up the spiral staircase together. At some point their hands touched and they walked to her bedroom holding hands as if it was the most natural thing in the world. When they reached her door, they looked at their hands as if they were inanimate objects belonging to neither one of them. Then Barbara blushed and laughed self-consciously. "I'm sorry. I don't know how that happened! I haven't held hands with anyone since my Janie was eight years old."

Mike looked at her seriously; tears sneaked out the corners of his eyes. With a choked voice he whispered, "I don't know how it happened either, but I'm glad it did. I haven't held hands with anyone since my children were small. Barbara, you are far more to me than just a friend."

He held her face gently and kissed her lips lightly. "Good night, my dear Barbara."

She covered his hands with hers and whispered softly through her tears, "Sleep well, my dear friend," and she kissed him back.

They embraced briefly and felt electrical charges burst through their middle-aged bodies. Barbara and Mike simultaneously stepped back from each other, a natural reaction to avoid another shocking electrical surge. They looked at each other with ambivalent longing and decided to go to their separate bedrooms while they still could...with a lot more than sugar plums dancing through their heads!

The next day Barbara and Mike felt young at heart and as if they were walking on clouds. Everyone noticed and there was much winking and back slapping for Mike. He took it good-naturedly. Velia and Alejandro hosted a wonderful barbecue fiesta. Their daughters and daughters-in-law helped with the food preparations. It was a festive day of joy at the beautiful mountain chalet. The children played gaily and there was music and dancing just as Mike had predicted.

Caesar had driven most of the guests back to their villages in very crowded Suburban rides before darkness fell on the mountain. Seat belts were not a priority in the Honduran mountains.

Mike and Barbara said awkward good nights and went to bed early since they had to rise very early the next morning for the long drive to El Progresso.

Velia prepared travel food for them. The trip was long and tiring but uneventful. Barbara and Mike were pleasant with each other but avoided being together alone. Their obvious desires were a frightening complication for both of them.

At the bus station, Caesar brought her bags to her as Mike quickly purchased a ticket for her to the capital. The bus was due in five minutes. If all went well, she should be back home by Wednesday night. Barbara had decided to surprise her family...so she made no phone calls. "*Gracias*, Caesar, for the safe driving through the mountains."

He murmured, "*Gracias*, *Señora* Barbara, and safe travels to you. *Hasta luego*."

She turned to Mike. "Thank you for *everything*, you've become so special to me. I'm really going to miss you. I'll see you in a couple weeks, please take good care of yourself."

Mike blinked back his tears. "You take good care of yourself and remember my advice about your health. I hope to see you again soon, Nurse Barbara." He kissed her hand as the bus rumbled into the depot.

She couldn't resist gently touching his weathered bearded face, and whispered, "I'll be back, and I'll think of you often while I'm gone."

Mike stood alone in the crowd and watched till the bus was out of sight. Then he returned to Caesar and they started the journey back, returning to the mountain clinics he'd dedicated his life to.

Caesar looked at his boss and said, "Nurse Barbara *es* nice *señora*. We all miss her now, right, Doctor Mike?"

Mike stared blindly out the passenger window, wondering if he'd ever see her again and answered, "Yes, Caesar, we'll all miss her now."

Barbara was amazed at how easily the travel back to Tegucigalpa had been, compared to her memory of going to Rebita a few months earlier on the bus with Alvie and Ethel. She thought, "Perhaps I've become accustomed to the challenges of travel in Honduras. Besides, the roads are quite good once we are down in the valleys."

Barbara arrived in the capital with several hours to spare before her flight to the USA. She went to the Peace Corps office, retrieved her passport and was granted two weeks' leave. She also answered questions regarding her need for a new generator for the clinic in Rebita and Pablo's murder.

At seven p.m. her plane embarked on the flight bound for New York City.

She felt like she'd been away for light years while it had really been eight months.

Chapter Twenty-six

Barbara slept soundly during the seven-hour flight and arrived at JFK Airport feeling refreshed. She'd already decided against calling Janie, rationalizing, "I'll see her at the wedding; besides, I'd only add more stress to her already hectic schedule." Instead she bought a ticket for the early bird flight to Lewiston. Without delays she'd be home by ten a.m. Still she had three hours to spend in the airport. She was glad to see shops opening up and did a little shopping…underwear, toiletries, two new shirts, two pair of slacks and a new pair of shoes.

When the hair salon finally opened, she still had an hour until her departure. Barbara asked, "How fast can you wash, trim and style hair?"

The perky young bleached blonde beautician looked at her hair and rolled her blue eyes framed by black mascara and heavy blue shadows. "If that's all you want, thirty minutes or less."

"Okay, let's do it, my flight leaves in an hour." Barbara had already changed into one of her new outfits and had thrown her old clothing away. All her other new things were carefully packed in her carry-on luggage. She wore her new shoes and they fit perfectly. Barbara felt like a million bucks. Obviously, the little beautician didn't think she looked like it.

"I hate to knock other people's work, but, honey, who the hell has been whackin' your hair? My God, it's a mess!" The beautician's Brooklyn accent was definitely authentic.

"I confess, I've been cutting it myself," Barbara answered. "And I'm not a beautician."

"No shit, Dick Tracy!" The girl rolled her eyes in disgust.

"You see…I've been living in a remote jungle in Central America. There was no one but me to cut my hair. I work for the Peace Corps."

"Yeah really, like my grandma does, too."

"Really, I do. But please just do what you can with my hair…I have to catch my flight." Despite her tarty remarks, this girl was likable and personable.

"Did you ever think about frosting your hair to cover the gray? And what about a little make up? You'd look so much younger and healthier with a little color," the blonde beautician asked.

"No color, I'd only have to deal with roots. I've neither the time nor patience for that."

Luckily for Barbara, the girl worked as fast as she talked. Twenty minutes later she spun Barbara's chair around. "It's a great cut. I hardly know myself with such a sleek look!"

"Okay, what about a little make up? I can do your face in twelve minutes. That would leave three minutes for you to pay and fifteen to get to your gate. What'd ya say?"

Barbara smiled and nodded. "Let's do it."

Ten minutes later, Barbara gasped when she looked in the mirror. "You're an artist, a magician…I almost didn't recognize myself. Thank you. How much for the hair and the make up?"

"I have to admit you look better than I ever thought you would, good luck to you. Hey, are you really in the Peace Corps?"

Barbara quickly showed her Peace Corps photo identification card, paid the bill and left a twenty-dollar tip for the girl. "Thanks, you did a great job. I don't want to miss my flight. Good-bye."

Between the photo identification and the tip the beautician's eyebrows went up, her heavily made-up eyes became wide as saucers and her mouth dropped open in shock….as Barbara left the shop, she shouted, "And good luck to you!"

Barbara was the last one to board, relieved to have accomplished so much during her layover: all necessary things she was glad to have checked off her to-do list before reaching home. It was a clear day and Barbara felt a tinge of hometown pride when the plane circled low on the perimeters of Lewiston. She thought, "It looks exactly the same. *But* I'm not the same…guess I'll find out if I can still fit into my old life. And an uneventful flight, which of course is the best kind, brought me home. I wonder if this may be an omen predicting the tone for Bobby's marriage and my visit home. I wonder. I hope."

Barbara went straight for a taxi with her two carry-on bags. She was ringing her parents' front doorbell by eleven a.m.

Her mother opened the door. She looked the same until she recognized Barbara, then turned white as the blood drained from her face. "Barbara! *Barbara!* Oh my goodness, I can't believe it!" She quickly flung the door open and hugged her daughter with a strength that clearly defied her age.

Barbara had feared her mother was about to faint and felt relieved by the strength of her embrace. "It's so good to see you again, Mom. I hope I haven't surprised you too much showing up like this. Where's Dad?"

"He's off doing a few errands for me...weddings, even for the groom's family, always create last-minute extras. We went through this just last year, but this wedding's a little different. We all have to travel out to Cleveland...Barbara, you've lost too much weight, but you still look lovely. I like your new hair style. You must be exhausted and hungry. How was your trip? Does anyone know you're coming? What a lovely, lovely surprise!"

Barbara relaxed and laughed. "A surprise that nearly made you faint! No, I didn't tell anyone I was coming, I didn't want to cause disappointment if something came up at the last minute and I wouldn't have been able to come. I'm glad you like my new hair style; I just had it cut at the airport this morning while waiting for my connecting flight to Lewiston. What can I do to help prepare for Bobby's wedding? You look wonderful, Mom."

"How about a glass of iced tea? Please tell me what you liked the most and the least about your work in Honduras. Oh, Barbara, it's so good to have you home again." Her mother set her iced tea on the table and gave her another unexpected hug. "I missed you more than you'll ever know; it's a thrill for me to finally have my girl back home."

Barbara smiled and kissed her mother's cheek. "I missed you too, Mom. And it's great to be home. To answer your questions, I think what I like most about nursing in Honduras is feeling genuinely needed and appreciated. The Hondurans are so warm, kind and friendly. The hardest thing is being away from you and the family and adjusting to the tropical heat. Now what about the wedding? What's Ashley like? She must be pretty special to have stopped Bobby cold in his tracks! How's he holding up, anyway?"

"Bobby's ecstatic. He'll be so pleased you came home for the wedding. We really haven't met Ashley face to face yet. Bobby showed us photos and he introduced us to her on the telephone. She's very sweet and very beautiful. Her son looks enough like Bobby to be his own child. Danny is a smart little boy with good manners, according to Bobby. We haven't met him yet either. We've seen pictures and talked with him on the phone."

"Has anyone planned a dinner to be hosted by the groom's family?"

"Yes, of course, it's all taken care of, tomorrow night in Cleveland. We have reservations at a highly recommended restaurant on the lake."

"I want to pay for that. As the groom's only surviving parent, it's my responsibility." Barbara sat quietly, suddenly very concerned about the hastily planned wedding and the fact no one in the family had even met the bride yet, except Bobby, and it sounded like he might be blinded by love.

"It doesn't matter to us who pays for the dinner, dear. Now don't worry, Bobby is a big boy and he's had plenty of girlfriends. We'll just have to trust his judgment on this. Would you like to take a rest and freshen up a bit before everyone gets here? You might as well use the guest room upstairs. No sense in opening up your house before we come back from the wedding. We leave at five a.m. for Cleveland tomorrow. First I'll fix you a quick sandwich. Is turkey and Swiss with tomato on wheat okay?"

"Mom, that sounds heavenly. I am hungry. I really missed my favorite foods, too."

"Well, I must say I've never seen you so thin. What will you wear to the wedding? I doubt any of your clothes will fit you now."

"That's why I don't want to sleep more than one hour. I'll have to run down to the Jan Charles Shop and get a couple things for Cleveland. And, Mom, I'm only home for two weeks. I'm not opening my house up. I'll check on it, but I'm not worried, I know you and Dad have taken good care of it. I know you're right about Bobby, but I just don't want him to make a mistake. I'm really anxious to meet Ashley and Danny. They must be nervous about meeting all of us, too. Well, I'll see you in an hour. Thanks, Mom. The sandwich and tea were perfect. Remember, just one hour, okay?" She gave her mother another hug and went upstairs for a short nap.

Barbara's mother was busy starting preparations for her daughter's favorite dinner. She always worked much faster when she was upset. And upset was only a mild description of her current state of mind. Her thoughts raced. "Just look how skinny the girl is! She could be an ad for the anorexia clinic. Only staying for two weeks and not opening her home up! What about us? Doesn't she know we need and appreciate her too?" Pent-up tears were flowing down her cheeks when Barbara's father came home.

"Mama, what's happened? Why are you cooking so much food? Why do you cry?" He took the pealing knife from her hand and gently dried her face with a tissue. He held her in a familiar loving embrace.

She snuggled her white hair against his broad chest and continued to sniffle. After all these years of marriage, she still believed he was the best gift

God had ever given her. A few seconds later she took a deep breath and finally said, "I'll fix you a cup of tea. Please sit down for a minute; I have to talk to you."

He sat down at the kitchen table, curious about what could have caused such distress in his usually unflappable wife.

She said, "Barbara's home, arrived around eleven. When I opened the door I was so shocked to see her, I nearly fainted. She's terribly thin and I don't know why but I thought she was home to stay…I guess I just chose to believe she was back for good when I saw her because I wanted her to be. But she's only here for two weeks. She came home for Bobby's wedding. Barbara's changed; I don't know…she's somehow grown away from us. She's not our little girl anymore."

Barbara's father smiled ear to ear. "Mama, just listen to yourself. This is good news, she's home. We'll put some meat on her bones while she's here. It's good she's found a purpose for her life. The poor kid never had anything except her children and they're all grown and independent now. We've always had each other. Eric has his own life. Let's not give Barbie a hard time. Let's enjoy our girl while she's here."

"Of course, you're right. It's just so hard. Oh dear, look at the time, it's been an hour and a half and she only wanted to sleep one hour. I better go wake her up. She has to shop this afternoon for a couple new outfits for the wedding." She stopped and gave her man a kiss on the cheek as she was leaving the kitchen and said, "Thanks for setting me straight."

"Anytime, Mama, anytime." He gave her a playful pat on her backside as she walked away. "Tell her to hustle. I want to see my girl!"

Barbara hurried downstairs with her mother. "Oh Dad, it's great to see you again. You look wonderful. Easy to see Mom's taking good care of you as usual. Mmm, what's that smell? Mom, you're cooking my favorite, jansons frestelse, you're going to spoil me while I'm home." Barbara took another deep breath. "Mmm, and I'm going to love every minute of it!" She kissed her mother's cheek. "Thanks, Mom."

Dad held her out at arm's length and shook his head from side to side, and gave her an emotional bear hug. "You are way too skinny, young lady. We're gonna put some meat on your bones while you're home."

"Okay, Dad, whatever you say. May I borrow the car to do a few errands?" Barbara mockingly rolled her eyes and briefly felt like she was sixteen again. "Now that takes me back a few years, asking for the car keys! And where are my house keys? I'll stop by the house and grab a pair of dress shoes for the wedding. Do you need anything else while I'm out? Dad, I'll talk to you when I get back. If I don't hurry I won't have time to do my errands before the wedding."

Her mother handed her the keys for her house and her father gave her the car keys. "You be careful with that car, it's a fine machine, been dependable as a Swiss watch for ten years now."

"Yes, Dad, I'll be careful. See you later. And thanks for the car." She kissed his cheek and was on her way.

First she stopped by her house for the safe deposit key. She had to prepare Bobby's wedding gift and that meant cashing a certificate of deposit and buying a ten-thousand-dollar cashier's check. The same as she'd given Billy and Liz for their wedding last fall.

She bought another check for twelve thousand for her parents as payment for their first year of taking care of her home. She knew it must be difficult to stretch their small pension checks and Social Security to cover all their expenses every month. She also knew they were so stubborn and proud that they'd never say a word about it. And they'd have to accept this check because they earned it.

Next visit was the dress shop; she found two dresses that would work, one for the wedding and one for the rehearsal dinner she'd host the next night. Her next stop was the gift shop for a silver picture frame and a special wedding card. She stopped by her house again and chose two pair of heels that would work with the new dresses. Barbara felt accomplished and ready for the wedding when she pulled the car into her parents' driveway in time for dinner.

The heavenly aroma of the frestelse drifted to the driveway through the open kitchen window; there were also two unfamiliar cars in the driveway. Barbara left her bags in the locked car and walked into the kitchen.

Jessica almost knocked Barbara over in her excitement to greet her. "Jessica, let me see what you look like in love. Oh, darling girl, you're beautiful! It's so nice to see you again, I've really missed you."

Barbara began to feel claustrophobic as Jessica clung to her. "Are you all right, Jess?"

"Yes, I'm fine. It's just I can hardly believe you're really here. I've been so worried about you. You look great, Mom. I like your hair but you're way too skinny! Have you been sick?"

Barbara smiled as she pulled free. "Only homesick! So tell me about your Michael."

"I'll do better than that, I'll introduce...." Jessica was interrupted by Grandmother Malone...walking as fast as she could with her arms extended for an embrace.

"Barbara, Barbara, what a grand surprise to have you home with us again. I've missed you, dear. I do hope you're back to stay and have got that silly Peace Corps stuff out of your system!"

"Mother Malone, it's wonderful to see you, too. You look great, at least ten years younger than when I left. Living with Jessica must be as good for you as it is for her." They exchanged their well-established superficial hugs.

Abruptly Grandmother Malone turned around in a flash of anger. "Who told Barbara about my treatments? I can't trust any one in this family!" She stomped out to the front porch.

Jessica and Barbara followed her. "Grandmother, I haven't told anyone, not even Michael. Although, I think maybe *you* just made an announcement!"

"Mother Malone, what treatments? I don't have a clue what you're talking about. No one has told me anything at all about you. I've only been home a few hours." Barbara walked over to the tall, proud and so often haughty woman who was her children's *other* grandmother, took her hand and gently said, "Let's go in and enjoy Mom's fantastic jansons frestelse. The smell of the spices, anchovies and potatoes have me near drooling!"

Inside Jessica stood beside a handsome, well-dressed young man who radiated warmth, confidence and love for her daughter. "Mom, this is Michael."

"Hello, Michael, it's nice to finally meet you. I've heard so many good things about you. I hope you like Swedish casseroles. This has long been my favorite dinner and what can I say but my mother's spoiling me? I love it!"

"It's good to meet you again, Mrs. Malone. I did meet you years ago when I came to study groups at your house, but I was just another kid in the crowd back then."

He had a winning smile. Barbara hoped it was sincere, and answered, "Well, I'm sure we've all changed since those days...."

Barbara felt relieved to hear her father call everyone to dinner. It was a relaxed and happy meal, even Mother Malone was mellow. For Barbara the food was heavenly. She carefully observed Jessica and Michael. They did seem like a happy, well-matched couple...there was just something about him. She wasn't quite sure what it was, maybe just an intuitive feeling...only thing was, she'd learned long ago to trust her intuitions because she was usually right on target.

Barbara knew for sure she didn't want Jessica to be hurt. Her mind wondered. "Does he think Jessica has money? Sooner or later he'll have to realize that any wealth she inherits will be tied up tightly in life trusts. And what there is is a far cry from a fortune."

Barbara sat back in her chair, enjoying a cup of decaf tea, reflecting on the small talk buzzing around the table, answering appropriately when asked direct questions. However, her mind was thousands of miles away in the Honduran mountains and a doctor named Mike with a long gray ponytail....

Chapter Twenty-seven

The next day Mother Malone, Michael and Jessica arrived promptly at seven a.m. Dad and Mom finished checking the house before locking up; everything was loaded in the trunk. They were off for the long drive to Cleveland; it was an overcast day with rain predicted. Michael offered to lead the way since he'd been to Cleveland many times and had even worked there for a year after college.

The rain started by eleven a.m. By twelve thirty, it was pouring when they stopped for a quick lunch at a Bob Evans Restaurant. They were still at least three hours from Cleveland.

Michael was still driving his car with Jessica and Grandmother Malone and leading the way. Barbara was the designated driver in her parents' car for the last leg of the journey. The heavy rain made visibility very difficult for her elderly father. Michael drove at a considerably slower speed due to the weather. Barbara couldn't help but appreciate his thoughtful common sense.

They finally arrived at the Sheraton. The young desk clerk informed them the up-and-coming film actress Miss Janie Malone had checked in an hour later. "Would you perhaps be relatives of Miss Malone?"

Barbara smiled. "Yes, I'm her mother."

Her parents answered, "Grandmother and Grandfather."

Mother Malone said, "Grandmother."

Jessica said, "Sister."

Michael said, "Future brother-in-law."

Barbara forced a smile. "Would you call Janie's room and ask her to come to my room in ten minutes? We need a little time to freshen up and unpack. Have a Mr. and Mrs. Bill Malone arrived yet?"

The clerk quickly scanned her computer guest registry. "Not yet. But they do have a reservation. Would you like me to give them your room number too, Mrs. Malone?"

"Yes, please. And thank you."

The bellboys politely took the service elevator with their luggage and somehow still managed to be at their assigned rooms before the Malone clan arrived. As Barbara was finishing her unpacking, her excitement about seeing her other children and meeting Ashley and Danny was mounting.

There was a knock on her door. She expected to see Janie but there stood Jessica with two diet cokes. "Hi, Mom, thirsty?" She walked in and plopped on the bed.

"Well, what do you think of Michael? I couldn't read you, but then I never could. You're a tough one; you've always been very good at hiding your feelings."

As they sat sipping their drinks, Barbara answered carefully, "Michael seems like a nice young man and he certainly seems to be devoted to you. So, of course I like him. He was very helpful in getting us to this hotel without getting lost even once. You can't knock a guy like that! And he definitely wants to marry you."

Jessica watched her mother closely. In a strained voice she asked, "Why don't you just say it? You don't like him. He *seems* to be nice, *seems* to be devoted."

"Darling, I don't even know him; I've only spent a couple hours with him. And how I feel about him is not really the issue here. Why should you care so much what I think? You're the one who'd be living with him. Are you having second thoughts? I only want you to be happy." Barbara walked over to Jessica and hugged her troubled daughter. "I know you'll make the right decision. You're a very smart girl. Always have been."

"Sometimes he seems almost like a stranger. I just don't know what to think of Michael. He can be so charming, I don't know, can't really put it into words. Oh well, we're here for good old Bobby."

"One quick question, what's this treatment that had your grandmother so upset?"

Jessica's expression slowly changed to a clever smile. "Oh that, there's a fairly new cosmetic procedure available. A plastic surgeon's dream…fast cash and only lasts for a year or two and needs done again. You could see by looking at Grandmother that it works but she's very sensitive about it."

Barbara laughed. "Obviously! It's ironic she undergoes this procedure to look younger and gets angry when given an innocent compliment about looking younger…."

"That's Grandmother Malone!" Jessica said with a devilish grin.

"So, how is it really going for you living with her? Are you happy there, Jess?"

"Surprisingly, yes, I am. I think I'd feel guilty if I didn't live there and I'd be over checking on her all the time anyway. Besides we get along grandly," Jessica answered.

Another knock on the door…this time it was Janie. She was stylishly dressed, thin as usual and gorgeous. The sisters and mother affectionately hugged each other. They closed the door, declaring their forever love and argued who had missed the other more. Then they stood back and sized one another up, all talking and laughing at the same time.

Finally Barbara demanded silence and a right to speak first. "I'm pulling rank on you two and after all I *am* the mother here! Janie, you look beautiful and confident. A dynamite combination, it's no wonder your career is going so well…once those idiot casting directors gave you a well-deserved chance at long last. It's wonderful to see my two girls together again; I've really missed you both."

"My turn, 'cause I'm the baby sister and I'll pout if I don't get my own way!" Janie stated with a threatening firmness.

Jessica mockingly rolled her eyes. "Some things never change!"

"And what do you mean by that?" Janie asked.

"Nothing. Just kidding." Jessica held her hands up in front of her face in fake self-defense, teasing her little sister just as she had always done.

"You're right about that, Jessica, some things never really change." Janie started to punch her sister with the bed pillows.

Barbara sighed and sat down to watch her girls work off steam, shaking her head from side to side. "Clearly some things never do change." She smiled as she watched but felt distant and removed from the rumpus.

"Okay, you two, enough is enough. Either you settle down and behave in a civilized manner or I'm calling building security!" Barbara stated in a firm clear voice.

The sisters promptly stopped roughhousing, sat on the edge of the bed and in a pretend military attention pose, they saluted their mother. "Yes, Mom. We're sorry."

Janie became serious. "Mom, are you all right? You've lost so much weight. I love your new hairstyle. And your make-up is great. Wow. What a difference a few months can make. So tell me about Honduras."

"And what's happening in your life, Jessica? I want to hear everything from both of you," Janie emphatically stated.

Barbara answered first. "I'm well, only homesick for all of you. It's taking me awhile to get onto the native cuisine. And I had my hair cut and styled in JFK yesterday while waiting for a connecting flight to Lewiston. The beautician also sold me the make-up. In Honduras I cut my own hair and wear no make-up; it's far too hot and humid in my village. There is only one phone at the police station and it doesn't work all the time. The village has no electricity. We have a generator at the Peace Corps Compound, which provides us with electricity for ceiling fans in the clinic and a few lights, ceiling fans, and a small refrigerator in my cottage. Except the generator was stolen about ten days before I came home...."

Jessica and Janie exchanged concerned glances. "Stolen?"

"I'll tell you more about that later. The people are so kind, generous and happy. They make me feel appreciated and needed like I've not felt in Lewiston since you were babies. Enough of that! We have an official wedding dinner in two hours. Aren't you excited to meet Ashley and Danny? How was your flight, Janie?"

"My flight was routine, extra security is necessary but a royal pain. *Yes*, I must say I'm anxious to meet them. They sounded delightful when I talked to them on the phone. Mom, your comments on Honduras are so positive...does that mean this is just a visit home? You're going back, aren't you?" Janie asked.

Jessica and Janie watched their mother closely. "Well, of course I'm going back. I have a two-year commitment to fulfill. I'm needed there and I've made some dear friends. It's been an eye-opening experience and I've grown as a person. It's been very challenging at times, but I do love it."

"Good grief, Mom, the Peace Corps should hire you for publicity, you'd be the best advertisement they'd ever find. Only the problem is you're really serious." Janie stared at the floor, obviously preoccupied.

Jessica put her arm around her mother. "There's no way we can make you feel needed in Lewiston? Sure, we can all take care of ourselves, but no one but you can be our mother...I'm sorry we've pretty much ignored you for so many years. If you'd come back, I promise things would be different."

Barbara covered Jessica's hand with her own and said, "I never thought you were ignoring me. That's what children do—they grow up, leave home and find their way in the world."

Janie walked over to them, sat down on the floor and laid her head on her mother's lap. "I think I understand why you're doing this Peace Corps thing. At least it's real." Janie had her head turned away from them. She was glad they couldn't see her tears. Her mother stroked her hair just like she'd done when Janie was a little girl. It was comforting.

Jessica glanced at her sister as she walked across the room. "Janie, what's wrong? Why the tears? Oh, Janie." She went back to her sister, leaned over and gave her a soft kiss on the cheek.

Janie took a deep breath and sighed. "I've just missed my family so much…it's such a relief to finally be together again."

Barbara looked at her watch. "My God! Look at the time. Girls, we have to hustle! We can't be late for a dinner we're hosting! We'll have more time together this weekend."

They agreed to meet in the lobby in thirty minutes. Jessica called Grandmother Malone. Barbara called her parents. Everyone was ready for the hotel transport to the restaurant except Billy and Liz. The desk clerk motioned to Barbara. He handed her a message received only minutes earlier. "Flight delayed. Now diverted to Buffalo for landing because of torrential rains and wind in Cleveland area. Will rent car and drive to Cleveland as soon as possible. Sorry to miss dinner tonight. See you all tomorrow. Bill and Liz."

She read the message aloud to the family. Everyone understood their dilemma but felt disappointed nonetheless. The bell captain approached them. "Your van has arrived."

As the hotel van approached the restaurant, Jessica said, "I can't wait to see Bobby again and meet his enchantress!"

No one else said a thing as they quietly climbed out of the van. But her words echoed their thoughts. Barbara was relieved they had arrived before Ashley, Bobby and her family. The private dining room was beautifully decorated for the occasion. The furniture was exquisite, the paintings and window coverings had obviously been carefully chosen. She thought, "If the food is half as good as this place looks, then we're in for a fantastic dining experience."

A few minutes later Ashley and Bobby arrived accompanied by a handsome little boy. Bobby was *shocked* to see his mother. He ran over and gave her a giant bear hug. "Mom, I can't believe it. I never expected you to be at our wedding. This is great! Ashley, darling, I'd like you to meet my mom, the Peace Corps volunteer. And this is your first grandson, Mom, meet Master Danny."

She turned to Ashley and took both the girls' hands in hers. "It's so good to meet you. I've heard so many wonderful things about you and I can see everything was accurately reported to me. Welcome to our family, dear Ashley."

Then she turned to Danny and lowered herself to her knees, to be eye level with the child. "I'm Bobby's mother, and I'm so happy he finally has a little boy. Now I can be a grandmother. It's great to meet you, Danny." She shook his hand briefly. He withdrew his hand and stared sullenly at the floor with both hands stuffed firmly in his pockets

He muttered softly, "It's nice to meet you, *but* I already have a grandmother."

"Well, lucky you, now you'll have two," Barbara answered seriously.

"But I only need one." He continued to stare at the floor; there were entirely too many strangers standing around for Danny to feel at ease. He didn't understand why he and his mommy liked Bobby so much, but they both did. And this lady was Bobby's mommy.

Danny glanced shyly at this new grandmother lady. She did seem nice. He reluctantly decided to give her a chance and with a guarded smile said, "*Maybe* two grandmothers will be okay."

"Thank you for giving me a chance, Danny. I'll see you later."

Everyone seemed to be talking at once. Barbara looked for Ashley and found her surrounded by Mother Malone, Jessica and Janie. They were engaged in an animated conversation. A stranger would've had a hard time believing they'd met only a few minutes earlier. Bobby was engaged in conversation with Morfar and Mormor. Michael was chatting with a pretty waitress. Barbara joined the girls, curious to talk with the bride-to-be.

Ashley gave Barbara a warm embrace. "I've heard so much about you that I feel like I know you already. This wedding must seem sudden to you. It does to us too. Thank you for raising such a wonderful man. I feel like Bobby is my soul mate and we were blessed to have found each other. I love him so much, when I came back to Cleveland after my temporary position at his firm ended…I was lost. Even with Danny and my grandmother as anchors, without Bobby I felt like a ship lost at sea. I'm so happy you've come all this way for our wedding."

Barbara graciously smiled at Ashley; she truly did have the voice of an angel. "I understand what you mean, my dear. It would've been a shame if you'd each gone your separate ways once you found each other. Did you know Bobby wrote to me about you before he'd even worked up the courage to ask you out on your first date? He was so impressed with you and rightfully so, I might add."

Ashley smiled. "No, I didn't know, that's very sweet, isn't it?"

Bobby walked over and put an arm around each of them. "So, how are my two best girls doing? Mom, you've lost way too much weight. Are you well? How did you manage to get home? I can't tell you how much it means to have you here for our wedding."

Barbara grinned, relieved to see Bobby looking so handsome, happy and settled. "One question at a time please. First I'm fine, haven't adjusted very well to the native cuisine. When I heard you were getting married, I wanted to be here so bad that my new friends helped me get to the bus station to begin the journey home. I didn't want to miss my son's wedding. You have a beautiful wife and son, Bobby. You have my blessings and best wishes." She lightly kissed their cheeks and said, "We'll talk more later; I'll let you mingle now."

Within ten minutes Grandma Miles and Ashley's mother, Joyce, arrived. Dr. Collins walked in a few minutes later. He'd made it clear that he'd prefer to bring a date and only reluctantly agreed to come alone. Introductions were made without incident. Ashley breathed a sigh of relief.

Barbara and the rest of the Malones were amazed that Ashley could even be related to her parents. However, everyone adored Grandma Miles.

Joyce walked over to Barbara. "So you and I are going to mothers-in-law to each other's children. Interesting predicament, wouldn't you say?"

Barbara looked at her closely. She answered carefully, not knowing if Joyce was teasing or serious. "Yes, I suppose it is. What does being a mother-in-law mean to you, Joyce?"

"Not a damn thing, if you want to know the truth, I'm just making conversation. I'd seriously like to know what possessed you to join the Peace Corps at this stage of your life."

Barbara was taken off guard with Joyce's confrontational style of conversation. "I feel good about Bobby and Ashley's marriage. I feel like they are well suited for each other and wish them a lifetime of love and friendship. I joined the Peace Corps after my husband's death. I needed a change and I wanted to use my nursing skills to help people."

Joyce's tone changed. "I have the same thoughts on my daughter and your son's relationship. I think you're a remarkable person to be in the Peace Corps at your age, but I don't get it. Don't take this the wrong way, but why did you have to go so far away? The classifieds are full of ads for nursing jobs right here in the US. Hey, it's been a pleasure. I'll catch you later." She pointed to her empty glass, shrugged and was off for another drink.

Jessica casually walked by her mother and whispered, "Brace yourself; Dr. Collins is one hell of a nasty man."

Barbara walked over to Ashley's father. "It's nice to meet you, Dr. Collins. I'm Bobby's mother, Barbara."

He looked at her briefly and mumbled, "Yeah, yeah, nice to meet you too."

"Your daughter is an accomplished and beautiful young lady. You must be very proud of her. I think she and Bobby are very well suited for each other."

"I am proud of my daughter, could've been prouder, but she's a very stubborn girl. And what makes you think they're so well suited? How long have you known my daughter to make such an assessment?" Dr. Collins demanded.

"I've only met Ashley today and my first impressions are usually very accurate. Bobby wrote to me about her soon after they'd met, even before their first date," Barbara answered.

"Well, I guess I'm glad your family is so accepting of Ashley. We're not a very close family, but I want her to be safe and secure, she is my only child."

"You also have that wonderful little grandson, Danny," she innocently replied.

Dr. Collins responded coldly, "I have no grandchildren. I have only my daughter, Ashley. Bastard children do not count in *my* family."

His heartless bluntness shocked Barbara, especially since she had met Danny only an hour earlier. She took a deep breath and said in an even low tone, "Never in my life have I met such a cold, egotistical fool as you, Dr. Collins. Your attitude makes *you* the real bastard in your family. By refusing this child, you are missing out in one of the greatest joys of life, being a grandfather. It is your loss. I was thrilled when little Danny hesitantly accepted me as his new grandmother. He is my first grandchild. I hope to make some wonderful memories with him."

Dr. Collins turned to her. "Are you quite finished?"

"For now, I am."

"Good. I believe I've heard more than enough from you today. It is entirely my own business and no concern to you, Mrs. Malone," he replied with a sharp edge to his voice.

She quietly fumed at him, "I beg to differ with you, Doctor. Now that I'm Danny's grandmother, he is very much my concern too. I can't respect anyone who misuses his own family and that child, sir, is your own blood whether you like it or not!"

Before Dr. Collins could respond, Morfar's voice boomed over a loudspeaker, "Welcome everyone. It's been a pleasure for our family to meet Ashley's family. Thank you for comin' tonight. Bobby's brother, Billy, and his wife, Liz, have been delayed and will not arrive till late tonight. Their flight was rerouted to Buffalo due to weather. They send apologies and look forward to meetin' you tomorrow. Reverend Waters just arrived. He's goin' to lead us in a quick walk through rehearsal for the weddin'. Dinner will be served immediately after you've all learned your parts. Now concentrate, 'cause I'm startin' to get real hungry."

The Malones immediately applauded and cheered Morfar as they always did when he did the honors for any celebration. Since a simple service was planned, the rehearsal was soon over. Reverend Waters agreed to stay for dinner and offered the blessing. Then Morfar stood and shouted, "Enjoy!"

Joyce and Dr. Collins, sitting at opposite ends of the table, simultaneously sighed audibly, expressing their joint disapproval. Jessica leaned toward Bobby and whispered, "How did Ashley turn out so sweet with such snooty parents?"

Bobby grinned, gently elbowed his sister and whispered, "Not now. We'll talk about that later."

Mormor and Grandma Miles were seated beside each other. Joyce was beside Grandmother Malone. Barbara smiled to herself. "Grandmother Malone could certainly handle the cynical Joyce."

All the young people were clustered together. Danny was seated between Ashley and Morfar. He'd always been a wizard with children. It was then she realized she had been seated next to Dr. Collins. She took a deep breath and silently prayed, "Please help me, God." She felt some anger at herself for burning a bridge of communication with him earlier. Just what she'd always taught her children not to do.

"Hello again, Dr. Collins. I guess we'll be seated next to each other for dinner."

"Indeed." He stood and gallantly held her chair. "It is my good fortune to dine with a woman who is not afraid to speak her mind."

"Thank you, Doctor." She noticed his glances toward Danny and her father. "You know it's not too late. He's a little charmer and very bright. His whole world is about to change. You could be part of it."

"Mrs. Malone, I believe you have said quite enough on that subject. You might be glad to know that *I am thinking about the whole concept for the first time*. It *was* much less complicated not to acknowledge his existence." Dr. Collins glanced at Danny again.

Danny noticed him looking and made eye contact. Then he smiled, a smile that could melt an iceberg.

Barbara waved at Danny and blew him a kiss. She spoke very softly, "Doctor, anyone who can resist that smile must have a chunk of granite for a heart."

Dr. Collins smiled back at his grandson and waved. Ashley glanced over just in time to see the exchange; she gave her son an affectionate hug and a radiant smile of gratitude to her father.

"So I understand you're in the Peace Corps living with some jungle tribe. How did a woman your age come to join the Peace Corps? I thought it was a place for college kids to get experience."

"You're right, it is mostly younger workers, but they're happy to get experienced bilingual volunteers, too. I joined after my husband died last summer. Our children were all living independently in distant cities and I needed a change. I wanted to help truly needy people."

"Remarkable. I know plenty of independent widows with grown children who'd *never* consider the Peace Corps."

"Well, it's definitely not for everyone. At times it can be grueling but always rewarding."

After dinner Barbara found her way to Ashley's grandmother. Before she could say a word, the old woman embraced her and said, "Finally, I get to meet the famous mother of Ashley's Bob. You must be one special lady raising such fine children and then going off to join the Peace Corps. Welcome to Cleveland. I'm Grandma Miles."

"It's a pleasure to meet you; I've heard some wonderful stories about you."

"Don't believe everything you hear, only the good parts. So, how long did it take you to travel back to the States from the mountains of Honduras? I visited Honduras once, a long time ago. I traveled with my husband for his work after Joyce started college. I remember it was a beautiful tropical country...we had such a grand time traveling together." She wiped a few stray tears. "Sorry, I get too emotional taking all this darn medicine. He's been gone near twenty years and I still miss him terribly. But I'm sure you know what that's like...."

Barbara instinctively squeezed Grandma Miles' hand. "I must agree with you about the tropical beauty of Honduras. I traveled for two and a half days just to reach Tegucigalpa from my assigned village but my flight was only seven hours to JFK. What do you think about your Ashley and my Bobby?"

"I think they were made for each other. And did you notice the astonishing resemblance of Danny to Bob? I've never seen Ashley so happy," Grandma Miles answered quietly.

"I've never seen Bobby look so happy either. He's really needed a personal life so that every little thing in the office doesn't bother him so much. I'm glad I was able to get home and see their glow. It's truly a joy to witness such unabashed adoration."

"I'm happy I lived long enough to see my only grandchild marry for love and friendly companionship. It's been lovely chatting with you, but I'm very tired and tomorrow is *the* big day. Good night Barbara, I'll see you at the wedding." Grandma Miles signaled to her housekeeper. A few minutes later she was whisked away via the waiting limousine.

Barbara noticed Dr. Collins leave immediately after the meal; Joyce remained a captive of Grandmother Malone. Michael remained on the sideline and continued to flirt with the pretty waitress. Barbara looked at Jessica and was sadly relieved that she too had noticed her wandering fiancé. Indeed!

Ashley quietly walked to Barbara's side and shyly tucked her arm through Barbara's. "I'm so happy you could be here, what shall I call you?"

"What would you like to call me? I believe Liz calls me Mother and calls her own mother Mom. Barbara is another option. I'm very flexible. Whatever you're most comfortable with." She patted Ashley's hand reassuringly.

"I couldn't help but notice you seemed to make my father squirm during dinner and he couldn't leave fast enough after dessert. He told me he'd been paged and had to rush to the hospital. I've heard that one before! But he looked, smiled and waved at Danny during dinner. He's never so much as acknowledged Danny's existence before. Whatever you said to him...thank you. It's a start."

"Since I'll be an official grandmother as of tomorrow, I felt I had a right to say whatever I pleased regarding my grandson. Excuse me, my dear, but your father can be an outrageous bigot at times. I may have given him some food for thought."

Ashley couldn't help smiling. "I know I'm going to love being part of this family. Thanks for talking some sense into my father." She leaned over and lightly kissed Barbara's cheek. "Thanks...Mother. I'll see you tomorrow."

During the ride back to the Sheraton, everyone heartily agreed that Ashley and Bobby made a great couple and they all adored little Danny and Grandma Miles. Everyone also agreed Dr. Collins was a rude, nasty, self-centered man.

Grandmother Malone said, "And her mother, Joyce, what a piece of work! Ashley was a very lucky young lady to have her Grandma Miles raise her. Otherwise, I can't imagine how confused she may have grown up to be. Her mother is argumentative, cynical and condescending beyond anyone I've ever had the misfortune to meet."

They all said good night in the lobby, agreeing to meet for breakfast in the dining room at nine a.m. Barbara stopped at the desk to see if Billy had arrived yet. She wrote a note to be given to them when they checked in,

> *Welcome Liz and Billy. Sorry about the hassles with your flight. We missed you at the rehearsal dinner. Pleasant dreams. We're meeting in the dining room at nine for breakfast.*
>
> *Love, Mom... Yes, I'm here!*

Liz and Billy arrived exhausted at two thirty-five a.m. It had been a long arduous trip. The desk clerk gave them the note after they checked in. Liz read the note, momentarily unable to speak; she taped Billy on his arm, waving the note. "Read this."

He scanned the note and smiled. "Well, I'll be...." Billy almost forgot how tired he'd been feeling. He and Liz happily wheeled their bags to the elevator, anticipation mounting to see the whole family in the morning.

Chapter Twenty-eight

The Malones, Mormor and Morfar filled their alcove of the dining room with warmth and excitement. Bobby and Danny also joined them for breakfast.

Billy and Liz hugged Barbara with delight. "It's a double prize, my brother's wedding and seeing you, Mom. Driving half the night was definitely worth it. How are you? You've lost so much weight. Are you home to stay?"

Barbara kept her arms around their shoulders. "It's wonderful to see you both again. I'm fine, I've just not adjusted to the native foods too well yet. And no, I'm home for two weeks to visit and for the wedding. That's all. My work is there and I signed a two-year contract. I didn't want to miss Bobby's wedding…besides I was just a little homesick. So, tell me, how are you? I was really surprised to read about your new interest in gardening, Billy!" She gave his shoulder an extra squeeze and smiled.

"No complaints. Liz and I enjoy our teaching…most days, anyway. We've developed a stable routine to keep up with school and housework during the week and usually do something fun on the weekends. We've both become certified scuba divers." He grinned at Barbara. "And *yes*, we have our garden. I do enjoy it more than I ever thought I could. It's really quite lovely, we'll show you pictures later."

Bobby asked if any of the bridesmaids were interested in going to the house with him to help Ashley get ready for the wedding and try on their wedding dresses. All three girls jumped up at once and said, "Give us ten minutes to get our things together and we'll meet you in the lobby."

Billy looked at his brother. "So, how's the man of the hour holding up?"

Bobby smiled confidently and answered, "I feel like I'm right where I'm supposed to be and that's a damn good feeling."

Barbara and the grands had been talking with Danny. He was already more comfortable with them just as they were with him. He was a bright, delightful, sweet child with excellent manners.

Billy hugged his brother and wished him well. "I'm sorry we didn't make it last night. Seems like everyone was favorably impressed with Ashley, and Danny *is* a great little boy."

Bobby told his brother, "You know, I'm going to adopt Danny as soon as I can. Wait till you meet Ashley, she's simply wonderful. We've both been lucky to have found good women."

"I was curious why she didn't have any of her friends as bridesmaids in the wedding…why future sisters-in-law she hadn't even met?" Billy asked.

"Ashley said she wanted the wedding to focus on her future. She preferred the three sisters-in-law because they'll be her future. Old friends symbolized the past. She has her own ideas about things. She's an only child, like Liz, and loves the idea of family."

The wedding was in the beautifully decorated Miles mansion where the heavy oak sliding doors between the two rooms were slid into their casements and rows of white folding chairs had been set up to accommodate the guests.

To Barbara's surprise, Eric and his family had flown in from California. The cousins from North Carolina, Alice and her husband, as well as Charlie and his family from Lewiston, came for Bobby's wedding. They were all even more astonished to see Barbara!

The ceremony was enchanting, Ashley was radiant and Bobby looked like a handsome prince. Danny was darling as the ring bearer in his white tuxedo. Billy and the three bridesmaids were beautiful. Barbara thought, "This will be an easy wedding for the photographer to get beautiful wedding pictures with such good-looking subjects."

Dr. Collins looked pompous and proud as he walked Ashley to the altar. Her mother didn't shed a tear, though Grandma Miles cried tears of joy for her Ashley.

The reception was noisy and festive. The huge veranda had been set with party tables for eight all covered with crisp white linen tablecloths, matching napkins and lovely china place settings. Name cards at each table included a thank you for helping them celebrate their marriage, signed by Ashley and Bob (Bob?), with an official engagement photo. Each table included four one-time-use cameras with notes attached asking the guests to take photos of each other.

A large tent with a portable hardwood floor had been set up in the back yard. *Everything* had been decorated to the ninth degree. Bows of white ribbons and netting were tastefully displayed with bouquets of exquisite orchids on every table as well as in large vases on side tables…their fragrance filled the air.

A contemporary combo dressed in black suits and the female singer in a long black gown provided the perfect background music. They had a vast repertoire that easily accommodated all requests. The total ambiance was one of perfection. The catered dinner was beyond delicious with a menu that would satisfy any palate. The wedding photographer seemed to be everywhere at the same time.

After the dinner, Barbara complimented Joyce and Grandma Miles on the lovely wedding and reception. They graciously accepted the compliment but gave most of the credit to Ashley's father. Grandma Miles insisted all the Malones come to brunch the next day. Barbara promised to give her a count later in the evening of how many would be able to attend.

She found Dr. Collins talking to Billy. Billy's nose twitched and red blotches were breaking out on his neck—a sure sign he needed rescued from Dr. Collins' condescending web. Barbara interrupted their conversation without an apology, she put her arm across Billy's shoulder. "Hello, you two. Billy, I just saw a lonely looking bridesmaid school teacher over there who told me she'd love to dance if she only had a partner."

He looked relieved. "Thanks, Mom, see you later." Then he turned around and said, "Good talking with you, Dr. Collins."

Barbara smiled as she watched Billy make his retreat. "Dr. Collins, this has been an incredibly beautiful wedding and reception. Thank you, our family truly appreciates your generosity. It's given Ashley and Bobby a foundation of excellent memories to begin their lives together."

"Thank you, Mrs. Malone. That's very kind of you to say. But one thing I've noticed about you is you seldom lack for words. You're really quite smooth. That was a flawless rescue for Bill," the doctor replied without a trace of a smile.

"Thank you…I think." She turned to watch the dance floor. There were only about sixty people at the wedding and at least forty were dancing. They all looked so happy. Barbara stood there in Cleveland with a contented smile on her face thinking of the *fiestas* in Honduras, which seemed like a world away….

Dr. Collins touched her elbow lightly. "Would you dare dance just once with the father of the bride?"

A surprised Barbara shrugged and smiled. "Why not?"

He said, "I couldn't help notice as you watched the reception, you seemed to be a million miles away, and from the look on your face, it was a much happier place than this."

"Well, for a surgeon, that's pretty fair observation skills. Everyone looked so happy dancing that it reminded me of my village in Honduras. The people are so poor, but when they have their *fiestas*, they look like the happiest people in the world. And that happiness is contagious."

"I've never met anyone like you before. It appears you've raised four good young people. And I'm even starting to believe that maybe this was a good step for Ashley. I certainly hope so for her sake and the boy."

"Thanks for the dance. And it's good to hear you finally acknowledge Danny's existence. At least that's the first step of beginning a relationship. Thanks again for the lovely wedding." After the dance, Barbara quickly walked away to say hello to Charlie and talk with Alice and Eric.

Alice held Barbara's hand. "I just can't believe you're really here. You've changed, Barbara, and it's not just the weight loss, you have a faraway glow to you. Yes, I can see it clear as day."

"Oh, Alice, you're so silly, it's just jet lag," Barbara protested.

"Jet lag, my ass! We've been friends too long. I *know* you're holding out on me.

When you're ready to tell me, I'll be all ears." Then she started to teasingly sing, "Glow little glowworm..." and squeezed Barbara's hand reassuringly. "You know you'll always have a friend in Pennsylvania."

Barbara hugged her friend and promised to call as soon as they returned to Lewiston from the wedding.

The young people danced for hours. The bridesmaids and Ashley acted like long-time girlfriends...their futures forever more intertwined.

Fifteen of the Malone family agreed to attend the brunch the next day. Exhausted, Barbara and the grands went back to the Sheraton about midnight. They'd noticed little Danny and his great-grandma excused themselves and said their goodnights about ten p.m.

An exquisite catered brunch was served on Sunday morning. A smaller but still lively group made conversation slightly easier than during the reception. Bobby and Ashley had left at eight a.m. Sunday morning for Niagara Falls for a two-day sampler honeymoon.

Brunch champagne was served after everyone had finished eating. Grandma Miles rang a bell for silence and toasted, "To the union of our families. May the blessed love that brought Bob Malone and Ashley Miles Collins together always be our mutual bond. To family!"

That afternoon, back at the Sheraton, hasty and tearful goodbyes were said as everyone prepared to head home. Eric, Joanne and family were waiting for transport to the airport. Meanwhile Erica flooded Barbara with questions about her village in Honduras. Her older brothers became very attentive, too. They were amazed that the children rarely even owned a pair of shoes and just went barefoot. The lack of electricity and phone service were amazing to these high-tech California children. Their biggest surprise was how much Barbara loved serving in the Peace Corps.

Mormor and Morfar were clinging to every minute they could with Katie's two children, otherwise known as the North Carolina cousins. They had grown to be fine young people, but their Pennsylvania grandparents weren't travelers and had rarely seen them since Katie had died of cancer five years, seven months ago.

Promises were made with good intentions to stay in closer touch, but not one of them believed they'd really do it. Life just gets too busy.

When they arrived back in Lewiston late Sunday night, everyone went straight to bed, unpacking and even showers postponed to morning.

The next day, wrapped in an old bathrobe, Barbara lingered over her second cup of hot tea, listening to her parents rehash every aspect of the wedding. She quietly smiled. She'd listened to different versions of the same conversation all her life. Finally, she excused herself to shower and unpack.

Barbara had lunch with Alice every day that week and enjoyed meeting her baby granddaughter. Barbara, true to her nature and the solid friendship she and Alice shared, never responded to direct questions or comments about references to her "faraway glow."

Every night she dined with Jessica and the grands. She almost enjoyed watching from the sidelines as Jessica told Michael, "I need some space in this relationship. We're definitely *not* ready to be engaged, but I'd like to think we could remain friends. And here's your ring, I can't keep it the way things are with us now."

Michael did not act very friendly when he left the house that night. Barbara put her arm around Jessica's shoulder. "Are you sure about this, Jessica?"

"Yes, Mom, I am. I couldn't be happy with a man I couldn't trust and I couldn't trust Michael. He was pushing me towards setting a wedding date...I don't know, Mom, the better I got to know him, the less I thought I knew him. Does that make any sense?"

"Yes, it certainly does. Congratulations for making a sensible and mature choice. I'm *very* proud of you."

All the grands breathed a sigh of relief, too. They'd all had funny feelings regarding Michael, but nothing to base their free-floating anxieties on until the weekend in Cleveland.

Barbara enjoyed several phone conversations with Billy and Liz, also Janie as well as Bobby, Ashley, Danny and Grandma Miles. Barbara felt she'd had a good visit home.

She paid her parents for taking care of her home, over their protests. "I refuse to take no for an answer, you've earned it and it's one less thing for me to be concerned about, knowing I can count on you. Thanks, Mom and Dad." She quietly left an extra fifty dollars to cover the telephone calls she'd made.

Leaving was hard for everyone. Grandmother Malone, Jessica and her parents went with her. They all cried. Jessica and Grandmother Malone accepted an invitation to have a cup of tea with Mormor and Morfar when they returned from the airport. They all agreed Barbara seemed happier than they'd seen her in many years. She had a sense of purpose now. Though each of them knew they'd done a lot more talking than she had and they really knew little more about her life in Honduras now than they did before her visit home.

Barbara's luggage was loaded with favorite grocery non-perishables. She slept with the hint of a contented smile during the uneventful flight back and was relieved to arrive in Tegucigalpa feeling somewhat rested. She decided to stay one night in the city, visit the Peace Corps office that day to check for any updates she should be aware of. Barbara planned to take an early bus the following day. She'd also have time to do some additional shopping for badly needed staples for her kitchen.

The Peace Corps office staff greeted her as if she were a celebrity. The secretary said, "Barbara Malone! You really came back! I thought you would, but there were those who said," and she rolled her eyes toward her boss. "No way, when she's safe in the USA. That's where she'll stay." Then she whispered teasingly, "You owe me ten dollars, sir."

Barbara smiled. "Well, I thought I'd signed a two-year contract...."

"Of course you did, please come in and have a seat. Would you like a glass of tea or a Coca-Cola?" The Honduras field manager was trying hard to make her feel appreciated.

"Tea would be lovely, thank you. I'm sorry you lost ten dollars because of me, sir. I just didn't want to miss my son's wedding and I think I also needed a break. I feel refreshed and ready to go again. Is there any news on a new generator for the clinic in Rebita?"

"Well, it's good to have you back on board. I've heard good things about the work you've been doing in Rebita. I'm very sorry you've had to work under such adverse conditions, dealing with the outlaw element. My sympathy regarding the murder of your friend Alvira. Bullet wounds, death and theft. It's a shame, a real shame. The Hondurans are such peaceful, kind and generous people and then these hooligans.... Yes, the generator arrived only two days ago. We have special transport arranged for the day after tomorrow. It should get to Rebita about the same time you do. The driver knows how to install it."

"Thank you, sir. I do appreciate your sympathy about Alvie. And also your speedy action on a generator. However, our compound guard was killed by government soldiers when they came to steal the generator. They also stole our VCR and large-screen television. It had been a gift to me and I gave it to the village. It was stored in the village church and we had monthly movie nights. The villagers loved it. The outlaws killed Alvie by accident when she saved a child caught in the crossfire...only after they'd been ambushed inside the village by government soldiers. Well, the *banditos* are the ones who gave it to me."

The field manager raised his eyebrows questionably. "And why would the outlaws give you a gift, Barbara?"

"I was forced to do emergency surgery to save the younger brother of the gang's leader. We were lucky. And, of course, I had no space or need for such a large television."

"Be careful, Barbara, with your political perceptions. Grudges can go very deep in Honduras. And everything is not always as it seems."

"I appreciate your warning. I'll be careful." At the same time she thought, "And I know what I saw. I know what I see happening in the villages...."

That night she stopped to visit her host family, Maria, Jose and family. They insisted she dine with them. Maria worried over her new thinness and insisted she eat seconds of everything. Maria and her family were well and again Barbara was treated as a celebrity.

Their current Peace Corps volunteer was a very young man, broke with no independent income. He was quickly becoming disillusioned. Barbara went for a short walk with him after dinner and offered him encouragement.

He'd heard of her in his training class and listened closely to her bits of wisdom and he thanked her for taking time to talk to him. He told her she'd inspired him and he'd stay, that her courage had rekindled the spirit that had brought him this far.

The next morning she hurried into the Peace Corps office and anonymously contributed five hundred dollars to the young man's account. Barbara then took a cab to the bus station since her cumbersome bags made walking to the station nearly impossible. Her second bus trip to Rebita was not as exciting as the first. Rebita was no longer an unknown entity. She missed the chatter of Alvie and Ethel, her traveling companions on that first trip only eight and a half months ago. Yet it seemed like so long ago. At least she'd see Ethel when she reached Valencia. Barbara sighed and her thoughts lingered on Dr. Mike Kane. "How will he react when he sees me again? He certainly sends mixed messages. Maybe I send confusing messages to him, too. I just don't know. He's definitely a kind but complicated person. Well, perhaps everyone is."

The trip seemed to be going faster this time. The bus was just as crowded, but she still dozed on and off. She daydreamed of her children and as always when she thought of them, she prayed for their safety and guidance.

By early evening they'd arrived at Valencia and she found a driver to take her to the Peace Corps compound. Ethel opened the door, looking every bit her age but healthy and energetic. She grabbed Barbara and gave her a gigantic hug. Ethel had lost weight too, though not nearly as much as Barbara. "I heard you'd gone home and I knew you'd be back. We older ones respect our commitments. Dr. Kane was afraid you'd never come back what with so many terrible things happening to you up in those mountains. I told him not to worry that you'd be here. So, how was the wedding? I'm sure it was lovely. Did he pick a good one? How's the family?"

It felt safe and wonderful to be with Ethel again. "I was remembering our first trip out here with Alvie after training as I rode the bus today. It's so good to see you again. I guess I needed the break at home. The wedding was beautiful and so was the bride. She has a darling five-year-old son, so now I'm a grandmother, too. Thank God, everyone seems to be well," Barbara answered.

"Tomorrow is Dr. Kane's day in Valencia, so why don't you stay an extra day and let him see you with his own eyes. He's really been quite concerned about you. I can understand why when I see how thin you still are after two weeks at home." Ethel spoke with a soft but firm voice.

"I'm very confused by that man. He can be so kind and so totally obstinate at times. And *why* does he talk to you about me?"

"Think about it, Barbara, I'm your friend. I'm a nurse. And who else is he going to talk to about you? In case you haven't noticed, the jungle can be a bit isolating for us *gringos*!" Ethel replied.

Barbara yawned. "All right, I get it…I'm so tired. Where shall I sleep tonight?"

Ethel gave her a piercing stare, as if asking, "Well?"

"Okay, okay! I'll stay tomorrow night too. Good night now. I'll shower in the morning. I'm exhausted."

The next morning Ethel left for the clinic while Barbara slept late. She finally woke up at ten and showered, feeling rested. Ethel had rescheduled Barbara's transport for the following day.

Barbara looked out and saw Mike's SUV. Ethel sent a message to the cottage. "Get pretty. Company coming for lunch."

Barbara looked in the mirror and shrugged. "At least I still have a decent hair cut. This is about as good as it's going to get." She did set the table for lunch, put a dab of perfume on and a touch of lipstick.

Before long she heard footsteps on the porch. Ethel came in first and winked at Barbara. Then Mike walked in and stopped cold. Obviously, Ethel hadn't told him she was here.

"Hi Mike, I'm back. How are you?" Barbara smiled hesitantly.

"Barbara, you look lovely! Welcome back to our mountains. Ethel insisted you'd come back, but I couldn't believe her." Finally he smiled. His long gray hair was pulled into its usual ponytail.

Ethel suggested, "Why don't you two have some iced tea and sit down to the table here, eat a bite of lunch and catch up. You're acting like lovesick kids!"

They both blushed and laughed, as Barbara kicked Ethel lightly under the table and gave her a look of consternation.

"So how are things in Rebita since I left?" Barbara asked.

"I haven't been there, but from what I understand 'quiet,' which is good, of course. I'm scheduled there tomorrow; could I offer you a ride?"

"Well, that sounds good to me…I'll have to cancel my scheduled ride."

"I've already taken care of that for you," Ethel said with a broad smile.

Immediately after a quick lunch Ethel excused herself and went to her bedroom to sleep. The lunch and *siesta* hours flew by.

Barbara and Mike sat on Ethel's lumpy sofa; he wanted to know everything about the wedding and her visit home. She told him story after story.

A surprised Barbara asked, "Aren't you getting bored listening to me go on like this?"

He laid his head back on the sofa, covered her hand with his and said, "Not yet. You tell a good story, Nurse Barbara."

Barbara sat there feeling a bit stunned at first. Then she leaned her head back on the sofa, hand in hand with her friend, Mike. She realized she felt totally relaxed for the first time in years. She thought, "It's a strange thing, but I finally found a place and someone that feels like *home*." Barbara dozed off with a contented smile on her face.

The End